HER RETURN
TO KING'S BED

BY
MAUREEN CHILD

laging and manufacturing processes conform to the legal environmental regulations of the country of origin.

Printed and bound in Spain
by Blackprint CPI, Barcelona

MILLS
BOON®

Published in Great Britain 2013
by Mills & Boon, an imprint of Harlequin (UK) Limited,
Eton House, 18-24 Paradise Road, Richmond, Surrey TW9 1SR

© Maureen Child 2013

ISBN: 978 0 263 90494 9

51-1213

Harlequin (UK) policy is to use papers that are natural, renewable and
recyclable products and made from wood grown in sustainable forests. The
keeping and manufacturing processes conform to the legal environmental

Maureen Child writes for Mills & Boon® Desire™ and can't imagine a better job. Being able to indulge your love for romance as well as being able to spin stories just the way you want them told is, in a word, perfect.

A seven-time finalist for the prestigious Romance Writers of America RITA® Award, Maureen is the author of more than one hundred romance novels. Her books regularly appear on the bestseller lists and have won several awards, including a Prism, a National Readers' Choice Award, a Colorado Romance Writers Award of Excellence and a Golden Quill.

Maureen believes that laughter goes hand in hand with love, so her stories are always filled with humor. The many letters she receives assures her that her readers love to laugh as much as she does.

Maureen Child is a native Californian, but has recently moved to the mountains of Utah. She loves a new adventure, though the thought of having to deal with snow for the first time is a little intimidating.

To my husband, the man who is always there when
I need him and who still makes me laugh every day.
I love you.

One

"A jewel thief?" Rico King demanded of his chief of security. "Here in the hotel?"

Franklin Hicks scowled. The man was late thirties, stood six foot five and boasted a shaved head and sharp blue eyes. "Only explanation. The guest in bungalow six—Serenity James—reported that some of her diamonds are missing. I've already interviewed the maid and room service."

Bungalow six. Rico could have pulled up the map of the hotel on his computer, but there was no need. He knew every inch of his place. He knew that the bungalows were set apart from the main hotel—for privacy, since a lot of his clientele insisted on seclusion. People like Serenity James, an up-and-coming Hollywood darling who, in spite of her name, lived life on the edge.

The actress might claim to want to avoid photographers and nosy guests, but according to security, there were men streaming in and out of her bungalow at all hours. Any one of them could have made off with the diamonds. He hoped it would be that easy.

"What about Ms. James's 'guests'?" Rico looked up at the other man. "Did you talk to them, as well?"

Snorting, Franklin admitted, "We're still running them all to ground, but I don't think it was one of them, boss. If those diamonds were taken by one of her 'guests,' they'd have helped themselves to more than just the one necklace. Whoever took the diamonds was picky about it. Took the stones that would be easiest to pry out of their settings and sell. Smells like a professional job to me. Besides, you have to remember we've had two more reports of stolen property in the last few days. Gotta be a pro."

"Not good news," Rico mused.

His hotel, the Tesoro Castle, had only been open for a little more than six months. It was new, fresh and exclusive and had quickly become the hot spot for celebrities and the überwealthy who were looking for a private getaway spot. Tesoro Island sat in the middle of the Caribbean, but it was privately owned. No one landed here—private yacht or cruise ship—without permission of the owner, Walter Stanford.

Which meant that those seeking privacy had nothing to fear from paparazzi, except for the occasional overachiever who used telephoto lenses from a boat anchored far offshore.

Tesoro was lush and secluded, and the Castle was like Disneyland for adults: there were infinity pools, the best spas in the world and sweeping ocean views from every room. The hotel had deliberately been built small, to keep it a select destination. There were only a hundred and fifty rooms, not counting the private bungalows scattered across the grounds. The interiors were opulent, service was impeccable and the island itself carried an air of dreamy seduction. For those who could afford it, Tesoro promised a world of languid pleasures for all of the senses.

And damned if Rico was going to allow his hotel's reputation to be stained. If there was a professional thief operating in his place, then that thief would be found.

"Security cameras?" Rico demanded.

"Nothing." Franklin scowled as if the word tasted bitter. "Another reason to go with the professional thief theory. Whoever it was, they knew how to bypass the cameras."

Perfect.

"Set up a meeting with your men. I want eyes and ears everywhere. If you need to hire more security," Rico said, "call my cousin Griffin. King Security can have more men here tomorrow if we need them."

Franklin bristled. He'd once worked for Griffin King and his twin, Garrett, and had decided to leave in favor of being chief of security here on the island. He clearly didn't care for the suggestion that there might be something he couldn't handle. "I won't need more men. The team I've got is the best in the world. Now that I know we're looking for a pro, we'll find him."

Rico nodded. He understood pride and he knew that Franklin's had been pricked. He was in charge and having a professional thief on the grounds was a direct slap in the face. But pride notwithstanding, if Rico decided they needed more help, Franklin would get extra men whether he liked it or not.

This hotel had been Rico's dream. Built to his exact

specifications by King Construction, the Tesoro Castle was the epitome of luxury hotels. He'd been working toward this project for all of his adult life. He owned several hotels and each in its own way was spectacular. But this place on Tesoro was his crowning achievement. He'd do whatever he had to do to protect his name and his investment.

Shaking his head in irritation, Rico turned and stared out his office window at the view spread out below him. The island of Tesoro, Spanish for "treasure," was aptly named.

Miles of unspoiled beaches, aquamarine ocean, thick jungles with amazing waterfalls hidden away in the stands of trees. Sunshine every damn day and unlike most of the Caribbean, the trade winds blew across Tesoro almost constantly, keeping the heat—and flying insects—at bay.

Rico had spent months with Walter Stanford, negotiating for his own slice of the old man's paradise. Hell, he'd even had some of his cousins come in and talk to the older man for him. Of course, Rico mused, that had worked out for Sean King, since he'd married Walter's granddaughter Melinda.

After the negotiations, the months spent building this place and the time and expense of furnishing and staffing this hotel to get it just right…irritation blossomed into quietly restrained fury. No one was going to ruin this place.

His guests came to Tesoro looking for beauty, privacy and security and he would see that they got it.

Just the thought of jewel thieves on the island had him gritting his teeth and flexing his hands into fists that had no one to punch. He supposed it was only natural that thieves would find their way here to Tesoro, where the rich flocked in droves. Just as it was natural that when he found whoever was behind this, he'd see them locked away for decades.

But a professional thief risked a lot to make a play on Tesoro. The island was too small. Too difficult to get to and to leave from. And since no ships had left the harbor in days, whoever the thief was, he was still on the island and he still had the stolen property on him.

Jewel thieves.

Suddenly, those two words began to echo over and over again in his mind as warning bells started clanging inside his head. Even then, though, Rico assured himself that the little voice inside his head had to be wrong.

No way would she risk that.

Not even *she* would have the nerve to chance facing him again.

But what if she had?

"Boss?"

"What?" Rico glanced over his shoulder at Franklin.

"You want me to contact Interpol about this?"

The international police force with hundreds of member countries didn't make arrests or have its own jail, but it could and did provide much-needed data on suspected thieves, killers and just about any crime imaginable.

"No," he said, ignoring the look of surprise on his head of security's face. Instead, he turned back to look out the window over the playground he'd built for the rich and famous. Rico's brain was racing with possibilities and his adrenaline surged at the idea that he just might be at the threshold of the revenge he'd waited five years to take.

No chance in hell he'd bring Interpol into this before he knew whether or not his gut instinct was right or not.

"We'll handle it on island," he said, never taking his gaze from the horizon, where the sunlight glinted off the water in bright shards. "Once we've got the thief, we'll decide what to do then."

"Your call," Franklin said, then he left, closing the office door behind him.

"Yeah, it is," Rico told himself aloud. And if this jewel thief turned out to be the woman who'd stolen from him once before…Interpol would be lucky if there was anything left of her to hand over.

"Papa, please. Leave now before it's too late." Teresa Coretti glanced from her father to the closed door of his suite and back again.

She was so anxious just being here on Tesoro, even her nerves had nerves. But she'd had to come. The moment she'd realized where her father and brother had gone on their supposed vacation, Teresa had had no choice.

"How can I leave?" her father asked with an exaggerated shrug and a smile. "I've not finished my holiday."

Holiday.

If only.

If Nick Coretti was really taking a sabbatical from his avocation, no one at the Tesoro Castle would have lost any of their possessions. No, her father could call this a holiday if he wanted to, but the truth was he was working. As he always was.

Dominick was a shorter, older, Italian version of George Clooney. His tan was permanent, and his sharp brown eyes missed nothing. His black hair was gray-streaked, but that only seemed to give him an air of distinction. He was polished and always a gentleman. He had been a faithful husband until Teresa's mother's death ten years ago.

Since then, he had used his considerable charm to smooth his way into high society, where, he said, "the pickings are always worth the effort." He loved women; women loved him. And he was the best jewel thief in the world—not counting Teresa's brothers, Gianni and Paulo.

Her father was always on the lookout for his next job. She should have known that he would never have been able to resist the allure of Tesoro. For him, it was the mother lode.

The problem was, this fabulous hotel belonged to Rico King and that was really not a good thing.

It had been five years since she'd seen Rico and just thinking his name sent a ripple of heat along her spine. Like it was yesterday, she could see those blue eyes of his as he stared down at her. She could almost taste his mouth on hers and hardly a night went by that she didn't dream of his hands sliding across her skin.

She'd spent so much time trying to get Rico out of her mind as well as her life—and here she was. On *his* turf.

Warily, she turned her head for a quick look outside to the terrace, as if half expecting to see Rico standing there. Glaring at her.

But the elegantly furnished deck was empty save for the glass-topped table, the chairs and matching chaise and a silver bucket holding her father's favorite brand of champagne. Which, she thought, brought her right back to the problem at hand.

"Papa," she started, "I asked you to stay away from Rico King, remember?"

Nick flicked an imaginary piece of lint from the elegantly tailored suit jacket he wore, then smoothed one hand along the side of his perfectly styled hair. "Of course I remember, my angel. And as promised," he continued, wagging a finger at her, "I have refused all temptation to relieve Mr. King of his valuables."

Teresa sighed. "That's not what I meant, Papa. Tesoro is Rico's. Being here, stealing from his guests, you might as well be lifting *his* wallet. You're tempting fate, Papa. Rico is not exactly an understanding man."

"Ah, Teresa," Nick said, carrying his crystal flute to the terrace where he refilled his glass and took a sip before continuing. "You were always too nervous. Too…" He paused, tipped his head back and tried to come up with the right word. Finally, he added sadly, *"Honest."*

A wry smile curved Teresa's mouth. Where else but in her family would honesty be considered a fatal flaw? She'd lived on the fringes of the law since she was a child. Before she was five, she could identify a plainclothes police officer as well as a possible mark with alacrity. While other children played with dolls, Teresa learned to pick locks. When her girlfriends were taking driver's education, Teresa studied with her uncle Antonio, the master safecracker.

She loved her family, but she'd never been comfortable with stealing for a living. At eighteen, she had broken it to her father that she had gone on her last job. Instead, she became the first Coretti in memory to go to school and be legally, gainfully employed.

Her father still considered it a tragic waste of her talents.

While her mind raced, she watched her father settle on the chaise and stare off at the resort spread below.

Rico had built something amazing here, she thought, but that didn't surprise her. He was a man who never settled for less than the best, no matter the circumstances. She'd learned that when she first met him so long ago in Cancún.

At his hotel, Castello de King—King's Castle—Teresa had been one of the innumerable chefs in the immense hotel kitchens. In her first real job after culinary school, she was excited simply to be a part of the hustle that took place in that amazing kitchen. Teresa had believed that working in that hotel was the best thing that had ever happened to her—until she met Rico himself.

She'd worked late one night and before heading to her apartment, Teresa had treated herself to a little relaxation. She'd carried a glass of wine out to one of the beach lounge chairs and sat to enjoy the night, the moon on the water and the lovely sensation of being absolutely *alone*.

Then *he* had appeared, walking along the water's edge, moonlight shining on his dark hair and making the white shirt he wore seem to glow. He'd worn tan slacks and his bare feet had kicked through the water with every step. She couldn't seem to look away from him. He was tall and dark and as he came closer, she realized he was *gorgeous*. He was also her employer. Rico King, playboy, gazillionaire, hotelier and at the moment, as alone as she.

In an instant, her mind replayed that scene.

He glanced up as if sensing her gaze on him and when he saw her, he smiled and headed for her. "I thought I was alone on the beach."

"So did I," she managed to say.

"Shall we be alone together?"

Teresa still remembered that faintest hint of an accent coloring his words. His eyes were a piercing blue, his hair as black as the night and his smile was temptation personified. She couldn't have said no to him even if she had tried—which she hadn't. Rico had sat on the sand beside her and they'd shared her glass of wine and spent the next couple of hours talking.

Teresa came out of the memory and mentally warned herself to stop reliving the past. To stop indulging in thoughts of him and what might have been. She was here on Tesoro—in Rico's hotel—for one reason only: to get her family out of there before Rico discovered them. If only her father had listened to her. But Nick Coretti was a force of nature and when the prize was rich, no risk was too much.

Rico *would* find them. Teresa knew that man too well to think that he would allow jewel thieves to operate freely in his place. It was only a matter of time. Which meant that she had to get the Coretti family off Tesoro. Fast.

Teresa followed her father to the terrace. The sunlight was bright, the sky a brilliant blue and a soft breeze carried the scent of tropical flowers as it lifted her hair off her neck.

"Papa, you don't know Rico like I do. He *will* catch you."

Her father snorted, then shook his head and chuckled. "*Bellissima,* no Coretti has *ever* been caught. We are too good at what we do."

True, she thought, but the Corettis had never come up against an adversary like Rico before, either. Yes, various police forces from several countries had tried and failed to pin a crime on the Corettis. But their interest in the family of thieves had been purely professional.

For Rico, this would be personal.

"Papa, you have to trust me on this." She laid one hand on his arm. "Please, let's get off the island while we still can."

He clucked his tongue at her. "You have made far too much of this man you once cared for. Always you believe he is searching for you. Searching for *us*."

"He did search for me, remember?"

Nick waved that away. "You pricked his pride when you left him, my darling. It is understandable. No man would care for losing such a lovely woman from his life. But it's now five years. I believe it's time you stop worrying about this man."

Five years or five minutes. Rico was the kind of man who *never* left a woman's thoughts.

Besides, her father didn't know everything that had happened between her and Rico. Some things she hadn't been able to share, not even with her family.

Watching her father now, looking like the lord of the manor as he stared out over the luxurious view spread below him, she thought that under any other circumstances, he and Rico might have been friends. They were two of the most stubborn, willful men she had ever known.

And realizing that meant she had to admit she was fighting a losing battle. Dominick Coretti would never leave a job half-finished. And now that he had begun to infiltrate the guests at the Castle, he wouldn't leave until he was good and ready.

Which made him a sitting duck for Rico. Every hotelier in the world knew the Corettis. They weren't invisible. They were simply so good at what they did, there was never any evidence against them. They were high profile, wealthy and they didn't hide in out-of-the-way spots. Nick Coretti, like all of those who came before him, believed in living his life to the fullest. The fact that he did it with other people's money didn't change anything.

Ordinarily Teresa might have worried that coming here herself would give up the game because Rico would notice her. But her family was here. In plain sight. And now diamonds were missing. Rico would put the two together.

Her father stood, poured more champagne and stepped to the wrought-iron lace of the balcony railing. He might have been enjoying the view, but Teresa knew him well enough to know that he was looking not at the resort, but at its guests. He would be scoping them out, looking for his next target—assuming he hadn't already chosen one.

For all his charm, Dominick wasn't a man to be crossed. As head of the Coretti family, he might as well have been a general ordering his troops around. When he made a plan, that was it. The rest of the family fell in line.

Except for Teresa. As a kid, she'd been intrigued by the Coretti family legacy. As a teenager, she'd begun wishing that they could stay put in their house outside Naples. That she could *belong,* instead of traipsing all over Europe. They never stayed in one place more than a month and only came back to their home base occasionally, so it was impossible to make friends. Teresa and her brothers had been homeschooled and along with the usual—history, math and such—had taken classes on lock picking, safecracking and forgery. By the time the Coretti children were adults, they were each prepared to carry on the family dynasty.

That was when Teresa had taken her stand. Her father had raged and argued, her mother had wept and her brothers hadn't really believed she would do it. But in the end, Teresa had become the one Coretti in generations who *hadn't* joined the family business. Which made her a puzzle to her brothers and an irritation to her father.

"You're making too much of this, Teresa," he chided now with a sad shake of his head. "This is no different from any other job, and when we have finished, we will be gone. With no one the wiser."

"You're wrong, Papa," she argued again. "You don't know Rico as I do. He's a dangerous man."

Dangerous to *her,* anyway.

That got Nick's attention. "Did this man harm you in some way? If he did—"

"No." She interrupted him quickly. The problem, she thought, was that the Coretti family had a history with Rico that her father knew nothing about. And now wasn't the time to tell the story. "He didn't hurt me. But Papa, he won't allow thieves to operate in his place. He'll find you and when he does…"

"What can he do?" Nick laughed a little and sipped at his champagne. "He will have no proof of anything. You should know better, Teresa. The Coretti family is not so easy to catch."

"Obviously it is not as difficult as you might wish." A deep, familiar voice spoke up from directly behind her.

Teresa went absolutely still.

She would know that voice anywhere.

With a weird mixture of dread and anticipation, she slowly turned and looked into the eyes of Rico King.

Two

"What's the meaning of this?" the older man in the room demanded, striding in from the terrace to face Rico. "Who are you? What are you doing in my suite?"

"Papa," Teresa said, rising from her chair, "this is Rico King."

"Ah," Nick mused with a half smile. "Our host. Still, this doesn't give you the right to intrude uninvited."

Rico steamed silently and hated the fact that he had to *force* his gaze away from Teresa's to meet her father's. The glint in the other man's eyes told Rico the older Coretti had known exactly who Rico was. This was all part of the game. "The fact that you're a thief on my property gives me all of the rights I need."

"*Thief?*" The older man bristled and puffed up until his chest was so full of air, Rico wouldn't have been surprised to see him lift off the floor and float about the room.

"Papa, please." Teresa stepped in between the two men like a referee interrupting a prizefight. Facing Rico, she said, "We'll leave. Right away."

"You're not going anywhere," he told her and felt that bubble of righteous anger fuel him again.

Five years, he told himself. Five long years wondering where the hell she was. If she was dead or injured. If she was laughing at him from some other man's bed. No. She wasn't leaving. Not until he was good and ready for her to be gone. And at the moment, he didn't know just when that might be.

She went pale and her brown eyes shone with too many banked emotions to identify. If he had cared to try. Which he didn't, he assured himself. Instead, Rico dismissed her and focused his gaze on the other man in the room.

Dominick Coretti was stylish, confident and even now Rico could see the gleam of exhilaration in his eyes. He was already trying to think of a way out. A way to salvage a situation that had turned on him unexpectedly. Well, there was no way out for him—unless he did exactly as Rico wanted.

"I am insulted that you would think me a thief," Nick began, clearly sticking to his routine of outraged guest. "And I will not stay where I am clearly unwelcome. My family and I will book passage off the island by this evening."

"Your family will not be allowed to leave until the jewelry you've taken has been returned."

"I beg your pardon—"

"There is no pardon here," Rico told him flatly. Oh, he had to hand it to the man. He was pulling off the insulted-guest routine so well that if Rico hadn't been sure of his facts, he might have believed him. Problem was, there was no doubt in Rico's mind just who the Coretti family really was.

"Once the jewelry is returned," he said with a knowing smile, "you and your son can leave. My *wife* will remain with me."

"Wife?" Nick echoed.

"Wife?" Teresa yelped.

Finally, Rico looked to her again and was pleased to see stunned shock on her beautiful features. Her eyes were wide, her mouth open and color had rushed in to fill her pale, honey-toned cheeks.

"That's crazy."

"It's true."

"You said nothing to me of marrying this man," her father accused.

"It wasn't important," she argued without even glancing at the other man.

Those three words slapped at Rico and only served to fan the flames of his anger. *Not important.* Their marriage. Her running out on him. Her family stealing what was his. *Not important.* Anger was rife inside him and he struggled to keep his tone and his expression from revealing his feelings. "That's not what you said at the time."

"How is it I was not told of this marriage?" The accusatory tone in her father's voice singed the air.

"Papa—"

Rico didn't believe the other man's outrage for a second. He knew all about the Corettis. He'd done his research over the last several years. And though the private investigators he'd hired hadn't been able to locate Teresa, they'd come up with quite a bit of very interesting information. Enough to see the whole damn family locked away, if he wished.

So, no, he didn't believe Nick's performance. He knew that thieving had been a way of life for the family for generations. Lying was their stock in trade.

"I'm not playing this game," he said simply, quietly.

"Game?"

He glanced at the older man, then shifted his gaze back to the woman who haunted him. "As I said, return the jewelry you stole and you and your son can leave the island. Teresa will stay here. With *me,* until you bring me the gold dagger that was taken from me five years ago."

"You cannot hold my daughter here against her will," Nick said, the steel in his voice telling Rico this was a man accustomed to being obeyed.

"It's that," Rico said, staring at the other man now, "or I go to Interpol."

Nick waved that threat away with a negligent, well-manicured hand. "Interpol doesn't worry me."

"Once I hand over the information I have gathered on your family over the years, I think you'll feel differently."

Dark brown eyes narrowed. "What information?"

"Enough to end you," Rico promised, ignoring Teresa's soft gasp.

"Impossible," Nick blustered, but concern glinted in his eyes. "There has never been evidence found against my family."

"Until now." Rico gave him a smile. "Private investigators can go where the police can't. And if the law should receive this information from an anonymous source…"

Nick Coretti—or Candello, as he was registered here—looked as if he'd been cornered. And he had.

Now the years of hiring the best private investigators in the world and collecting data and evidence were finally paying off—just as he'd known it would one day. Rico had been methodical as only a King could be when faced with an enemy. Add to that heritage the Latin blood that swam in his veins and revenge tasted sweeter than he had even imagined.

"Your sons are not always as careful as their father," he said, watching suspicion and then a cautious wariness shine in Dominick Coretti's eyes.

"You're bluffing."

Rico smiled slightly and, without taking his gaze from Nick's, said, "Teresa, tell your father I don't bluff."

"He doesn't, Papa," she whispered and the sound seemed to echo in the plush suite. "If he says he has evidence, he does."

A frown crossed Nick's face then and Rico knew he had the man's attention.

"What is it you want?"

"I've already told you. I want what your family stole from me five years ago."

Nick shot a look at his daughter. "I think you stole something from me, as well."

He hadn't *stolen* Teresa, Rico thought. He'd let his heart rule his head for the first and last time in his life. And just look where that had gotten him.

"Fine, then," he said. "Call it an exchange. You return my property and I will return yours."

He knew he was being insulting and he just didn't give a royal damn.

"Property?" Teresa hissed the word as her back went poker straight and her shoulders squared as if for battle.

She lifted her chin and looked up at Rico. "I'm no one's property. Least of all *yours*."

He inclined his head in a nod. "Don't bother being offended. I'm not interested in keeping you."

She reacted as if she'd been slapped.

Rico ignored her. "You can go as soon as I have the Aztec dagger back in my possession."

Not only had Teresa used him and then vanished, she'd done her disappearing act right after the centuries-old dagger had gone missing from Rico's collection. He knew, thanks to information his P.I.s had gathered, that Teresa's brother had stolen it from him. And he wanted that dagger. It was a ceremonial dagger, used in the Aztecs' religious sacrifices, that Rico's great-great-however-many-greats-grandfather had found in an archaeological dig more than two hundred years ago. Not only was it ancient and a piece of history—it had been handed down in his father's family for longer than anyone could remember—and Rico would have it returned.

Once he had that—and his personal revenge on Teresa—he could be done with her and the past.

As if Nick wasn't in the room with them, Teresa took a single step closer to him before stopping herself. Staring up into his eyes, she said, "I got a divorce five years ago. I hired an attorney in Cancún and he filed the papers. He sent me the final decree."

"It was a fake," he said sharply.

Rage escalated as he remembered her attorney, a good friend of Rico's, coming to him, telling him about Teresa's divorce plans. Because that attorney had owed Rico, he'd given his allegiance to him rather than his client. Together, they'd faked a divorce decree and let her believe the marriage had been dissolved. Of course, he had tried to use the address she gave the lawyer to find her. But she had disappeared again, losing herself somewhere in Europe.

There had been a few times over the last five years that Rico had regretted his decision. But at the time, he'd been too tormented by the way she'd left. Too furious at the way she'd used him only to vanish, to let her go. And still too…enamored of her to allow that disappearance to be final.

Now he was glad he'd done it. For the satisfaction of seeing her shock, if for nothing else. She had thought herself in charge. Assumed that she had left him behind in her tangle of lies.

Even now, he knew she was wondering how he'd found her here. How he'd managed to pluck her from the hundreds of guests currently staying at the Castle.

It hadn't been hard.

As owner of the hotel, he had access to the guest registry and finding Teresa had been surprisingly easy. She'd signed in under the name Teresa Cucinare—Italian for "cook." Once he suspected her of the thievery, he had zeroed in on her, then confirmed his suspicions with a quick talk with the front desk.

When his employee had described Teresa Cucinare as drop-dead gorgeous with wide brown eyes and a dimple in her right cheek, Rico knew he had her.

Five years, three months and ten days.

Not that Rico was counting or anything. But he knew down to the damn minute when this woman—*his* woman—had disappeared.

He'd spent a lot of time thinking about what he would say to her. What he would do when he finally found

her. And now here she was and all he could do was
stare at her.

He finally allowed himself the time to simply drink
her in. From the top of her head down her incredibly lush
and curvy body to the tips of her red-painted toes, displayed so nicely in her high-heeled sandals.

Hunger roared to life inside him and smothered even
the rage and frustration that had been Rico's constant
companions these last five years. She'd married him.
Used him. And then left him looking like a damn fool.
There was no forgiveness for that, Rico told himself.

But damn, she looked even better now than she had
when they were together. Clearly, the last five years
hadn't been difficult ones for Teresa Coretti.

Coretti.

When he'd married her, he'd had no idea that her last
name was infamous throughout Europe. He'd discovered
that much later, after she had gone. He'd been able to follow her trail as far as Italy, but after that, it was as if she'd
gone up in a puff of smoke. She was as adept at protecting herself as the rest of her family was. The police had
never been able to pin a crime on the Corettis and Rico
hadn't been able to find her, no matter how many P.I.s
he'd hired in so many different countries he'd lost count.

But all of that was over now. He had her. Here. At his
place. And damned if she'd get away from him again.

"Rico—"

Her voice was low, breathless, sexy enough to jolt
through him like a bolt of lightning. Damn, Rico hated
to admit—even to himself—that he was still affected
by her. Five years and he still wanted her more than his
next breath.

But this time that want, that need, would be assuaged on *his* terms.

"Been a long time," he finally said, keeping his gaze fixed with hers.

"I know—"

"What amazes me—" he spoke quickly, interrupting whatever she might have said "—is that you had the guts to show up here."

"If you'll let me explain…"

"Why? So you can spout whatever lies you've rehearsed for this occasion?" He shook his head. "I don't think so."

"Now, I think we can all discuss this in a civilized manner."

Rico's gaze darted to Teresa's father. Dominick Coretti. Head of a family of thieves and no doubt the man who had taught his daughter her precarious sense of honor. Studying him, Rico had to give the man credit. Caught red-handed, Nick Coretti looked unflappable. As if nothing more important had happened than his champagne had gone flat. This despite the fact that everyone in the room *knew* that he'd been outmaneuvered.

"Civilized?" Rico repeated. "Is it civilized to steal from others? Is it civilized to use your daughter to keep a man busy so that you can steal from him?"

Nick's eyes narrowed. "I don't use my children."

"Just train them, do you?" Rico sneered.

"That's enough." Teresa took a breath and then, deliberately turning her back on Rico, she faced her father. "Papa, will you excuse us?"

The older man looked from his daughter to Rico and back again. "Are you certain, Teresa?"

"I'll be fine," she assured him. "Please."

"Very well." Nick tugged at the lapels of his suit, lifted his chin and met Rico's gaze. "I will not be far."

"That would be best," Rico told him. "And I would advise that you not consider trying to leave the island."

Nick stiffened, clearly insulted. "I would not slink away like a coward, leaving my daughter behind."

Rico wasn't so sure, but since he was anxious to get the man out of the room, he didn't say so aloud. Instead, he waited until Nick had left the suite before saying to Teresa, "The harbor's closed. He won't get out."

"He wouldn't leave me," she said stiffly.

"Honor among thieves, you mean?" Rico snorted a laugh. "Hard to believe coming from the woman who used me just long enough for her family to steal what was mine."

"I didn't—" She stopped, shook her head and muttered something he couldn't catch before she looked up at him. "What did you mean when you said we're not divorced?"

"Just that. The decree your lawyer sent you was a forgery."

She huffed out a breath and folded her arms across her chest. "A forgery." Swinging her long fall of hair back behind her shoulder, she fired a glare at him. "And I'm guessing that was your idea."

"It was."

She sucked in a gulp of air. "You've got a lot of nerve calling my family cheats and liars. You're no better."

"That's where you're wrong," he told her, moving in closer, pleased when she scurried back a step or two. "I never stole from you. I never lied to you. I didn't *use* you."

"Maybe not," she countered, "but you tricked me. You let me believe we were finished. And why? So you could find me and what, keep me locked in a dungeon here on the island?"

He gave her a small smile. "Sadly, I have no dungeon here at the hotel. But I'm sure I can come up with something appropriate."

"You can't be serious." Teresa gave a quick look to either side of her, as if expecting help to come riding to her rescue. But there was nothing. They were still alone in the luxury suite and the tension simmering between them grew thicker by the moment.

"I've never been more serious." He leaned in close to her ear and whispered, "You're still my wife."

He'd waited for this moment. To have her in front of him, telling him to his face that their marriage had been nothing but a lie. That it had been a ruse to allow her family access so they could steal from him.

And now that the moment was here? It was every bit as sweet as he'd dreamed it would be.

She turned her head slightly and glared at him. "You know as well as I that you can't keep me prisoner, Rico."

He shrugged and tucked his hands into the pockets of his black jeans. As his gaze locked with hers, he said, "I won't have to. You'll stay with me of your own accord."

"Why would I do that?"

"I've already told you and your father that I have enough evidence to put the Coretti family in jail for centuries."

"You would do that just to get even with me?"

"Don't doubt it for a moment," he said tightly. "You would be surprised what I might do to someone who deliberately used me. Cheated me."

"I didn't cheat you," she started. "When I found out my brother had—"

"I'm not interested in your explanations," Rico spoke up, cutting her off as he moved in close enough to lay both hands on her shoulders. The feel of her again after all this time was almost too much for him. He steeled himself against his body's instinctive reaction to being with her and focused instead on that still-hot ball of rage in the pit of his stomach. "The time to explain was five years ago, Teresa."

She flinched and he knew his words had been a direct hit. Oddly, that knowledge didn't give him as much pleasure as it should have. "All I want from your family now is what's rightfully mine."

Her eyes widened and as if he could read her thoughts, he shook his head. "No, Teresa. I'm not talking about you. I'm talking about the Aztec dagger your brother took from me. I want it back. And until I get it, you're not going anywhere."

Three

Teresa could have sworn she actually *felt* a lock tumble on the box Rico had trapped her in. He was right. No matter what he wanted or asked or demanded of her, she'd give it, because she couldn't risk her family going to prison.

She felt more vulnerable with Rico now than she had on the night she'd first met the staggeringly sexy man on a deserted Mexican beach. And back then, one look at Rico and her knees had gone weak. Now, though, she couldn't risk showing any weakness at all. The man in front of her might still be her husband—but he was a stranger.

She'd tried to keep up with him, of course. She hadn't been able to rid her mind or heart of his memory, so she'd fed the need to see him by reading tabloids and looking him up on Google. And though it had chewed at her heart to see him squiring some beautiful model or actress around, it had also met the need she had to see his face. He hadn't exactly lived the life of a monk since the last time she'd been with him. But she couldn't hold that against him, could she, since they were divorced.

Or so she'd thought.

"I can't believe we're still married."

His mouth curved into a brief, sardonic smile. "Believe it, Teresa."

She shook her head. "But I paid the attorney. He sent me the final decree."

"Esteban came to me when you hired him," Rico told her. "He owed me a debt."

"And you used me as his payment?"

"You can actually accuse *me* of using *you?*" There was no smile now, only fire flashing in his blue eyes as if the anger churning inside was manifesting into actual flames. "I think we both know the real truth."

She couldn't blame him for believing what he did, but it just wasn't accurate. "I didn't use you, Rico. I wouldn't."

"I would find that easier to believe if you hadn't vanished—along with a valuable antique."

She pushed one hand through her hair, fingers tangling in the thick, black mass. Even now, she could kick her brother Gianni. Five years ago, she'd specifically asked her family to leave Rico alone, but Gianni hadn't been able to help himself. Instead, he'd taken the gold Aztec dagger that Rico prized above everything else. And in doing that, Teresa's brother had made Teresa's decision for her.

"I didn't know the dagger had been stolen until you told me that last morning."

"And I should believe you?"

She sighed. "Believe me or don't."

"Your family took it."

"One of my brothers, yes." God, she was shaking. See-ing him again was so hard. Harder than she would have thought. Seeing him look at her with an angry distance in his eyes was even more difficult.

There had been a time when his eyes shone with pas-sion and something more. Five years ago, she had been swept into a romance so wildly unexpected it had almost been a fairy tale.

And it had all ended with a shattering crash. Much like Cinderella finding herself facing midnight—unwill-ing to see the magic end.

"I can't believe we're still married. Or that you would go to so much trouble just to punish me."

"You should have known that I wouldn't let you go," he told her.

"I suppose I should have." Teresa looked into his eyes again, hoping to see…what? Love? Passion? Once, she'd seen everything she had ever dreamed of in his eyes. But those days were gone and she had no one to blame but herself. She never should have allowed herself to fall in love with him. And when she did, she never should have kept her identity a secret. Never should have run without at least *trying* to explain. But rewriting the past was a futile mental exercise. Nothing would change what had happened. Nothing would bring back the magic she had once found in Rico's eyes. Because all she read in those blue depths now was a cool detachment that tore at her even as it forced her to adopt a defensive posture.

"What was the point of holding on, Rico? I would

have thought you'd be happy to let me go after the way things ended."

"You took what was mine," he said simply, his features as stony and aloof as an exquisitely carved statue.

For one heart-stopping second, Teresa thought he might have been talking about *her*. That he had considered her important enough to him that he'd purposely kept them legally tied together. Then, as she continued to stare into blue eyes that refused to warm, she admitted the truth to herself. His holding on to her had nothing to do with *her*—it was all about the dagger that Gianni had stolen.

She closed her eyes briefly and wished herself anywhere but here. When she opened her eyes again, though, she was still looking at Rico, still feeling his icy stare dig right through her.

"I didn't know my brother was going to steal the dagger."

He laughed. "You think I believe you?"

"Probably not," she admitted. "But I wanted you to know that."

"Five years later, you decide to try honesty." He shrugged her statement off. "You and your family. Very versatile. You'll even make a wild attempt at the truth if you think it will serve better than a lie."

"This isn't about my family," she argued. "This is about me. And I'm trying to tell you the truth of what happened."

"*Thank you*," he said, sarcasm dripping from the words. "Now I know. It changes nothing." Rico moved past her, walking to the terrace that overlooked the hotel he'd built and the surrounding grounds.

When she followed him, he didn't even look at her

when she spoke. "How long do you plan on keeping me here?"

"Until your thieving family returns my property."

She flushed and was grateful he hadn't seen it. Hard to argue with the truth, no matter how much she'd like to. "This is only about the dagger then?"

"Oh," he said, turning to face her. "It is about much more than that."

The warm, soft trade winds blew across the terrace, ruffling Rico's collar-length black hair. His eyes were shuttered, emotion carefully hidden beneath a veneer of contempt.

She shivered a little at the ice in his gaze and remembered a time when his eyes had held nothing but heat when he looked at her. A time when the two of them hadn't been able to keep their hands off each other. A time when passion had sizzled in the air and hunger was never sated. But the past was as ephemeral as the trade winds, blowing through her heart and mind and passing all too quickly.

"What exactly is it that you want from me, Rico?"

"I want *you,*" he said flatly.

The ice inside her melted in a flash, dwarfed by a rush of heat that boiled her blood and fried her bones. "You what?"

"I want you here," he said, leaning casually against the railing. Feet crossed at the ankles, arms folded across his chest, he added plainly, "In my bed."

"You do?" Had she read him completely wrong? Had he really kept their marriage alive because he still felt something for her? Was this his way of telling her that he wanted them to be together again?

"For one month," he qualified, splintering whatever

rainbow-and-unicorn thoughts that were still revolving through her mind.

"What?"

"You heard me," he said. "And you're lucky I'm not demanding the *five years* that you were gone."

She blinked.

"You will stay here for one month. You will share my bed like a good wife."

"You are *not* going to blackmail me into sex."

"Of course not. But we will sleep in the same bed. And when we *do* have sex again, Teresa, it will be your idea," he said, giving her a knowing smile. "You remember how good it was between us…"

Oh, she really did.

"So blackmail won't be necessary."

He was probably right, God help her.

"As I was saying," Rico continued, "at the end of that month, your brother returns my property and I let you go—with a *real* divorce this time. More," he added when she opened her mouth to speak, "I'll give you the evidence I hold against the Coretti family. You can destroy it yourself."

Wow. Her brain had a lot to sift through: everything he'd said, the cold way he'd said it and the right way to react. Her thoughts tumbled over each other in a crash of confusion until she was finally able to concentrate on the single word that stood out from the rest.

"Destroy?" she asked. "You'd turn it all over to me?"

"I will," he assured her, then lifted one shoulder in a casual shrug. "And I don't lie."

She frowned at the little slap, but instead of arguing the point, she turned her mind to what he'd promised. If she could destroy any evidence on her family, the Corettis would be safe again. But as her father had said, no one before Rico had ever managed to catch them in the act. How could she be sure that Rico had what he said he did?

"How do I know you have anything for us to worry about?"

"As you told your father not long ago, I don't bluff." He pushed away from the railing. "I have enough on them to make any law enforcement agency do a dance of joy as they close a cell door on your father and brothers."

A knot tightened in the pit of her stomach. Rico was a man who said what he meant and always meant what he said. If he promised retribution, then it would be delivered with a vengeance. If he said he could lock her family away, the cell door was as good as shut.

Her heart felt as if it were being squeezed by a cold fist. Looking into his eyes only made the chill she felt go deeper. Though he stood no more than three feet from her, the distance separating them could just as easily have been measured in light-years. "This is about revenge, then?"

"Absolutely." He smiled, but it was an empty echo of the smile she remembered. The smile that still haunted her dreams. "Did you expect me to declare my love? To have spent the last five years pining away for the woman who stole from me and vanished?"

"Pining away?" she repeated with a short laugh. "Please. I've seen the pictures of you in the magazines. Actresses. Models. Socialites. You didn't look like you were crying on their shoulders, either."

One corner of his mouth quirked. "Jealous?"

Desperately. "Hardly."

His gaze narrowed on her. "A thief from a family of thieves. Why should I believe you?"

"I didn't steal from you," she argued, beginning to feel a flutter of outrage building inside.

"Your family did, which makes you as guilty as they."

Okay, she had to give him that. She was a Coretti, after all, despite the fact that she'd never taken part in one of their jobs. "So it's revenge on my entire family that you're after?"

"No, Teresa," he said, moving closer, lifting one hand to cup her cheek. The tender touch was muted by the hard glint in his eyes. "From your family, I want only my property. From you…I want only the pleasure we'll find together during the next month."

Everything inside her rippled and pulsed. Just those few words were enough to build a fire in her blood. How was it fair that he had been with countless women over the last five years while she had lived like a nun? How was it fair that he could whisper the word *pleasure* and have her ready to fall into bed with him?

"And if I'm not interested in sex with you?" she asked, with a mental *hah!* "Would you force me?"

His blue eyes flashed a warning. "You think I would—*could* do that?"

"No," she murmured, shaking her head for emphasis. "I don't."

He nodded. "Good."

"But," she said quickly, "apparently you're not above blackmailing me into your bed."

"You're my *wife*. You belong in bed with me. And as I've told you, I don't have to blackmail you into sex. Soon, you'll be *begging* me to take you," Rico told her with a smile. "And I will be happy to acquiesce. Think of it. You spend the month with me and I don't see your family locked away."

"I don't remember you being so hard…" Her words trailed off as she shook her head sadly.

"A lot has changed in the last five years," he told her.

Her eyes were golden-brown and dreamy, just as he remembered them. Her scent was the same, too, faintly floral with a hint of summer nights. His hands itched to hold her and he told himself he was just eager to get started on the revenge for which he'd waited so long.

But it was more than that and he knew it.

The memory of this one woman had tormented him enough that no other woman had ever come close to erasing Teresa from his mind. It was time now to exorcise that memory so he could move the hell on.

"Do you agree to my terms?" He asked the question because he wanted to hear her say yes. He wasn't the kind of man to take a woman against her will—and it pissed him off that she could even suggest it to him. But he wasn't above making sure the woman he desired didn't have much choice, either. At least in Teresa's case.

She was the only woman who had stayed with him, thoughts of her eating away at him day and night. And it wasn't just her betrayal that made her so unforgettable. No, it was more than that, though the fact that she'd lied to him and used him gnawed at Rico constantly.

She was the woman who had made him *feel* more than he ever had. Hell, he'd *married* her when he had been sure that he'd never want to be with one woman for the rest of his life. With Teresa, though, he hadn't second-guessed anything. He'd listened to his heart and thought her a gift. He'd married her because he hadn't been able to imagine his life without her. He'd let down his guard around her and had ended up paying for that.

After she had vanished, he'd figured out that she hadn't been a gift, but a curse. Now he was going to get past the old anger and sense of betrayal. He was going to use her to pave his way to the future.

A future *without* Teresa Coretti.

"So?" he asked, a casualness he didn't feel coloring his tone. "What is it going to be, Teresa? Do you stay with me for a month or do you wave goodbye to your family as the jail doors slam shut?"

She lifted her chin, fixed her gaze on his and whispered, "I'll stay."

Teresa was surprised Rico had let her out of his sight.

Although, she told herself an hour later, maybe she shouldn't have been. He knew all too well that she wouldn't do anything to endanger her family. So of course she would agree to his terms. And of course she wouldn't make a break for freedom. And of course she would end up having sex with him. How could she not? Teresa had been dreaming about Rico for five years. Sleeping beside him wouldn't be enough and she knew it as well as he did.

She walked along the dock, headed for the boat launch where her father and brother waited. Rico had made arrangements for her family to be taken from the island to St. Thomas. From there, they could take a plane back to Italy and hopefully retrieve Rico's dagger from Gianni's collection. Thankfully, her brother hadn't sold the dagger, as he did most things the Coretti family liberated from their owners. Gianni had a small, priceless collection of his own and she knew that dagger was a part of it.

In one month, her family would be back to return the antiquity and free Teresa.

A soft breeze caressed her and tossed a long lock of her hair across her eyes. She plucked it free, plastered a fake smile on her face and studied her family as she approached them.

Her father was cool and calm—nothing shattered the reserve Dominick wore as elegantly as the three-piece suits he preferred. But Paulo looked agitated. He paced back and forth in front of their father, gesticulating wildly and arguing. Though his words were caught by the wind and carried away from her, Teresa had no problem guessing what he was saying. He was furious and she knew that her brother in a temper was someone to avoid. Though there was no chance of that now. She had to face them both, give them Rico's ultimatum and then watch them go.

"Cara," her father murmured as she came closer. "You're leaving with us after all?"

"No, Papa," she said and withstood the urge to throw herself into her father's arms for a hug she badly needed. "I'm staying here."

"For how long?" Paulo demanded.

"A month."

"Hell with that!"

She looked up at her older brother and winced when she saw just how angry he was. He was tall and dark and right now his brown eyes were flashing with fury. "Paulo, you being mad isn't helping me."

"I'm supposed to just accept this?" he asked. "Just leave you here with that man for a month?"

"Yeah. We all have to accept it." Reaching out, she gave Paulo a brief hug and felt better when he squeezed her back. Paulo and Gianni had always looked out for her. Since she was the baby of the family *and* a girl, it was to be expected, she supposed. So naturally Paulo would have a hard time seeing her caught in a web he couldn't get her out of.

"Like it or not," she said, looking from her brother to her father, "Rico is still my husband."

"Yeah, and I want to know how *that* happened," Paulo muttered.

"Me, as well," her father said.

"I'll tell you everything when I leave here, okay?" Teresa took a deep breath and blew it out in a rush. "Look, the important thing to remember is that Rico won't hurt me."

"No, just trap you."

"Paulo…"

"Color this any way you choose, Teresa," her brother said, "but the hard truth is, he's using *us* to get you back into his bed."

She winced and tried not to look at her father. Maybe Paulo was right—but what her brother didn't know was that Teresa was torn about her own reaction to the situation. Yes, Rico wanted his dagger back, but was it also possible that he wanted *her,* too, even if he couldn't admit it to himself?

"Surely not," Dominick muttered.

"Why else would he keep her here for a month?" Paulo threw his hands high in disgust. "He knows we could get hold of Gianni and have that damned dagger back here by tomorrow. He's doing this deliberately. To keep Teresa where he wants her."

"This is not acceptable," her father said shortly.

"Papa, we're *married.*"

"This does not give him the right to—"

Thankfully, he didn't finish the sentence. There was

only so much more Teresa could take today. Besides, she knew Rico well enough to know that nothing would change his mind. Firing a glare at her big brother, she said, "One month. Then you can return the dagger Gianni stole and Rico will let me leave. *With* the evidence he's gathered about us."

Paulo pushed one hand through his hair. "I still don't like it."

"I don't either," she admitted, "but we don't have a choice."

"I won't leave you here with him," her father said softly. "I won't use my child to bargain for my own safety."

"What Papa said," Paulo muttered. "If your ex wants to throw us in jail, let him."

She loved them both for wanting to make the sacrifice, but she couldn't allow it. "You'd all go to prison for years."

"But you didn't do anything wrong," Paulo argued. "Not right that you should be the one to pay this price."

Teresa fought down a tide of guilt that seemed to swell up from the bottom of her heart. If that were true, she thought, she wouldn't be in this mess in the first place. She had been wrong. She'd lied to Rico from the beginning and then she'd run away rather than tell him the truth.

"Gianni stole the dagger, that's true," she said, with a glance over her shoulder at the Tesoro Castle up on the hill behind her. "But I'm not entirely innocent in this either."

"This doesn't feel right, Teresa," Paulo told her, "leaving you here. With *him*."

Shaking her head, she looked back at her brother. "He's still my husband, remember?"

Her father gave her a long look. "Not for much longer."

"One month, Papa. I'll tell you everything at the end of the month."

One of the island's launch boats fired up its engine, shattering the quiet and bringing home the fact that soon Teresa would be alone with a man who'd waited five years for revenge. Sadly, she was both concerned about that…and aroused.

Talking to her family again, she said, "Don't worry. I'm not in any danger. Rico's angry, but he would never hurt me."

"He's keeping you here against your will," her father reminded her.

"I'm staying because I choose to stay, Papa," she said.

He frowned, glanced at the launch boat that would take them to St. Thomas, then turned back to her. "We've already tried to call Gianni. He's not answering his phone. We'll find him, though, and get the dagger your *husband* requires."

Briefly, she wondered where her oldest brother had vanished to this time. Gianni hadn't been around much in the last couple of years and when he did spend time with the family, he was even more secretive than usual.

"Wait a month before returning, Papa. Rico means what he says."

"I will wait," Nick answered with a hard look at Paulo, who was grumbling under his breath. "If you're sure you want to do this."

Want was a strong word, she thought. Oh, she *wanted* Rico, there was no denying that. But if she had any real choice, would she choose to stay with a man who could barely stand to look at her? Probably not. But the truth was, they were all out of options.

"I'm sure," she said and hoped her voice sounded stronger than she felt at the moment.

"I still don't like it," Paulo muttered.

"Neither do I," their father agreed, then stepped close enough to draw his daughter into the circle of his arms. He held her tightly for a long moment and Teresa snuggled in, taking the comfort he offered before he leaned back to look at her. "You are the one who decided to not be a part of the family business, Teresa. It is not right that you are the one to pay for your legacy."

She forced a smile she didn't feel. "It's only a month, Papa. Then I'll really be free. And so will my family. That's all that matters."

He huffed out an exasperated breath then snapped, "Take the bags to the boat."

With a last look at his sister, Paulo scooped up their luggage and headed down the dock.

"You're certain you'll be safe here?"

"I will," she lied. Of course, she wasn't worried about Rico actually *hurting* her. Not physically, anyway. But every time he looked at her through eyes that spat fury, a new emotional wound opened up inside her.

Nodding, Nick looked up to the white hotel on the crest of the hill behind them, as if he could see straight into Rico's eyes. When he turned back to his daughter, he sighed. "I should have listened to you, *cara,* about staying away from this man. I swear to you now, when this month is over, Rico King will be nothing but a bad memory. For all of us."

He had never been a *bad* memory to Teresa, though. And she knew that after another month with him, most likely spent in his bed, she would never again be able to pry him out of her mind. But her father didn't need to know that her heart was still uncertain when it came to the man who was now pulling their strings like a master puppeteer.

"It'll be fine, Papa."

Still frowning, he nodded. Then he kissed her forehead and stepped back. "One month, Teresa. We will come back for you in one month."

She nodded too, though her heart was breaking. Her family was leaving and any minute now she would be alone with the one man who could shatter her heart and soul. "I'll see you then."

She watched them board the small craft and stood on the dock, gaze locked on the boat until it was no more than a smudge on the horizon. Then she turned and stared up at Rico's castle—wondering what kind of dungeon he had in store for her.

Four

A half hour later, her family had left the island and Teresa was exactly where Rico wanted her. In the bedroom of the home he'd had built for himself on the island. Just beyond the hotel, there was a rise of land that overlooked the ocean on one side and the forest on another. Rico had known the moment he'd seen it that this was where he would build his house.

And though he had furnished it and staffed it and lived in it for almost a year now—it had felt empty to him until today. Now *she* was here and the palatial home felt…crowded.

He watched her walk around the room, stepping tentatively, as if she expected land mines to be lying beneath the gleaming bamboo floor. White linen curtains rippled and danced in the island breeze that wafted through the open windows. Birds in the trees beyond sang in harmonies that lent a peaceful air to this confrontation that was *anything* but peaceful.

In her red silk shirt and dark blue slacks, she looked like a jewel dropped from the sky against the background of his room's white walls and furnishings. He waited for her to speak. To say *something* about what had happened five years before. Hell, to beg him to release her. But she gave him nothing, and a part of him wasn't surprised.

Narrowing his gaze on her, he blurted out, "Was it all a lie? Right from the beginning?"

She turned so quickly her dark hair swung out around her in a curtain of silky movement. "What do you want me to say?"

Tricky question.

"I want the truth, but somehow I doubt I'll get it," Rico said, never taking his gaze off the woman across the room from him.

"Then why should I say anything?" she countered. "You wouldn't believe whatever I told you."

How the hell could he? He kept his distance purposely. He didn't quite trust himself when he was too close to her. The need in him roared for satisfaction and the anger was just as raw.

Oh, he'd never hurt her. He didn't hurt women. But damn it, he didn't want to blackmail her into staying with him, either. Damn her for bringing him to this. And damn her for putting him here, in this position. Soon enough, though, he would have her panting to have him making love to her once again. Then he would remind her just what she'd given up by disappearing so long ago.

No other person in the world had managed to twist Rico up like she had. She'd dug so deeply inside him, there was no room for anyone else. He had his family, of course. The Kings were loyal down to the bone.

But there hadn't been another woman in his life since Teresa and his body was clamoring for what he'd denied it for too damn long.

Sure, he'd gone out with women. Had even brought a few of them back to his rooms at the hotel. But he'd never brought one to his home before. Never taken one into his bed. Not since Teresa.

He knew what it looked like to the world at large, but the world saw what it wanted to see. A billionaire playboy. The man with a succession of gorgeous women on his arm. But those women never touched him. Never shared his bed. And none of them would admit to it, because none of them could stand letting the public know that *they* hadn't been able to coax a King into their beds.

So as Teresa had lied to him, Rico had lived a lie for five long years and now that the end was in sight, he wanted her so badly he was hard as stone. So yeah, better he keep his distance.

"Try me. Tell me why. Why any of it?"

"Telling you why won't change anything, Rico. Why go there?"

"We never *left* there."

She shrugged and walked to the French doors opposite his bed that led to the terrace. She stared out and he knew the view she was looking at. The white sand beach. The aquamarine ocean beyond. The banyan trees and the double-wide hammock strung between them. There was a stone patio out there, surrounded by so many different varieties of flowers it took the breath away even as it urged you to breathe deeply, to savor the scents and tastes on the wind. There was a boat at his private dock, a yacht that Rico took out when he needed complete privacy and time to think. And when it was still and quiet enough, you could hear the waterfall in the nearby forest that splashed over rocks worn smooth by time and the relentless rush of the river.

He'd built his treasure, his paradise on Tesoro. And now that she was here—it felt complete.

"There's nothing I can say to you, Rico."

"There's plenty you could have said five years ago," he countered.

She blew out a breath and shook her head. "If I give you a reason, will it make this better for you?"

Nothing would. Nothing could. "Give it a shot."

"Fine," she said, crossing her arms over her chest in a classic self-defensive posture. "I slept with you because you were gorgeous. Famous. Rich. What girl wouldn't go to bed with you?"

A fresh spurt of anger shot through him even as he identified the lie in her words. She was too dismissive. Too careless to be telling him any kind of truth. But this lie would serve him as no truth could.

"Good. Then the next month will be easy for you," he said, at last crossing the room in long, slow strides that had her automatically backing away. "I'm still famous. Still rich. So being with me again won't be a hardship for you."

He saw her pale slightly. Then she stiffened her spine and squared her shoulders.

"I'm ready to pay my debt." She glanced at the bed, then to him. "Now?"

God, yes.

"No." He enjoyed the flicker of surprise he caught in her eyes. "I've already told you, I don't bargain for sex,

Teresa. When we come together again, it will be because
you *need* me. Not because you are paying a bill owed by
your family." She flushed and the color was lovely on
her skin.

By the time he was finished with her, she'd be plead-
ing with him to take her. "Your things have been brought
here from your suite at the hotel."

"Here? To your house?"

"Here. To my *room*," he corrected. "Our room—for
the next month, anyway."

She stiffened her spine but flattened her lips together
to keep from saying whatever was stuck in her throat.
Didn't matter, he told himself. Nothing mattered now.
Nothing but finally getting the revenge he'd promised
himself so long ago. And still, he had to ask. "One more
question."

"Only one?"

"Were you planning your family's theft from the beginning?"

"Would it matter if I said no?"

He thought about that for a second or two. "No, because how could I believe a thief?"

She winced and he almost felt guilty—almost.

"Get dressed. We're going to dinner."

She frowned and couldn't stop herself from asking,
"Dinner?"

Her surprise told him he had caught her off guard.
Good. Now all he had to do was keep her there. "Be
ready in an hour."

After he left Teresa in his room, Rico stalked down
the long hallway leading to the front of the house. He
didn't notice the throw rugs in bright tropical colors or

the sunlight glancing in through the front windows to lie on the gleaming tile floor. His mind was too busy, his emotions choking him too completely to be interested in the mundane. Right now all he could think about was the fact that Teresa was back with him. And what that was going to mean.

In long strides, he marched down the long, elegant hallway directly to the library. Once there, he sealed himself inside, walked to his desk and sat down behind it. Snatching up the phone, he hit the speed dial and waited for the connection to be made.

"Hello?"

His cousin Sean's voice sounded clipped and a little harassed. Rico smiled. "Catch you at a bad time, Sean?"

A huff of resignation came before Sean King said, "No. Just recovering from my latest heart attack. Mel had another false alarm."

In spite of everything going on, Rico had to grin. Sean King had, since marrying Melinda Stanford, become a changed man. Wasn't so long ago that Sean himself would have laughed at the image of himself as devoted husband and father-to-be. Now, though, he was the prototypical family man. And since Melinda's due date was only a week or two away, he never let his wife out of his sight. Every sigh she made sent Sean into a tailspin, and watching his anxiety escalate over the last several months had been *very* entertaining. While Melinda was sailing through her pregnancy, it was about to kill Sean.

"I swear," Sean said under his breath, "sometimes I think Mel's doing it on purpose. I'm sitting here watching the game and she lets out this little whimper-slash-groan. I jumped up so fast I knocked my beer over and dumped a whole bowl of popcorn on the floor. The dog loves me."

Rico laughed. "If it's this bad before she goes into labor, how will you survive the real thing?"

"Once it actually *happens* I'll be fine," Sean argued. "It's this waiting and waiting that's making me nuts. And between you and me, I think Mel's doing this stuff just to watch me jump."

She probably was. Melinda was great, but she did love keeping her husband on his toes. "I'm sure she's as nervous as you are."

"Who's nervous?" Sean replied. "I'm not nervous. I'm just hyperprepared." He grumbled something under his breath then added, "Right now, she's eating ice cream and laughing at me."

In the background, Rico could hear Melinda's laughter and the excited barking of their dog, Herman. Soon they would have their child and be even happier than they were already. Hard not to be jealous of that.

"You're a lucky man," Rico told him.

"Yeah, and she never lets me forget it," Sean said, laughing. "So what's going on?"

Secrets were impossible to keep inside the King family. So naturally Rico's brothers and cousins all knew about his marriage to Teresa—and the fact that the divorce had never gone through. Hell, with a lot of the Kings now living across Europe, Rico had had unpaid "detectives" keeping their eyes open looking for Teresa so that Rico could finally end what was still lying between them.

The King family was tight. And since Sean had led the King Construction project to build this hotel and Rico's home—then stayed on Tesoro when he married Melinda—the two cousins had grown even closer. They'd spent many nights having a drink together, talking about work and family and what Rico would do if he ever caught up to Teresa Coretti King.

Now that he finally had, Rico had to talk to his cousin about this. He took a breath and said simply, "She's back."

"She?"

"Teresa."

There was a long pause and Rico knew his cousin was as dumbstruck as he'd been just a couple of hours ago. Idly, he picked up a pen off the desktop and flipped it between his fingers.

"Are you kidding me?" Sean's voice ratcheted up a notch or two before he stopped and talked to Melinda. "Rico's wife showed up. Yeah, I'm finding out." When he came back, he asked, "She just showed up at the hotel?"

"Not alone. She was with her father and brother—who were doing what they do best."

"Oh, crap. They were pulling jobs on your guests?"

"Yeah. Serenity James lost a necklace and there were a few others hit, as well." Just thinking about it infuriated Rico all over again. Of course he'd made sure the Corettis turned over the stolen property before they left the island, but the fact that thefts had occurred at all seriously pissed him off. "They returned the jewels before they left."

"Before you tossed 'em off the island, you mean."

"That's about it."

"And you didn't alert the police because…"

"Because I made a deal with Teresa."

"Oh, man, do I want to know what it is?"

Rico tossed the pen to the desktop and watched it roll off the far edge. Leaning back in his chair, he outlined his plan for revenge and waited for Sean's reaction. It didn't take long.

"So basically you took her prisoner?" A yelp from Melinda in the background caused Sean to say, "I know, Mel. I'm finding out." Then he asked, "Okay, so where's Teresa now?"

"In my bedroom."

"Oh, for God's sake, Rico—"

"She's still my wife, Sean." He prepared for a battle. He'd talked to his cousin many times about the frustration he'd felt over the years. Now that his revenge was at hand, though, Rico almost felt…guilty about wielding it. So he'd called his cousin for some backup. Which, it appeared, he wasn't going to get.

"She's your wife but you haven't seen her in five years."

"You don't have to remind me," Rico said, flipping the pen between his fingers.

"So what're you planning to do? Lock her up?" Sean asked. "Chain her to the bed?"

"I hadn't considered it, but…" Now that erotic image seared itself on his brain as he considered it.

Fine. He was kidding. Probably. Although the thought of Teresa chained to his bed awakened a mental image that suddenly made him completely uncomfortable. Pushing out of his chair, Rico paced the perimeter of the room. Even the air of home seemed different now, with Teresa here. She was just up the stairs and it was taking everything he had to keep from storming up there. He knew she would see his hunger for her, but it would only mirror what she was feeling and push her closer to coming to him.

Sean sighed. "What's the plan?"

"Just what I said." Rico stopped at the wide front window overlooking the meticulously landscaped front yard.

"She stays with me for one month. Then her family returns the dagger and I divorce her."

"Uh-huh." Sean blew out a breath. "Until that happens, what're you gonna do with her?"

He knew what he *wanted* to do with her. His body was rock hard and just knowing Teresa was upstairs, in a room with a wide, comfortable bed, made even breathing difficult. But he had time. His wife would be here, with him, for a solid month and in that time he would find a way to finally and completely get Teresa out of his mind for good.

But for now, "We're going to dinner at the hotel."

Sean snorted. "Sure. When your missing wife reappears after five years of running from you, you want to put off revenge long enough to have a dinner date."

"It's not a date." Even the word had Rico scowling.

"Then what is it?"

"It's dinner." Rico slapped one hand to the wall beside the window and glared out at his yard. "I'm not romancing her. I'm not courting her. We both have to eat and I don't want her out of my sight. Don't make more of this than there is, Sean."

"Sure, sure. Not a date. Just revenge foreplay. Got it all planned out, huh?" There was a distinctive smile in Sean's voice that irritated Rico beyond measure.

"Is there something wrong with a plan?"

"Nope," Sean said. "Just be prepared, cousin."

"For what?"

"For when your plan blows up in your face."

Teresa's stomach was in knots. Just being with Rico was tearing her up. And waiting for whatever was going to happen next was making her a little crazy. Who knew what he would do? She never would have expected to be held hostage and since he'd surprised her once, she had to wonder what else was ticking through his mind.

Oh, she had known the minute she slipped from their suite at the Castello de King five years ago that she had made him her enemy. It had broken her heart at the time, but over the last five years, she had tried to heal. Tried to forget the fact that she had run away from a man who had loved her. And though her inner wounds had healed over, the scar tissue was still tender. Being here with him now, Teresa knew that even more pain was headed her way. There was no chance to avoid it. When this month with him was over, that was it. All dreams would be dead. All hope gone.

So should she treat this month as the punishment Rico considered it—or should she embrace it and pack in as many memories as she could? Enough to last her a lifetime?

"If I turn this around," she whispered into the quiet room, "and look at this month as a gift from the fates…" What? She wouldn't be in pain later? She'd get the happy ending to her fairy tale?

"No," she told herself, refusing to even begin to blow a bubble of hope that was doomed to burst. "But at least this time with him will be easier. For both of us."

She almost laughed. Nothing about this was going to be easy, no matter how she colored it. The man she had loved so desperately wanted her—but only for the revenge she could provide. There was no happily ever after in her future. But she still had the choice to either accept this coming month as he'd described it—a punishment— or to look at it as one last thing she could share with Rico.

The door to the bedroom opened on a hush of sound

and she turned to look at the man standing in the doorway. He took her breath away. In this palace of tropical pastel colors and varying shades of white, he stood apart. Dressed entirely in black—slacks, long-sleeved shirt, shoes—he looked…dangerous. And she knew he was. At least, to her own sensibility. His black hair was too long, curling around the collar of his shirt. His blue eyes shone against his tan. His mouth was a grim slash. He tucked his hands into the pockets of his slacks, leaned one shoulder against the doorjamb and fixed his gaze on her.

She felt that look as surely as she would have a touch. Heat washed through her and her breath came in short, sharp gasps. Oh, she was in very deep trouble here. And she couldn't even really regret that he had ensured she stay with him. How could she? She'd missed him for five years. Now that she was with him again, how could she *not* enjoy it?

"You're ready. Good. We're leaving." He straightened up, turned and walked out of the room, clearly expecting her to follow.

She glanced into the mirror and gave herself a quick look. She was wearing a lemon-yellow dress, with narrow straps over her shoulders, a deeply cut back and a full skirt that ended just above her knees. Her long black hair was drawn back into a tumble of curls that fell down between her shoulder blades and the gold hoops at her ears winked in the light. She looked good and she knew it.

Yet Rico had almost looked *through* her. As if she hadn't seen her at all. As if she was no more important to him than any of the other furnishings in his lovely home.

She was nothing to him now.

And so the pain began.

* * *

Once they were at his hotel, Rico stalked across the main dining room. He kept one hand at Teresa's back as if to assure himself she wouldn't bolt. But the feel of her bare skin beneath his palm was a fire that wouldn't be denied. Heat spilled up his arm and through his chest to spread lower until simply walking was an agony. The low back of her dress showcased the pale honey tone of her smooth skin and made a man's gaze dip lower, to the curve of her behind. Then Rico's mind took over, just to drive him completely around the bend.

Nice job, he told himself silently. *You're supposed to be punishing her and instead, you're torturing yourself.* Yeah. This month was going to be a piece of cake.

While the maître d' hustled to escort them to his private table, Rico's gaze slipped around the room. Black tablecloths, candles on every table, the flames flickering in the soft wind drifting in through the opened windows that allowed the scent of flowers to wash over the room. Muted conversations, the clink of crystal and classical music being pumped through the stereo system all came together to make King's Castle on Tesoro's dining room the elegant sanctuary it was. Waiters moved swiftly, silently through the maze of tables. Champagne corks popped, wine was poured and the finest food in the world was served. He had built this, following the vision he'd had to create a lush, sensual retreat. A place where reality took a backseat and dreams came to life. Where sensual pleasures were enhanced and fantasies sprang to life.

Now he himself was caught up in one of those fantasies.

He noticed the furtive glances of other men as they

passed and he knew they were admiring Teresa. Well, hell, who could blame them? She was beautiful, but more, there was an inherent pride in the way she held herself. The tilt of her chin, the flash in her eyes. He knew they saw all of that, because he had seen the same the first time he met her—when he had known he had to have her.

That need was as fresh tonight as it had been so long ago.

The booth at the back of the restaurant had a view of the entire room, yet remained set apart. Private. *His.* He felt her shiver as they stepped into the shadows and he hid a smile. He liked knowing that she was off balance. Rico had the power here and he wasn't going to give it up. Sensing Teresa's nerves smoothed the jagged surfaces of the simmering anger and raw need clawing at Rico's insides.

She gave the maître d' a smile and then slid across the burgundy leather seat. Rico's heartbeat skittered wildly, but he buried the reaction to her smile and told the tuxedoed man beside him, "Champagne."

"Right away." He scurried off and Rico slid into the booth beside Teresa.

"Champagne?" she asked.

"We're celebrating, aren't we?" He leaned back and laid one arm across the back of the bench seat. "After all, it's been five years. A reunion deserves champagne, don't you think?"

"Reunion." She laughed a little under her breath, but the sound didn't mask her anxiety. "Is that what this is?"

"You have been in the wind for five years, Teresa," he said, his voice low enough that only she could possibly hear him. "I think we both deserve to mark this… *occasion.*"

In seconds, a waiter appeared tableside and uncorked the champagne. After pouring some for Rico and getting a nod of approval, he poured two glasses and then disappeared, leaving them alone again.

Teresa took a long sip, then sat back, closed her eyes and sighed.

That soft, breathy sound shot through Rico like a bullet. His body was hard as stone and his mind was struggling to keep the memory of her betrayal sharp and clear so that his body and heart couldn't surrender again. He'd already lived through that once. He wouldn't do it again.

"I'm surprised your father agreed to the deal I offered him."

Her eyes opened and brown eyes met blue. "Did you think he wouldn't?"

He shrugged. "I have no idea how a thief thinks."

She sucked in a breath. "Are you going to be throwing that word around for the whole month?"

"It's appropriate, don't you think?" He paused for a sip of his champagne and let the bubbles slide down his throat. In the flickering candlelight, her golden-brown eyes glittered. "If not for your family's occupation, we wouldn't be here."

Her eyes never left his face. "And you'll never let me forget it."

"Why would I?" He set the crystal flute down and stared at her, meeting her accusing glare with one of his own. He was the one who had been cheated, lied to, stolen from. How she had the nerve to act like the injured party was beyond him. But he wasn't going to let her get away with it. "You don't like the word *thief?* Which would you prefer? Criminal? Burglar? Or perhaps *cat burglar* would be more specific."

Her fingers swept up and down the slender stem of her champagne flute. His gaze caught the motion and fixated on it. He imagined that small, dainty hand sliding across his body and it took everything he had not to reach out and grab her. Drag her to him across the bench seat and haul her across his lap where she could *feel* what she was doing to his body. He wanted his hands on her again. He needed to feel the flash and heat of her body against his.

This month was either going to satisfy his need for payback—or kill him.

"The Coretti family has been doing what they do for generations."

Just like that, it was as if ice water had been poured in his lap.

"And that makes it all right?"

"I didn't say that."

"You used me for your family's sake and then left when the job was finished."

Her eyes went soft and then hard again in a blink. As if she'd deliberately shut out whatever it was that had caused that momentary weakness. "I've told you. I didn't know they were going to take the dagger until the job was done."

"Very convenient."

"Nothing convenient about it," she muttered, then lifted her chin and met his gaze squarely. "If you think it was easy for me to leave you, you're crazy."

"Easy or not, you did it," he said and as memory and anger roared into life inside him, his accent became more pronounced. He heard it in his whispered words, but couldn't seem to tame it. "I have never been used before or since. That makes you *special*, Teresa. And I won't rest until you've returned my property and paid for what you did."

"I have paid," she told him and her voice sounded unbelievably weary. "For five years, I've paid for what I did, Rico. But it doesn't matter what I say, does it? You won't believe me."

"No," he agreed. "I won't. That's the downside of being a liar. Even when you claim to be telling the truth, no one will listen."

How the hell could he? She'd ripped him in two when she disappeared. Never before or since had he allowed a woman to slip into his life as Teresa Coretti had. She'd crept past his defensive shields and burrowed her way into his heart. His soul. In the short time they were together, she'd given him more than he had ever hoped to find.

Then she'd been gone.

And the cold that had filled him once he'd learned that she and her family had used him had never really ebbed. Being beside her now, he felt sexual heat, but even that wasn't enough to burn off the stinging chill of the memory of her betrayal.

All around them, couples leaned across tables, laughing and talking in soft murmurs that added to the romance of the room. But here at his table, there was a distance between him and Teresa that might as well have been a brick wall.

"Then why are we here?" she asked after several long moments of silence. "If you don't want to talk to me or hear my side of things, why didn't you just lock me in your bedroom?"

Good question. But the answer wasn't one he was ready to give her. How could he admit to her that having her standing there in his room had pushed every one of his buttons? She'd been too close, the situation too intimate. He'd needed time. Time to think about exactly how he wanted this to go. Time to get his own raging need under control. Because he wouldn't be led around by his sexual desire. This time, where Teresa was concerned, he wouldn't allow his brain to be clouded by desire.

"Have to eat." His tone was dismissive and the sentence short and sharp. He wanted her to know that it didn't matter to him that she was sitting beside him smelling like hot summer nights.

"Fine. We'll eat." She took another long drink of her champagne, then sighed heavily. "Then maybe you can tell me exactly what you expect of me for the next month."

His body stirred. Oh, he expected plenty. "I think you already know."

She closed her eyes briefly. "I suppose I do. Not getting enough action from the models and actresses you squire around?"

One eyebrow arched. "Been keeping track of me? Flattering."

"Not really," she said with a sniff. "It's hard not to know what you're up to when you're splashed across magazines and newspapers—complete with pictures of you and the bimbo of the week."

"My life is none of your business." He scowled at her and left it at that. He didn't care for the disapproval in her voice. She was the one who had walked out. Who was she to pass judgment on anything he did? Let her think what she would. Her opinion of him meant less than nothing, didn't it?

"You're right. It's not my business. But answer one question for me. Why didn't you just let me go five years ago? Why stop the divorce and go to the trouble of sending me a forged decree?"

His fingers clenched around the delicate crystal stem and Rico had to force his grip to relax before the glass simply shattered in his hand. When he finally spoke, his voice was low and even, despite the anger churning within.

"You ran. From *me*." His gaze caught hers and he noticed the flicker of…was it shame shining in her light brown eyes? If so, he was glad to see it. "I'm a King, Teresa. We don't lose. Ever."

She pulled in a long, shuddering breath. "So this is a game? A competition? I can leave but only when *you* say so?"

"If this is a game, it is one you devised," he reminded her. "But it is one I will win."

"You're wrong," Teresa said softly, with a slow shake of her head. "No one's going to win."

His heart fisted in his chest and that tight knot of pain told him she was probably right. By the time they were through, there would be no winners.

Only survivors.

"Are we interrupting?"

He knew that voice. Scowling, Rico turned to the man standing beside his table. He slanted a hard look at his cousin Sean, then smiled at the lovely, *very* pregnant woman by his side.

"Would it matter if I said yes?" Rico asked his cousin.

"No," Sean said.

"Yes." Melinda spoke up at the same time. She gave her husband's arm a light swat, then shrugged and looked at Teresa. "We are interrupting, but honestly, I just had to get out of the house."

Sean wore slacks and a long-sleeved white shirt. Melinda's long black hair was pulled back into a ponytail gathered at the base of her neck. Her blue eyes looked tired and she was dressed in a long skirt and a clingy top that emphasized her pregnancy.

"You mentioned you were going to dinner," Sean put in, already helping Melinda slide across the leather seat. "And we thought that sounded like a great idea."

He settled at the end of the booth, directly opposite Rico, and gave him a grin. Rico blew out a sigh, but short of tossing his cousin out, there was no way to get rid of him. Besides, Melinda was much too nice to be treated badly because of her idiot husband.

"Hey, champagne!" Sean spotted the bottle nestled in a silver ice bucket and signaled to a waiter for another glass. Remembering his wife, he also ordered a bottle of sparkling water.

While they waited, Rico looked at Teresa. "This is my cousin Sean King and his beautiful wife, Melinda Stanford King."

"Stanford?" Teresa asked. "Any relation to Walter Stanford? The man who owns this island?"

"He's my grandfather."

Rico watched Teresa curiously as the two women fell into an easy conversation. She had known about Walter Stanford. So she'd done some research on Tesoro before arriving on the island. To help her family? Or to find out more about Rico and where he was living now?

She laughed at something Melinda said and the delicious sound settled over him like a warm blanket. Seeing her now, he wasn't looking at his betrayer, but simply a woman so lovely it took his breath away. And he realized that the tightness in his chest was easing.

Maybe it was a good thing Sean had horned in on dinner. Having the other couple here was definitely easing the tension at the table. Though it would no doubt return when the evening was over and they were back at Rico's house.

"So," Sean asked with a smile as the waiter arrived and poured Melinda a glass of the sparkling water. "What's new?"

Rico glared at him. Sean's sense of humor could be irritating at the best of times. Tonight was not the best of times.

"I should ask that of you," Rico said. "When we spoke earlier, you were watching a game. What made you decide to come here instead?"

"This promised more action than what was happening in that game. Dead boring." He took a sip of champagne, then leaned his head toward his wife. "Besides, Mel's getting a little twitchy. Waiting for the baby to make a move can make you restless. Thought she'd have a good time getting out of the house."

"Please," Melinda said with a laugh. "It wasn't just *me* trying to get out for the evening. You were going stir-crazy."

"Maybe a little," Sean allowed and draped one arm around her shoulders.

Shaking her head at her husband, Melinda turned to Teresa. "Sean tells me you've been living in Europe the last few years. What do you do for a living?"

Rico slanted a look at her and waited for her answer. He, too, was interested in how she'd spent her time the last five years. When he'd known her, she'd been one of the chefs at his Cancún hotel. Had she kept her love for cooking, or had that been part of the ruse she'd used to get close to him? How could she be so familiar to him and yet feel like such a stranger?

Teresa glanced at him briefly, as if she'd guessed what he was thinking. Then she turned her full attention to Melinda. "I'm a chef. I've been working at different restaurants in Europe for the last few years."

Melinda frowned a bit. "No home base?"

"No," Teresa said with another glance at Rico. "I move around a lot."

To avoid being found, no doubt, he thought, even though he wondered why. It wasn't as if she had known he was looking for her. So why hadn't she gone back to her family? The ones who had been important enough to her to betray her husband?

"That sounds great," Melinda said. "I love living on the island. Couldn't imagine being anywhere else." She reached out and caught Sean's hand in hers. "I do love to travel, though, so I envy you that. But I really can't empathize with the chef thing. I'm a terrible cook."

"True," Sean put in. "She made tacos last week and even the dog wouldn't eat them. And he'll eat anything."

"Thank you," Melinda said wryly.

Her husband gave her a hard, fast kiss. "Didn't marry you for your cooking abilities," he said with a grin. "We can hire cooks."

"Thank goodness. Or we'd starve," Melinda put in. "Though right now, I'm looking too well fed to be starving."

"You look gorgeous," Teresa said.

"That's what I've been telling her." Rico smiled gently at his cousin's wife. "A pregnant woman is nothing but beautiful."

"And big," Melinda put in. "Don't forget big."

"When're you due?" Teresa asked.

"Officially? A week." The woman winced and shifted position uncomfortably. "But it feels like any minute to me."

Sean shivered dramatically. "Don't say that. At least wait until we get home again."

Melinda patted his hand. "Sean's practiced making the hospital drive from our house five times."

"Smart," Teresa said.

Rico snorted.

Sean sneered at him.

"The hospital is only ten minutes away," Melinda said with an indulgent smile for her husband.

"There could be traffic," he said, defending himself.

"On Tesoro?" Rico laughed and shook his head at his cousin. "The landmass is so small, if you were on the other side of the island it would still only take you twenty minutes to reach the hospital."

"Fine, fine." Sean poured his wife another glass of sparkling water, then topped off his own champagne. "Just wait until *your* wife is pregnant. Then we'll see how funny you think this is."

Silence dropped over the table with a thud of awkwardness. Teresa winced. Melinda slapped her husband's arm again. Rico frowned and Sean took a deep drink of his champagne. "Going to be a long night."

Five

Going to be a long night.

Sean King's words echoed over and over again in Teresa's mind as she waited in Rico's bedroom hours later. He'd already promised that they would sleep in the same bed. But there was no way she could relax until he was here.

She figured she now knew how a sacrificial virgin must have felt just before being tied to an altar stone. Of course, she was no virgin—that ship had sailed long ago. But the nerves were there. The anxiety about what she should do. He'd said nothing would happen between them unless she initiated it. So. *Should* she?

In spite of the anxiousness holding her in its grip, Teresa was…aroused. And she'd thought that over the years she had managed to bury what she'd felt for Rico. She had never met another man who could stir up her insides with a single look. She had thought that Rico was her one chance at happiness and when she'd left him, she had accepted that she would never have him again.

Now she was here, and Teresa was forced to admit, at least to herself, that the thought of going to bed with Rico again had her body burning in anticipation.

It had been so long since he'd touched her. So long since she'd felt the intimate slide of his body into hers. The mental images crashing through her mind made her legs tremble so badly that she was forced to drop into the closest chair. Teresa took a deep breath and let it out slowly, hoping for calm. Calm, though, was impossible to find.

She looked around his bedroom, noting that the space was done in shades of soothing white, from cream to ivory and every shade in between. There were splashes of color in the paintings on the walls and the jewel-toned pillows stacked on the bed wide enough to qualify as a soccer field. The bamboo floor gleamed like old honey in the soft lighting. The chair she sat in was one of two drawn up before a now cold fireplace of river stone. A table between the chairs held a carafe of lemon water, left there by one of Rico's efficient yet nearly invisible staff.

She poured herself a glass of water and drank half of it down, hoping to ease her dry throat. But there was no help there, either. She wasn't thirsty, she was *needy*.

Oh, she hated to even let that thought race through her mind. Hated knowing that her body and heart were still vulnerable to Rico even after five years.

When she'd first met him, he had been open, warm. He'd drawn her in so easily, sweeping her into an affair and a romance and into marriage before she'd even had time to notice how quickly things were moving between them. Even if she had noticed, she wouldn't have cared. It had all felt so right. As if they'd somehow been fated to find each other. She had *loved* completely, for the first time in her life, and she had hoped it was forever.

Now his warmth was gone, covered by a veneer of ice that put a hard glint in his pale blue eyes, and Teresa knew that she was to blame for the change in him. She set her water glass aside and scrubbed her hands up and down her arms, as if she could chase away the chills dancing along her skin. Despite the sexual heat simmering inside her, the cold sensation of impending disaster just wouldn't dissipate.

"Where is he?" she muttered aloud, more to hear a sound in the stillness than for anything else. "What's he waiting for?"

Why wasn't he storming into the bedroom and finding a way to make her beg for him?

Another rush of heat swamped her and she pushed up from the chair. Her knees were weak, but her will was strong. Whatever game Rico was playing, she wasn't going to cooperate. She refused to sit still and worry herself into what her mother used to call a state. Rico expected her to just sit here in this lush *cell* and await his arrival. No doubt he knew exactly what she was going through and was enjoying it.

"But what choice do you have?" she murmured. "Where could you go, even if you were willing to run away again? You're on an *island,* for heaven's sake."

Even if she could, she wouldn't have run. Not again. Everyone made mistakes, she assured herself, but only really foolish people made the *same* ones over and over again.

Muttering, grumbling and trying to get a grip on her

own skittering hormones, Teresa stepped out of the bedroom onto the flagstone terrace.

Instantly, the flower-scented breeze wrapped itself
around her as it rattled the leaves on the surrounding
trees, sounding like hushed whispers in the dark. At the
edge of Rico's property, the ocean sighed into shore,
moonlight shimmering on the surface of the water. It
was perfect. Dreamlike. She only wished she wasn't too
tense to enjoy it.

"Planning to run again?" Rico asked from behind her.

As she whirled around to face him, he continued,
"There's nowhere to go this time, Teresa. You can't get
off the island until I *let* you go."

He was backlit by the room behind him and in his
black clothes, with his black hair and his face in darkness…he looked like a shadow of doom. He wasn't,
though. Because ghosts or shades or whatever you wanted
to call them didn't give off heat as Rico did. Even from
across the patio, she was dazzled by it.

"I wasn't running," she managed to say. "I was waiting."

"For?" He stepped out of the bedroom and walked
across the patio toward her. Moonlight shone in his eyes,
but his luscious mouth was a grim line and his body language was anything but relaxed.

"I was waiting for you, Rico, and you know it," she
said. "I've been here. Alone. For two hours. Is making
me wait part of the thrill for you?"

"Thrill?" He moved in so close, she instinctively
took a step back. But the metal railing around the patio
stopped her retreat and dug into the small of her back.
"You think I'm enjoying this?"

"I think you're loving it," she told him as nerves gave

way to the Italian temper her parents had gifted her with. "You had to wait five years, but you're finally getting back at me."

"Did you expect anything less?"

Had she? On those rare occasions when she'd allowed herself to imagine meeting Rico again, she'd never wondered what he'd say to her. What she could possibly say to him. Her imaginings had been more rich fantasies of desire and the passion that still haunted her. In her dreams, she and Rico hadn't wasted a lot of time *talking*. But she was rapidly discovering that reality was much harder to live with than fantasies.

Teresa stared up into his eyes and knew she was in no position to be angry at him. Though temper still simmered inside her, it was slowly draining away. After all, this was her fault. She was the one who'd lied to him so long ago and those lies had eventually brought them here. To this moment.

"No," she said. "I suppose not."

"Why did you come to Tesoro, Teresa?"

She pushed her hair back from her face with one hand, then let it fall to her side again. "When I realized my father and Paulo had come here, I tried to get them away before you found them. That's all."

"I don't think so." He moved in closer and she leaned back because she couldn't move with the railing pressing against her spine. He slapped both hands down on the iron on either side of her, effectively caging her between his arms, and then bent his head until his eyes were boring into hers. She looked into those so familiar and yet so different eyes and saw nothing soft or tender or loving. All that shone back at her was temper and ice.

"I think you came because you *wanted* me to catch you at last. Because you couldn't stay away."

"You're wrong." She shook her head, determined to deny his words. If he was right, then she was a monumental fool.

"Am I?" His voice dropped to a husky whisper that hinted at intimacy. "You could have phoned your father. Warned your brother to leave. Instead, you came here, to my place."

All right, yes. She could have phoned. Could have tried to talk to her family long-distance from the safety of her apartment in Naples. Oh, she'd told herself that they wouldn't listen to her if she called. That she would have to convince them in person. But what if Rico was right? What if her hunger to be near him again had sent her right into his revenge plan?

Oh, God, she hoped not. Because that would mean her feelings for him were still too rich, too deep for her own good.

"Think about it, Teresa," Rico urged, his mouth just a breath away from hers. "You came to me. And now that I have you…"

Her insides swirled and heat rushed through her in a blink. Her throat went dry and her breath locked in her chest. Funny, but his idea of revenge—keeping her in his bed for a month until she surrendered to the want clamoring inside her—was just what she'd been dreaming about ever since she'd left him. The punishment for her would be when the month was over and he gave her the divorce she had thought she'd gotten years ago.

He brushed his lips across hers. Once. Twice. Just the barest touch of his mouth to hers and fireworks exploded inside her. She shivered and watched as he pulled away, then straightened, taking a step back from her.

"Now that I have you," he repeated, "we do this *my* way."

"What is your way, Rico?"

"That you'll find out soon enough." He turned toward the bedroom. "Come. It's late and I'm tired."

Tired?

She was still struggling for breath as she watched him go. Her knees were rubbery and her head was spinning. Her heart was racing and at the core of her, she felt hot and achy. A barely there kiss had reduced her to this—and hadn't seemed to affect Rico at all.

She was tangled up in knots and he was *tired.*

Teresa pulled in a deep breath and let it out slowly as she followed Rico. Whatever he had planned for her, it looked as though it wasn't going to happen tonight. So it seemed she was just going to have to learn to live with the jittering nerve endings and the screaming hormones. Because she wasn't about to let him know just how much his kiss had awakened in her.

He already had the power here. No point in crowning him a true King.

For the next few days, Rico was like a man holding on to a live electrical wire. His body was in a constant state of burning. He was touchy. Jumpy. And so damned horny he wondered if a man could die from *want.*

The plan had been to keep Teresa with him at all times, taking every chance to touch her. To kiss her. To make her so crazy she'd beg him to take her. Joke was on him though, as he was the one suffering.

He walked into the tropical bar, glancing around at the

crowd gathered beneath rainbow-colored umbrellas. Not far away, waves rushed to shore, leaving frothy footprints in their wake. Surfers rode the waves and tanned beauties lay stretched out under the sun on royal-blue chaises that looked like sapphires on the white sand. And here in the bar, conversations were loud, laughter was bright and liquor flowed as freely as the sea.

He scanned the faces gathered there and finally found the one he sought. Teresa was behind the bar, helping Teddy, the bartender, serve drinks. Rico wasn't sure why it irritated him to find her there, helping. But it did. Hell, she was supposed to be miserable. Instead her eyes were shining, her smile wide and welcoming, and when she laughed at something a customer said to her, everything inside Rico tightened into a fist.

Before he could go to her, though, a hand came down on his arm and he looked to his left. Serenity James, Hollywood's latest darling and Rico's current annoyance, smiled up at him.

She tossed her caramel colored hair back from her shoulders to make sure her no doubt surgically enhanced breasts in her impossibly small bikini were displayed to their best advantage.

"Rico, I've been hoping to see you," she said, her voice a breathy promise of sex in silk sheets. "I wanted to thank you for finding my diamonds."

The diamonds she was wearing right now. Apparently in the young actress's eyes, beachwear also demanded accessories clearly worth more than half a million dollars. The stones glittered against her tanned skin and she ran one fingertip over the diamonds, as if to reassure herself they were still where they belonged.

"It was my pleasure," he said politely, though it cost

him. He flicked a glance at Teresa, still laughing with her customer. She was supposed to be suffering, he told himself. Instead, she was making herself at home on Tesoro. He'd noticed over the last few days just how often she lent a hand to one of the staff. The bar today, yesterday it had been some crisis in the kitchen and before that, he'd caught her helping one of the maids whose service cart had been upended by a drunken guest.

Teresa was ingratiating herself with everyone on the island. Including Sean and Melinda King. He knew that Melinda and Teresa had spent some time together since their shared dinner that first night. According to Sean, Teresa was wonderful, being good company and keeping Melinda from worrying about the unknown terrors of her impending labor.

She was winning hearts and minds everywhere. And she was making him just a little insane. His plan was going nowhere fast and time was slipping by. Meanwhile, he was trapped with the empty-headed actress smiling up at him as if she wanted to take a bite out of him. Perhaps at some point in his past he would have been tempted to allow her to do just that. But since meeting Teresa, no other woman interested him in the slightest.

So he gritted his teeth and focused on getting rid of Serenity James as quickly and discreetly as possible.

"As a guest at Castello Tesoro," he said, "you are my priority, Serenity. We want you to be happy and enjoy your time on the island."

"Well, that's the nicest thing anyone's said to me all day." She threaded her arm through his and steered him off to her table. "Join me for a drink so I can thank you again."

Annoyance scratched at the base of his spine, but he

kept his professional smile firmly in place. There was no way out of this and Rico knew it. He was used to playing host to the wealthy and the spoiled. And sometimes that meant temporarily burying his own wants and needs to keep the guests happy. Besides, Teresa wasn't going anywhere.

He took a seat beside the actress at her table. While Serenity told him all about her latest movie and asked him where she could find some real "action" on the island, Rico's mind wandered to the brunette behind the bar.

For three days and nights, they'd shared his home. His bedroom. His *bed*. Every night he lay beside her in the dark and called on every reserve of willpower he possessed to keep from touching her and taking what he still thought of as *his*. His mind filled with images, memories, of burying his body deep within hers. Tension coiled so hard and fast inside him it was a wonder he slept at all. But he would finally fall asleep, only to wake up with Teresa curled up against him, her arm flung across his chest, her head nestled on his shoulder. The scent of her filled his lungs and made waking both pleasure and agony.

Though she went to sleep clinging to the edge of the bed like the last leaf on a tree in autumn, by morning, Teresa was all over him.

She wasn't being tortured by his plan.

He was.

Serenity dragged the tips of her bloodred nails across the back of his hand. But rather than the seductive sensation she no doubt hoped it was, all Rico felt was irritation. He drew his hand back and gave her a smile. "If there's anything we can do to ensure your stay is a pleasant one, you must tell me."

Instantly her grass-green eyes flashed with interest and more. No, that wasn't what he'd meant, but women like Serenity saw only what they wished.

"Now that you mention it," she said on a throaty purr, "why don't you and I go to my cottage right now and have a private party? We could get to know each other better and—"

Before he could speak, he heard Teresa's voice come from directly behind him.

"A private party?" she repeated, coming around to sit on the arm of Rico's chair. She laid one arm around his shoulders and he felt her breast press against him as she leaned in.

Curious as to what she was up to, he didn't say a word to stop her.

"Shouldn't you be behind the bar mixing drinks?" Serenity asked coolly, her gaze moving up and down Teresa's outfit of cotton-candy-pink T-shirt, white shorts and flip-flops with dismissal.

"Oh," Teresa cooed, "I'm much more than a bartender, Ms. James."

Rico was enjoying himself. Teresa's hand slid back and forth across his shoulder, then moved up to the nape of his neck, where her fingers threaded through his hair with slow strokes. His skin was sizzling and every drop of blood in his body suddenly rushed south.

"Now, if you don't mind," Teresa said, giving the other woman a sweet smile, "my *husband* and I have other plans."

"Husband?" Serenity looked from Rico to Teresa and back again. "You're *married*?"

Rico bit back an oath as the actress's voice hitched high enough to be heard at the surrounding tables. His marriage had never been public knowledge. His and Teresa's time together had been so short that not even the media had caught on to it before she had disappeared from his life. Now, though, that looked as if it was about to change.

"Well, damn it," Serenity said on a full-bottom-lip pout, "you could have *mentioned* it." When she stood up in a huff, she punched her breasts out to make sure he could appreciate what he'd be missing, then turned and sashayed—the only word to describe the swing of her hips and the long stride of golden legs—out of the bar.

When she was gone, Teresa made a move to get up, but Rico caught her around the waist and dragged her down onto his lap. Her sexy, curvy behind nestled on top of him and Rico knew a whole new world of discomfort. He groaned, but held her in place. Yes, there was pain, but there was also need and want and a hunger like he hadn't known in five years. She wiggled, trying to get up, but her movements only fanned the flames licking at him.

"Let me up," she said in a whisper. "People are watching."

"You made sure of that when you walked up and rubbed yourself against me," he told her, enjoying the memory almost as much as the feel of her sitting on him.

"I didn't—" She broke off. "Fine. I did."

"Question is," he asked, "why?"

She looked down into his eyes and seemed to consider whether she would answer or not. After a long minute or two, she tore her gaze from his and muttered, "You looked like you wanted to be rescued."

"Ah." He hid a satisfied smile. He hadn't needed saving. Teresa had chased off the actress for her own reasons. Maybe his plan of seduction was actually working better than he had thought. "That's another lie. You're very good at it, by the way, but not good enough."

"Well, if I read you wrong and you *didn't* want to be saved from a conversation with that vacuous twit, I'm so very sorry."

A smile ticked up the corner of his mouth. "Twit? Have you met Ms. James before, then?"

"I don't need to talk to her to recognize the type," Teresa said, studying her fingernails now as if the secrets of the universe were scribed there.

"Which is?"

She shrugged and that little movement had her shifting on his lap again. Rico had to hiss in a breath to keep from groaning aloud. It was the sweetest kind of pain he'd ever known and he was in no hurry to ease it.

"She's pretty and has great boobs, which she probably paid a fortune for, and that's about it."

Rico smirked at her. "You can tell this with a glance?"

"Absolutely," she said. "But if you want to chase Ms. Boobs, just say so."

He shook his head. "I'm not interested in Serenity."

"Not how it looked from the bar." And she was back to studying her nails.

"You were jealous."

She stiffened in outrage and glared at him for good measure. "I don't know what you're talking about."

"Yes, you do." He dropped one hand to her thigh and relished the feel of her sun-warmed skin, bared by her white shorts.

She shivered and tried to scoot to one side, but his other arm wrapped around her waist held her exactly where he wanted her. He continued to stroke her thigh and felt the tremble shaking her slide under his own skin, as well.

Surrounded by guests enjoying the beach, Rico felt as if he and Teresa were alone. Only the two of them in this moment. And hell, it would have been much easier on him if they *had* been alone. Then he could just stretch her out on the sand, strip her clothes off and give in.

"You are lying again. To me. To yourself."

She huffed out a breath and squirmed on his lap, which only served to make him harder and her more aware of it. Instantly, she stilled. "What do you want to hear, Rico?"

"The truth," he said, in a direct challenge. "That you didn't like seeing that woman with me."

She laughed, but the sound lacked her usual musical quality and came off as strained instead. "If I were the jealous type, the last five years of seeing your picture in magazines and newspapers, always with a different woman, would have drummed that right out of me."

"So you tell yourself. And yet…"

Teresa took a breath, slanted her eyes to his and murmured, "Fine. I didn't like the way she was pawing at you. Heck, she was practically drooling. Happy now?"

Short answer was yes. A longer answer would take more time. At least a couple of hours. In his bed. Even his taste for revenge was muted by the fire inside him. All he wanted, all he could think about, was getting her naked and—if he didn't stop thinking about it he'd never be able to walk out of the bar.

Reluctantly, he relaxed his hold on her and she quickly got to her feet. She looked down at him and her eyes were bright, her mouth parted as her breath came fast and hard. He caught one of her hands in his and rubbed his thumb across her knuckles. She pulled her hand free a moment later and he allowed it.

"I'll see you back at the house," he said quietly. "One hour."

She swallowed hard and suddenly looked just a little… anxious. "Rico—"

"One hour, Teresa. Then we settle this between us."

She gave him a brief nod, then moved back to the bar. Alone, Rico stared out at the sea, trying to empty his mind of every wicked thought and desire that raced through it. What he needed was a cold shower, but what he wanted was more heat. Teresa's heat. The fire he had only ever experienced with her.

And soon he would have it.

Six

Teresa was standing on his bedroom terrace when he arrived. The tropical breeze smelled of saltwater and flowers. The sound of the ocean was like a heartbeat in the distance and the dappled shade from the surrounding trees danced and shifted with the wind that lifted her hair from her shoulders in soft waves.

Her heart was pounding. Every nerve in her body was standing straight up and buzzing. She felt electrified from the inside out. She couldn't sit still. Couldn't stand without moving, pacing. Could hardly breathe through the knot of anticipation lodged in her throat.

Back at the beach bar, when she'd been sitting on Rico's lap, she'd felt the hard proof of his desire for her. And even there, surrounded by strangers, she'd wanted nothing more than to turn in the chair, straddle him and—
Oh boy, she was in very serious trouble.

Feeling this way for your husband was one thing. Wanting the man who only wanted to use you then discard you was simply a road map to misery. God, she remembered so clearly what it was like to be loved by Rico King. To be the reason his eyes warmed when she walked into a room. To know that he was right there if she stretched out her hand. To have his arms come around her in the middle of the night, making her feel safe and treasured.

And she knew what it was like to lose all of it.

Now she would have to lose it *again,* and Teresa didn't know if she'd be able to bear it this time. Because she'd already lived through years of emptiness without him, so this time when she left, she knew exactly the kind of cold, dark place that would be waiting for her. She'd do anything to avoid that wide chasm of utter loneliness again. But there was just no way out.

Her careening thoughts skidded to a halt when she actually *felt* Rico's presence. Slowly she turned to see him standing in the open doorway, watching her. The wind caught his hair and tossed it across his forehead. His blue eyes were fixed on her and his mouth was tight, as if he wished he were anywhere but here. And yet…there was heat and tension spiraling between them, binding them together with invisible tendrils of desire and need.

Whatever else also lay between them—lies, betrayal, anger—this was just as real. This living, breathing passion that was so strong it was pushing her to take the first steps toward him even now. It didn't matter why he wanted her. Only that he did. She couldn't take another moment without feeling his hands on her. She'd wanted for so long and now she could *have.*

He held his ground, half in the bedroom, half out, and

waited for her to come closer. Every step was a test in courage. Every breath a victory. She couldn't look away from his eyes and when she saw a flash of heat dazzling there, she crossed the last of the space separating them in a dash.

Teresa threw herself at him and he caught her, encircling her in his arms, holding her tightly to him so that she could feel every ridge and plane of his body. She felt the thick hardness of him pressed against her middle and instantly she went hot and wet.

Here, her mind whispered. *Here* was where she belonged. Where she always wanted to be.

What sounded like a growl erupted from his throat as he threaded his fingers through her hair, tipped her head back and held her for his kiss. She met him eagerly, hungrily. Their mouths fused, tongues twisting and dancing in a frenzy of need. Breathing was short and labored. Hands slid up and down burning bodies and when he suddenly turned and walked her backward toward the bed, she kept pace.

Teresa fell back onto the mattress and kept her arms around Rico's neck, as if a part of her was afraid that he would stop now. Take that one step away and return to that careful, cold distance between them just to torture her. But she wouldn't let him. Not this time.

Every night she slept beside him and every morning she woke up entangled with him, feeling the heat of his body pouring into hers just before he bolted from the bed and left her there. Alone.

She was done.

Let the revenge begin.

She didn't care *why* she was there anymore. Or even

why he wanted her there. It was enough that Rico was with her again, laying his body atop hers.

Finally he tore his mouth from hers, looked down into her eyes and whispered, "You're wearing too many clothes."

"You, too."

Nodding, he rolled to one side of her and got up just long enough to yank his clothes off and toss everything to the floor. Teresa did the same. Her T-shirt, shorts and sandals were on the floor in seconds and her bra and panties quickly followed. Then she was naked, standing in front of him as the sunlight streaming through the terrace doors caressed their already-heated bodies in a golden warmth that seemed to soak deep into their bones. That light was reflected in his eyes as he looked at her and Teresa shivered in response.

He was beautiful. Just as she remembered him. His body was tanned and every muscle was sharply defined. He was also hard and ready and glancing at his erection made Teresa quiver deep inside. Right where she wanted him.

As if reading her thoughts, Rico reached for her, then tumbled her back onto the mattress. Heated skin met the cool silk of the duvet beneath her and seemed to heighten every one of her senses to overload.

Rico's hands skimmed over her body. Her breasts, her nipples, her abdomen and finally lower, where he cupped her heat and rubbed the heel of his hand against her until she was writhing beneath him.

Her gaze still locked on his, she watched as her responses to him fed the flames dancing in those pale blue depths. She chewed at her bottom lip and a soft moan slipped from her mouth as he dipped first one finger and then two into her heat.

Teresa sighed at the blissful sensation of his touch on her body again. Everything was so familiar and yet so new. Almost as if this was their first time together. Her hands moved over his shoulders and down his arms, stroking, loving the feel of his skin beneath her hands. He was so hard and strong and so warm to the touch.

He bent his head to her breast and as she watched, he took one of her already-peaked nipples into his mouth. She gasped at the first touch of his lips and tongue. She moaned as his teeth scraped across the sensitive tip and then she arched into him as he suckled her.

His hand stroked her core while his mouth drove her even closer to the edge. Again and again, he drew on her breast, as if he could taste all she was. She felt that drawing sensation down to her bones and all she could think was, *yes. This is all just as it should be.*

This was what had tormented her dreams for so long. The memories of his touch, his caresses, his mouth, his hot breath dusting across her skin. All she needed now to feel complete was his body pushing into hers, locking them together as they were meant to be.

He lifted his head as if he'd heard or sensed her thoughts. Staring into her eyes, he whispered, "You feel so good, Teresa. As I remembered and more."

"Rico…" That single word came out strangled as knots of need lodged in her throat and breathing was more and more difficult.

Her hips lifted into his hand and his thumb brushed across one particular spot of sensation that had her reaching blindly for him. He kissed her again and again, mouths meeting and parting, breath mingling, their heavy sighs coming in tandem.

Teresa struggled to find her breath as Rico drove her toward a climax she didn't want to experience without him inside her. "Be with me, Rico. Be *in* me."

He hissed in a breath, dropped his forehead to hers for a moment and then eased up enough to look into her eyes. "No, Teresa. When I have you, it will be *my* way."

Her heart broke a little even as her body was clamoring for more. "Don't," she urged, framing his face in her hands. "Don't use what's between us for payback."

His hand on her core stilled and her body ached.

"If I wanted to torture you," he said softly, kissing her mouth, her nose, her eyes, "I would step away now and leave you hungering for me as I hungered for you so long ago."

Guilt rushed in and chewed at her heart. She had walked out on the man she loved without explanation. Without apologies. Just disappeared one day and as far as he knew, never looked back. But it hadn't been easy for her. She'd left a piece of her soul behind when she'd slipped away from his life. A piece she could never reclaim.

"Rico, I hungered, too," she whispered and felt the sting of tears in her eyes. "I didn't want to leave you. I had to—"

Sunlight shone in the black of his hair and glittered across his blue eyes. Outside the terrace doors, the surrounding trees were filled with birds screeching and singing. Inside, silence was as heavy as stone.

He shook his head. "No more. The past is gone. What we have is now. This month and no longer."

There it was. He couldn't have been clearer. From

the first time he'd proposed this blackmailed month to this very moment, Rico had laid down his expectations. One month. No longer. Her insides twisted and her heart wept, but her body was more interested in the *now.* In the completion of the orgasm that had been promised.

"This month, then," she said softly and thought that she saw, however briefly, a flicker of regret in his eyes. But in the next moment, it was gone anyway.

She smoothed one hand across his face as he touched her again, sliding his fingers deep inside her. He stroked her inside and out, increasing the rhythm of his caresses until all thought but one was chased from her mind. She needed.

All she could see was his eyes. Those blue depths that were filled with so many colliding emotions she couldn't identify them. All she felt was the tightening coil inside her, threatening to explode.

"Rico, please. Now. Be with me." She bucked against him and tossed her head from side to side. Her heartbeat clamored in her chest and it felt as though every muscle in her body was clenched. Feet planted on the mattress beneath her, she moved into his hand, seeking more, needing more.

When he stopped touching her and pulled away, she groaned tightly. "Don't stop. Please. Don't stop."

"I'm not," he said through gritted teeth. "I couldn't even if I wanted to."

She heard a drawer open and close, then the distinct sound of a foil wrapper being ripped open. She opened her eyes, looked at him in time to see him sheathe himself and her mouth went dry again. He was the most beautiful man she had ever seen. How had she ever had the courage to leave him and what she'd found with him? How would she ever survive without him again?

But those thoughts and the millions of others that would no doubt torment her for years to come had no place here now. Here there was only she and Rico. And the passion rising in the room.

Teresa lifted her arms to him and parted her legs in welcome. His body covered hers and in the next breath he entered her, sliding into her heat in one long, smooth stroke. She sighed in soul-deep pleasure at the feel of him within her once more. So long. It had been so very long.

Teresa's head tipped back on the mattress and she lifted her legs higher, wrapping them around Rico's waist, holding him to her, taking him as deeply as she could. She wanted to savor the moment. Imprint the feel of him inside her on her brain so that the sensation became a part of her. So that she would never truly feel alone again.

"Look at me," he whispered and Teresa opened her eyes to stare into his. Her own desire was reflected back at her and matched by what was shining in his gaze.

He set a rhythm that she eagerly met and as they looked into each other's eyes, they raced toward completion together. Teresa shouted his name as pleasure, raw and wild, crashed over her and as her arms locked around him, she heard him groan, felt him stiffen as his own release claimed him.

And locked together, they tumbled over the edge and willingly fell into oblivion.

A half hour later, Teresa was feeling wonderful. Sprawled across a bed, her lover—her husband—lay beside her. Every inch of her body felt well used. Her heart was full and in that moment, her mind raced with possibilities.

Maybe this month wouldn't be the end after all, she thought, refusing for now to remember Rico's words, *This month and no longer.* Maybe it could still be different. Maybe this time with him would be a beginning. A fresh start. A time for them to meet as equals and realize that what they had found together was too precious to throw away. Maybe there could still be a happily ever after.

But not, she knew, until the past had finally been put to rest.

"Rico," she said, voice soft in the quiet room, "I want you to know that when I left five years ago—"

"Stop." He cut her off with one sharp word. Turning his head to meet her eyes, he said, "I'm not interested in remembering old lies—or hearing new ones."

His cold tone was like a verbal slap. "I wasn't going to—"

"Teresa," he said on a sigh, "this changes nothing between us, so don't look at me with stars in your eyes."

God, she had been. And she should have known better. But how was she supposed to protect her heart against hope?

"I need a shower." Rico pushed off the bed, gave her a quick look and said, "That was good, thanks."

"Thanks?" Stunned, she looked up at him. "That's it? Just *thanks?*"

He shrugged. "Were you expecting outpourings of love and devotion?" He smiled briefly and shook his head. "All we share now is sex and this hotel, Teresa. And that only for the next month."

Hurt crowded around her heart and squeezed painfully. Just a short while ago, he had been a part of her, sharing something *amazing,* and now he'd draped that icy demeanor over himself like a damn cloak. There was distance in his voice and a careless attitude that tore at the last remaining shreds of five-year-old dreams.

"That wasn't just *sex*, Rico." There was more between them than that. Wasn't there?

He met her gaze thoughtfully for a long second or two. Then he said simply, "Yes, it was."

Turning his back on her, he stalked toward the spa-like bathroom and tossed over his shoulder, "You should get cleaned up. We're expected for dinner at Sean and Melinda's."

Then he closed the bathroom door behind him and left her, suddenly cold and very much alone, in the middle of the bed.

Dinner was an eternity.

Pretending as if nothing was wrong only built the tension inside Rico until he felt as though he would *snap*. He'd finally escaped to the patio of Sean's home, where he stood alone in the starry darkness. Solar lights made circles of gold on the neatly tended lawn. Mature trees surrounded the house and yard and a stone walkway led down to the ocean.

He listened now, letting the soothing charge and retreat of the surf sink into him, hoping to relax some before rejoining the others inside. It wasn't easy to act as though all was well. It went against his nature to be less than honest. He was uncomfortable with pretense. Lies were tangled webs, snaring everyone who came close. And the lies Teresa had told so long ago were still strangling him.

Rico had never been one to accept lies. When he was a boy, his mother had concocted stories with impunity to get whatever she wanted. He'd never been able to believe a word she said because lying had become second nature to her. When Rico was eleven, she had at last given him up to be raised by his father, Mike King. He remembered his father coming to him several months later, asking him if he missed his mother. The sad truth was, he hadn't missed her at all, because he'd never really known her.

Her lies and impossible-to-believe stories had ensured that she was a mystery, even to her son. When she died ten years ago, she had still been a nebulous figure to Rico. He had no idea who she had been. What she'd believed. If she'd loved him at all. The lies had clouded everything.

Truth was much cleaner. Much more…efficient.

But lies kept entangling him.

For example, the lie he'd told himself: that having Teresa back in his bed would rid him of the remains of his desire for her. Instead he wanted her now more than ever.

And that shook him.

Then there was the lie he had told Teresa: that it had been simply sex that they'd shared. It cost Rico to admit it, but he couldn't hide the truth from himself. What he'd just experienced with Teresa was something else again. His whole damn body felt as if it were burning up from the inside. The tension that had been clawing at him since he'd first seen Teresa here on the island was as raw and fresh as ever. He felt as tightly wound as he ever had and he knew that his revenge plan had suddenly turned on him.

He turned away from the garden view and looked at the well-lit house behind him. Through the wide bay window in the huge kitchen, he could see Teresa with Melinda, and the two women seemed to be having a good time. No one would guess that only a couple of hours ago, Teresa had been wild in his arms. Or that he'd seen hurt in her eyes when he'd dismissed what they'd shared.

But he knew, and the memories were choking him.

"Plan not going so well?"

Rico glanced at Sean as his cousin walked out to join him on the patio. "What makes you say that?"

"For starters, you're strangling that poor, innocent beer bottle."

Rico cursed under his breath and carefully eased his grip on the bottle neck. "I've a lot on my mind."

"Yeah." Sean looked over his shoulder at the two women standing in the home King Construction had built for his family. "It's pretty clear just what's on your mind."

"Stay out of this, Sean." Even Rico heard his accent thicken as his voice dropped to a dangerous tone. He'd spent most of his early youth in Mexico with his mother. Much later he had gone to California to live with his father's family. And still, at emotional or stressful times, the music of an accent appeared in his speech.

Sean lifted both hands in false surrender. "Hey, I'm out. What you do to screw up your world is your business."

Annoyance flared and Rico scowled at the other man. He loved his family—all of them. But he knew their flaws and the worst one was that in the King family, even when they were "butting out," they had their say. You never had to wonder what your brothers or cousins were thinking, because there hadn't been a King born yet who could keep his opinion to himself. Every last one of them was sure he was right and didn't care who knew it. Made for some interesting family get-togethers and some very loud discussions.

Scowling, Rico took a sip of beer that he didn't want

and willed the icy brew to cool off the fires within. It didn't help any. "How's Melinda feeling?"

"Oh, nice change of subject. Very subtle." Sean snorted and leaned one hip on the patio railing. His gaze still focused on his wife through the wide bay window, he sighed. "She's nesting. I swear, Rico, the more nervous I get, the more *serene* she gets."

"Probably in self-defense," Rico mused. "Watching you go crazy with worry, she can either go with you or…"

"Yeah." Sean scraped one hand over his face. "Okay, yeah, I am going a little nuts. But damn, Rico. I'm about to be a *father*. That's just scary as hell."

"It must be." For one incredibly brief instant, Rico's mind dredged up an image of Teresa, pregnant with his child. Then that image shattered and he mentally swept up the shards and disposed of them.

"I mean," Sean was saying, "what the hell do I know about being a father? What if I mess it up?"

"You won't."

"Yeah? My dad wasn't the best role model in the world."

True. Sean's father, Ben King, had many sons and had never married any of their mothers. He had done his best by his children, but he hadn't always been around for them. Rico could understand Sean's doubts even as he knew that Sean would never let down his children or his wife.

"You're better than that."

"I'd like to think so," Sean admitted, then he gave a shaky laugh. "But the God's truth is, this is…huge. My kids will be looking to *me* for answers, about life and the world and—" He shook his head and took a long pull of his beer. "Okay, freaking out a little, I guess."

"It's understandable." Rico slapped his cousin on the back. "But some of your brothers are fathers. Surely they can give you some tips."

Sean laughed a little and shook his head. "Yeah, if you listen to Lucas, his Danny is ready for college and the kid's just about to turn three. And as for Rafe, his and Katie's daughter, Becca, is only a few months old. He's still as confused as I feel."

Chuckling in spite of everything, Rico reminded him, "In the last few years, how many of our brothers and cousins have begun multiplying? Think about it, Sean. If they can handle being fathers, so can you."

"How do I know *they're* doing it right?" Sighing, he admitted, "Nope, there's no hope for this kid. I'm all he's got and I don't know what the hell I'm doing."

All joking aside, Sean really did look as though he was worried about this, so Rico took pity on his cousin.

"You will love your son, Sean. That's all he really needs from you."

"Well, that much I can do for sure," Sean said with a nervous grin. Shaking his head again, he admitted, "You know, nothing in my life has ever made me so happy and at the same time scared me boneless as the idea of my son being born."

"I think," Rico told him, "that is how it is supposed to be." He used his beer to point at the kitchen window. "Besides, look at your lovely wife. Does she look worried? No. Because she has you. And because she knows that the two of you are making a family."

Sean blew out a breath. "When did you get so damn smart?"

Rico laughed at the idea. *Smart.* If he was smart, he wouldn't have wedged himself into his current situation with Teresa. "It's not being smart," he said. "It is knowing my family. And you will be a good father, Sean."

"Hope you're right." He grinned. "No backing out now. Hey, did I tell you Melinda and I are taking the baby to California for Christmas? Get a chance to let everyone meet our new son and I can show her around Long Beach…"

Rico was only half listening now. His focus was Teresa. She was wearing a short-sleeved green silk blouse and a pair of white slacks and she looked…edible. His insides twisted anew as fresh desire pulsed in his bloodstream. She smiled and tossed her hair back from her face. The line of her throat was elegant. The shine in her eyes was magnetic. Her lush body was everything a man dreamed of.

"Oh, yeah," Sean said on a laugh, catching Rico's attention. "Your plan's working real well. Damn, dude. You can help me, but you can't dig yourself out of your own mess."

Rico straightened up. He ignored Sean's teasing and snapped out, "Melinda."

Behind the glass, Sean's wife had doubled over, one arm wrapped around her belly. Teresa was hovering over her and throwing a frantic look to Rico.

"Holy—" Sean broke off and ran. "It's time. Get the car."

Seven

In fifteen minutes, the four of them were at the hospital and Melinda and Sean were taken away to the mysteries of the maternity ward.

Then time started ticking past so slowly that Teresa almost thought they'd stepped into some vortex where time had actually stopped.

The waiting room was long and narrow. It had mint-green paint, beige linoleum floors and the most uncomfortable chairs she had ever experienced. And why, she asked herself, did all hospitals smell the same? In America, Italy, even here on this beautiful tropical island, hospitals stank of antibacterial cleansers and fear. She wrapped her arms around herself, stood up and walked out to the light-filled hallway. Across from her was a nurses' station, manned by one very tired-looking woman. Teresa didn't bother to ask any questions, mainly because Rico had been plaguing the poor woman for hours now and Teresa just didn't have the heart to bother her more.

During the long night, anxious husbands and excited grandparents had come and gone from this waiting room, and still she and Rico waited. Teresa took a seat in the narrow, nearly empty lobby, ignored the small television on the wall playing an old movie she had no interest in and stared instead at Rico, who hadn't stopped pacing since they arrived. She could understand that.

She'd realized from the moment she met him that as a King, he didn't accept inactivity easily. He was a man who took charge. Who stepped in to do what needed doing. It was part of his nature. His heritage. And now he was in the position of being able to do *nothing*.

Helplessness was not something he was even remotely familiar with.

"You might as well sit down," she finally said. "This could take a long time."

"It has already been *hours*." Frowning, he glanced at her, then fired a hard look at a passing nurse. "How much longer? And how can we know if no one will tell us anything?"

Teresa took a chance and threaded her arm through his. When he didn't shrug her off, she called it a win and smiled to herself. "Let's take a walk."

"What?" He looked down at her. "Where? I don't want to go far—what if…?"

"We won't be far," Teresa said, touched that he cared for his family this much. It was these few moments, when he was unguarded, that allowed her a glimpse of the man she'd met so long ago. This man was the Rico she remembered. The stranger was the man who had jumped out of bed as if it were on fire.

"Didn't you tell Sean that nowhere on this island was far from anything?"

"Good point." He blew out a breath and scraped one hand through his hair. "All right, then. I could use some fresh air."

"And I think the nurses could use a break, too." Teresa patted his arm as they walked past the nurses' station. She paused there only long enough to say, "We're going outside for a few minutes. If Sean comes out looking for us, tell him we'll be right back."

"I will." Her gaze fixed on Rico, she said, "You take your time."

Teresa laughed, but Rico's expression didn't change in the slightest. He still wore a frown that would send most people scrambling for a place to hide. Shaking her head, Teresa led him to the elevator, then punched the button for the main floor. The two-story building wasn't large, but it spread out over quite an area. It was the only medical facility for the islanders. Without it, people who needed serious medical help would have had to board a boat for St. Thomas.

She'd learned a lot in the last few days. Rico's employees were eager to talk about him and the island paradise where they lived. They had told her all about what the Kings had done for Tesoro since moving here. For example, they had donated enough money to see to it that the small hospital now boasted top-of-the-line, state-of-the-art equipment. They'd hired more doctors and nurses and made it possible for most emergencies to be handled on island.

They'd rebuilt the dock and improved the harbor, making it easier for charter ships, as well as local fishermen, to pull into port. In town they'd arranged for more of

the islanders to sell their wares to the tourists who now
flocked to Tesoro. The Kings had done good things on
the island and everyone here seemed to appreciate it. But
Teresa knew that if she commented on any of this to Rico,
he would shrug off her admiration and call it simply good
business. He was a complicated man and maybe that was
one reason she was so drawn to him. Because at the heart
of it, very few men were complicated.

At the ground floor, Rico practically lunged off the
elevator and Teresa had to hurry to keep up with him.
Outside the night was quiet, the wind was soft and the
sound of the ocean rumbled in the distance. It felt good
to get out of the claustrophobic waiting room. It felt even
better to have Rico beside her.

Teresa took a long, deep breath and blew it out again.
"Nice to get out of the hospital for a while."

"Yes." Rico looked back over his shoulder at the
brightly lit entrance. "But not for too long. I want to be
nearby when—"

"We will be." Teresa took his hand and was pleased
when he didn't pull away. Small victories. She led him
across the side yard, their steps muffled by the thick
grass. "But waiting for hours can be hard. You have to
get out now and then."

He snorted, but the tension in him eased a bit as the
trade winds continued to rush past them, carrying the
scents of flowers and the sea with them. "And how do
you know so much about women in childbirth?"

Teresa smiled and squeezed his hand. Whatever else
was between them, for the moment they were on the same
side, allies against the unknown.

"I grew up all over the world," she said finally, tipping

her head back to look up at the night sky, dazzled with stars. "Our home was in Italy, but we were rarely there."

"I wondered why I have more of an accent than you do."

She shrugged as if it didn't matter, when the truth was all of her life she had longed for a place to call home. Even her own apartment in Naples wasn't home. Just another temporary refuge.

"Hard to adopt a particular accent when you're never in one place long enough to pick up the rhythms of the local speech."

"Hmm…"

His noncommittal answer told her that he was thinking about the Coretti family and their tradition of thievery keeping them on the move. But she wasn't going to talk about her family now and ruin this momentary truce.

"Anyway, we were living in New York and my mother's sister was having a baby. I was about sixteen, I guess."

"And you waited as we are now?"

"We waited. For hours." She sighed and shifted her gaze from the skies to him. "It seemed to take forever."

"And did your father fill his time by stealing from the patients and doctors?"

She stopped dead and turned to face him. Her gaze met his and she was sorry to see the stony glint in his eyes again. "Can you never let it go, Rico? Not even for a while?"

"Why should I?" he demanded.

"Because I'm not my father." Her voice was quiet but strong. Her gaze never left his as she added, "I've never stolen anything in my life. I'm not a thief."

A muscle twitched in his jaw as if he were fighting an

internal battle over what to say and what to hold back. Then he blurted, "So just a liar, then?"

The verbal slap hit home and she winced. It seemed that their momentary truce had ended and her sorrow was quickly swallowed by impatience. He was determined to see her only as treacherous and Teresa had no idea how to change his mind.

"And you've never lied? Are you that perfect, Rico?"

"Not perfect," he countered. "But I don't lie to the people who matter to me."

"Ah," she said, crossing her arms over her chest and giving him a sharp nod. "So you're a picky liar. Only a select few. I'm guessing women?"

"Mostly," he admitted and didn't look bothered by the admission at all.

"And that's okay?"

"I didn't say that."

"You didn't have to." She shook her head and asked, "What about me? Did you tell me pretty lies when we met?"

His jaw clenched and it looked as though he were grinding his teeth into powder. "You're the one who lied to me, remember?"

"So you were honest with me, but not with other women." She laughed shortly. "Well, hell, Rico. You're wasting your time being a hotelier when you should be a saint."

Furious now, she let her temper reign because that was so much easier than dealing with the disappointment and regret threatening to choke her. Teresa spun around and took two steps away from him before he caught her with one strong hand and whipped her back around to face him.

"I never claimed to be a saint," he muttered, his accent suddenly flaring into life and coloring his words with a seductive tang he probably didn't intend at the moment. "But I never lied to *you*."

"What about the phony divorce papers?"

He frowned, gritted his teeth and kept quiet, silently admitting he had no answer for that.

Taking a deep breath, she looked up into his eyes and searched for the man she loved behind that wall of ice he'd built between them. "I didn't want to lie to you, Rico. I didn't want to leave you, either. But there was nothing else I could do. Can't you understand lying to protect someone?"

"I can't understand a family who demands that kind of loyalty."

"Really?" She tipped her head to one side and met him, glare for glare. "Because the King family isn't loyal?"

"We don't cheat for each other," he snapped. "We don't lie to protect each other."

"But you would if you had to."

His mouth flattened into a grim slash and his eyes narrowed. She could see that he was thinking about it, considering…and not really enjoying the answer he was coming up with.

She took a long breath. "Rico, I'm not asking you to forget what happened five years ago. But maybe you could try to see it from my side."

"Your side? All I know of your side is one thing." He released his hold on her, shoved his hands into his pockets and stared over her head at the surrounding trees. "You chose them over me."

"They're my family."

His gaze shot to hers. "And I'm your *husband*."

"Do you really think it was easy for me?"

"All I know is that you did it," he ground out. "Easy or difficult, you made your choice and we were both forced to live with it."

Pain squeezed her heart and radiated out to every square inch of her body. There was nothing she could say to that. No excuse. No plea for understanding. Rico would never see what she had done as anything less than betrayal.

Their gazes locked, unspoken tension practically humming between them in the soft island air. The ocean was a murmur of sound and somewhere in the distance an animal's screech sounded out.

There was so much to say and so little all at the same time. Teresa had hoped that they might find a way to reach each other again, but for every step forward she took, Rico moved that much farther away. He was slipping away from her even as she stood beside him. Missing the feel of his touch, Teresa scrubbed her palms up and down her arms in a futile attempt to ease the chill of the cold that was deep inside her.

"Teresa," he asked quietly a moment later, "what happened?"

"What?" She shook her head and looked at him in confusion.

"With your aunt," he said, reminding her of the story she had been telling. "What happened?"

It took her a second, but a smile curved her mouth as she looked at him. Nothing had been solved. They were still on opposite sides of the same battle. But his question told Teresa that Rico, too, missed their all-too-brief truce. So she willingly played along and dipped back into her memories.

"After what seemed like forever, she had a baby boy. I saw him when he was just a few minutes old." Her smile brightened. "Luca was so tiny. And he looked just furious at the indignity of being born."

Rico smiled with her and for one long moment, it was almost as if they were…united. And it was so good Teresa didn't want that moment to end, though she knew it would. For whatever reason, Rico had decided to put their argument aside and go back to their earlier, almost friendly position. She was more than willing.

"Then I will try to be patient as we wait for the newest King to make his arrival."

"They know it's a boy?"

"They do," he said, nodding. "Just last month I helped Sean paint the baby's room."

"Melinda showed me the nursery. You guys did a nice job. I love the blue and chocolate-brown." She stopped and laughed a little. "Wow. I just realized it was only a few hours ago that we were at Melinda's house and it feels like days."

He nodded, looked past her at the hospital entrance and said, "The waiting takes a toll."

"It does." She followed his gaze and said, "We should really get back."

"Yes. We should." He looked as reluctant to end this alone time as she felt and Teresa told herself not to make more of it than there was. Still, a tiny nugget of hope settled into a corner of her heart and wouldn't be budged.

He took her hand in his and the warmth of his skin washed through her. She held that feeling to her and told herself to remember. To etch that sensation into her heart and mind so that one day soon, when he was far out of reach, she'd be able to take out this memory and relive the feel of her hand in his.

When he led her back to the hospital, they were silent, even their footsteps muffled on the grass.

By dawn, their wait was over.

Sean strutted down the long hallway to the waiting room and greeted them both with a wide grin stretched across his face.

"Melinda's great and so is our son." He slapped his hands together and scrubbed his palms before shoving both hands through his hair. "It was—Melinda was—*amazing.*"

Rico bolted out of his chair, crossed the room and gave his cousin a brief, hard hug before stepping back and slapping Sean on the shoulder. "Congratulations! You're a father!"

"Terrifying, man," Sean told him with a shudder. "I won't lie."

Teresa winced a little at that word, half expecting a knowing glare from Rico. She was surprised, and pleased, when it didn't come. She walked to Sean and gave him a hug. "Do we get to see him?"

"Absolutely." Sean grinned at both of them again. "I came to get you so you can admire and stare with awe at the newest King."

Rico took Teresa's hand again as they followed Sean along the corridor and she had the feeling he hadn't even noticed doing it. The move had just come naturally. As if he'd needed to be linked with her for the occasion. That nugget of hope grew just a bit in spite of the fact that she tried hard to prevent it.

The hospital was small, so it didn't take long to get to the nursery. There were only three newborns nestled into clear bassinets. And only one of those three was a boy. While Sean stared at his son with the bemused expression of someone who had survived a battle when he hadn't expected to, Teresa just looked at the baby. He was perfect. Tiny and pink-cheeked and so beautiful she felt a knot of envy lodge in her throat.

"He's a good-looking baby, Sean," Rico said softly and his hand tightened imperceptibly on Teresa's.

"Yeah." Sean rocked on his heels and finally tore his gaze from his son. "He really is. You want to go see Melinda?"

They did and once in the private hospital room, Teresa and Rico stood on either side of the new mother's bed.

"He's beautiful," Teresa said.

"I know!" Melinda smiled and sighed, then unnecessarily smoothed the blanket and sheet covering her. "I can't believe he's finally here."

"What's his name?" Teresa asked, looking from one new parent to the other.

"Stryker," Sean announced with a secretive smile for his wife.

"It was my father's name," Melinda added, beaming at Sean. "My grandfather was really pleased when we told him what we were going to name the baby. And it means a lot to me, too."

"It's a big name for such a little guy," Sean mused.

"I think he will grow into it," Rico told him, with another slap on the shoulder. "Stryker King. It sounds strong."

"Yeah." Sean had a silly grin on his face. "It does."

Teresa watched Rico and his family and wished that she really belonged in that circle of familiarity. But she was a temporary blip on the King family radar. She wouldn't be here to watch Stryker grow up. She wouldn't be here to build on the friendship she and Melinda had begun. In less than a month, she would be gone and the island would go on without her. As would Rico.

She took a breath and held it. To distract herself, she glanced around. The private room was a pale yellow and a single bedside light glowed, throwing soft shadows across Melinda's features. She looked tired, but more happy than Teresa could have imagined.

Melinda grinned up at them and reached for Rico's hand. "I'm so glad you guys stayed. But you must be exhausted."

"You're the one who did all the work," Teresa pointed out.

"Hey, I was here too, you know," Sean chimed in.

His wife gave him a smile usually reserved for heroes. "You were, sweetie, and you were great." Then she sighed and leaned back into her pillow. "I am tired, but I'm so wired right now there's no way I could sleep, you know?"

"Well, if you are not tired, I'm willing to bet that you are at least hungry," Rico said.

"Oh, God." Melinda laughed. "I'm so hungry if I had any chocolate syrup to drown them in, I'd eat the sheets right off the bed."

Teresa laughed.

"But the nurse tells me that breakfast isn't served for another couple of hours…" She glanced at her husband. "I'm going to get Sean to go home and bring me a nutrition bar. Or a bag of cookies. Or both."

"I think we can do better than that." Rico leaned over the metal bed rail and kissed Melinda's forehead. Then he straightened and looked at Sean. "I will have our chef prepare something and it will be here within a half an hour."

"Oh, boy! You are a god among men, Rico," Melinda said on a sigh of gratitude.

"That has been said," he allowed.

"That's breakfast for *two,* right?" Sean put in hopefully.

"Of course."

"Feel better already." Sean grinned. "Of course, making himself the hero here, there'll be no living with him now. Good luck to you, Teresa."

A strained silence erupted suddenly as everyone in the room remembered at once that Teresa was on Tesoro only temporarily. Taking a breath, she swallowed hard and said, "Congratulations again, Melinda. Your baby is gorgeous."

"Thanks." She took Teresa's hand and held it for a second or two, offering silent support. "Once I get out of here, come to the house. I'll tell you all of my horror stories."

"Can't wait." Teresa smiled, then walked around the end of the bed to join Rico.

"We will see you soon." Rico lifted one hand to Sean and slipped out the door, drawing Teresa with him.

As they walked down the hall and passed the nurses' station for the last time, Teresa said, "That was nice of you. Sending them breakfast, I mean."

"It is a small enough thing to do." He tried to shrug it off and hit the elevator button for the ground floor. In moments the doors had opened again and they were striding out of the hospital into the cool of early morning.

"You really don't like being told you're nice, do you?" She studied his profile.

"Only because I'm not. And you would have said the same yesterday."

Her steps faltered a bit, but she caught herself and hurried on. True, after he'd climbed out of bed the day before and looked at her with ice in his eyes, she wouldn't have called him nice. But he had a heart, she knew he did. She'd just seen evidence of it. And five years ago he had offered that heart to her.

Was she solely to blame for the changes in Rico? And if so, how could she undo it?

Once they were in his car and buckled up, she asked, "How will Sean get home? We brought him here."

"I'll have someone bring his car to the hospital for him."

Teresa smiled. "Nice again."

He blew out a breath and glanced at her. "Expedient."

"You can't convince me, Rico." She shook her head and relaxed back against her seat, giving in to the fatigue that had suddenly begun to drag at her. "You're a nice guy and that's not a bad thing."

"Don't make me what I'm not, Teresa," he warned and fired up the engine. "It won't serve either of us."

Sunrise streaked the sky with soft colors that grew bolder nearer the horizon. The ever-present wind sighed through the opened car windows.

She understood what Rico was trying to tell her. But in the soft light of the breaking dawn, she looked at him and saw him for *exactly* what he was.

The love of her life.

Eight

A week later, Rico stood in his office at the hotel, staring out the window at the sprawling view beyond the glass. From here he could see most of the village, the harbor and all the way to the horizon. He wasn't noticing the inherent beauty of the view at the moment though. Instead, he was trying to focus on the myriad problems facing him.

Running a luxury resort such as Castello Tesoro meant that there were small crises in the making at all times. Usually he accepted them as simply a part of his world. But with Teresa back in his life, he was less focused and so, less prepared to handle it all.

In the last few days, he had already dealt with a small fire caused by a candle left burning in one of the bungalows. No injuries, thank God, but a chaise and several throw pillows were toast. Then there was the tourist who broke an ankle jumping from the top of a waterfall on the property. He was in pain but he was lucky he hadn't broken his neck instead. Naturally, the hotel would pay for his hospital bills and Rico was arranging for private transport back to the States.

There were the small, everyday problems, as well: sunburns, jellyfish stings, drunks and the occasional brawls between guests. It was the sort of thing you expected to deal with as a hotelier. What you *didn't* normally come up against was an executive chef with appendicitis.

Rico turned his back on the window and faced his general manager, standing on the opposite side of his desk. "How long will Louis be out of commission?"

"According to the doctor, at least a week." Janine Julien, a woman of about sixty with the organizational skills of a general, tapped her computer tablet. Janine had been with him since Cancún. She'd chosen to leave her home in Mexico for the island of Tesoro and Rico had been pleased by the decision. The woman kept her finger on the pulse of the hotel and was often able to anticipate and prevent problems before they happened.

"Louis will be fine," she added. "But with him out of commission for a while, I'm more concerned about what's going to happen here. As you know, the hotel is booked solid for the foreseeable future. There's a wedding scheduled this weekend and I can't stress enough how much time Louis spent with the bride's mother going over the selected menu. She is *not* going to be happy."

"We have other chefs." Rico shrugged. "They are more than capable."

"Sure they are," Janine agreed. "But Louis keeps the kitchen running. He's more than a chef. He's the one voice amid the chaos that people listen to. We've got a problem, Rico."

He had more than one, he told himself grimly. But at the moment, straightening out the mess in the hotel kitchen took precedence over Teresa.

"And I think I've found the solution."

"What?" Rico came around his desk and perched on the front edge. Folding his arms over his chest, he asked, "A solution already?"

The woman met his gaze and said, "Your wife."

Since she had been here on the island, Teresa had become known to everyone. If they'd been surprised to discover he was married, no one had mentioned it. Rico only hoped they were as discreet when the marriage was over and Teresa was gone from the island and his life.

That thought made him frown, so he pushed it aside and turned his focus back to the older woman.

"What about Teresa?"

"She was in the kitchen helping the staff prepare when Louis collapsed." Shaking her head, Janine said, "I happened to be there, too, to discuss the individual cakes for the upcoming wedding. I saw how she took charge." Shaking her head, she continued, "I was flustered, I'll admit it. But Teresa? She checked on Louis, had someone call the hotel doctor, then had another chef drive him to the hospital. And while all of this was going on, she got the kitchen moving again."

Janine shook her head, still clearly impressed with what she'd witnessed. "Everyone was shaken, but Teresa just stepped up and took charge. No one questioned her. They got back to work, and in spite of what had happened to Louis, the staff never missed a step. She's still down there now, running things. I thought you should know."

Rico didn't know whether to be grateful or furious. Once again Teresa had proven herself to him and to his staff. She wasn't cowering in his room, as a proper hostage should be. Instead, she was making herself a part of the fabric of Castello Tesoro. He knew, too, that the fabric would unravel once she was gone.

And she would be gone.

He couldn't risk believing in her again. Couldn't take the chance of keeping her here with him, knowing that her thieving family might show up at any time. But that wasn't the truth at all. He didn't give a damn about Teresa's family and knew he could handle them if they ever showed up on Tesoro again.

This was about *her*. The woman he'd once married. The woman he had trusted. Believed in. Only to be betrayed.

Well, if she was trying to ingratiate herself with him now, it wouldn't work. Of course he'd allow her to help; he wasn't an idiot and a talented chef didn't fall out of the sky when needed. But her help was all he was interested in.

Pushing up from the desk, he barked out orders. "Contact the hospital. Take care of Louis's bill and get him whatever he wants. I'll go see him later."

"Right." Her gaze tracked him as he stalked across the room toward the office door. "Where are you going?"

"To the kitchen." He glanced over his shoulder at her. "I'll see for myself if Teresa is working out as head chef or not."

A few minutes later Rico stood in a doorway, watching the choreographed confusion in the gigantic kitchen and couldn't help but be impressed. The first thing he noticed was that the classical music Louis insisted on piping through the room had been replaced by rock, with a beat that kept the entire staff moving from station to station at a busy pace. The pastry chefs worked at a mound of dough, the salads were being prepared at a long marble counter and the prep chefs were busily preparing tonight's soup selections, as well as setting up the ingredients for the rest of the menu.

And in the middle of the chaos stood Teresa. Her black hair was pulled back and tucked up under a chef's hat. She wore a white coat over her street clothes and directed traffic in the big room like a traffic cop at a particularly busy corner.

She paused to take a sip of a sauce, then directed the chef to add something else. She inspected the pastry chefs' work and grinned at them in approval. Someone shouted a question and before they'd finished speaking, she was there, lending a hand.

Rico shook his head as he watched her. Sunlight poured in from the skylights in the roof and that golden light seemed to follow Teresa wherever she went. She shone, plain and simple. He was impressed. He didn't want to be, but there it was. Teresa had stepped in when she was most needed and was taking charge of what could have been a disastrous situation.

Everyone knew that the chefs in any big kitchen had rivalries and jealousies driving them. Without Teresa, there would have been a power play with several of the chefs making a bid to step into Louis's position. With her, the kitchen was running as well as or better than it had before.

Frowning to himself, he had to admit that there was much more to this woman than he had long believed. She wasn't here of her own free will. He had practically kidnapped her, blackmailed her, holding the freedom of her family over her head. Yet instead of standing by and watching disaster strike his hotel, she had jumped in, unasked, to save the day. Why? He had to wonder.

Unnoticed, he watched her and as he did, something within him stirred. Not the heat of desire that was a continuous, overwhelming pulse tearing through him. This was something else. There was warmth beneath the heat and a rush of feelings that he'd been denying for five long years.

As soon as he sensed that warmth settling around his heart, he bit off an oath and walked away.

It had been great to be back in a big kitchen.

Teresa had told Melinda that she'd spent the last five years working in a series of different restaurants around the world. And it was true. But they were small places—mom-and-pop diners, coffee shops and bakeries. She'd worked in a patisserie in Paris, a bakery in Gstaad and a pretzel shop in Berlin. She'd spent time in Italian restaurants in Florence and tea shops in London.

But not since she left Rico in Mexico had she worked for a five-star restaurant. Truthfully, when she had first disappeared from his hotel in Mexico, Teresa had worried that he would track her down and find her, so she'd hidden away in small eateries that most people overlooked. But after some time, she had simply gravitated to those places as if she were punishing herself by refusing the opportunity to do what she did best—run a big kitchen.

But today that had changed. She felt terrible that Louis had taken ill, but she also had to admit that she had loved the challenge of stepping into his shoes, however temporarily. She'd worked tirelessly for hours and when the guests had all been served and the ovens shut down, she'd stayed late to supervise the massive cleanup required.

By the time she was ready to go back to Rico's house and her gilded cage, Teresa was exhausted. And felt better than she had in far too long. She let herself in through the front door and quietly shut it behind her. A smile was still on her face as she headed down the long, slate-tiled hallway toward Rico's bedroom. As she passed the shadow-filled living room, his voice stopped her.

"Why did you do it?"

"Rico?" The room was dark, save for the pale, watery light spilling in from the night beyond the wide windows. "Why are you sitting down here in the dark?"

She heard a click and instantly, a fire blossomed to life in the gas hearth. Multicolored slate tiles in shades of blues and grays made up the fireplace insert. Leaping flames and fiery light jumped around the room, highlighting the man who stood before it. "I want to know why you helped out in the kitchen, Teresa. You didn't have to. It wasn't up to you to prevent a disaster."

She walked into the room, hardly noticing the brightly patterned throw rugs scattered over the floor. She paid no attention to the oversize brown leather couches and chairs or to the gleaming oak tables between them. She barely glanced through the wide window providing a spectacular view of his yard that swept down to an ocean that frothed with phosphorescent light.

"I wanted to help."

"I know that. What I don't know," he repeated, "what I need to know, is *why?*"

"Is it really so hard to understand, Rico?" she asked, walking close enough to him to stare up into eyes that were shadowed in the low light, yet danced with the reflections of the flames.

"Yes," he whispered, gaze locked on her, moving over her features as if he'd never seen her before. "You had no reason to. I forced you to stay here on the island when you had no wish to. I've threatened your family with imprisonment and have made you a hostage. So yes, it is hard for me to understand why you would step in during a crisis at my hotel."

Teresa shook her head sadly. He couldn't see how much she loved him. Or if he did, he chose to not recognize it. So how could she explain that for her, there hadn't been a choice at all? "I wanted to help *you,* Rico. Louis got sick and I was right there, so I helped."

"What are you trying to do to me?" His voice was low, deep and rough. As if every word had to scratch its way past his throat.

"Do to you?" She huffed an impatient breath. "Nothing, Rico. I'm here for a month. Would it be easier on you if I sat in a corner and cried over being trapped here by a man who clearly can't stand to be around me unless I'm in his bed?"

"Maybe," he muttered thickly as he shoved one hand through his hair. "I don't know anymore."

Teresa didn't even know what she was feeling now. Impatience, irritation, a swell of love that was so rich and deep it filled her entire body and throbbed in her heart.

"Rico, would you rather I just sit on your bed naked, awaiting your pleasure? Would that be hostage-like enough for you?"

"Yes. No. *Yes,*" he ground out, then continued in a ragged voice, "if you behaved as if you were frightened or worried, that would make more sense to me. Instead you make yourself a part of things here, even knowing you won't be staying."

"If it would help, I could whimper for a while."

He snorted. "You wouldn't know the first thing about whimpering."

A small smile curved her mouth. "At least you know me that well."

All trace of amusement drained from his features and his eyes flashed in the firelight. "Once I thought I knew you better than anyone I have ever known."

Her heart ached at the wistful tone in his voice. How much she had destroyed when she'd left. How much she'd given up, never to find again. How much they had both missed in the last five years because of a twist of fate. If Gianni hadn't stolen that dagger... If she had told Rico the truth about her family when she first met him...

But *ifs* were nebulous creatures and changed nothing.

"You did know me, Rico."

"No." He shook his head and reached for her, dropping his hands onto her shoulders and pulling her up close. "I thought I did, but you weren't real. You weren't mine."

"I was, though," she argued, *willing* him to believe it.

"Not then," he answered. "Your heart was torn, your loyalties tested too deeply for you to have been mine alone. But tonight, you *are* mine."

He was right. In spite of her love for him, she *had* been torn between Rico and her family. Maybe she'd been too young to appreciate what she had found with him. She only knew that if faced with the same decision today, she would do it all differently. She would tell Rico everything and trust him to do the right thing.

God, she'd been an idiot.

She was in love with her husband and that was the one thing she could never tell him.

Rico had been waiting for her for hours. Convinced that she had an ulterior motive for offering her help when it was most needed, he'd worked it over and over again in his mind and still was no closer to discovering what her plan might be. She had to know that he hadn't changed his mind. That no matter how much she integrated herself into life on the island, he would still watch her leave at the end of the month.

She'd become friends with his cousin and his wife. The hotel staff was in love with her and he couldn't even walk into his own damned home without catching her scent. The memory of her laugh. The hush of her sighs.

When she left, it would tear a gaping hole in his life, but she *would* leave. That was their bargain and he would hold up his end. He would give her the divorce she had paid for five years ago and he would never again trust his heart to a woman.

Because even now she was keeping something from him. He didn't know what, but it was easy to read in her golden-brown eyes that she was deliberately *not* telling him everything. What her secret might be this time, he had no idea. And it bothered him more than he wanted to admit that she was *still* hiding things from him.

But through the frustration and the irritation, one thing continuously rang true. He hungered for her. He wanted her now more than ever. And the whole time he'd been here, in the dark, waiting for her, his mind had devised all manner of things he wanted to do with her when she returned. Now that she was here, in front of him, smelling so good, he drew in breath after breath just to taste her scent…Rico didn't want to wait even the length of time it would take to get to the bedroom.

"You're driving me insane, Teresa." His hand cupped her cheek, then slid around to the back of her head.

"You're not alone in that," she told him and went up on her toes.

He kissed her, hard, taking her mouth in a rush of desire and all-encompassing need. She tangled her tongue with his, leaning into him for support and wrapping one leg around his hips, pulling him closer. He ground his body against hers, letting her feel the hard, hot, demanding part of him, and she groaned into his mouth, feeding the frenzy.

The staff was gone for the night. The house was theirs. And in the dancing, firelit shadows, he shoved the hem of her T-shirt up so that he could cup her breasts. Through the fragile lace of her bra, he stroked his thumbs across her nipples, eliciting a moan of pleasure from Teresa's throat.

That soft sound stoked the fires inside him into a blaze that quickly engulfed him. Rico could hardly breathe for the need crouched in his chest. He flicked her bra open and cupped both of her breasts in his palms.

She held on to him, fingers grasping at his shoulders as she pushed herself into his touch. "Rico, more. I want more."

So did he. But he wanted her naked.

"Clothes," he murmured, letting her go briefly. "Off. Now."

"Oh, yes." Nodding, she pulled her T-shirt up and over her head, then tossed it aside. He watched her step out of her shorts, displaying the lacy, pale pink thong she wore beneath them.

His mouth went dry and his pulse skyrocketed. He kept his gaze locked with hers as he quickly tore off his own clothing and threw it to the floor. When he was naked, her gaze dropped to his erection and she sighed in anticipation.

She reached out one hand to curl her fingers around him and he hissed in a breath at the first touch of her hand. She smiled up into his eyes and stroked, rubbed and caressed him until his eyes were rolling back in his head and he had to fight for every breath.

Body taut, tension coiled, he was so close to exploding he couldn't risk her fingers on him another minute. He caught her hand in his and shook his head. "Enough."

"No," she said breathlessly with a shake of her head. "It's not nearly enough."

He had to smile. His Teresa was a passionate one and he loved that about her. No simpering, coy females for him. Rico appreciated that his woman wanted as hungrily as he did.

His woman.

That thought echoed in his mind until he deliberately shut it down.

He pulled her up against him, enjoying the feel of her lush, curvy body pressed to his. Again, she hooked her leg around his waist and he felt the heat of her core against his hard length. He groaned tightly and backed her up until she bumped into the arm of the leather couch. When she went to fall back onto it, he caught her, turned her in his arms and eased her down until she was bent over, her luscious, beautiful behind displayed to him.

She propped herself up on her elbows and looked back at him over her shoulder. She wiggled her hips suggestively, licked her lips, took a breath and said, "Touch me, Rico."

Her welcome, her *passion* undid him. He reached down and tugged that thong from her and rubbed her tender flesh with strong strokes. She moaned again and pushed her hips up, bracing her feet apart on the floor, giving him easy access to drive them both over the edge.

His brain splintered, thoughts dissolving under an onslaught of pure sensation that tore through him. Rico had never lost control of himself this way. Never allowed a woman to reach past his well-built defenses to glimpse the man he was beneath the sophisticated veneer. But Teresa did it without even trying.

Rico's finely honed control simply snapped. He couldn't wait another minute. Couldn't be denied the ecstasy of being surrounded by her wet heat. He bent over her, letting her feel how badly he wanted her. She turned her face to him and their tongues met in a fast, delving exploration, then he straightened and positioned himself behind her.

Her breath came fast and hard. She threw her hair out of her face and turned her head to watch him. Her eyes gleamed and she licked her bottom lip with a long, slow swipe of her tongue.

He ran his hands up and down her back, following the line of her spine and the curve of her behind until she was groaning with need and twisting beneath his grip.

His thumbs swiped down into the heat of her and spread her inner core to his gaze. She was hot and damp and as he stroked her she moaned, "Rico, please. Touch me. Touch me."

He did, stroking her inside and out as his own body screamed for him to enter her. To claim her as his.

Heart racing, his blood thrummed in his veins and urged him on. Teresa looked back at him again, her breath coming harder, faster, and she whispered, "Hurry."

He grinned at her eagerness. His Teresa had never been shy about lovemaking. When they were first together, they had christened every room in his suite over the Cancún hotel and what they had done on his terrace one memorable morning still woke him up at night, wanting to do it all again.

"Please," she muttered, bracing herself on the leather cushions and wiggling her hips in invitation. "Now, Rico. Do it now."

"Now," he agreed and pushed himself into her depths.

She cried out his name at his entry and everything in him fisted painfully. She was so hot, so tight and felt so right. He rocked in and out of her body, hating every retreat and welcoming every surge as the blessing it was.

Again and again, he pushed them both higher and higher, the rhythm they set breathtaking. The only sounds in the room were their heavy breathing and the hiss and snap of the fire.

He leaned over her, cupped her breasts in his hands and tweaked her nipples as his body continued to plunge into hers. She groaned and rocked back into him, doing all she could to match his movements.

She humbled him, aroused him and left him shaken to the heart of him. Desire pumped like a wildfire through his body even while his mind stood apart and realized how precious she was. How special to him. How his life would be even emptier once she was gone from it.

But Rico didn't want to think now. Didn't want to recognize future or past. All that existed was the present. This moment snatched out of time where he and Teresa could be who they were destined to be. Two halves of a whole.

That thought staggered him, so he pushed it aside. He gave himself over to the sensations cresting inside him. Rico looked down at her and saw her bite down on her bottom lip as she fought to claim the release that was so close to each of them.

He felt her internal muscles clench and strain around him and knew her climax was only moments away. He gave her everything he had and when she shrieked his name, he buried himself as deeply as he could inside her and then joined her on that steep slide into completion.

Nine

When he could think again, when he could *move,* Rico gently disentangled their bodies, then helped her shift position onto his lap as he took a seat on the couch. Wrapping his arms around her, he held her carefully, as if she was fragile and likely to break.

Which, he realized, was ironic, considering what the two of them had just done. But Teresa had always brought out his protective tendencies. It seemed that had not changed. Right now she was warm and trembling in his arms, still reacting to the explosive climax that had shattered them both. And though his body was sated, Rico already wanted her again.

"That was," she said on a sigh, "*incredible.*"

"Yes, it was." He let his head drop to the back of the couch. His eyes closed and a groan lodged in his throat as he realized what had just happened. What he'd done without even thinking about it. But then, that was the problem, wasn't it? He *hadn't* been thinking at all. "It was also incredibly stupid."

"What?" She looked up at him, her hair a wild tangle around her face, her mouth puffy from his kisses and her eyes still shining with satisfaction. "What do you mean? How was any of that stupid?"

He blew out a breath and met her gaze. "I lost control."

"I know," she said, giving him a slow, sexy, very tempting smile. "I liked it."

"So did I," he admitted. He lifted his head, stared into her eyes and added, "But I didn't stop for a condom."

"Oh. *Oh.*" She bit her lip, took a breath and said, "All right, that was stupid. But this wasn't only your fault, Rico. I wasn't thinking either."

"Small consolation." Rico had never lost control like that. But then, only Teresa had ever touched him so deeply that his brain shut off and let his body take over.

"If it helps any, I'm healthy." She laid one hand on his chest. "I haven't been with anyone since you."

Those words rattled around in his mind and then slipped down to center around his heart. He shouldn't have cared, but he did. Shouldn't have been pleased, but he was. For five years he had imagined his *wife,* thinking herself divorced, being with other men. Letting them kiss her, taste her. Giving to them what had been only his. To know that none of those torturous imaginings had been real was a gift he hadn't expected.

He dropped one hand to the curve of her breast and slowly stroked his fingertips across one hard, dusky nipple. She sighed in reaction and he felt his groin leap to life again. So did she and she smiled knowingly. That small smile touched something inside him that he didn't want to explore too closely.

It was enough that she was here. With him. For right now. He hadn't looked to the future since the night she'd disappeared from the hotel in Mexico. Instead, his thoughts had always gone back to when she had been there beside him. Smiling, laughing, giving him a secretive look that told him she wanted him as badly as he wanted her.

Rico had never planned on giving her a confession about their time apart, but since she had been so open with him, he could do no less and still retain any sense of honor in his own mind. If he was honest with himself, he would have to say that he'd enjoyed having her think that he had moved on to other women. But now, especially with what had just happened between them and with her admission, he couldn't let her go on believing his lie of omission.

Lie. He was only now seeing that as much as he hated being lied to himself, he was as guilty as anyone when it came to convenient untruths.

"I have not been with anyone since you, either." He watched surprise flash in her eyes and pleasure quickly followed.

"But—" She shook her head. "All of the pictures of you with models and actresses…"

"Things are not always what they seem." He ran one hand up and down her bare back in long, slow strokes, loving the feel of her skin beneath his palm.

"All right, then answer me this." She took a breath, blew it out, and asked, "Why haven't you been with any of those women?"

He laughed shortly. "Because unlike you, I *knew* I was still married."

She flushed and the soft color filling her cheeks made her look even lovelier, though he wouldn't have thought that possible.

"And you?" he countered. "What kept you from other men?"

She was silent for several long, tense seconds before she said, "You're the only man I wanted."

Heat spilled through him instantly. He realized that he *wanted* to believe her. He wanted to think that she had missed him as desperately as he had missed her for the last five years. But if she felt so strongly about him, how could she disappear from his life? How could she have lied to him about who she was? And how could she have stayed away for so long?

She leaned her head against his chest and he knew she could hear his heartbeat slamming against his ribs. Since she'd arrived on Tesoro, Teresa had tried to explain her past actions to him and he hadn't been interested in listening. Now, though, he wanted to know. Needed to hear her explanation, whatever it was. And yet he had to wonder if he would be able to believe her.

His mind was a rushing torrent of contradictory thoughts. His blood burned in his veins. His body was hard and ready to take her again.

What this woman could do to him was dangerous.

What he had just done to her, he reminded himself, was unforgivable. Even if they were both healthy, he thought, no condom meant there was a chance at an unexpected pregnancy. And they had to talk about the possibilities.

"Teresa," he said softly, turning her face up to his. "I must know. Are you taking birth control?"

"No." She shook her head, then laid her hand over his, holding his hand to her breast. "I'm not. But don't worry, Rico. Everything will be fine. What are the odds I could be pregnant from one time?"

It depended on whether or not the gods had a sense of humor, he supposed. He remembered how not too long ago he'd actually imagined Teresa pregnant with his child. Now, through his own stupidity, there was a chance that would happen.

"I was never much of a gambler, because the odds are usually against you." He shook his head, still having a hard time believing that he had put them in this position. "I must apologize to you. For losing control of myself."

"Don't," she said, meeting his eyes. "Don't you dare apologize. I wanted this. I wanted you. I'm glad you lost control, Rico, and if I am pregnant…we'll deal with the situation if it presents itself."

Deal with it.

He didn't know exactly what she meant by that, but he knew very well what would happen if she was pregnant with his child. They would stay married. The divorce he'd promised her would never happen.

And that would mean he would have to find a way to live with the still-rich memories of her betrayal. His chest tightened as if iron bands were wrapped around his body, squeezing mercilessly.

How could he spend his life with a woman he couldn't trust? Would he ask himself every day if *today* was the day she would bolt?

Shaking his head, he wrapped his arms around his

wife and wondered if passion would be enough to save a marriage born in deception.

A few days later Teresa and Rico went into the village to shop for gifts for Melinda and her new son.

The day was warm, the wind was soft and two of the small launches used to transport guests from St. Thomas were docked at the harbor.

Tesoro village looked, Teresa thought, like a movie set. It was too perfect to be real. The street was narrow and lined on either side by brightly painted shops. From pastels to jewel tones, each building was as different as the wares it offered.

There was a bakery, and the scent of cinnamon wafted through its open door to tempt pedestrians. There were souvenir shops, a chocolatier that Teresa really wanted to visit, and every other kind of shop you could imagine, all catering to the wealthy tourists who came to the island to vacation. At the end of the winding street there was a small grocery store that mostly served the locals and there was a spectacular view of the ocean from every point on the tidy street. The shops huddled close to the freshly swept sidewalks. Windows gleamed, reflecting the bright light of the sun, and terra-cotta pots positioned outside the tidy stores held trailing bouquets of brightly colored flowers.

There was so much to see, Teresa swung her head from side to side in an attempt to miss nothing. "It's so pretty," she said, with a glance up at Rico, walking beside her. "Like a postcard."

"That's been said," he agreed. "In fact, Sean and I hired photographers to take photos of this street at different angles and at different times of the year. Then Walter picked the ones he liked and we had postcards made to be sold in all of the shops. Proceeds go directly to the island, and the citizens here vote on how the money's spent."

She just stared at him for a moment, letting the surprise she felt show on her features. "In Mexico you stayed out of local politics. Said you only wanted to run your hotel. You weren't interested in joining committees or getting involved with the other hoteliers or the tourist industry."

He shrugged and shifted his gaze to pass over the main street, now crowded with a few of the tourists staying at his hotel. "Everything changes."

She sighed, staring up at his profile. "Not everything," she murmured, knowing that her feelings for him would never change. Of course, she also knew that Rico wouldn't believe her even if she was foolish enough to admit to still loving him. So she kept that piece of information to herself.

"There were two boats in the harbor," she pointed out. "I mean, besides the local fishing boats."

He nodded, tucked her arm through his and started walking again. "Sometimes there are more hotel guests coming in from St. Thomas than usual."

"No cruise ships are allowed to stop here, right?"

He glanced at her. "How did you know that?"

Well, because when she found out that Rico had bought land on Tesoro with the intention of building a hotel, she'd spent a lot of time researching the island. She'd wanted at least to know what he was doing and where he would be living—even if she couldn't be with him. Which was how she had known that Melinda's grandfather owned the island outright. And that it was one of the bigger privately held islands in the Caribbean.

Walter liked keeping his island as private as possible, but he also was aware that the shopkeepers needed to make a living. So he'd compromised and allowed small ships to bring in tourists to stay in the hotel and give the islanders a steady income while at the same time protecting Tesoro from being overrun with too many people.

When she first read about him and his stubborn refusal to welcome cruise ships, she had thought the older man was shortsighted, not letting his island progress. But looking at the village now, she could appreciate his decision. She imagined these tidy streets jam-packed with crowds of people—snapping pictures, drinking too much, dropping trash on the pretty streets—and actually shuddered at the mental image. Walter had been smart to protect this place.

Now, to answer Rico's question, she hedged a little. "I read up on the island when I found out my father and brother had come here."

He scowled at her and she was sorry to see that bringing up her family had instantly soured his mood. But better that than letting him know she'd been keeping tabs on him for years.

"I admit, I was surprised that your family chose to come here for a 'job.'" Rico started walking again and Teresa kept pace. "It's a small island—thieves are spotted more easily, and, as it turns out, *caught* more easily, as well."

True, her father's ego would be bruised for years over Rico actually catching him. Police departments all around the world had been trying and failing to do it for years.

But Rico was different. As tenacious as he was, she had known that coming into contact with him again would bring disaster down on the Corettis. Which was exactly why she had warned her family off. Rico King was nobody's fool. His eyes were too sharp to miss anything and he wasn't one of those wealthy types who only occasionally stepped in to keep an eye on what belonged to him. Rico was hands-on. He would know everything happening with his properties.

Especially since he'd been robbed himself, he was on a higher alert than most people would have been.

Still, she hadn't been all that surprised when her father and brother had come to Tesoro.

"My father enjoys a challenge," she said, and couldn't help the small smile that curved her mouth. Whatever else Dominick Coretti was, he had always been a warm and loving father.

"He should try *not* stealing then," Rico told her flatly. "Give himself a real challenge."

"Don't think I haven't suggested it." Teresa lifted her face into the wind and sighed as the cool air slid past. "But…"

"Once a thief, always a thief?"

Teresa let that statement go because it was pointless to argue with him about the Coretti family business. He would never understand the centuries-old legacy that Dominick was so determined to keep alive. Teresa's worry was that her father wasn't getting any younger and perhaps his skills weren't as good as they had been once—though she would never suggest such a thing to him in person.

She didn't want to see her family in prison, though. And heaven knew the Corettis had more than enough money to retire. It wasn't, she thought, the actual stealing that her father loved so much as the adventure of having every day be a different one. Of finding a way into a heavily guarded estate. Of out-thinking security parameters and disabling electronic surveillance equipment. He *liked* pitting himself against an adversary, so thinking of a way to get her father to hang up his black gloves was going to be difficult.

That was a problem for the future, though. She only had a little more than two weeks left with Rico. She could spend that time arguing with him over the Coretti family business…or she could simply enjoy what she had while she had it.

"Oh, my." She stopped dead in front of a shop window, drawing Rico to a stop, as well. "How beautiful."

In the jewelry shop window, on a bed of black velvet, sat rings, bracelets, earrings and necklaces, all set with blue-green stones that Teresa had never seen before. They shone in the sunlight like pieces of the sea, trapped forever in settings of gold and silver. Pure avarice struck her and the Coretti legacy reared its ugly head as she curled her fingers into her palms to keep from trying to grab them all right through the glass. "They're beautiful."

"They are." Rico stood beside her, but in the reflection of the glass, she saw that he was looking at her, not the jewelry. "They're Tesoro topazes. The gemstone is found only on this island."

"So jewel prospecting is a pretty good job on this island, then?"

He laughed shortly and she suddenly found his eyes even more appealing than the glittering stones and precious metals spread out in front of her. "Occasionally a hotel guest will stumble on a find while out for a hike. But the islanders know where to look for the best stones."

"It would be fun," she mused as her gaze swung back to the shop window. "Like a treasure hunt."

"The jewelry you see here is Melinda's work," he said after Teresa spent another minute or two practically drooling on the glass.

"Melinda?" Teresa looked at him.

"She makes the jewelry and it's sold here."

"She's incredibly talented," Teresa murmured. "And I think I'm more than a little envious."

"On the other hand," Rico told her, capturing her hand in his again, "you are a chef and Melinda is a miserable cook. So for survival's sake, I would choose your gifts over hers."

A flush of pride and pleasure filled her and just for a second or two she allowed herself to fully enjoy the look in his eyes and the warmth of his hand in hers. But even as she watched, the gleam in his eyes faded slightly. So she spoke up and kept her tone light.

"Well, then," Teresa said with a half smile. "Guess it would be pointless to buy her that lovely bracelet as a new-mom present. I mean, since she made it."

"True." He pulled her hand through the crook of his arm and steered her along the street after she gave one last look at the shop window. "When Sean and Melinda became engaged, he bought her a ring and only later found out that she had made it herself."

Teresa laughed at the image and enjoyed the fact that just for now, they were smiling together. Taking a walk, enjoying the day, as if reality had taken the day off. It was almost as it had been five years ago. But, of course, it couldn't last.

When Rico's cell phone rang, she felt a quick flash

of annoyance. Just when things were going so well. She stopped and waited as he glanced at the screen.

"It is the hotel," he said, then answered it. "Yes?"

His gaze shot to hers and Teresa was disappointed to see his easy expression drain away to be replaced with the cold, cautious one she'd become so accustomed to.

"What is it?" Her voice was as resigned as she felt.

"A phone call," he said. "From your father. The hotel is forwarding it to my cell."

"My father?" She hadn't heard from her father since the day he left. Mainly because Rico had commandeered her cell phone—no doubt so she couldn't make escape plans. She took the phone from him and tried not to worry at what might have happened to make her father call. "Papa?"

"Bellissima, are you all right?" Nick's voice was hurried, anxious. "I have not heard from you and when I try to call your cell, I get only your answering machine."

"I, um, lost my phone," she said, with a quick look at Rico, who only seemed amused. Yes, she'd lied *again*. But she couldn't very well tell her father that Rico had commandeered her phone to ensure that she didn't call her family to plot an escape.

"Good, good. I am glad you are all right. This King person, he is treating you well?"

"I'm fine, Papa. Rico has been very…" She paused and caught his eyes. One black eyebrow lifted, as if he was waiting to see exactly what she would tell her father about their time together. "…*kind*."

He snorted.

Her father only muttered something in Italian that she thought it was better Rico hadn't heard. Then he spoke again.

"When this is all over, *cara,* you will tell me all about how you could marry this man without telling your papa."

"I will," she promised, though she knew that conversation wouldn't be a pleasant one. No man wanted to hear that his daughter had been so swept away by passion that marrying a man she hardly knew had seemed like the rational thing to do.

"But for now," her father continued, "there is a small *problema, mi cara.*"

"Problem?" she repeated for Rico's benefit, and his scowl deepened accordingly. "What's wrong?"

Her father huffed out a breath. "We cannot find Gianni," he admitted finally. "He, too, is not answering his phone—why do my children plague me with machines they do not bother to use?—and he has not been in touch with us. He is not here in Italy and no one has seen him in weeks."

Her brother could be anywhere in the world. If he didn't want to be found, no one would be able to locate him. But why wasn't he answering his phone? It wasn't like him to simply disappear without telling the family when he would be back.

There were only two weeks left in Rico's ultimatum, and if Gianni didn't return Rico's dagger at the end of the month…the Coretti family would end up in jail. As to what Rico would do with *her,* she couldn't even guess.

"Did you try reaching him at his apartment in London?" she asked, keeping her gaze now firmly away from Rico's.

"*Si, si.* Of course we tried. Paulo is traveling, trying to run Gianni to ground." He sounded completely disgusted with the whole situation. "Paulo is in Monaco right now. If he finds Gianni there, he will call me immediately. I am going to Gstaad. He had a woman there last year and perhaps…"

That was the trouble with having a wandering family. They all had connections all over the world. Gianni could be anywhere. But the fact that he wasn't answering his phone had Teresa more than a little worried. What if he had been arrested somewhere? What if he was right now sitting in a jail cell and *couldn't* call?

She chewed at her bottom lip as she considered the possibilities. Then she realized that if one of the Coretti family had been arrested, it would have made all of the news programs. So clearly Gianni wasn't in jail. So where, exactly, was he?

"Papa, if you can't find him in Switzerland," she said, "call Simone in Paris. She might know where he is."

"Ah, of course!" Her father sounded joyful at the suggestion. "Simone and Gianni…" And off he went again in fluent, musical Italian.

Teresa stole a glance at Rico and was sorry she had. He didn't look happy. His blue eyes were almost cobalt and a muscle in his tightly clenched jaw twitched with his effort to control his anger.

"You will be well, *bellissima,*" her father said when he had wound down. "All will be taken care of. But we *might* need a little more time…"

Oh, no. "Hold on, Papa."

Taking a breath, she covered the phone with her hand and spoke to the man glowering beside her. "Paulo and my father are having a hard time finding Gianni," she explained.

"He's the one who took my dagger?"

"Yes," she said shortly. "And it seems he's disappeared, at least *temporarily*. They're looking for him, but Papa says they might need a little more time and—"

Shaking his head, he snatched his phone from her and said tightly, "Signore Coretti. You have no more time. There are two weeks left. If my dagger is not returned, the evidence I hold goes to Interpol."

She could hear her father's loud blustering and his shouted demand, "And what of Teresa? What happens to my little girl?"

She held her breath, waiting for the answer to that question. Rico's gaze met hers and she saw no softening in those cold blue depths. No warmth on his features when he said, "She will no longer be your concern. As she is my *wife*, I decide what will happen."

He shut off the phone and dropped it into his shirt pocket. Looking down at her, he repeated, "Two weeks, Teresa."

"And then?"

"We will see when the time comes." He took her hand in his, but it wasn't a comforting grip. More like a jailer's hold on a flight risk. "For now, let us go to the chocolatier for Melinda's gift."

She followed after him because she had no choice. But the truth was, she'd have followed him anyway.

There were only two weeks left. And whatever his plan for Teresa entailed, she knew it didn't include staying with him.

So while her family panicked and searched the globe for Gianni…Teresa was going to try to enjoy the moments she had left with the only man she'd ever love.

Ten

Two days later, Rico arrived home earlier than usual.

Ever since that phone call from Dominick, there'd been new tension between him and Teresa. It was as if they both realized that time was running out and neither of them knew quite how it would end.

Over the last couple of weeks so much had changed between them that Rico wasn't comfortable with his old plan of revenge and payback. Now he was more focused on Teresa herself and what they might have found together. Though the complication of the Corettis still stood between them.

He knew she was worried about her family. Anxious at the thought of her brothers and father going to prison. And yes, he knew that it was his threats that had brought them all to this point.

The difference was that now he hated to see her on

edge. Hated knowing that it was because of *him* that she had to fear for her family. And he really hated that he was falling under her spell again.

He couldn't trust her, but that didn't seem to matter. Old feelings were back and they were growing into something even bigger than they'd once been.

Scrubbing one hand across his face and then shoving that hand through his hair, he tried to find a way through this mess of his own design. But there was nothing. He had backed himself into a corner.

Moving quietly through his darkened house, he headed unerringly for the bedroom where Teresa would be waiting for him. A sharp tug of pleasure dragged at the edges of his heart at the knowledge. Oh, he was in deep trouble.

His steps faltered as he heard low-pitched voices—one of them a man's—coming from his bedroom. Rico went instantly still. Someone was in his bedroom, with Teresa. What the hell? She wasn't screaming for help, which only fed the flames of suspicion burning inside. On alert now, he eased closer to the partially closed door and peered inside.

Everything in him urged Rico to charge into that room and find out who the mystery bastard was. But this time his mind won over his instincts. He had to know what was going on and if he slammed in, the hurried conversation would end. So instead he moved closer and listened.

"Bastien, you have to *go*," Teresa said, her voice hurried, yet determined.

"Not without you." The man's voice was deep and adamant.

Rico's blood rushed to his head and he curled his fists at his sides. But before he could give in to the jealousy pouring through him as though from a tap turned on full blast, Rico peered into the room and saw an older man, dressed all in black. His gray mustache covered half his face and his bushy gray brows were wiry.

So, not a romantic encounter.

"Your father sent me to get you away," the man insisted, tossing a nervous glance over his shoulder at the open terrace doors. "He cannot find Gianni or the dagger."

Teresa sighed. "My brother wasn't in Paris, either?"

"No." The old man lowered his voice even further, but his insistence was sharp. "We are still looking, but your father does not wish you to stay with this man—your husband—any longer. He worries for your safety."

Rico scowled at the door. As if he was a danger to Teresa? Insult slammed into him but was buried deep as he waited for her reply.

"Tell my father I'm safe, Bastien. And I can't leave the island."

"*Si,* you can. I have a fishing boat waiting at the harbor." The older man reached out and took her hand. "From the mainland, we board the plane your father has waiting. It will take us to him."

Anger flared so bright and hot, Rico could hardly see. Teeth clenched, his jaw muscles felt tight enough to snap. He could already feel what would happen next. Teresa was going to do it again. She would run to save her family. She would break her word and disappear. Again.

He took a step forward, intending to stop her before she got one step outside his house, but he halted suddenly when Teresa spoke.

"You don't understand, Bastien," she said, words tumbling from her in a rush. "I *won't* leave. I gave my word to Rico and I won't break it. Not again. He's my husband

and I…*care* for him. I won't hurt him by disappearing one more time, Bastien. I agreed to stay here for a month and I'm going to."

Rico laid one hand on the doorjamb to steady himself. His world had just been rocked. Teresa had shocked him straight to the bone. She cared for him. *Love?* Did she still love him? While he stood there outside the room, something flickered to life in the center of his chest. Warmth filled him along with the territorial urge to go to her, hold her tightly to him and sweep her into bed, where he would damn well *keep* her for the rest of their time together.

He shifted position slightly so he could see Teresa better. Her long, thick hair was pulled back into a ponytail at the back of her neck. She was wearing the dark green nightgown he loved to strip from her, with a short white robe over it, loosely belted at her waist. Her long, tanned legs were bare and planted wide apart as if in a fighting stance. But it was the expression on her face that caught and held his attention. She looked…fierce. She was defying her father's attempt at a rescue. In favor of Rico.

This time she had chosen *him*.

"Your father will not be happy." The older man was speaking again.

"My father is the one who taught me that once your word is given, it is sacred," Teresa told him. "I won't cheat Rico. Tell my father to find Gianni. He still has two weeks to bring the dagger here."

Through the anger at Dominick's duplicity rose a new and unexpected feeling inside Rico. Trust. That warmth rushing through him was enveloping as he watched the woman who was his wife. And though he warned himself to be wary, he knew that something between them had shifted tonight.

Gathering together the threads of his anger, Rico pushed the door open and stepped into the room. Both Teresa and the older man whipped around to face him. She looked stunned and embarrassed. The man she'd called Bastien just looked worried. As he should.

"Get out," Rico said, voice tight with the effort of holding on to the anger churning in his gut.

The man didn't need to be told twice. He scuttled for the terrace doors and only stopped at the threshold when Rico spoke up again.

"Leave the island tonight," he advised. "If I see you here tomorrow I'll have you arrested for trespassing."

One bob of the man's head told Rico he was understood. In another second, the man was gone and he and Teresa were alone in the room.

"I can explain," she said quickly.

"You don't have to." Rico looked down at her and felt that rush of warmth again. She was beautiful. She was proud and defiant and she was his. For now, anyway. "I heard everything before I came in. Your father sent him."

She blew out a breath before lifting her chin high enough that she met his gaze. "Yes. Bastien is a family friend. Sort of an honorary uncle, I guess."

"Uh-huh." Despite everything, he felt a quick flash of irritation for Nick Coretti. Yet how could he blame the man for trying to save his daughter? Rico or any of the Kings would have done the same for one of their family. Though it burned that the older man had almost put one over on him. Would have, if Teresa hadn't chosen to stay.

"So your father arranged this *escape.*"

"He's worried about me," Teresa told him with a heavy

sigh of frustration mingled with exasperation. "He can't find Gianni or the dagger."

"Are you certain that it is *you* he's worried about?" he asked. "Or is he more concerned with the idea that he and his sons are going to prison?"

She flushed and a spark of anger lit her eyes briefly. "Of course he's thinking about that, too. But sending Bastien was about *me*."

Scowling, Rico said, "Maybe. But it was a foolish thing to do."

He pulled his phone from his pocket, handed it to her and said, "Call him."

She took a deep breath and held it. Then she punched in her father's number and listened to it ring. "Papa?" She flicked a glance at Rico. "Yes, Bastien was here. I wouldn't go with him."

Rico heard the older man's shout and almost smiled. He, too, hated it when a plan fell apart. As his own plan concerning Teresa had, he thought grimly. But he'd consider that and the ramifications later. For now...

"Let me talk to him." He held out one hand and waited until Teresa slapped the phone onto his palm. Dominick was still shouting at his daughter when Rico interrupted him.

"Do not try something like that again," he warned, holding Teresa's gaze while he listened to Nick Coretti sputter.

"She is my daughter. I want her safe," Nick said finally.

"I understand that," Rico told him, and he meant it. He would do whatever he had to do to keep a member of *his* family safe. But that didn't mean he was going to let Nick off the hook. "Teresa is safe with me. But if you try to get her off the island again, I'll make sure you and your sons are locked up forever."

The man on the other end of the line was quiet for a long moment, then said, "Agreed."

"Good." Rico looked into Teresa's eyes and added for both her and her father's benefit, "I am a man of my word. At the end of the month, once I have my dagger, I'll hand over the evidence I hold."

"And," Nick said firmly, "you will release my daughter."

He should. It was part of the deal he'd made. Not to mention the fact that he had spent the last five years working to get his errant wife out of his mind and heart. But now, looking at Teresa, Rico knew that he couldn't let her go.

Yes, he'd given his word. But he couldn't, *wouldn't* let Teresa leave him and disappear again. She was a part of him. A part of his life here on the island and without her...no.

It was unthinkable. But he couldn't very well say that to her father. So instead he said only, "We made a deal. I will stick to it—as you should."

He ended the call and felt the world beneath his feet tilt precariously. All his life Rico had done his best to be a man of his word. To avoid lies and deception. And now the only way he could get out of a bargain he had struck was to break every one of his personal rules.

Which meant he had to find another way out of this.

"He's scared," Teresa said as explanation, dragging him out of his thoughts and back to the present.

"I know." He reached for her before he could stop himself, cupping her cheek in the palm of his hand. "Any father would be. What I want to hear is why you didn't go with Bastien."

She was silent for a few seconds, as if she was considering just how to say what she needed to say. Finally she said quietly, "Five years ago, I made the choice I thought I had to. But tonight I didn't want to repeat the same mistake."

He stiffened slightly, as he always did when reminded of that time five years past. He'd shut her down whenever she had tried to tell him about the night she had left. He hadn't wanted to hear this before, but now he needed to. Rico had to know why she'd left him. Why she'd run—so he could believe that she wouldn't do the same now.

The bedroom was cool and dimly lit from the moonlight pouring in through the open terrace doors and the twin bedside lamps casting golden light across the bed and floor.

"Tell me." His words were short and clipped, but they seemed to release her from a tension that had coiled inside her for too long.

When her eyes met his again, they were damp, looking like gold coins drenched in water. If her tears spilled over, it would tear at his heart, he knew. Rico steadied himself, then took her hand and led her to the bed. Sitting down, he drew her with him and repeated, "Tell me."

"I'm glad you're finally willing to listen."

"I wasn't ready before," he told her. "I am now."

Nodding, Teresa tried to smile, but gave that up quickly. "All right, but first you have to know that when I was eighteen, I told my father that I wasn't going to be a thief. That I wanted a different kind of life."

He hadn't expected to hear that and as he thought about it, he laughed shortly.

She glared at him.

"Sorry," he muttered. "I was just imagining how your father must have taken that decision."

A reluctant smile curved her mouth. "Not well. He was horrified. And disappointed. But in the end, though he didn't understand my decision, he respected it."

Rico silently gave Nick Coretti half a point of admiration for backing off and giving his daughter the room she needed to grow her own way. Not that he was willing to forgive the old thief or anything.

"I took that job at your hotel," she said, starting off slowly, her soft voice hesitant, as if she wasn't sure how to put it now that he'd given her the chance. "And I asked my family to stay away." She smiled wryly. "Usually they did as I asked, not wanting to bring down suspicion on me in a place where I happened to be working. But that was before I took a job with Rico King."

She shook her head and caught his eyes again. "The temptation was too much. The richness of your guests at the Castello de King was enough of a draw all on its own, but there was more. They knew about your dagger. There had been some piece written about it—"

Rico remembered that. Someone had done an interview with him for a national magazine article on the Cancún Castello and during the meeting the reporter had seen the Aztec dagger in a case on his desk. There had been questions and photos and apparently that had been enough to attract the attention of professional thieves.

He hadn't worried about it at the time, because his security at the hotel was top-of-the-line. But the Corettis, he was discovering, were very worthy adversaries. "I remember that article. Go on."

She nodded and threaded her fingers together in her

lap, restlessly tugging at them until he laid one hand on top of hers to hold her still.

"My oldest brother, Gianni, loves antiquities. He couldn't resist the lure of that dagger and where he went, so did my father and Paulo." She looked up at him again and held on to his hand tightly. "I swear I didn't know they were going to hit the hotel until after it was done."

Staring into those wide-open, pale brown eyes shining with misery and regret, he could only nod. Rico believed her. But then, if he hadn't been in such pain over losing her, he would have believed her long ago.

Satisfied, she kept talking. "When you discovered the dagger missing, I just...had a feeling. Then you contacted the police and were vowing to hunt down the thieves no matter what it took."

He remembered that, too. His fury at being robbed. The crushing need to retrieve something his father had passed on to him.

"While you were with the police, I searched through the guest register and found my family under one of their more familiar assumed names."

Familiar. Assumed. She had grown up quite differently than he had. Now he saw that lying, to Teresa, had been second nature. Just the way things were done. And he had to admire her for breaking away from the only life she had ever known. What kind of strength was that, to turn your back on your family? Your legacy?

"Gianni was already gone with the dagger," she was saying and Rico came out of his thoughts to listen to the rest of the story.

"My father and Paulo were packing." She winced. "They had already sent what they'd taken from your guests by overnight mail to our home in London."

And those, Rico told himself, were diamonds, rubies and emeralds that would never see the light of day again. *At least,* he told himself wryly, *not in their original settings.*

"I begged my father to call Gianni, to get him to return the dagger, but it was too late. My brother had boarded a plane right after—" She broke off.

"Right after stealing from me," Rico finished for her.

"Yes. There was no way to reach him and I'm not sure I would have been able to convince him to return the dagger even if I could have talked to him." She sighed and shook her head, pulling one hand from his to push a stray lock of hair behind her ear. "Maybe if I had confessed that we were married—" she mused. "But I just couldn't do it. You were furious, I knew I would have to leave you and there wasn't a point in telling my family and hurting my father over a marriage that would be ending anyway."

He gritted his teeth and she saw him fight for control. When he finally found it, he spoke again. "This explains the robbery," Rico said quietly. "And why you didn't tell your family about us. It does not tell me why you ran from me. Why you chose them over what we had together."

She pulled in one long, shuddering breath and slid off the bed to stand up. Facing him, she wrapped her arms around her middle, accidentally opening the fall of her robe, giving Rico a glimpse of luscious, tanned skin and the tops of her breasts beneath her nightgown. He had to force himself to focus on what she was saying.

"I left my father and Paulo packing and went back to our suite. Do you remember how you were? What you were saying?"

"No," he said. All he recalled clearly was the helpless

anger that had had him in a choke hold, strangling him with a sense of helplessness that no King could accept.

"I do," she said softly. "You told me that if it was the last thing you ever did, you would hunt down those thieves. You would see them in prison for a lifetime." She tightened her grip around her middle and held on as if clutching a lifeline in a choppy sea. "You said you would do whatever it took. That you and I would find them. Together. Then you asked if I had seen anything, heard anything unusual around the hotel."

"And you lied to me."

"Yes." She swallowed hard and nodded. "I lied. To protect my family."

"Why, Teresa?" he asked, though he already knew the answer. Her father. Her brothers. Her connection with them ran deep. Perhaps deeper than the link she had had with a new husband and the promise of a future too vague to be real.

"Because I couldn't help you track them down, Rico. I couldn't do what you needed me to do, but I couldn't stay and *not* help you, either. I would have been living a lie every day, praying that you wouldn't discover my secret." She shook her head so wildly her ponytail swung behind her head like a pendulum. "It was a disaster. Any choice I made, I hurt someone I loved. I didn't want to lie to you, but I thought that *one* lie was better than a lifetime of them."

"You should have told me," he said, pushing up from the bed to lay both hands on her shoulders. "You should have trusted me."

She laughed now and the sound wasn't musical at all. It was like shards of glass being ground under steel wheels.

"Trusted you? I should have told you that the thieves were my family and please don't prosecute?"

He frowned at her as her words resonated inside him.

"Would you have believed that I had nothing to do with the theft?" she demanded, all traces of tears gone from her eyes now, replaced by sparks of rising temper. "The first thing you said to me when you found me here was that you thought I had married you only to give my family access to your blasted dagger."

Now it was his turn to feel a rush of shame. Yes, he had convinced himself years ago that Teresa had only married him to help her family's thieving. But that had never made sense and he'd known it even while he'd allowed the thought to drive him insane. The Corettis were, if nothing else, *excellent* thieves. They didn't need to use Teresa. They'd gotten past his security and out of the country almost before he'd known he'd been hit.

No, blaming Teresa had been his pride talking. The wound she'd left when she disappeared had festered until that convenient lie he'd told himself had simply been a way of deflecting the truth.

That she'd chosen another over him.

"You're right," he said, his voice hardly more than a hush.

She blinked at him and shook her head. "Excuse me?"

One corner of his mouth lifted briefly. Of course she would be surprised. He hadn't given her any reason to think he would be on her side in *any* argument.

"I said, you are right. I would have accused you. I would have been wrong, though." He slid his hands up to hold her face between his palms. His gaze bored into hers as he willed her to believe him. "I know you weren't a part of it. And I can even understand a little now why you made the choice you did."

She huffed out a breath. "Thank you."

"But I need to know why you chose differently to-night, Teresa."

Leaning into him, she said solemnly, "Because I didn't want to hurt you again, Rico. Because this time *you* were more important. This time I had to trust you."

"Good answer," he murmured and bent down to kiss her. He'd meant only to plant a brief, hard kiss on her lips.

But at the moment of contact, Teresa wrapped her arms around him and held on. She opened her mouth and tangled her tongue with his and they were linked, as they were meant to be, always.

Rico groaned and held her tighter. Lifting her off her feet, he turned back to the bed, laid her down and then lay down beside her. Rising up on one elbow, he looked down into golden-brown eyes. Then he kissed her again and lost himself in the arms of the only woman in the world who held his heart.

Rico met Sean for lunch at a small restaurant near the harbor. It had been two days since Teresa had turned down a chance at escape. Two days since she had chosen *him* over her family. He liked knowing that she was on his side in this, but he had to wonder how long that would last if her family didn't return the dagger.

Because if that happened, he would go through with his threat. He would hand over all of the evidence he'd collected over the last several years to Interpol. And once he did that, he would lose Teresa. How could he expect her to stay with the man who had imprisoned her family? No, he knew damn well she would never forgive him for that.

And if they *did* deliver the dagger as promised, then he would have to hold up his end of the bargain and not only release Teresa, but divorce her, as well. He couldn't keep her here without going back on his word and couldn't let her go without losing a piece of his soul.

Time was ticking past. With every beat of his heart, that internal clock moved on, pushing them toward the end of the month. Toward the end of his time with Teresa.

He couldn't stand that thought.

This month had started out with him holding her against her will, yes. But that had changed, hadn't it? She didn't act like a hostage—with the run of the island, working in the hotel kitchen, coming to his bed eagerly. Whatever it was that was still humming between them, it was something that would die the moment he sent her family to prison.

"You look like hell." Sean sat back in his chair and sipped at a bottle of beer.

"Thank you. It is good to have family to turn to in times of trouble." Rico picked up his own beer and took a long swallow, hoping to ease the knot in his throat. It didn't work. "How are Melinda and Stryker?"

Sean's grin lit up his face. "Great. Seriously great." He shook his head. "The baby's keeping us both up all night, every night, but I don't even mind. Right now I'm like a zombie, but I've never had so much fun."

A pang of envy rippled through Rico, but he ignored it. No point in wishing for things that weren't going to happen. *Unless,* a voice in his mind whispered, *Teresa is already pregnant. Then your problems are over, aren't they? You stay married. You keep her with you. And you have the family you've always craved.*

He straightened in his chair as that nebulous idea took root in his mind.

"So." Sean spoke up and Rico came out of his thoughts. "You said you wanted to talk. What's going on?"

"That is a question with too many answers."

"Pick one."

"I am trying to decide what to do about Teresa."

"Ah," Sean said, smothering a laugh. "The brilliant plan falling apart? Wow. Wish I'd seen that coming. Oh. Wait. I *did*."

Rico sneered at his cousin. "Very helpful, thank you. There is nothing better than an *I told you so* at just the right moment."

"Happy to help." Sean reached for a nacho loaded with beans and cheese, then popped it into his mouth, crunching with a grin on his face.

"Right." He should have known his cousin would love this. A King liked nothing better than an entertaining "I was right, you were wrong" chat. Shaking his head, he leaned forward, bracing his arms on the glass-topped table. The bright yellow table umbrella shaded them from the noonday sun and all around them hotel guests were either boarding day boats for fishing trips or sitting at the bar having tropical drinks. "Her father hired a man to help her escape. Seems he hasn't found her brother yet and he wants more time."

"Escape? Okay, I'm guessing she didn't go anywhere, yes?"

"She stayed." Rico took a sip of his beer. "She wouldn't leave."

"Interesting." Sean smiled, then narrowed his eyes.

"Aside from the failed rescue, do you think her father's stalling deliberately?"

"It's possible," Rico admitted, thinking back to the sound of Dominick Coretti's outraged voice. "But I don't know that he would take this kind of risk with his family. So if I assume he really does need the extra time, what do I do about it?"

"What do you want to do?"

Rico sent his cousin an exasperated glare. "If I knew that, would I be asking for your opinion?"

Sean laughed. "Okay, no. I'm no fan of Teresa's family—they're thieves." He shrugged. "But you locking up her family isn't going to score you points with her, either."

"Yes, I know that, as well." Talking to his cousin was supposed to help him straighten out his thoughts.

"So go with your gut, Rico." Sean was still smiling. "You want Teresa. She wants her family safe. Do what you have to do to make everyone happy."

"Let the thieves go free?"

"It's family, man," Sean said, smile fading into a thoughtful frown. "Look at the Kings. What haven't we been willing to do to keep family safe?"

He was right, Rico knew. And the answer, it seemed, was simple after all. A King would risk anything for family. And Teresa—not to mention the child she might be carrying—was his family.

Eleven

Another week of her month was gone and Teresa felt as though she was listening to the inexorable tick of a countdown in her head. Every morning she woke up beside Rico and every evening the heat between them sizzled anew. And every day gone was one less that she had with him.

Sitting on a chaise on the beach below Rico's house, Teresa curled her feet up under her on the floral cushion. She swept her gaze across Rico's private slice of the Tesoro paradise and sighed. A yacht was docked at Rico's private pier and the brass fittings winked in the bright sunlight. "Oh, God, I don't want to leave."

She loved it here. Loved the easy, relaxed way of life on the island. She loved having the wild beauty surrounding her wherever she went. She loved working in the hotel and she'd already made some good friends here. The hotel staff, Sean and Melinda.

But mostly she loved being with Rico. For so long she'd yearned to be with him again and now it was as if she was living in a perfect dream world.

But the sad part about dreams was that eventually you woke up and the dream shattered.

A wind off the ocean buffeted her, waves crashed against the shore, sending spray into the air, and Rico's boat creaked noisily as it rose and fell with the surging sea. Out on the horizon, dark clouds gathered, promising a coming storm, and birds in the tree behind her chattered as if in warning.

The wind kicked up, sending grains of sand stinging into her skin like tiny bullets. She hardly noticed since the pain around her heart went so much deeper.

What was she going to do without Rico in her life?

"I was looking for you."

His deep voice coming from right behind her didn't surprise Teresa. It was as if she'd conjured Rico out of thin air just by thinking about him. She hoped it would work that well in the coming years, but somehow she doubted it.

"You weren't worried, were you?" She tipped her head back and shaded her eyes with one hand. "I thought I already proved to you that I'm not going to leave the island before the end of the month."

He sank into a crouch beside her and reached out one hand to tuck her hair behind her ear. That one slight touch sent shivers of anticipation rattling through her body. He gave her a half smile and shook his head.

"You did," he said with a nod. "You gave me your word. I wasn't worried. I just wanted to see if you'd like to take a ride around the island."

His hair blew in the ever-present wind, the white shirt

he wore was open at the throat and the sleeves were rolled up. His black jeans looked worn and comfortable. He was also barefoot and, for some reason, that only heightened his sex appeal. The man was a walking orgasm.

"With you?"

He gave her another half smile. "No. With Sean."

"Funny." She nodded, held out one hand to him and let him help her up from the chair.

For the last week, Rico had been attentive, seductive and *romantic* in a way she hadn't experienced since they were first together. Every day he had a new adventure for the two of them. They had spent one day out on his yacht, alternately swimming in the ocean and climbing aboard to dry off and make love. They'd had a romantic seaside dinner in the village and finished the evening off by dancing in the moonlight. One day he had even taken her treasure hunting for Tesoro topazes.

There had been picnics on the beach and lazy swings in the hammock. Long walks and sitting together at night in front of a fire built more for romance than warmth.

It had been a perfect week. Perfect in ways that made her miserable to think of losing Rico forever. But in all the time they had spent together, not once had he talked about the possibility of her staying. Not once had he hinted he *wanted* her to stay. And not once had he said that he didn't want the divorce he had promised her.

So though she was being romanced, she had finally figured out that Rico was simply saying goodbye to her. A long, drawn-out, incredibly sweet and romantic goodbye.

And that broke her heart.

Still, she wouldn't let him see that she knew what he was doing. Wouldn't let him know that her heart ached to be with him. That the thought of leaving made her feel as though she had been hollowed out and left an empty shell.

If he could make these last few days together special, then the least she could do was join him in the pretense. There would be plenty of time later for the tears that seemed to be constantly near the surface. So for now she smiled up at him and let him see only the pleasure she felt at being beside him. "Are we going in a car or on your boat?"

"For what I want to show you, we'll have to take the car."

"I'd love to."

She bent to pick up her sandals and then followed him from the beach and across the manicured lawn to the driveway in front of his home. A small red sports car sat in the shade of several trees, waiting for them.

Once they were in the car and buckled in, Rico fired up the engine and steered the car out of the driveway and down to the main road. But instead of heading toward the hotel and the village, he turned left and sped along the narrow, paved road.

"You've been here nearly three weeks," he said, his voice carrying over the growl of the engine. "And I thought you might like to see the rest of the island."

Before you go.

He didn't say it, but he didn't have to. She knew exactly what he meant. A bubble of pain opened up in the center of her chest, but Teresa fought it down. Being here with Rico was too nice to spoil with thoughts of what was going to happen all too soon.

"Thanks. I would."

She'd seen a lot of Tesoro from his boat and he had taken her to the foot of the hills to search for topaz. But there was still so much she hadn't seen. Still so much she hadn't done. Leaving tore at her and she turned away from him so he wouldn't see the sorrow in her eyes.

Instead, she looked at the landscape as they passed. As they got farther from the village and the hotel and Rico's house, the land changed, shifted. Stands of jungle were so thick the trees looked like a solid green wall. Even the sunlight barely made it through the leafy foliage. It was like driving through a green tunnel. Then they emerged into the light again and Teresa gasped at the beauty spreading out on either side of the car. Meadows with wildflowers dancing in the breeze. Patches of farmland, even a small vineyard. And at the edge of the island, a beach with sand so white it hurt the eyes to look at it and the ocean beyond.

"It's so gorgeous here." She leaned in to Rico to make sure he heard her.

He grinned, whipping his hair back from his face as he turned to smile at her. "It is. And what I'm going to show you now will take your breath away."

That happened just looking at him, Teresa thought. But she was so glad to see pleasure in his eyes, in the easy curve of his mouth, she only said, "I'm ready."

He laughed and stepped on the gas, sending the little red car hurtling along the road at a speed that brought a laugh from her throat.

The road wound on and Teresa hoped the ride would never end. She could spend eternity like this, she told herself. Beside Rico, off on an adventure together, with the wind in their hair and the sun on their faces. But eventually Rico pulled the car over and turned the engine off.

She looked around and saw a wall of rock spilling

down into a patch of trees that looked cool and shad-owed. "Where are we?"

"You'll see." He got out of the car, came around to her side and opened the door. "Just leave your sandals here. You won't need them."

Then, taking her hand, he led her into the cool shade of the stand of trees. Birds sang, the wind blew and under it all, she heard the steady roar of the ocean. But as Rico led her on, her bare feet making no sound on the sandy ground, that roar became louder and she noticed it didn't have the sighing rhythm that she'd become used to. "What is that?"

He looked at her and grinned. "One moment and you'll see for yourself."

Using a series of timeworn rocks as steps, he led her down a narrow path through the trees. The roaring sound was even louder now and Teresa thought she knew what to expect. She was only half-right.

Stepping out into a clearing, she saw the waterfall she'd guessed was their destination. But she hadn't been prepared for the sheer beauty of the place. It was de-serted. Private. Water spilled from a rock overhang into a pond below that then drained down into a river whose twists and turns were swallowed by the jungle surround-ing them.

Trees shielded the pond from most of the sunlight. Grass and vines clung to the rock face on either side of the waterfall itself, and the surface of the pond below frothed with the power of the surging water slamming into it.

He smiled at the expression on her face, then turned and led the way along the rocks until they reached the pond.

"This is so beautiful," she said, looking up at him. "Thank you for bringing me here."

His smile faded slowly as he looked at her. "I wanted to see it with you. It's too far out from the hotels and the village for many of the tourists to know about. And most of the locals don't come here." He turned his gaze on the waterfall and the surrounding beauty before looking back at her. "So it's where I come when I want to be alone with my thoughts."

And he'd brought her here. Shared this with her. Her heart was touched and broken all at once. Who would he share his secrets with when she was gone? How would she bear it, knowing that one day he'd leave her memory behind and move on for good with some other woman?

"Teresa?" His brow furrowed and he set both hands at her waist. "Are you all right?"

No. "Yes. I'm fine." She nodded, plastering a smile she didn't feel on her face. "I should have brought a bathing suit."

His eyes flashed and his lips curved in a wicked, completely tempting smile. "Here you won't need one."

A swirl of excitement fluttered to life in the pit of her belly and she went with it. As Rico undressed, so did she, and in a few short seconds, they were jumping into the pool at the base of the waterfall, swimming toward the curtain of water dropping from the overhang.

She hooked her arms around Rico's neck and pressed close to him, loving the feel of his skin against hers. The cold, clear water fell over and around them, sealing them into a bubble of privacy that seemed to lock the rest of the world away. Here it was only the two of them. And that was just as she wanted it.

When he kissed her, Teresa gave him everything she

had, everything she was. She poured her heart into the kiss and hoped he could feel her love in her touch.

His hand dropped to her core and slowly rubbed her center until she was writhing in his arms. The cold water on her skin and the heat he engendered with his touch combined to make Teresa feel as if she were about to splinter. And when her climax hit, she clung to him, their mouths fused, their breath sliding from one to the other and just for that perfect moment, they were *one*.

Much later, after making love in a patch of sun-warmed grass, the two of them lay sprawled together beside the waterfall. The roar of the water was the only sound and Teresa was torn between sheer happiness and the grief of knowing that all too soon this time with her husband would end.

"What will you do when the month is up?"

She tipped her head back to look up at him. "I don't know. Go back to my apartment in Naples, I suppose."

Features grim, he nodded and said, "I've been thinking about this, as well, Teresa."

"Really?" Was he going to ask her to stay? Could he put aside what had happened between them five years ago and allow for a future? Hope, that treacherous little beast, jumped up and down inside her.

"Yes." He went up on one elbow and looked down at her. All trace of the romantic was gone from his expression. His features were drawn and tight and the hope inside her withered a bit in response.

This couldn't be good.

"I've been thinking that you should not leave the island."

And just like that, hope was back. She smiled up at

him and felt the strangling knots around her heart loosen a little for the first time in years.

"You want me to stay?" *Please say yes.*

"Yes," he said. "At least until we know if you are pregnant."

This was why she rarely allowed hope to inflate inside her like an oversize balloon. Because when the inevitable happened and that balloon popped, the fall back to reality was a crushing one.

Rico didn't want her. He wanted the child they might have made together. So much for fresh chances. For starting over. He couldn't let go of the past and she couldn't change it for him, so they were at a standstill.

"That's why you want me here," she said, for her own benefit more than his. She needed to hear herself say it. "Because I might be pregnant."

"You will admit, there is a good chance you are." He laid one hand against her flat abdomen as if already claiming the child that *might* be inside her. "And if you are, you will stay here. With me. No divorce."

She pushed away from him and scrambled to her feet. Looking down on the gorgeous man sprawled naked in the sunshine, she felt only disappointment. Regret. And a deep, bone-searing sorrow that would probably be with her for the rest of her life.

"But the only way you want me is if I'm pregnant." God, it cost her to say those words.

"I did not say that," he countered, coming to his feet in a slow, languid movement.

"You really didn't have to," she muttered, pushing her still-damp hair back from her face with both hands. "God, I'm an idiot."

"Teresa? Surely you see that we are good together. Staying married wouldn't be a hardship on either of us."

His tone was so reasonable. The look on his face so patient. Teresa wanted to scream.

Shaking her head, she reached for her clothes and tugged them on while she talked. "No, Rico. I won't be part of a marriage that's described as *not a hardship*."

"You are deliberately misconstruing what I said."

"I don't think so," she countered, shooting him a quick glare while she hopped on one foot to pull on her shorts. "I think you said just what you meant."

He got dressed too, but with more casual, easy movements than she managed. "You are overreacting."

"Really?" She hooked her bra and then grabbed her shirt. Pulling it on, too, she asked, "Then what would your reaction be if I asked you to forget about prosecuting my family?"

He went still as stone, his pale blue eyes fixed on her, looking like chips of ice.

"Could you let them go?" She already knew the answer but she had to hear him say it.

Then he surprised her. Again.

"If I let them go," he said shortly, his voice as cool as the gleam in his eyes, "what do I get out of it?"

She threw her hair back out of her eyes. "I'll stay with you."

"For how long?"

This cost her. Humiliation flushed her cheeks as she realized she was blackmailing her husband into keeping their marriage alive. He wanted her. The passion between them was strong. And this last week she'd seen a side of him she hadn't seen since five years before. Maybe, she told herself, if she stayed and they were together long enough, love would eventually win the day.

"Forever," she said simply, surrendering her last ounce of pride. "Or for as long as you want me."

He took a long, deep breath and steadied himself. His eyes were shuttered, emotions sheathed to keep her from reading whatever he was thinking. It seemed to take forever before he finally said, "It's a deal. The Corettis go free and you stay here. With me."

She should have been happy. This was exactly what she had wanted so badly. To be able to remain with Rico here on the island. But getting it this way left her feeling as empty as she had during the previous five years. She could only nurture that small, now silent surge of hope and pray that eventually it would prove enough to conquer Rico's heart at last.

That hadn't gone at all as he'd planned.

Rico had spent the last week being the most attentive husband in the world in an attempt to get her to beg him to let her stay. That way he could keep his word to her family and hold on to his pride at the same time.

But she'd turned the tables on him.

Pacing the perimeter of his office two days after their sojourn at the waterfall, he felt caged. As if somehow he had wandered into a trap of his own making and now there was no way out.

"It was telling her that I wouldn't let her leave if she was pregnant," he muttered, scraping one hand across the back of his neck.

But he didn't know how he could have handled that any differently. Yes, he wanted her. Yes, he *loved* her still. But he couldn't tell her that without handing her all of the power in the negotiation that was sure to follow. So instead he got a wife who had once again become a hostage for her family.

She had traded her freedom for theirs and now he would never know if she would have chosen to stay simply because she loved him.

"Idiot." He kicked his desk for good measure as he made another pass around the room and the resulting pain was only what he deserved.

When his secretary buzzed through, he answered angrily, "I don't wish to be disturbed."

"I know, sir, but there's a man here to see you. He says it's urgent."

Scowling, Rico demanded, "Who is he?"

"He says his name is Gianni Coretti and that you're expecting him."

Twelve

Rico felt a surge of both anger and satisfaction. At last there was a target for the fury writhing inside him. "Send him in."

Gianni Coretti was tall, with short black hair, sharp brown eyes and the look of a man who didn't have much patience. Good, Rico thought. Then they were well matched. Gianni was wearing a well-cut suit and looked more like the head of a corporation than an infamous thief.

He crossed the room in several long strides and offered his hand. Rico merely looked from the outstretched hand and back up to the man's eyes. He gave nothing away, though mentally he was shouting, *Why are you early? I still have four days with Teresa!*

Which was ridiculous, of course. The whole point of this bargain he'd begun what felt like a lifetime ago was to have the Aztec dagger returned. That piece of family history that had been entrusted to him by his father. That's what he should be interested in. Instead all he could think was, if Gianni was here with the dagger, then Teresa would go.

But no, a voice in his mind whispered. She wouldn't. She'd bargained herself away for his assurance that he wouldn't see the Corettis jailed. Teresa was going to stay.

For all the wrong reasons.

Damn it.

"I've heard quite a bit about you from my father and brother," Gianni was saying as he let his hand drop to his side.

One eyebrow lifted. "Not flattering, I imagine."

"Not in the slightest," Gianni agreed with a grin. "But that's not important now, is it? I have what you asked for." He reached into his suit jacket and from the inner pocket pulled a cloth-wrapped item. "You can have it as soon as I have the evidence you gathered against my family."

Rico only crossed his arms over his chest and braced his feet wide apart. "Let me see the dagger first."

Gianni chuckled and shook his head. "This is what is wrong with the world today. No one trusts anymore."

Amused, Rico pointed out, "Says the thief."

"Touché, and yet it saddens me that the world has become such a cynical place."

He hadn't expected to almost like Teresa's brother, but damned if he didn't. "Makes stealing more difficult, does it?"

"There is that," Gianni acknowledged as he carefully unwrapped the ancient dagger he'd stolen five years before. "This...is magnificent." His gaze locked on the antiquity, he smiled as if watching a lover. "Intricate carvings, jewel-encrusted handle—but it's the *history* behind this piece that sings to me." He glanced at Rico. "And to you, I believe."

"Yes," Rico admitted, barely glancing at the once all important dagger. "It has been in my family for generations and we have all, at one time or another, felt the hum of history in that blade."

Gianni nodded, still studying the dagger. "When I took this from you, all I saw was its beauty. The jewels, the gold." He shrugged. "I am a mercenary man, trained to appreciate the finer things."

"That belong to others."

"As you say." Gianni shrugged that off and continued while Rico listened, oddly fascinated. This should have been a short meeting. An exchange and then a fast goodbye. Instead, Teresa's brother was acting as though they were old friends settling down for a visit.

"As I was saying," Gianni mused, looking down at the dagger in his hand, "when I first took the dagger, all I saw was its worth. But I couldn't bring myself to fence it. Couldn't sell it. It became a part of my collection and also, it became a sort of talisman."

"What do you mean?" Interested in spite of himself, Rico waited for an answer.

"As I held this dagger in my hands, for the first time in my life I felt the history of a piece." He turned it, studying it thoughtfully. "And I began to see that I had not been taking *things* from people. I had been stealing away pieces of their lives."

Surprised, Rico only stared at him. This was not the kind of thing he expected to hear from a professional thief.

"I, too, was shocked by this revelation," Gianni admitted with a wry smile. "It is not the sort of feeling a thief most appreciates."

"I don't think your father and brother share your philosophy."

"No." Gianni laughed and shook his head. "Not yet, anyway. But everything changes, does it not?"

He'd said that to Teresa not so long ago, Rico realized. And now all he could think was that *some* things would never change. He would always love her. And because he did, he realized what he had to do.

He had to let her go.

Rico had always thought that cloying cliché, "if you love something, set it free," was bull. He believed more in the "if you love something, hold on to it with both hands so you don't lose it" way of thinking. But now he understood that cliché. It tore at him to realize the hard truth, but there was no other choice for him.

Teresa had once again given up her own life for the sake of her family. She had once again made a sacrifice. The last time, he hadn't been a part of it. He had been left out of her choice altogether. Thinking back, he couldn't say what he might have done had she come to him with the truth. Would he have seen past his own anger at her lies? She'd kept so much from him back then. But had he been any more honest? They had fallen in love so quickly and their marriage was so new they hadn't had time to build the bridges of trust that would have seen them through bad times.

So. Would he have had her family arrested five years ago? He didn't know. He only knew what he should do *now*.

"Your ultimatum," Gianni said quietly, "had my family scrambling all over Europe to find me."

Rico laughed shortly and brought his mind back to the conversation at hand. "Your father thinks you should answer your phone."

Gianni grinned. "If I did that, he would call me more often."

"I feel the same about my own family at times." A shame they were meeting as enemies, since Rico had the feeling the two of them might have been friends.

"Well, then, we two have some business to conduct," Gianni said, holding the dagger so that the overhead light caught the blade and glinted like diamonds. "Here is your property. And now I would like to see this evidence my father claims you hold."

Rico nodded, walked to his desk and unlocked the top drawer. He took out a thick manila envelope and carried it to Gianni. Handing it over, he said, "That is everything I collected over five years." As a compliment of sorts, he added, "There wasn't much to be found."

Gianni grinned. "The Corettis are not easy to catch."

"I noticed," Rico said and took the dagger when it was offered.

The heavy gold weight felt solid, right, in his hands. He was relieved to finally have it back and yet…it felt like a hollow victory. He had set his sights on the return of his property and hadn't looked beyond that. Now he could see that retrieving his dagger could cost him the woman he loved.

Gianni opened the envelope and flipped through a few of the pages. He whistled low and long before looking up at Rico. "What you have here would have seen me and my family locked away for some time." He tucked the pages back inside and slapped the envelope against his palm. "Tell me, would you really have done it? Seen Teresa's family jailed?"

Setting the dagger down onto his desk, Rico pushed one hand through his hair and looked at the other man, standing quietly, watching him. It was past time for complete honesty, he thought. With himself as well as everyone else.

"Had you asked me that question two weeks ago," he said, "the answer would have been yes. Absolutely. Now…"

Gianni's eyes warmed as he smiled. "You *do* love her. My sister."

"I do."

"Which makes what I have to say next that much more uncomfortable. You have to release her from this bargain you and she struck."

"I know."

Gianni's eyebrows lifted high on his forehead. "You surprise me. I'd thought I would have to…convince you to uphold your end of the bargain."

"The bargain has nothing to do with this. Letting her go is the right thing to do," Rico said, a sharp stab of pain accompanying those words.

The thought of losing her broke his heart. But if he kept her here, he would never really *have* her. If she left… there might be a chance for them later.

"My father was right about you," Gianni said softly. "You are a dangerous man."

Before he could figure out what the other man meant by that, his office door flew open and Teresa stormed inside. She was wearing her white chef's uniform and as she slammed the door behind her, she snatched the hat from her head and tossed it aside.

"Teresa," her brother said warmly, "you look wonderful."

"Gianni, I'm not leaving," she said flatly.

"How did you know he was here?" Rico asked.

"Your assistant called to tell me when Gianni arrived. I had a soufflé in the oven and couldn't get away until just now."

Rico sighed and shook his head. She had friends all over the hotel and they were apparently willing to spy for her.

"Your brother was just leaving. As are you," Rico said. "The bargain is finished. Go back to your family."

She looked as though he'd slapped her and he winced. It wasn't his intention to bring her more pain.

"We talked about this, Rico," she reminded him, hands at her hips. "I'm staying."

"I've reconsidered." He ignored Gianni just as Teresa was. "We made a deal. The month is over."

"You can't mean this," she muttered. "What if I'm pregnant?"

"Pregnant?" Gianni scowled at Rico.

He waved the man's outburst away with one negligent hand and focused solely on Teresa. "Are you?"

Teresa chewed on her bottom lip, then grumbled, "No."

Disappointment welled inside him as his last hope at keeping her faded. But he had to do this for her. Damn it, he had blackmailed her into a monthlong affair. He would not blackmail her into being his wife. Since reason wasn't working with her, he released the anger churning inside him.

"You think I *want* you to be a sacrifice for your family? *Again?*" He shook his head. "No, Teresa. You'll go and you'll do whatever it is you want to do without worrying about trading your life for theirs."

"No one asked her to sacrifice—"

"Be quiet, Gianni," she snapped and took two furious steps closer to Rico.

He saw the fire in her golden eyes and loved her even more. She was magnificent in her fury as she was in every other aspect of her life. This woman was everything to him. And his only chance to prove that was to force her to go.

"I don't want you here," he blurted out.

She sucked in a gulp of air and fired another glare at him as she shook her head. "You're *lying,* Rico. You said you didn't lie to those you care about, but you're lying now."

"Teresa, I think we should—" Gianni said patiently.

"*Basta!* Enough!" She snapped the words out and held up her hand, palm out toward her brother. Gianni shrugged and leaned one hip against Rico's desk, settling in to watch the show.

"You're an idiot," she said, frowning at Rico.

Gianni laughed.

Rico scowled and murmured, "Thank you."

"I'm not *sacrificing* myself by staying here, Rico," she said, coming closer now, keeping her gaze fixed on his. "I'm staying because I *love* you."

A flare of heat swelled in his chest and Rico breathed easy for the first time since she had stormed into his office. Maybe there was light in his darkness after all. "I love you, too. I always have."

Tears swamped her eyes and a tremulous smile curved her mouth. Reaching up, she laid her hand on his cheek and sighed when he turned his head just far enough to plant a kiss in the center of her palm.

"What about before, Rico? The past. Will that always be there between us?"

That was one thing he was sure of. "I don't care about the past, Teresa. All that matters to me is the future. *Our* future."

"And my family?"

He slid a glance at Gianni, still watching them with a bemused expression on his face. "If I can handle the Kings, I think I can live with the Corettis." He pointed a finger at the other man. "As long as they stay out of my hotels."

"Agreed." Gianni nodded.

"But you were going to let me leave," Teresa complained, drawing his attention back to her. "Why?"

"Because you had to *want* to be here. With me. It had to be your choice," he whispered now, as if only the two of them existed. "But if you had left, I promise you I would have followed."

Her smile wobbled, then grew more bright. "Really?"

"I would have traipsed all over Europe and beyond, romancing you, seducing you, winning your heart until you chose to come home. With me."

"Home?"

"Our home. Here. On Tesoro."

"Our home, Rico, is anywhere we're together." She went up on her toes and kissed him lightly. "You are my family, Rico. And I will always choose you."

Gianni cleared his throat and stood up, interrupting. "I will tell Papa what happened here. He'll be disappointed that you're not coming home, but I think he'll understand."

Teresa went to her brother and hugged him tightly. "Thank you, Gianni."

He shrugged and kissed her forehead. "You should know," he said, talking to Rico now, "Papa will probably want another wedding for you two—since we weren't invited to the first one."

"Yes, about that," Teresa said.

"Doesn't matter now, little sister," he said, "as long as you're happy. And I can see that you are."

She grinned at him, then watched as he walked to the cold fireplace on the far wall. "Gas?" he asked.

"The switch on the wall," Rico told him, knowing just what the other man was going to do.

Gianni hit the switch, gas flames erupted and he went down on one knee in front of it. Carefully, he tossed the envelope of evidence onto the flames and watched as it burned. When it was nothing but curling paper and ash, he stood again to face his sister and Rico.

"Now that's done, I can go."

"Where, Gianni?"

"London, for now." He went to her and pulled her in close for another hug. Then, looking from her to Rico, he said, "You don't have to worry about me anymore. The reason Papa couldn't get me on the phone this month is that I've been in talks with Interpol."

"What?"

He smiled at Teresa's shock. "In exchange for immunity, I'm going to work with their people. Help them catch thieves for a change." He shrugged. "Could be fun. And I think I might be able to talk Paulo and Papa into doing the same."

"Good luck with that," Rico said on a laugh.

"It's worth a try," Teresa said and beamed at her brother. "I'm so proud of you, Gianni."

"Imagine. *Me*. Working for the police." Shaking his head, he walked to the door and paused only long enough to look back at Rico and say, "Treat her well, Rico. I'll be in touch."

When he was gone, Rico grabbed Teresa, pulled her against him and just held on. Burying his face in the curve of her neck, he inhaled her scent and dragged it so deep inside him he would never take another breath without tasting her on it.

"I love you, Teresa Coretti King."

"I'm going to want to hear that a lot," she said, leaning back to look up at him. "I love you so much, Rico. I always have. Living without you was so horrible—"

"Shh. That's done. It's gone. Neither of us will ever have to feel that misery again, that's all that matters."

"Being here. With you. On Tesoro. It's perfect." She leaned her head on his chest and whispered, "Take me home, Rico. To *our* home."

"First," he told her as he stepped away, "I have something for you."

"All I need is you, Rico."

He grinned at her. God, he felt freer than he had in years. Just hearing her say that filled him with the kind of joy he had never really expected to feel again. But this had to be done. "Trust me. This you need."

He walked to his desk, opened the top drawer and took out a small velvet box that he had looked at every day for the last five years. When he brought it to her, he opened it and Teresa gasped.

"It's your ring," he said unnecessarily. "The one you

left behind with your note, telling me only that you had to leave."

"Oh, God." She stared at the yellow diamond and clapped one hand over her mouth. "It almost killed me to take that ring off, Rico. It—you—meant everything to me." Shaking her head, she murmured, "You kept it. I can't believe you kept it all this time."

"Sometimes," he said, "I admit, I thought about selling it or even tossing it into the sea."

"Oh, God…"

"But something kept me from it," he admitted as he plucked the ring from the velvet and slid it onto her finger. He sealed it there with a kiss, then met her eyes, now drenched again in what he knew were tears of happiness. "I think a part of me knew that we would find our way to each other again.

"Because you are my one. My only. And now the ring—and you—are back where you belong."

"And this time," Teresa whispered as she lifted her face for his kiss, "my romantic, wonderful husband, it's forever."

"It is a deal," he said with a smile, then kissed her with all the love he held in his now healed heart.

* * * * *

Leo was aware that some people called him hard… Unfeeling.

But he did what he did knowing how many employees around the world depended on the Cavallos for their livelihoods. It irked the hell out of him to think that another man was temporarily sitting in his metaphorical chair.

How was he going to survive being back-burnered for two months? Did he even want to try becoming the man his family thought he could be? A balanced, laid-back, easygoing guy?

He rested his free arm across the back of the sofa and closed his eyes, reaching for something Zen. Something peaceful.

Damn it, he didn't want to change. He wanted to go home.

At least, he had until he met Phoebe. Now she was what he wanted.

* * *

A Billionaire for Christmas is part of the No.1 bestselling miniseries from Desire™: Billionaires and Babies:

Powerful men… wrapped around their babies' little fingers.

A BILLIONAIRE
FOR CHRISTMAS

BY
JANICE MAYNARD

MILLS
BOON

Published in Great Britain 2013
by Mills & Boon, an imprint of Harlequin (UK) Limited,
Eton House, 18-24 Paradise Road, Richmond, Surrey TW9 1SR

© Janice Maynard 2013

ISBN: 978 0 263 90494 9

51-1213

Harlequin (UK) policy is to use papers that are natural, renewable and recyclable products and made from wood grown in sustainable forests. The logging and manufacturing processes conform to the legal environmental regulations of the country of origin.

Printed and bound in Spain
by Blackprint CPI, Barcelona

Janice Maynard came to writing early in life. When her short story *The Princess and the Robbers* won a red ribbon in her third-grade school arts fair, Janice was hooked. She holds a BA from Emory and Henry College and an MA from East Tennessee State University. In 2002 Janice left a fifteen-year career as an elementary teacher to pursue writing full-time. Her first love is creating sexy, character-driven, contemporary romance. She has written for Kensington and NAL, and now is so very happy to also be part of the Mills & Boon® family—a lifelong dream, by the way!

Janice and her husband live in beautiful east Tennessee in the shadow of the Great Smoky Mountains. She loves to travel and enjoys using those experiences as settings for books.

Hearing from readers is one of the best perks of the job! Visit her website, www.janicemaynard.com, or email her at JESM13@aol.com. And of course, don't forget Facebook and Twitter. Visit all the men of Wolff Mountain at www.wolffmountain.com.

For my mother, Pat Scott, who loved Christmas
as much as anyone I have ever known.

One

Leo Cavallo had a headache. In fact, his whole body hurt. The drive from Atlanta to the Great Smoky Mountains in East Tennessee hadn't seemed all that onerous on the map, but he'd gravely miscalculated the reality of negotiating winding rural roads after dark. And given that the calendar had flipped only a handful of days into December, he'd lost daylight a long time ago.

He glanced at the clock on the dashboard and groaned as he registered the glowing readout. It was after nine. He still had no idea if he was even close to his destination. The GPS had given up on him ten miles back. The car thermometer read thirty-five degrees, which meant that any moment now the driving rain hammering his windshield might change over to snow, and he'd really be screwed. Jags were not meant to be driven in bad weather.

Sweating beneath his thin cotton sweater, he reached into the console for an antacid. Without warning, his brother's voice popped into his head, loud and clear.

"I'm serious, Leo. You have to make some changes. You had a heart attack, for God's sake."

Leo scowled. *"A mild cardiac event. Don't be so dramatic. I'm in excellent physical shape. You heard the doctor."*

*"Yes, I did. He said your stress levels are off the charts.
And he preached heredity. Our father died before he hit
forty-two. You keep this up, and I'll be putting you in the
ground right beside him…"*

Leo chewed the chalky tablet and cursed when the road
suddenly changed from ragged pavement to loose gravel.
The wheels of his vehicle spun for purchase on the uneven
surface. He crept along, straining his eyes for any signs of
life up ahead.

On either side, steep hillsides boxed him in. The head-
lights on his car picked out dense thickets of rhododendron
lining the way. Claustrophobic gloom swathed the vehicle
in a cloying blanket. He was accustomed to living amidst
the bright lights of Atlanta. His penthouse condo offered an
amazing view of the city. Neon and energy and people were
his daily fuel. So why had he agreed to voluntary exile in a
state whose remote corners seemed unwelcoming at best?

Five minutes later, when he was almost ready to turn
around and admit defeat, he saw a light shining in the darkness. The relief he felt was staggering. By the time he finally pulled up in front of the blessedly illuminated house,
every muscle in his body ached with tension. He hoped the
porch light indicated some level of available hospitality.

Pulling his plush-lined leather jacket from the backseat,
he stepped out of the car and shivered. The rain had slacked
off…finally. But a heavy, fog-wrapped drizzle accompa-
nied by bone-numbing chill greeted him. For the moment,
he would leave his bags in the trunk. He didn't know exactly where his cabin was located. Hopefully, he'd be able
to park closer before he unloaded.

Mud caked the soles of his expensive leather shoes as
he made his way to the door of the modern log structure.
It looked as if it had been assembled from one of those kits
that well-heeled couples bought to set up getaway homes in
the mountains. Certainly not old, but neatly put together.

From what he could tell, it was built on a single level with a porch that wrapped around at least two sides of the house.

There was no doorbell that he could see, so he took hold of the bronze bear-head knocker and rapped it three times, hard enough to express his growing frustration. Additional lights went on inside the house. As he shifted from one foot to the other impatiently, the curtain beside the door twitched and a wide-eyed female face appeared briefly before disappearing as quickly as it had come.

From inside he heard a muffled voice. "Who is it?"

"Leo. Leo Cavallo," he shouted at the door. Grinding his teeth, he reached for a more conciliatory tone. "May I come in?"

Phoebe opened her front door with some trepidation. Not because she had anything to fear from the man on the porch. She'd been expecting him for the past several hours. What she dreaded was telling him the truth.

Backing up to let him enter, she winced as he crossed the threshold and sucked all the air out of the room. He was a big man, built like a lumberjack, broad through the shoulders, and tall, topping her five-foot-nine stature by at least four more inches. His thick, wavy chestnut hair gleamed with health. The glow from the fire that crackled in the hearth picked out strands of dark gold.

When he removed his jacket, running a hand through his disheveled hair, she saw that he wore a deep blue sweater along with dark dress pants. The faint whiff of his aftershave mixed with the unmistakable scent of the outdoors. He filled the room with his presence.

Reaching around him gingerly, she flipped on the overhead light, sighing inwardly in relief when the intimacy of firelight gave way to a less cozy atmosphere. Glancing down at his feet, she bit her lip. "Will you please take off your shoes? I cleaned the floors this morning."

Though he frowned, he complied. Before she could say another word, he gave her home a cursory glance, then settled his sharp gaze on her face. His übermasculine features were put together in a pleasing fashion, but the overall impression was intensely male. Strong nose, noble forehead, chiseled jaw and lips made for kissing a woman. His scowl grew deeper. "I'm tired as hell, and I'm starving. If you could point me to my cabin, I'd like to get settled for the night, Ms....?"

"Kemper. Phoebe Kemper. You can call me Phoebe." Oh, wow. His voice, low and gravelly, stroked over her frazzled nerves like a lover's caress. The faint Georgia drawl did nothing to disguise the hint of command. This was a man accustomed to calling the shots.

She swallowed, rubbing damp palms unobtrusively on her thighs. "I have a pot of vegetable beef stew still warm on the stove. Dinner was late tonight." And every night, it seemed. "You're welcome to have some. There's corn bread, as well."

The aura of disgruntlement he wore faded a bit, replaced by a rueful smile. "That sounds wonderful."

She waved a hand. "Bathroom's down the hall, first door on the right. I'll get everything on the table."

"And afterward you'll show me my lodgings?"

Gulp. "Of course." Perhaps she shouldn't have insisted that he remove his shoes. There was something about a man in his sock feet that hinted at a level of familiarity. The last thing she needed at this juncture in time was to feel drawn to someone who was most likely going to be furious with her no matter how she tried to spin the facts in a positive light.

He was gone a very short time, but Phoebe had everything ready when he returned. A single place mat, some silverware and a steaming bowl of stew flanked by corn bread and a cheerful yellow gingham napkin. "I didn't know what you wanted to drink," she said. "I have decaf iced tea, but the weather's awfully cold tonight."

"Decaf coffee would be great…if you have it."

"Of course." While he sat down and dug into his meal, she brewed a fresh pot of Colombian roast and poured him a cup. He struck her as the kind of man who wouldn't appreciate his java laced with caramel or anything fancy. Though she offered the appropriate add-ons, Leo Cavallo took his coffee black and unsweetened. No fuss. No nonsense.

Phoebe puttered around, putting things away and loading the dishwasher. Her guest ate with every indication that his previous statement was true. Apparently, he *was* starving. Two large bowls of stew, three slabs of corn bread and a handful of the snickerdoodles she had made that morning vanished in short order.

As he was finishing his dessert, she excused herself. "I'll be back in just a moment." She set the pot on the table. "Help yourself to more coffee."

Leo's mood improved dramatically as he ate. He hadn't been looking forward to going back down that road to seek out dinner, and though his cabin was supposed to be stocked with groceries, he was not much of a cook. Everything he needed, foodwise, was close at hand in Atlanta. He was spoiled probably. If he wanted sushi at three in the morning or a full breakfast at dawn, he didn't have to look far.

When he finished the last crumb of the moist, delicious cookies, he wiped his mouth with his napkin and stood up to stretch. After the long drive, his body felt kinked and cramped from sitting in one position for too many hours. Guiltily, he remembered the doctor's admonition not to push himself. Truthfully, it was the only setting Leo had. Full steam ahead. Don't look back.

And yet now he was supposed to turn himself into somebody new. Even though he'd been irritated by the many people hovering over him—work colleagues, medical professionals and his family—in his heart, he knew the level of their concern was a testament to how much he had scared them all. One moment he had been standing at the head of a large conference table giving an impassioned pitch to a group of global investors, and the next, he'd been on the floor.

None of the subsequent few minutes were clear in his memory. He recalled not being able to breathe. And an enormous pressure in his chest. But not much more than that. Shaken and disturbed by the recollection of that day, he paced the confines of the open floor plan that incorporated the kitchen and living area into a pleasing whole.

As he walked back and forth, he realized that Phoebe Kemper had created a cozy nest out here in the middle of nowhere. Colorful area rugs cushioned his feet. The floor consisted of wide, honey-colored hardwood planks polished to a high sheen.

Two comfortable groupings of furniture beckoned visitors to sit and enjoy the ambience. Overhead, a three-tiered elk antler chandelier shed a large, warm circle of light. On the far wall, built-in bookshelves flanked the stacked stone fireplace. As he scanned Phoebe's collection of novels and nonfiction, he realized with a little kick of pleasure that he was actually going to have time to read for a change.

A tiny noise signaled his hostess's return. Whirling around, he stared at her, finally acknowledging, if only to himself, that his landlady was a knockout. Jet-black hair long enough to reach below her breasts had been tamed into a single thick, smooth braid that hung forward over her shoulder. Tall and slender and long-limbed, there was nothing frail or helpless about Phoebe Kemper. Yet he could imagine many men rushing to her aid, simply to coax a smile from those lush unpainted lips that were the color of pale pink roses.

She wore faded jeans and a silky coral blouse that brought out the warm tones in her skin. With eyes so dark they were almost black, she made him wonder if she claimed Cherokee blood. Some resourceful members of that tribe had hidden deep in these mountains to escape the Trail of Tears.

Her smile was teasing. "Feel better now? At least you don't look like you want to commit murder anymore."

He shrugged sheepishly. "Sorry. It was a hell of a day."

Phoebe's eyes widened and her smile faded. "And it's about to get worse, I'm afraid. There's a problem with your reservation."

"Impossible," he said firmly. "My sister-in-law handled all the details. And I have the confirmation info."

"I've been trying to call her all day, but she hasn't answered. And no one gave me your cell number."

"Sorry about that. My niece found my sister-in-law's phone and dropped it into the bathtub. They've been scrambling to get it replaced. That's why you couldn't reach her. But no worries. I'm here now. And it doesn't look like you're overbooked," he joked.

Phoebe ignored his levity and frowned. "We had heavy rains and high winds last night. Your cabin was damaged."

His mood lightened instantly. "Don't worry about a thing, Ms. Phoebe. I'm not that picky. I'm sure it will be fine."

She shook her head in disgust. "I guess I'll have to show you to convince you. Follow me, please."

"Should I move my car closer to the cabin?" he asked as he put on his shoes and tied them. The bottoms were a mess.

Phoebe scooped up something that looked like a small digital camera and tucked it into her pocket. "No need," she said. She shrugged into a jacket that could have been a twin to his. "Let's go." Out on the porch, she picked up a large, heavy-duty flashlight and turned it on. The intense beam sliced through the darkness.

The weather hadn't improved. He was glad that Luc and Hattie had insisted on packing for him. They had undoubtedly covered every eventuality if he knew his sister-in-law. Come rain, sleet, snow or hail, he'd be prepared. But for now, everything he'd brought with him was stashed in the trunk of his car. Sighing for the lost opportunity to carry a load, he followed Phoebe.

Though he would never have found it on his own in the inky, fog-blinding night, the path from Phoebe's cabin to the next closest one was easy to pick out with the flashlight. Far more than a foot trail, the route they followed was clearly an extension of the gravel road.

His impatience grew as he realized they could have driven the few hundred feet. Finally, he dug in his heels. "I should move the car," he said. "I'm sure I'll be fine."

At that very moment, Phoebe stopped so abruptly he nearly plowed into her. "We're here," she said bluntly. "And *that* is what's left of your two-month rental."

The industrial-strength flashlight was more than strong enough to reveal the carnage from the previous night's storm. An enormous tree lay across the midline of the house at a forty-five-degree angle. The force of the falling trunk had crushed the roof. Even from this vantage point, it was clear that the structure was open to the elements.

"Good Lord." He glanced behind him instinctively, realizing with sick dismay that Phoebe's home could have suffered a similar fate. "You must have been scared to death."

She grimaced. "I've had better nights. It happened about 3:00 a.m. The boom woke me up. I didn't try to go out then, of course. So it was daylight before I realized how bad it was."

"You haven't tried to cover the roof?"

She chuckled. "Do I look like Superwoman? I know

my own limitations, Mr. Cavallo. I've called my insurance company, but needless to say, they've been inundated with claims from the storm. Supposedly, an agent will be here tomorrow afternoon, but I'm not holding my breath. Everything inside the house got soaked when the tree fell, because it was raining so hard. The damage was already done. It's not like I could have helped matters."

He supposed she had a point. But that still left the issue of where he was expected to stay. Despite his grumblings to Luc and Hattie, now that he was finally here, the idea of kicking back for a while wasn't entirely unpleasant. Perhaps he could find himself in the great outdoors. Maybe even discover a new appreciation for life, which as he so recently had found out, was both fragile and precious.

Phoebe touched his arm. "If you've seen enough, let's go back. I'm not going to send you out on the road again in this miserable weather. You're welcome to stay the night with me."

They reversed their steps as Leo allowed Phoebe to take the lead. The steady beam of light led them without incident back to his car. The porch light was still on, adding to a feeling of welcome. Phoebe waved a hand at the cabin. "Why don't you go inside and warm up? Your sister-in-law told me you've been in the hospital. I'd be happy to bring in your luggage if you tell me what you'll need."

Leo's neck heated with embarrassment and frustration. Damn Hattie and her mother-hen instincts. "I can get my own bags," he said curtly. "But thank you." He added that last bit grudgingly. Poor Phoebe had no reason to know that his recent illness was a hot-button issue for him. He was a young man. Being treated like an invalid made him nuts. And for whatever reason, it was especially important to him that the lovely Phoebe see him as a competent, capable male, and not someone she had to babysit.

His mental meanderings must not have lasted as long

as he thought, because Phoebe was still at his side when he heard—very distinctly—the cry of a baby. He whirled around, expecting to see that another car had made its way up the narrow road. But he and Phoebe were alone in the night.

A second, less palatable possibility occurred to him. He'd read that a bobcat's cry could emulate that of an upset infant's. And the Smoky Mountains were home to any number of those nocturnal animals. Before he could speculate further, the sound came again.

Phoebe shoved the flashlight toward him. "Here. Keep this. I've got to go inside."

He took it automatically, and grinned. "So you're leaving me out here alone with a scary animal stalking us?"

She shook her head. "I don't know what you're talking about."

"The bobcat. Isn't that what we're hearing?"

Phoebe laughed softly, a pleasing sensual sound that made the hair on his arms stand up even more than the odd noise had. "Despite your interesting imagination," she said with a chuckle, "no." She reached in her pocket and removed the small electronic device he had noticed earlier. Not a camera, but a monitor. "The noise you hear that sounds like a crying baby is *actually* a baby. And I'd better get in there fast before all heck breaks loose."

Two

Leo stood there gaping at her even after the front door slammed shut. It was only the realization his hands were in danger of frostbite that galvanized him into motion. In short order he found the smaller of the two suitcases he had brought. Slinging the strap across one shoulder, he then reached for his computer briefcase and a small garment bag.

Locking the car against any intruders, human or otherwise, he walked up the steps, let himself in and stopped dead in his tracks when he saw Phoebe standing by the fire, a small infant whimpering on her shoulder as she rubbed its back. Leo couldn't quite sort out his emotions. The scene by the hearth was beautiful. His sister-in-law, Hattie, wore that same look on her face when she cuddled her two little ones.

But a baby meant there was a daddy in the picture somewhere, and though Leo had only met this particular Madonna and child today, he knew the feeling in the pit of his stomach was disappointment. Phoebe didn't wear a wedding ring, but he could see a resemblance between mother and child. Their noses were identical.

Leo would simply have to ignore this inconvenient attraction, because Phoebe was clearly not available. And though he adored his niece and nephew, he was not the kind of man who went around bouncing kids on his knee and playing patty-cake.

Phoebe looked up and smiled. "This is Teddy. His full name is Theodore, but at almost six months, he hasn't quite grown into it yet."

Leo kicked off his shoes for the second time that night and set down his luggage. Padding toward the fire, he mustered a smile. "He's cute."

"Not nearly as cute at three in the morning." Phoebe's expression as she looked down at the baby was anything but aggravated. She glowed.

"Not a good sleeper?"

She bristled at what she must have heard as implied criticism. "He does wonderfully for his age. Don't you, my love?" The baby had settled and was sucking his fist. Phoebe nuzzled his neck. "Most evenings he's out for the count from ten at night until six or seven in the morning. But I think he may be cutting a tooth."

"Not fun, I'm sure."

Phoebe switched the baby to her left arm, holding him against her side. "Let me show you the guest room. I don't think we'll disturb you even if I have to get up with him during the night."

He followed her down a short hallway past what was obviously Phoebe's suite all the way to the back right corner of the house. A chill hit him as soon as they entered the bedroom.

"Sorry," she said. "The vents have been closed off, but it will warm up quickly."

He looked around curiously. "This is nice." A massive king-size bed made of rough timbers dominated the room. Hunter-green draperies covered what might have been a large picture window. The attached bathroom, decorated in shades of sand and beige, included a Jacuzzi tub and a roomy shower stall. Except for the tiled floor in the bathroom, the rest of the space boasted the same attractive hard-wood he'd seen in the remainder of the house, covered here and there by colorful rugs.

Phoebe hovered, the baby now asleep. "Make yourself at home. If you're interested in staying in the area, I can help you make some calls in the morning."

Leo frowned. "I paid a hefty deposit. I'm not interested in staying anywhere else."

A trace of pique flitted across Phoebe's face, but she answered him calmly. "I'll refund your money, of course. You saw the cabin. It's unlivable. Even with a speedy insurance settlement, finding people to do the work will probably be difficult. I can't even guesstimate how long it will be before everything is fixed."

Leo thought about the long drive from Atlanta. He hadn't wanted to come here at all. And yesterday's storm damage was his ticket out. All he had to do was tell Luc and Hattie, and his doctor, that circumstances had conspired against him. He could be back in Atlanta by tomorrow night.

But something—stubbornness maybe—made him contrary. "Where is Mr. Kemper in all this? Shouldn't he be the one worrying about repairing the other cabin?"

Phoebe's face went blank. "Mr. Kemper?" Suddenly, she laughed. "I'm not married, Mr. Cavallo."

"And the baby?"

A small frown line appeared between her brows. "Are you a traditionalist, then? You don't think a single female can raise a child on her own?"

Leo shrugged. "I think kids deserve two parents. But having said that, I do believe women can do anything they like. I can't, however, imagine a woman like you needing to embrace single parenthood."

He'd pegged Phoebe as calm and cool, but her eyes flashed. "A woman like me? What does that mean?"

Leaning his back against one of the massive bedposts,

he folded his arms and stared at her. Now that he knew she wasn't married, all bets were off. "You're stunning. Are all the men in Tennessee blind?"

Her lips twitched. "I'm pretty sure that's the most clichéd line I've ever heard."

"I stand by my question. You're living out here in the middle of nowhere. Your little son has no daddy anywhere in sight. A man has to wonder."

Phoebe stared at him, long and hard. He bore her scrutiny patiently, realizing how little they knew of each other. But for yesterday's storm, he and Phoebe would likely have exchanged no more than pleasantries when she handed over his keys. In the weeks to come, they might occasionally have seen each other outside on pleasant days, perhaps waved in passing.

But fate had intervened. Leo came from a long line of Italian ancestors who believed in the power of *destino* and *amore*. Since he was momentarily banned from the job that usually filled most of his waking hours, he was willing to explore his fascination with Phoebe Kemper.

He watched as she deposited the sleeping baby carefully in the center of the bed. The little boy rolled to his side and continued to snooze undisturbed. Phoebe straightened and matched her pose to Leo's. Only instead of using the bed for support, she chose to lean against the massive wardrobe that likely held a very modern home entertainment center.

She eyed him warily, her teeth nibbling her bottom lip. Finally she sighed. "First of all, we're not in the middle of nowhere, though it must seem that way to you since you had to drive up here on such a nasty night. Gatlinburg is less than ten miles away. Pigeon Forge closer than that. We have grocery stores and gas stations and all the modern conveniences, I promise. I like it here at the foot of the mountains. It's peaceful."

"I'll take your word for it."

"And Teddy is my nephew, not my son."

Leo straightened, wondering what it said about him that he was glad the woman facing him was a free agent. "Why is he here?"

"My sister and her husband are in Portugal for six weeks settling his father's estate. They decided the trip would be too hard on Teddy, and that cleaning out the house would be much easier without him. So I volunteered to let him stay with me until they get home."

"You must like kids a lot."

A shadow crossed her face. "I love my nephew." She shook off whatever mood had momentarily stolen the light. "But we're avoiding the important topic. I can't rent you a demolished cabin. You have to go."

He smiled at her with every bit of charm he could muster. "You can rent me *this* room."

Phoebe had to give Leo Cavallo points for persistence. His deep brown eyes were deceptive. Though a woman could sink into their warmth, she might miss entirely the fact that he was a man who got what he wanted. If he had been ill recently, she could find no sign of it in his appearance. His naturally golden skin, along with his name, told her that he possessed Mediterranean genes. And in Leo's case, that genetic material had been spun into a ruggedly handsome man.

"This isn't a B and B," she said. "I have an investment property that I rent out to strangers. That property is currently unavailable, so you're out of luck."

"Don't make a hasty decision," he drawled. "I'm housebroken. And I'm handy when it comes to changing lightbulbs and killing creepy-crawlies."

"I'm tall for a woman, and I have monthly pest control service."

"Taking care of a baby is a lot of work. You might enjoy having help."

"You don't strike me as the type to change diapers."

"Touché."

Were they at an impasse? Would he give up?

She glanced at Teddy, sleeping so peacefully. Babies were an important part of life, but it was a sad day when a grown woman's life was so devoid of male companionship that a nonverbal infant was stimulating company. "I'll make a deal with you," she said slowly, wondering if she were crazy. "You tell me why you really want to stay, and I'll consider your request."

For the first time, she saw discomfort on Leo's face. He was one of those consummately confident men who strode through life like a captain on the bridge of his ship, everyone in his life bowing and scraping in his wake. But at the moment, a mask slipped and she caught a glimpse of vulnerability. "What did my sister-in-law tell you when she made the reservation?"

A standard ploy. Answering a question with a question. "She said you'd been ill. Nothing more than that. But in all honesty, you hardly look like a man at death's door."

Leo's smile held a note of self-mockery. "Thank God for that."

Curiouser and curiouser. "Now that I think about it," she said, trying to solve the puzzle as she went along, "you don't seem like the kind of man who takes a two-month sabbatical in the mountains for any reason. Unless, of course, you're an artist or a songwriter. Maybe a novelist? Am I getting warm?"

Leo grimaced, not quite meeting her gaze. "I needed a break," he said. "Isn't that reason enough?"

Something in his voice touched her...some note of discouragement or distress. And in that moment, she felt a kinship with Leo Cavallo. Hadn't she embraced this land

and built these two cabins for that very reason? She'd been disillusioned with her job and heartbroken over the demise of her personal life. The mountains had offered healing.

"Okay," she said, capitulating without further ado. "You can stay. But if you get on my nerves or drive me crazy, I am well within my rights to kick you out."

He grinned, his expression lightening. "Sounds fair."

"And I charge a thousand dollars a week more if you expect to share meals with me."

It was a reckless barb, an attempt to get a rise out of him. But Leo merely nodded his head, eyes dancing. "Whatever you say." Then he sobered. "Thank you, Phoebe. I appreciate your hospitality."

The baby stirred, breaking the odd bubble of intimacy that had enclosed the room. Phoebe scooped up little Teddy and held him to her chest, suddenly feeling the need for a barrier between herself and the charismatic Leo Cavallo. "We'll say good night, then."

Her houseguest nodded, eyes hooded as he stared at the baby. "Sleep well. And if you hear me up in the night, don't be alarmed. I've had a bit of insomnia recently."

"I could fix you some warm milk," she said, moving toward the door.

"I'll be fine. See you in the morning."

Leo watched her leave and felt a pinch of remorse for having pressured her into letting him invade her home. But not so much that he was willing to leave. In Atlanta everyone had walked on eggshells around him, acting as if the slightest raised voice or cross word would send him into a relapse. Though his brother, Luc, tried to hide his concern, it was clear that he and Hattie were worried about Leo. And as dear as they both were to him, Leo needed a little space to come to terms with what had happened.

His first instinct was to dive back into work. But the

doctor had flatly refused to release him. This mountain getaway was a compromise. Not an idea Leo would have embraced voluntarily, but given the options, his only real choice.

When he exited the interstate earlier that evening, Leo had called his brother to say he was almost at his destination. Though he needed to escape the suffocating but well-meaning attention, he would never *ever* cause Luc and Hattie to worry unnecessarily. He would do anything for his younger brother, and he knew Luc would return the favor. They were closer than most siblings, having survived their late teen and early-adult years in a foreign land under the thumb of their autocratic Italian grandfather.

Leo yawned and stretched, suddenly exhausted. Perhaps he was paying for years of burning the candle at both ends. His medical team *and* his family had insisted that for a full recovery, Leo needed to stay away from work and stress. Maybe the recent hospital stay had affected him more than he realized. But whatever the reason, he was bone tired and ready to climb into that large rustic bed.

Too bad he'd be sleeping alone. It was oddly comforting when his body reacted predictably to thoughts of Phoebe. Something about her slow, steady smile and her understated sexuality really did it for him. Though his doctor had cleared Leo for exercise and sexual activity, the latter was a moot point. Trying to ignore the erection that wouldn't be seeing any action tonight, he reached for his suitcase, extracted his shaving kit and headed for the shower.

To Phoebe's relief, the baby didn't stir when she laid him in his crib. She stood over him for long moments watching the almost imperceptible movements of his small body as he breathed. She knew her sister was missing Teddy like crazy, but selfishly, Phoebe herself was looking forward to having someone to share Christmas with.

Her stomach did a little flip as she realized that Leo might be here, as well. But no. Surely he would go home at the holidays and come back to finish out his stay in January.

When she received the initial reservation request, she had researched Leo and the Cavallo family on Google. She knew he was single, rich and the CFO of a worldwide textile company started by his grandfather in Italy. She also knew that he supported several charities, not only with money, but with his service. He didn't need to work. The Cavallo vaults, metaphorically speaking, held more money than any one person could spend in a lifetime. But she understood men like Leo all too well. They thrived on challenge, pitting themselves repeatedly against adversaries, both in business and in life.

Taking Leo into her home was not a physical risk. He was a gentleman, and she knew far more about him than she did about many men she had dated. The only thing that gave her pause was an instinct that told her he needed help in some way. She didn't need another responsibility. And besides, if the cabin hadn't been demolished, Leo would have been on his own for two months anyway.

There was no reason for her to be concerned. Nevertheless, she sensed pain in him, and confusion. Given her own experience with being knocked flat on her butt for a long, long time, she wouldn't wish that experience on anyone. Maybe she could probe gently and see why this big mountain of a man, who could probably bench-press more than his body weight, seemed lost.

As she prepared for bed, she couldn't get him out of her mind. And when she climbed beneath her flannel sheets and closed her eyes, his face was the image that stayed with her through the night.

Three

Leo awoke when sunlight shining through a crack in the drapes hit his face. He yawned and scrubbed his hands over his stubbly chin, realizing with pleased surprise that he had slept through the night. Perhaps there was something to this mountain retreat thing after all.

Most of his stuff was still in the car, so he dug out a pair of faded jeans from his overnight case and threw on his favorite warm cashmere sweater. It was a Cavallo product... of course. The cabin had an efficient heat system, but Leo was itching to get outside and see his surroundings in the light of day.

Tiptoeing down the hall in case the baby was sleeping, he paused unconsciously at Phoebe's door, which stood ajar. Through the narrow crack he could see a lump under the covers of a very disheveled bed. Poor woman. The baby must have kept her up during the night.

Resisting the urge to linger, he made his way to the kitchen and quietly located the coffeepot. Phoebe was an organized sort, so it was no problem to find what he needed in the cabinet above. When he had a steaming cup brewed, strong and black, he grabbed a banana off the counter and went to stand at the living room window.

Supposedly, one of his challenges was to acquire the habit of eating breakfast in the morning. Normally, he had neither the time nor the inclination to eat. As a rule, he'd be at the gym by six-thirty and at the office before eight. After that, his day was nonstop until seven or later at night.

He'd never really thought much about his schedule in the past. It suited him, and it got the job done. For a man in his prime, *stopping to smell the roses* was a metaphor for growing old. Now that he had been admonished to do just that, he was disgruntled and frustrated. He was thirty-six, for God's sake. Was it really time to throw in the towel?

Pulling back the chintz curtains decorated with gamboling black bears, he stared out at a world that glistened like diamonds in the sharp winter sun. Every branch and leaf was coated with ice. Evidently, the temperatures had dropped as promised, and now the narrow valley where Phoebe made her home was a frozen wonderland.

So much for his desire to explore. Anyone foolish enough to go out at this moment would end up flat on his or her back after the first step. *Patience, Leo. Patience.* His doctor, who also happened to be his racquetball partner on the weekends, had counseled him repeatedly to take it easy, but Leo wasn't sure he could adapt. Already, he felt itchy, needing a project to tackle, a problem to solve.

"You're up early."

Phoebe's voice startled him so badly he spun around and managed to slosh hot coffee over the fingers of his right hand. "Ouch, damn it."

He saw her wince as he crossed to the sink and ran cold water over his stinging skin.

"Sorry," she said. "I thought you heard me."

Leo had been lost in thought, but he was plenty alert now. Phoebe wore simple knit pj's that clung to her body in all the right places. The opaque, waffle-weave fabric was pale pink with darker pink rosebuds. It faithfully outlined firm high breasts, a rounded ass and long, long legs.

Despite his single-minded libido, he realized in an instant that she looked somewhat the worse for wear. Her long braid had frayed into wispy tendrils and dark smudges underscored her eyes.

"Tough night with the baby?" he asked.

She shook her head, yawning and reaching for a mug in the cabinet. When she did, her top rode up, exposing an inch or two of smooth golden skin. He looked away, feeling like a voyeur, though the image was impossible to erase from his brain.

After pouring herself coffee and taking a long sip, Phoebe sank into a leather-covered recliner and pulled an afghan over her lap. "It wasn't the baby this time," she muttered. "It was me. I couldn't sleep for thinking about what a headache this reconstruction is going to be, especially keeping track of all the subcontractors."

"I could pitch in with that," he said. The words popped out of his mouth, uncensored. Apparently old habits were hard to break. But after all, wasn't helping out a fellow human being at least as important as inhaling the scent of some imaginary rose that surely wouldn't bloom in the dead of winter anyway? Fortunately, his sister-in-law wasn't around to chastise him for his impertinence. She had, in her sweet way, given him a very earnest lecture about the importance of not making work his entire life.

Of course, Hattie was married to Luc, who had miraculously managed to find a balance between enjoying his wife and his growing family and at the same time carrying his weight overseeing the R & D department. Luc's innovations, both in fabric content and in design, had kept their company competitive in the changing world of the twenty-first century. Worldwide designers wanted Cavallo textiles for their best and most expensive lines.

Leo was happy to oblige them. For a price.

Phoebe sighed loudly, her expression glum. "I couldn't ask that of you. It's my problem, and besides, you're on vacation."

"Not a vacation exactly," he clarified. "More like an involuntary time-out."

She grinned. "Has Leo been a naughty boy?"

Heat pooled in his groin and he felt his cheeks redden. He really had to get a handle on this urge to kiss her senseless. Since he was fairly sure that her taunt was nothing more than fun repartee, he refrained from saying what he really thought. "Not naughty," he clarified. "More like too much work and not enough play."

Phoebe swung her legs over the arm of the chair, her coffee mug resting on her stomach. For the first time he noticed that she wore large, pink Hello Kitty slippers on her feet. A less seductive female ensemble would be difficult to find. And yet Leo was fascinated.

She pursed her lips. "I'm guessing executive-level burnout?"

Her perspicacity was spot-on. "You could say that." Although it wasn't the whole story. "I'm doing penance here in the woods, so I can see the error of my ways."

"And who talked you into this getaway? You don't seem like a man who lets other people dictate his schedule."

He refilled his cup and sat down across from her. "True enough," he conceded. "But my baby brother, who happens to be part of a disgustingly happy married couple, thinks I need a break."

"And you listened?"

"Reluctantly."

She studied his face as though trying to sift through his half-truths. "What did you think you would do for two months?"

"That remains to be seen. I have a large collection of

detective novels packed in the backseat of my car, a year of *New York Times* crossword puzzles on my iPad and a brand-new digital camera not even out of the box yet."

"I'm impressed."

"But you'll concede that I surely have time to interview prospective handymen."

"Why would you want to?"

"I like keeping busy."

"Isn't that why you're here? To be *not* busy? I'd hate to think I was causing you to fall off the wagon in the first week."

"Believe me, Phoebe. Juggling schedules and workmen for your cabin repair is something I could do in my sleep. And since it's not my cabin, there's no stress involved."

Still not convinced, she frowned. "If it weren't for the baby, I'd never consider this."

"Understood."

"And if you get tired of dealing with it, you'll be honest."

He held up two fingers. "Scout's honor."

"In that case," she sighed, "how can I say no?"

Leo experienced a rush of jubilation far exceeding the appropriate response to Phoebe's consent. Only at that moment did he realize how much he had been dreading the long parade of unstructured days. With the cabin renovation to give him focus each morning, perhaps this rehabilitative exile wouldn't be so bad.

Guiltily, he wondered what his brother would say about this new turn of events. Leo was pretty sure Luc pictured him sitting by a fire in a flannel robe and slippers reading a John Grisham novel. While Leo enjoyed fiction on occasion, and though Grisham was a phenomenal author, a man could only read so many hours of the day without going bonkers.

Already, the idleness enforced by his recent illness had

made the days and nights far too long. The doctor had cleared him for his usual exercise routine, but with no gym nearby, and sporting equipment that was useless in this environment, it was going to require ingenuity on his part to stay fit and active, especially given that it was winter.

Suddenly, from down the hall echoed the distinct sound of a baby who was awake and unhappy.

Phoebe jumped to her feet, nearly spilling her coffee in the process. "Oh, shoot. I forgot to bring the monitor in here." She clunked her mug in the sink and disappeared in a flash of pink fur.

Leo had barely drained his first cup and gone to the coffeepot for a refill when Phoebe reappeared, this time with baby Teddy on her hip. The little one was red-faced from crying. Phoebe smoothed his hair from his forehead. "Poor thing must be so confused not seeing his mom and dad every morning when he wakes up."

"But he knows you, right?"

Phoebe sighed. "He does. Still, I worry about him day and night. I've never been the sole caregiver for a baby, and it's scary as heck."

"I'd say you're doing an excellent job. He looks healthy and happy."

Phoebe grimaced, though the little worried frown between her eyes disappeared. "I hope you're right."

She held Teddy out at arm's length. "Do you mind giving him his bottle while I shower and get dressed?"

Leo backed up half a step before he caught himself. It was his turn to frown. "I don't think either Teddy or I would like that. I'm too big. I scare children."

Phoebe gaped. Then her eyes flashed. "That's absurd. Wasn't it you, just last night, who was volunteering to help with the baby in return for your keep?"

Leo shrugged, feeling guilty but determined not to show it. "I was thinking more in terms of carrying dirty diapers out to the trash. Or if you're talking on the phone, listening to the monitor to let you know when he wakes up. My hands are too large and clumsy to do little baby things."

"You've never been around an infant?"

"My brother has two small children, a boy and a girl. I see them several times a month, but those visits are more about kissing cheeks and spouting kudos as to how much they've grown. I might even bounce one on my knee if necessary, but not often. Not everyone is good with babies."

Little Teddy still dangled in midair, his chubby legs kicking restlessly. Phoebe closed the distance between herself and Leo and forced the wiggly child to Leo's chest. "Well, you're going to learn, because we had a deal."

Leo's arms came up reflexively, enclosing Teddy in a firm grip. The wee body was warm and solid. The kid smelled of baby lotion and some indefinable nursery scent that was endemic to babies everywhere. "I thought becoming your renovation overseer got me off the hook with Teddy."

Phoebe crossed her arms over her chest, managing to emphasize the fullness of her apparently unconfined breasts. "*It. Did. Not.* A deal is a deal. Or do I need a written contract?"

Leo knew when he was beaten. He'd pegged Phoebe as an easygoing, Earth Mother type, but suddenly he was confronted with a steely-eyed negotiator who would as soon kick him to the curb as look at him. "I'd raise my hands in surrender if I were able," he said, smiling, "But I doubt your nephew would like it."

Phoebe's nonverbal response sounded a lot like *humph.* As Leo watched, grinning inwardly, she quickly prepared a serving of formula and brought it to the sofa where Leo sat with Teddy. She handed over the bottle. "He likes it sitting up. Burp him halfway through."

"Yes, ma'am."

Phoebe put her hands on her hips. "Don't mock me. You're walking on thin ice, mister."

Leo tried to look penitent, and also tried not to take note of the fact that her pert nipples were at eye level. He cleared his throat. "Go take your shower," he said. "I've got this under control. You can trust me."

Phoebe nibbled her bottom lip. "Yell at my bedroom door if you need me."

Something about the juxtaposition of *yell* and *bedroom door* and *need* rekindled Leo's simmering libido. About the only thing that could have slowed him down was the reality of a third person in the cabin. Teddy. Little innocent, about-to-get-really-hungry Teddy.

"Go," Leo said, taking the bottle and offering it to the child in his lap. "We're fine."

As Phoebe left the room, Leo scooted Teddy to a more comfortable position, tucking the baby in his left arm so he could offer the bottle with his right hand. It was clear that the kid was almost capable of feeding himself. But if he dropped the bottle, he would be helpless.

Leo leaned back on the comfy couch and put his feet on the matching ottoman, feeling the warmth and weight of the child, who rested so comfortably in his embrace. Teddy seemed content to hang out with a stranger. Presumably as long as the food kept coming, the tyke would be happy. He did not, however, approve when Leo withdrew the bottle for a few moments and put him on his shoulder to burp him.

Despite Teddy's pique, the new position coaxed the desired result. Afterward, Leo managed to help the kid finish the last of his breakfast. When Teddy sucked on nothing but air, Leo set aside the bottle and picked up a small, round teething ring from the end table flanking the sofa. Teddy chomped down on it with alacrity, giving Leo the opportunity to examine his surroundings in detail.

He liked the way Phoebe had furnished the place. The

cabin had a cozy feel that still managed to seem sophisticated and modern. The appliances and furniture were top-of-the-line, built to last for many years, and no doubt expensive because of that. The flooring was high-end, as well.

The pale amber granite countertops showcased what looked to be handcrafted cabinetry done in honey maple. He saw touches of Phoebe's personality in the beautiful green-and-gold glazed canister set and in the picture of Phoebe, her sister and Teddy tacked to the front of the fridge with a magnet.

Leo looked down at Teddy. The boy's big blue eyes stared up at him gravely as if to say, *What's your game?* Leo chuckled. "Your auntie Phoebe is one beautiful woman, my little man. Don't get me in trouble with her and you and I will get along just fine."

Teddy's gaze shifted back to his tiny hands covered in drool.

Leo was not so easily entertained. He felt the pull of Atlanta, of wondering what was going on at work, of needing to feel in control…at the helm. But something about cuddling a warm baby helped to freeze time. As though any considerations outside of this particular moment were less than urgent.

As he'd told Phoebe, he wasn't a complete novice when it came to being around kids. Luc and Hattie adopted Hattie's niece after they married last year. The little girl was almost two years old now. And last Valentine's Day, Hattie gave birth to the first "blood" Cavallo of the new generation, a dark-haired, dark-eyed little boy.

Leo appreciated children. They were the world's most concrete promise that the globe would keep on spinning. But in truth, he had no real desire to father any of his own. His lifestyle was complicated, regimented, full. Children deserved a healthy measure of their parents' love and attention. The Cavallo empire was Leo's baby. He knew on any given day what the financial bottom line was. During hard financial times, he wrestled the beast that was their investment and sales strategy and demanded returns instead of losses.

He was aware that some people called him hard…unfeeling. But he did what he did knowing how many employees around the world depended on the Cavallos for their livelihoods. It irked the hell out of him to think that another man was temporarily sitting in his metaphorical chair. The vice president Luc had chosen to keep tabs on the money in Leo's absence was solid and capable.

But that didn't make Leo feel any less sidelined.

He glanced at his watch. God in heaven. It was only ten-thirty in the morning. How was he going to survive being on the back burner for two months? Did he even want to try becoming the man his family thought he could be? A balanced, laid-back, easygoing guy?

He rested his free arm across the back of the sofa and closed his eyes, reaching for something Zen. Something peaceful.

Damn it, he didn't want to change. He wanted to go home. At least he had until he met Phoebe. Now he wasn't sure what he wanted.

Hoping that the boy wasn't picking up on his frustration and malcontent thoughts, Leo focused on the only thing capable of diverting him from his problems. Phoebe. Tall, long-legged Phoebe. A dark-haired, dark-eyed beauty with an attitude.

If Phoebe could be lured into an intimate relationship, then this whole recuperative escape from reality had definite possibilities. Leo sensed a spark between them. And he was seldom wrong about things like that. When a man had money, power and reasonably good looks, the female sex swarmed like mosquitoes. That wasn't ego speaking. Merely the truth.

As young men in Italy, he and Luc had racked up a number of conquests until they realized the emptiness of being wanted for superficial reasons. Luc had finally found his soul mate in college. But things hadn't worked out, and it had been ten years before he achieved happiness with the same woman.

Leo had never even made it that far. Not once in his life had he met a female who really cared about who he was as a person. Would-be "Mrs. Cavallos" saw the external trappings of wealth and authority and wanted wedding rings. And the real women, the uncomplicated, good-hearted ones, steered clear of men like Leo for fear of having their hearts broken.

He wasn't sure which category might include Phoebe Kemper. But he was willing to find out.

Four

Phoebe took her time showering, drying her hair and dressing. If Leo wasn't going to live up to his end of the bargain, she wanted to know it now. Leaving Teddy in his temporary care was no risk while she enjoyed a brief respite from the demands of surrogate parenthood. Despite Leo's protestations to the contrary, he was a man who could handle difficult situations.

It was hard to imagine that he had been ill. He seemed impervious to the things that lesser mortals faced. She envied him his confidence. Hers had taken a serious knock three years ago, and she wasn't sure if she had ever truly regained it. A younger Phoebe had taken the world by storm, never doubting her own ability to craft outcomes to her satisfaction.

But she had paid dearly for her hubris. Her entire world had crumbled. Afterward, she had chosen to hide from life, and only in the past few months had she finally begun to understand who she was and what she wanted. The lessons had been painful and slow in coming.

Unfortunately, her awakening had also made her face her own cowardice. Once upon a time she had taken great pleasure in blazing trails where no other women had gone.

Back then, she would have seen a man like Leo as a challenge, both in business and in her personal life.

Smart and confident, she had cruised through life, never realizing that on any given day, she—like any other human being—was subject to the whims of fate. Her perfect life had disintegrated in the way of a comet shattering into a million pieces.

Things would never be as they were. But could they be equally good in another very different way?

She took more care in dressing than she did normally. Instead of jeans, she pulled out a pair of cream corduroy pants and paired them with a cheery red scoop-necked sweater. Christmas was on the way, and the color always lifted her mood.

Wryly acknowledging her vanity, she left her hair loose on her shoulders. It was thick and straight as a plumb line. With the baby demanding much of her time, a braid was easier. Nevertheless, today she wanted to look nice for her guest.

When she finally returned to the living room, Teddy was asleep on Leo's chest, and Leo's eyes were closed, as well. She lingered for a moment in the doorway, enjoying the picture they made. The big, strong man and the tiny, defenseless baby.

Her chest hurt. She rubbed it absently, wondering if she would always grieve for what she had lost. Sequestering herself like a nun the past few years had given her a sort of numb peace. But that peace was an illusion, because it was the product of not living.

Living hurt. If Phoebe were ever going to rejoin the human race, she would have to accept being vulnerable. The thought was terrifying. The flip side of great love and joy was immense pain. She wasn't sure the first was worth risking the prospect of the last.

Quietly she approached the sofa and laid a hand on Leo's

arm. His eyes opened at once as if he had perhaps only been lost in thought rather than dozing. She held out her arms for the baby, but Leo shook his head.

"Show me where to take him," he whispered. "No point in waking him up."

She led the way through her bedroom and bathroom to a much smaller bedroom that adjoined on the opposite side. Before Teddy's arrival she had used this space as a junk room, filled with the things she was too dispirited to sort through when she'd moved in.

Now it had been tamed somewhat, so that half the room was full of neatly stacked plastic tubs, while the other half had been quickly transformed into a comfy space for Teddy. A baby bed, rocking chair and changing table, all with matching prints, made an appealing, albeit temporary, nursery.

Leo bent over the crib and laid Teddy gently on his back. The little boy immediately rolled to his side and stuck a thumb in his mouth. Both adults smiled. Phoebe clicked on the monitor and motioned for Leo to follow her as they tiptoed out.

In the living room, she waved an arm. "Relax. Do whatever you like. There's plenty of wood if you feel up to building us a fire."

"I told you. I'm not sick."

The terse words had a bite to them. Phoebe flinched inwardly, but kept her composure. Something had happened to Leo. Something serious. Cancer maybe. But she was not privy to that information. So conversation regarding the subject was akin to navigating a minefield.

Most men were terrible patients. Usually because their health and vigor were tied to their self-esteem. Clearly, Leo had been sent here or had agreed to come here because he needed rest and relaxation. He didn't want Phoebe hovering or commenting on his situation. Okay. Fine. But she was still going to keep an eye on him, because whatever had given him a wallop was serious enough to warrant a two-month hiatus from work.

That in itself was telling. In her past life, she had interacted with lots of men like Leo. They were alpha animals, content only with the number one spot in the pack. Their work was their life. And even if they married, familial relationships were kept in neatly separated boxes.

Unfortunately for Phoebe, she possessed some of those same killer instincts…or she had. The adrenaline rush of an impossible-to-pull-off business deal was addictive. The more you succeeded, the more you wanted to try again. Being around Leo was going to be difficult, because like a recovering alcoholic who avoided other drinkers, she was in danger of being sucked into his life, his work issues, whatever made him tick.

Under no circumstances could she let herself be dragged back into that frenzied schedule. The world was a big, beautiful place. She had enough money tucked away to live simply for a very long time. She had lost herself in the drive to achieve success. It was better now to accept her new lifestyle.

Leo moved to the fireplace and began stacking kindling and firewood with the precision of an Eagle Scout. Phoebe busied herself in the kitchen making a pot of chili to go with sandwiches for their lunch. Finally, she broke the awkward silence. "I have a young woman who babysits for me when I have to be gone for a short time. It occurred to me that I could see if she is free and if so, she could stay here in the house and watch Teddy while you and I do an initial damage assessment on the other cabin."

Leo paused to look over his shoulder, one foot propped on the raised hearth. "You sound very businesslike about this."

She shrugged. "I used to work for a big company. I'm accustomed to tackling difficult tasks."

He lit the kindling, stood back to see if it would catch, and then replaced the fire screen, brushing his hands together to remove the soot. "Where did you work?"

Biting her lip, she berated herself inwardly for bringing up a subject she would rather not pursue. "I was a stockbroker for a firm in Charlotte, North Carolina."

"Did they go under? Is that why you're here?"

His was a fair assumption. But wrong. "The business survived the economic collapse and is expanding by leaps and bounds."

"Which doesn't really answer my question."

She grimaced. "Maybe when we've known each other for more than a nanosecond I might share the gory details. But not today."

Leo understood her reluctance, or he thought he did. Not everyone wanted to talk about his or her failures. And rational or not, he regarded his heart attack as a failure. He wasn't overweight. He didn't smoke. Truth be told, his vices were few, perhaps only one. He was type A to the max. And type A personalities lived with stress so continuously that the condition became second nature. According to his doctor, no amount of exercise or healthy eating could compensate for an inability to unwind.

So maybe Leo was screwed.

He joined his hostess in the kitchen, looking for any excuse to get closer to her. "Something smells good." *Smooth, Leo. Real smooth.*

Last night he had dreamed about Phoebe's braid. But today...wow. Who knew within that old-fashioned hairstyle was a shiny waterfall the color of midnight?

Phoebe adjusted the heat on the stove top and turned to

face him. "I didn't ask. Do you have any dietary restrictions? Any allergies?"

Leo frowned. "I don't expect you to cook for me all the time I'm here. You claimed that civilization is close by. Why don't I take you out now and then?"

She shot him a pitying look that said he was clueless. "Clearly you've never tried eating at a restaurant with an infant. It's ridiculously loud, not to mention that the chaos means tipping the server at least thirty percent to compensate for the rice cereal all over the floor." She eyed his sweater. "I doubt you would enjoy it."

"I know kids are messy." He'd eaten out with Luc and Hattie and the babies a time or two. Hadn't he? Or come to think of it, maybe it was always at their home. "Well, not that then, but I could at least pick up a pizza once a week."

Phoebe smiled at him sweetly. "That would be lovely. Thank you, Leo."

Her genuine pleasure made him want to do all sorts of things for her...and *to* her. Something about that radiant smile twisted his insides in a knot. The unmistakable jolt of attraction was perhaps inevitable. They were two healthy adults who were going to be living in close proximity for eight or nine weeks. They were bound to notice each other sexually.

He cleared his throat as he shoved his hands into his pockets. "Is there a boyfriend who won't like me staying here?"

Again, that faint, fleeting shadow that dimmed her beauty for a moment. "No. You're safe." She shook her head, giving him a rueful smile. "I probably should say yes, though. Just so you don't get any ideas."

He tried to look innocent. "What ideas?" All joking aside, he was a little worried about having sex for the first time since... Oh, hell. He had a hard time even saying it in his head. Heart attack. There. He wasn't afraid of two stupid words.

The doctor had said *no restrictions,* but the doctor hadn't seen Phoebe Kemper in a snug crimson sweater. She reminded Leo of a cross between Wonder Woman and Pocahontas. Both of whom he'd fantasized about as a preteen boy. What did that say about his chances of staying away from her?

She shooed him with her hands. "Go unpack. Read one of those books. Lunch will be ready in an hour."

Leo enjoyed Phoebe's cooking almost as much as her soft, feminine beauty. If he could eat like this all the time, maybe he wouldn't skip meals and drive through fast-food places at nine o'clock at night. Little Teddy sat in his high chair playing with a set of plastic keys. It wasn't time for another bottle, so the poor kid had to watch the grown-ups eat.

They had barely finished the meal when Allison, the babysitter, showed up. According to Phoebe, she was a college student who lived at home and enjoyed picking up extra money. Plus, she adored Teddy, which was a bonus.

Since temperatures had warmed up enough to melt the ice, Leo went out to the car for his big suitcase, brought it in and rummaged until he found winter gear. Not much of it was necessary in Atlanta. It did snow occasionally, but rarely hung around. Natives, though, could tell hair-raising stories about ice storms and two-week stints without power.

When he made his way back to the living room, Allison was playing peekaboo with the baby, and Phoebe was slipping her arms into a fleece-lined sheepskin jacket. Even the bulky garment did nothing to diminish her appeal.

She tucked a notepad and pen into her pocket. "Don't be shy about telling me things you see. Construction is not my forte."

"Nor mine, but my brother and I did build a tree house once upon a time. Does that count?"

He followed her out the door, inhaling sharply as the icy wind filled his lungs with a jolt. The winter afternoon enwrapped them, blue-skied and damp. From every corner echoed the sounds of dripping water as ice gave way beneath pale sunlight.

Lingering on the porch to take it all in, he found himself strangely buoyed by the sights and sounds of the forest. The barest minimum of trees had been cleared for Phoebe's home and its mate close by. All around them, a sea of evergreen danced in the brisk wind. Though he could see a single contrail far above them, etched white against the blue, there was little other sign of the twenty-first century.

"Did you have these built when you moved here?" he asked as they walked side by side up the incline to the other cabin.

Phoebe tucked the ends of her fluttering scarf into her coat, lifting her face to the sun. "My grandmother left me this property when she died a dozen years ago. I had just started college. For years I held on to it because of sentimental reasons, and then much later..."

"Later, what?"

She looked at him, her eyes hidden behind dark sunglasses. Her shoulders lifted and fell. "I decided to mimic Thoreau and live in the woods."

Phoebe didn't expand on her explanation, so he didn't push. They had plenty of time for sharing confidences. And besides, he was none too eager to divulge all his secrets just yet.

Up close, and in the unforgiving light of day, the damage to the cabin was more extensive than he had realized. He put a hand on Phoebe's arm. "Let me go first. There's no telling what might still be in danger of crumbling."

They were able to open the front door, but just barely. The tree that had crushed the roof was a massive oak, large enough around that Leo would not have been able to encircle it with his arms. The house had caved in so dramatically that the floor was knee-deep in rubble—insulation, roofing shingles, branches of every size and, beneath it all, Phoebe's furnishings.

She removed her sunglasses and craned her neck to look up at the nonexistent ceiling as she followed Leo inside. "Not much left, is there?" Her voice wobbled a bit at the end. "I'm so grateful it wasn't *my* house."

"You and me, both," he muttered. Phoebe or Teddy or both could have been killed or badly injured...with no one nearby to check on them. The isolation was peaceful, but he wasn't sure he approved of a defenseless woman living here. Perhaps that was a prehistoric gut feeling. Given the state of the structure in which they were standing, however, he did have a case.

He just didn't have any right to argue it.

Taking Phoebe's hand to steady her, they stepped on top of and over all the debris and made their way to the back portion of the cabin. The far left corner bedroom had escaped unscathed...and some pieces of furniture in the outer rooms were okay for the moment. But if anything were to be salvaged, it would have to be done immediately. Dampness would lead to mildew, and with animals having free rein, further damage was a certainty.

Phoebe's face was hard to read. Finally she sighed. "I might do better to bulldoze it and start over," she said glumly. She bent down to pick up a glass wildflower that had tumbled from a small table, but had miraculously escaped demolition. "My friends cautioned me to furnish the rental cabin with inexpensive, institutional stuff that would not be a big deal to replace in case of theft or carelessness on the part of the tenants. I suppose I should have listened."

"Do you have decent insurance?" He was running the numbers in his head, and the outcome wasn't pretty.

She nodded. "I don't remember all the ins and outs of the policy, but my agent is a friend of my sister's, so I imagine he made sure I have what I need."

Phoebe's discouragement was almost palpable.

"Sometimes things work out for a reason," he said, wanting to reassure her, but well aware that she had no reason to lean on him. "I need something to do to keep me from going crazy. You have a baby to care for. Let me handle this mess, Phoebe. Let me juggle and schedule the various contractors. Please. You'd be doing me a favor."

Five

Phoebe was tempted. So tempted. Leo stood facing her, legs planted apart in a stance that said he was there to stay. Wearing an expensive quilted black parka and aviator sunglasses that hid his every emotion, he was an enigma. Why had a virile, handsome, vigorous male found his way to her hidden corner of the world?

What was he after? Healing? Peace? He had the physique of a bouncer and the look of a wealthy playboy. Had he really been sick? Would she be committing a terrible sin to lay this burden on him from the beginning?

"That's ridiculous," she said faintly. "I'd be taking advantage of you. But I have to confess that I find your offer incredibly appealing. I definitely underestimated how exhausting it would be to take care of a baby 24/7. I love Teddy, and he's not really a fussy child at all, but the thought of adding all this…" She flung out her arm. "Well, it's daunting."

"Then let me help you," he said quietly.

"I don't expect you to actually do the work yourself."

He pocketed his sunglasses and laughed, making his rugged features even more attractive. "No worries there. I'm aware that men are known for biting off more than they can chew, but your cabin, or what's left of it, falls into the category of catastrophe. That's best left to the experts."

She stepped past him and surveyed the large bed with the burgundy-and-navy duvet. "This was supposed to be your room. I know you would have been comfortable here." She turned to face him. "I'm sorry, Leo. I feel terrible about shortchanging you."

He touched her arm. Only for a second. The smile disappeared, but his eyes were warm and teasing. "I'm pretty happy where I ended up. A gorgeous woman. A cozy cabin. Sounds like I won the jackpot."

"You're flirting," she said, hearing the odd and embarrassingly breathless note in her voice.

His gaze was intent, sexy…leaving no question that he was interested. "I've been admonished to stop and smell the roses. And here you are."

Removing her coat that suddenly felt too hot, she leaned against the door frame. The odd sensation of being inside the house but having the sunlight spill down from above was disconcerting. "You may find me more of a thorn. My sister says that living alone up here has made me set in my ways." It was probably true. Some days she felt like a certified hermit.

Once a social animal comfortable at cocktail parties and business lunches, she now preferred the company of chipmunks and woodpeckers and the occasional fox. Dull, dull, dull…

Leo kicked aside a dangerously sharp portion of what had been the dresser mirror. "I'll take my chances. I've got nowhere to go and nobody to see, as my grandfather used to say. You and Teddy brighten the prospect of my long exile considerably."

"Are you ever going to tell me why you're here?" she asked without censoring her curiosity.

He shrugged. "It's not a very interesting story…but maybe…when it's time."

"How will you know?" This odd conversation seemed to have many layers. Her question erased Leo's charmingly flirtatious smile and replaced it with a scowl.

"You're a pain in the butt," he said, the words a low growl.

"I told you I'm no rose."

He took her arm and steered her toward the front door. "Then pretend," he muttered. "Can you do that?"

Their muted altercation was interrupted by the arrival of the insurance agent. The next hour was consumed with questions and photographs and introducing Leo to the agent. The two men soon had their heads together as they climbed piles of rubble and inspected every cranny of the doomed cabin.

Phoebe excused herself and walked down the path, knowing that Allison would be ready to go home. As she opened the door and entered the cabin, Teddy greeted her with a chortle and a grin. Envy pinched her heart, but stronger still was happiness that the baby recognized her and was happy to see her.

Given Phoebe's background, her sister had been torn about the arrangement. But Phoebe had reassured her, and eventually, her sister and brother-in-law gave in. Dragging a baby across the ocean was not an easy task in ideal circumstances, and facing the disposal of an entire estate, they knew Teddy would be miserable and they would be overwhelmed.

Still, Phoebe knew they missed their small son terribly. They used FaceTime to talk to him when Phoebe went into town and had a decent phone signal, and she sent them constant, newsy updates via email and texts. But they were so far away. She suspected they regretted their decision to leave him. Probably, they were working like fiends to take care of all the estate business so they could get back to the U.S. sooner.

When Allison left, Phoebe held Teddy and looked out the window toward the other cabin. Leo and the insurance agent were still measuring and assessing the damage. She rubbed the baby's back. "I think Santa has sent us our present early, my little man. Leo is proving to be a godsend. Now all I have to do is ignore the fact that he's the most attractive man I've seen in a long, long time, and that he makes it hard to breathe whenever I get too close to him, and I'll be fine."

Teddy continued sucking his thumb, his long-lashed eyelids growing heavy as he fought sleep.

"You're no help," she grumbled. His weight was comfortable in her arms. Inhaling his clean baby smell made her womb clench. What would it be like to share a child with Leo Cavallo? Would he be a good father, or an absent one?

The man in question burst through the front door suddenly, bringing with him the smell of the outdoors. "Honey, I'm home." His humor lightened his face and made him seem younger.

Phoebe grinned at him. "Take off your boots, *honey.*" She was going to have to practice keeping him at arm's length. Leo Cavallo had the dangerous ability to make himself seem harmless. Which was a lie. Even in a few short hours, Phoebe had recognized and assessed his sexual pull.

Some men simply oozed testosterone. Leo was one of them.

It wasn't just his size, though he was definitely a bear of a man. More than that, he emanated a gut-level masculinity that made her, in some odd way, far more aware of her own carnal needs. She would like to blame it on the fact that they were alone together in the woods, but in truth, she would have had the same reaction to him had they met at the opera or on the deck of a yacht.

Leo was a man's man. The kind of male animal who caught women in his net without even trying. Phoebe had thought herself immune to such silly, pheromone-driven impulses, but with Leo in her house, she recognized an appalling truth. She needed sex. She wanted sex. And she had found just the man to satisfy her every whim.

Her face heated as she pretended to be occupied with the baby. Leo shed his coat and pulled a folded piece of paper from his pocket. "Here," he said. "Take a look. I'll hold the kid."

Before Phoebe could protest, Leo scooped Teddy into his arms and lifted him toward the ceiling. Teddy, who had been sleepy only moments before, squealed with delight. Shaking her head at the antics of the two males who seemed in perfect accord, Phoebe sank into a kitchen chair and scanned the list Leo had handed her.

"Ouch," she said, taking a deep breath for courage. "According to this, I was probably right about the bulldozer."

Leo shook his head. "No. I realize the bottom line looks bad, but it would be even worse to build a new cabin from the ground up. Your agent thinks the settlement will be generous. All you have to provide is an overabundance of patience."

"We may have a problem," she joked. "That's not my strong suit."

Teddy's shirt had rucked up. Leo blew a raspberry against the baby's pudgy, soft-skinned stomach. "I'll do my best to keep you out of it. Unless you want to be consulted about every little detail."

Phoebe shuddered. "Heavens, no. If you're foolish enough to offer me the chance to get my property repaired without my lifting a finger, then far be it from me to nit-pick."

Teddy wilted suddenly as Leo cuddled him. What was it about the sight of a big, strong man being gentle with a baby that made a woman's heart melt? Phoebe told herself she shouldn't be swayed by such an ordinary thing, but she couldn't help it. Seeing Leo hold little Teddy made her insides mushy with longing. She wanted it all. The man. The baby. Was that too much to ask?

Leo glanced over at her, hopefully not noticing the way her eyes misted over.

"You want me to put him in his bed?" he asked.

"Sure. He takes these little forty-five-minute catnaps on and off instead of one long one. But he seems happy, so I go with the flow."

Leo paused in the hallway. "How long have you had him?"

"Two weeks. We've settled into a routine of sorts."

"Until I came along to mess things up."

"If you're fishing for compliments, forget it. You've already earned your keep, and it hasn't even been twenty-four hours yet."

He flashed her a grin. "Just think how much you'll love me when you get to know me."

Her knees went weak, and she wasn't even standing. "Go put him down, Leo, and behave."

He kissed the baby's head, smiling down at him. "She's a hard case, kiddo. But I'll wear her down."

When Leo disappeared from sight, Phoebe exhaled loudly. She'd been holding her breath and hadn't even realized it. Rising to her feet unsteadily, she went from window to window closing the curtains. Darkness fell early in this mountain *holler,* as the old generation called it. Soon it would be the longest night of the year.

Phoebe had learned to dread the winter months. Not just the snow and ice and cold, gray days, but the intense loneliness. It had been the season of Christmas one year when she lost everything. Each anniversary brought it all back. But even before the advent of Leo, she had been determined to make this year better. She had a baby in the house. And now a guest. Surely that was enough to manufacture holiday cheer and thaw some of the ice that had kept her captive for so long.

Leo returned, carrying his laptop. He made himself at home on the sofa. "Do you mind giving me your internet password?" he asked, opening the computer and firing it up.

Uh-oh. "Um…" She leaned against the sink for support. "I don't have internet," she said, not sure there was any way to soften that blow.

Leo's look, a cross between horror and bafflement, was priceless. "Why not?"

"I decided I could live my life without it."

He ran his hands through his hair, agitation building. His neck turned red and a pulse beat in his temple. "This is the twenty-first century," he said, clearly trying to speak calmly. "*Everybody* has internet." He paused, his eyes narrowing. "This is either a joke, or you're Amish. Which is it?"

She lifted her chin, refusing to be judged for a decision that had seemed entirely necessary at the time. "Neither. I made a choice. That's all."

"My sister-in-law would never have rented me a cabin that didn't have the appropriate amenities," he said stubbornly.

"Well," she conceded. "You're right about that. The cabin I rent out has satellite internet. But as you saw for yourself, everything was pretty much demolished, including the dish."

She watched Leo's good humor evaporate as he absorbed the full import of what she was saying. Suddenly he pulled his smartphone from his pocket. "At least I can check email with this," he said, a note of panic in his voice.

"We're pretty far back in this gorge," she said. "Only one carrier gets a decent signal and it's—"

"Not the one I have." He stared at the screen and sighed. "Unbelievable. Outposts in Africa have better connectivity than this. I don't think I can stay somewhere that I have to be out of touch from the world."

Phoebe's heart sank. She had hoped Leo would come to appreciate the simplicity of her life here in the mountains. "Is it really that important? I have a landline phone you're welcome to use. For that matter, you can use *my* cell phone. And I do have a television dish, so you're welcome to add the other service if it's that important to you." If he were unable to understand and accept the choices she had made, then it would be foolish to pursue the attraction between them. She would only end up getting hurt.

Leo closed his eyes for a moment. "I'm sorry," he said at last, shooting her a look that was half grimace, half apology. "It took me by surprise, that's all. I'm accustomed to having access to my business emails around the clock."

Was that why he was here? Because he was *too* plugged in? Had he suffered some kind of breakdown? It didn't seem likely, but she knew firsthand how tension and stress could affect a person.

She pulled her cell phone from her pocket and crossed the room to hand it to him. "Use mine for now. It's not a problem."

Their fingers brushed as she gave him the device. Leo hesitated for a moment, but finally took it. "Thank you," he said gruffly. "I appreciate it."

Turning her back to give him some privacy, she went to the kitchen to rummage in the fridge and find an appealing dinner choice. Now that Leo was here, she would have to change her grocery buying habits. Fortunately, she had chicken and vegetables that would make a nice stir-fry.

Perhaps twenty minutes passed before she heard a very ungentlemanly curse from her tenant. Turning sharply, she witnessed the fury and incredulity that turned his jaw to steel and his eyes to molten chocolate. "I can't believe they did this to me."

She wiped her hands on a dish towel. "What, Leo? What did they do? Who are you talking about?"

He stood up and rubbed his eyes with the heels of his hands. "My brother," he croaked. "My black-hearted, devious baby brother."

As she watched, he paced, his scowl growing darker by the minute. "I'll kill him," he said with far too much relish. "I'll poison his coffee. I'll beat him to a pulp. I'll grind his wretched bones into powder."

Phoebe felt obliged to step in at that moment. "Didn't you say he has a wife and two kids? I don't think you really want to murder your own flesh and blood...do you? What could he possibly have done that's so terrible?"

Leo sank into an armchair, his arms dangling over the sides. Everything about his posture suggested defeat. "He locked me out of my work email," Leo muttered with a note of confused disbelief. "Changed all the passwords. Because he didn't trust me to stay away."

"Well, it sounds like he knows you pretty well, then. 'Cause isn't that exactly what you were doing? Trying to look at work email?"

Leo glared at her, his brother momentarily out of the crosshairs. "Whose side are you on anyway? You don't even know my brother."

"When you spoke of him earlier...he and your sister-in-law and the kids...I heard love in your voice, Leo. So that tells me he must love you just as much. Following that line of reasoning, he surely had a good reason to do what he did."

A hush fell over the room. The clock on the mantel ticked loudly. Leo stared at her with an intensity that made the hair on the back of her neck stand up. He was pissed. Really angry. And since his brother wasn't around, Phoebe might very well be his default target.

She had the temerity to inch closer and perch on the chair opposite him. "Why would he keep you away from work, Leo? And why did he and your sister-in-law send you here? You're not a prisoner. If being with me in this house is so damned terrible, then do us both a favor and go home."

Six

Leo was ashamed of his behavior. He'd acted like a petulant child. But everything about this situation threw him off balance. He was accustomed to being completely in charge of his domain, whether that be the Cavallo empire or his personal life. It wasn't that he didn't trust Luc. He did. Completely. Unequivocally. And in his gut, he knew the business wouldn't suffer in his absence.

Perhaps that was what bothered him the most. If the company he had worked all of his adult life to build could roll along just fine during his two-month hiatus, then what use was Leo to anyone? His successes were what he thrived on. Every time he made an acquisition or increased the company's bottom line, he felt a rush of adrenaline that was addictive.

Moving slot by slot up the Fortune 500 was immensely gratifying. He had made more money, both for the company and for himself, by the time he was thirty than most people earned in a lifetime. He was damned good at finance. Even in uncertain times, Leo had never made a misstep. His grandfather even went so far as to praise him for his genius. Given that eliciting a compliment from the old dragon was as rare as finding unicorn teeth, Leo had been justifiably proud.

But without Cavallo...without the high-tech office... without the daily onslaught of problems and split-second decisions...who was he? Just a young man with nowhere to go and nothing to do. The aimlessness of it all hung around his neck like a millstone.

Painfully aware that Phoebe had observed his humiliating meltdown, he stood, grabbed his coat from the hook by the door, shoved his feet in his shoes and escaped.

Phoebe fixed dinner with one ear out for the baby and one eye out the window to see if Leo was coming back. His car still sat parked out front, so she knew he was on foot. The day was warm, at least by December standards. But it *was* possible to get lost in these mountains. People did it all the time.

The knot in her stomach eased when at long last, he reappeared. His expression was impossible to read, but his body language seemed relaxed. "I've worked up an appetite" he said, smiling as if nothing had happened.

"It's almost ready. If we're lucky we'll be able to eat our meal in peace before Teddy wakes up."

"He's still asleep?"

She nodded. "I can never predict his schedule. I guess because he's still so small. But since I'm flexible, I'm fine with that."

He held out a chair for her and then joined her at the table. Phoebe had taken pains with the presentation. Pale green woven place mats and matching napkins from a craft cooperative in Gatlinburg accentuated amber stoneware plates and chunky handblown glass goblets that mingled green and gold in interesting swirls.

She poured each of them a glass of pinot. "There's beer in the fridge if you'd prefer it."

He tasted the wine. "No. This is good. A local vintage?"
"Yes. We have several wineries in the area."

Their conversation was painfully polite. Almost as awkward as a blind date. Though in this case there was nothing of a romantic nature to worry about. No *will he* or *won't he* when it came time for a possible good-night kiss at the front door.

Even so, she was on edge. Leo Cavallo's sexuality gave a woman ideas, even if unintentionally. It had been a very long time since Phoebe had kissed a man, longer still since she had felt the weight of a lover's body moving against hers in urgent passion. She thought she had safely buried those urges in her subconscious, but with Leo in her house, big and alive and so damned sexy, she was in the midst of an erotic awakening.

Like a limb that has gone to sleep and then experienced the pain of renewed blood flow, Phoebe's body tingled with awareness. Watching the muscles in his throat as he swallowed. Inhaling the scent of him, warm male and crisp outdoors. Inadvertently brushing his shoulder as she served him second helpings of chicken and rice. Hearing the lazy tempo of his speech that made her think of hot August nights and damp bodies twined together beneath a summer moon.

All of her senses were engaged except for taste. And the yearning to do just that, to kiss him, swelled in her chest and made her hands shake. The need was as overwhelming as it was unexpected. She fixated on the curve of his lips as he spoke. They were good lips. Full, but masculine. What would they feel like pressed against hers?

Imagining the taste of his mouth tightened everything inside her until she felt faint with arousal. Standing abruptly, she put her back to him, busying herself at the sink as she rinsed plates and loaded the dishwasher. Suddenly, she felt him behind her, almost pressing against her.

"Let me handle cleanup," he said, the words a warm breath of air at her neck. She froze. Did he sense her jittery nerves, her longing?

She swallowed, clenching her fingers on the edge of the counter. "No. Thank you. But a fire would be nice." She was already on fire. But what the heck…in for a penny, in for a pound.

After long seconds when it seemed as if every molecule of oxygen in the room vaporized, he moved away. "Whatever you want," he said. "Just ask."

Leo was neither naive nor oblivious. Phoebe was attracted to him. He knew, because he felt the same inexorable pull. But he had known her for barely a day. Perhaps long enough for an easy pickup at a bar or a one-night stand, but not for a relationship that was going to have to survive for a couple of months.

With a different woman at another time, he would have taken advantage of the situation. But he was at Phoebe's mercy for now. One wrong move, and she could boot him out. There were other cabins…other peaceful getaways. None of them, however, had Phoebe. And he was beginning to think that she was his talisman, his lucky charm, the only hope he had of making it through the next weeks without going stark raving mad.

The fire caught immediately, the dry tinder flaming as it coaxed the heavier logs into the blaze. When he turned around, Phoebe was watching him, her eyes huge.

He smiled at her. "Come join me on the sofa. We're going to be spending a lot of time together. We might as well get to know each other."

At that very moment, Teddy announced his displeasure with a noisy cry. The relief on Phoebe's face was almost comical. "Sorry. I'll be back in a minute."

While she was gone, he sat on the hearth, feeling the heat

from the fire sink into his back. Beneath his feet a bearskin pelt covered the floor. He was fairly certain it was fake, but the thick, soft fur made him imagine a scenario that was all too real. Phoebe...nude...her skin gilded with firelight.

The vivid picture in his mind hardened his sex and dried his mouth. Jumping to his feet, he went to the kitchen and poured himself another glass of wine. Sipping it slowly, he tried to rein in his hunger. Something might develop during this time with Phoebe. They could become friends. Or even more than that. But rushing his fences was not the way to go. He had to resist the temptation to bring sex into the picture before she had a chance to trust him.

Regardless of Phoebe's desires, or even his own, this was a situation that called for caution. Not his first impulse, or even his last. But if he had any hope of making her his, he'd bide his time.

His mental gyrations were interrupted by Phoebe's return. "There you are," he said. "I wondered if Teddy had kidnapped you."

"Poopy diaper," she said with a grimace. She held the baby on her hip as she prepared a bottle. "He's starving, poor thing. Slept right through dinner."

Leo moved to the sofa and was gratified when Phoebe followed suit. She now held the baby as a barricade between them, but he could wait. The child wasn't big enough to be much of a problem.

"So tell me," he said. "What did you do with yourself before Teddy arrived?"

Phoebe settled the baby on her lap and held the bottle so he could reach it easily. "I moved in three years ago. At first I was plenty busy with decorating and outfitting both cabins. I took my time and looked for exactly what I wanted. In the meantime, I made a few friends, mostly women I met at the gym. A few who worked in stores where I shopped."

"And when the cabins were ready?"

She stared down at the baby, rubbing his head with a wistful smile on her face. He wondered if she had any clue how revealing her expression was. She adored the little boy. That much was certain.

"I found someone to help me start a garden," she said. "Buford is the old man who lives back near the main road where you turned off. He's a sweetheart. His wife taught me how to bake bread and how to can fruits and vegetables. I know how to make preserves. And I can even churn my own butter in a pinch, though that seems a bit of a stretch in this day and age."

He studied her, trying to get to the bottom of what she wasn't saying. "I understand all that," he said. "And if I didn't know better, I'd guess you were a free spirit, hippie-commune, granola-loving Earth Mother. But something doesn't add up. How did you get from stockbroker to this?"

Phoebe understood his confusion. None of it made sense on paper. But was she willing to expose all of her painful secrets to a man she barely knew? No...not just yet.

Picking her words carefully, she gave him an answer. Not a lie, but not the whole truth. "I had some disappointments both personally and professionally. They hit me hard...enough to make me reconsider whether the career path I had chosen was the right one. At the time, I didn't honestly know. So I took a time-out. A step backward. I came here and decided to see if I could make my life simpler. More meaningful."

"And now? Any revelations to report?"

She raised an eyebrow. "Are you mocking me?"

He held up his hands. "No. I swear I'm not. If anything, I have to admire you for being proactive. Most people simply slog away at a job because they don't have the courage to try something new."

"I wish I could say it was like that. But to be honest,

it was more a case of crawling in a hole to hide out from the world."

"You don't cut yourself much slack, do you?"

"I was a mess when I came here."

"And now?"

She thought about it for a moment. No one had ever asked her straight-out if her self-imposed exile had borne fruit. "I think I have a better handle on what I want out of life. And I've forgiven myself for mistakes I made. But do I want to go back to that cutthroat lifestyle? No. I don't."

"I know this is a rude question, but I'm going to ask it anyway. What have you done for money since you've been out of work?"

"I'm sure a lot of people wonder that." She put the baby on her shoulder and burped him. "The truth is, Leo. I'm darned good at making money. I have a lot stashed away. And since I've been here, my weekly expenses are fairly modest. So though I can't stay here forever, I certainly haven't bankrupted myself."

"Would you say your experience has been worth it?"

She nodded. "Definitely."

"Then maybe there's hope for me after all."

Phoebe was glad to have Teddy as a buffer. Sitting with Leo in a firelit room on a cold December night was far too cozy. But when Teddy finished his bottle and was ready to play, she had no choice but to get down on the floor with him and let him roll around on the faux bearskin rug. He had mastered flipping from his back to his tummy. Now he enjoyed the increased mobility.

She was truly shocked when Leo joined them, stretching out on his right side and propping his head on his hand. "How long 'til he crawls?"

"Anytime now. He's already learned to get his knees up under him, so I don't think it will be too many more weeks." Leo seemed entirely relaxed, while Phoebe was in danger of hyperventilating. Anyone watching them might assume they were a family…mom, dad and baby. But the truth was, they were three separate people who happened to be occupying the same space for the moment.

Teddy was her nephew, true. But he was on loan, so to speak. She could feed him and play with him and love him, but at the end of the day, he wasn't hers. Still, what could it hurt to pretend for a while?

She pulled her knees to her chest and wrapped her arms around her legs. Ordinarily, she would have lain down on her stomach and played with Teddy at his level. But getting horizontal with Leo Cavallo was not smart, especially since he was in touching distance. She'd give herself away, no doubt. Even with a baby between them, she couldn't help thinking how nice it would be to spend an unencumbered hour with her new houseguest.

Some soft music on the radio, another bottle of wine, more logs on the fire. And after that…

Her heartbeat stuttered and stumbled. Dampness gathered at the back of her neck and in another, less accessible spot. Her breathing grew shallow. She stared at Teddy blindly, anything to avoid looking at Leo. Not for the world would she want him to think she was so desperate for male company that she would fall at his feet.

Even as she imagined such a scenario, he rolled to his back and slung an arm across his face. Moments later, she saw the steady rise and fall of his chest as he gave in to sleep.

Teddy was headed in the same direction. His acrobatics had worn him out. He slumped onto his face, butt in the air, and slept.

Phoebe watched the two males with a tightness in her chest that was a combination of so many things. Yearning for what might have been. Fear of what was yet to come.

Hope that somewhere along the way she could have a family of her own.

Her sleepless night caught up with her, making her eyelids droop. With one wary look at Leo to make sure he was asleep, she eased down beside her two companions and curled on her side with Teddy in the curve of her body. Now she could smell warm baby and wood smoke, and perhaps the faint scent of Leo's aftershave.

Closing her eyes, she sighed deeply. She would rest for a moment....

Seven

Leo awoke disoriented. His bed felt rock-hard, and his pillow had fallen on the floor. Gradually, he remembered where he was. Turning his head, he took in the sight of Phoebe and Teddy sleeping peacefully beside him.

The baby was the picture of innocence, but Phoebe… He sucked in a breath. Her position, curled on her side, made the neckline of her sweater gape, treating him to an intimate view of rounded breasts and creamy skin. Her hair tumbled around her face as if she had just awakened from a night of energetic sex. All he had to do was extend his arm and he could stroke her belly beneath the edge of her top.

His sex hardened to the point of discomfort. He didn't know whether to thank God for the presence of the kid or to curse the bad timing. The strength of his desire was both surprising and worrisome. Was he reacting so strongly to Phoebe because he was in exile and she was the only woman around, or had his long bout of celibacy predisposed him to want her?

Either way, his hunger for her was suspect. It would be the height of selfishness to seduce her because of boredom or propinquity. Already, he had taken her measure. She was loving, generous and kind, though by no means a pushover.

Even with training in what some would call a nonfeminine field, she nevertheless seemed completely comfortable with the more traditional roles of childcare and homemaking.

Phoebe was complicated. That, more than anything else, attracted him. At the moment a tiny frown line marked the space between her brows. He wanted to erase it with a kiss. The faint shadowy smudges beneath her eyes spoke of her exhaustion. He had been around his brother and sister-in-law enough to know that dealing with infants was harrowing and draining on the best of days.

He also knew that they glowed with pride when it came to their children, and he could see in Phoebe the same self-sacrificial love. Even now, in sleep, her arms surrounded little Teddy, keeping him close though he was unaware.

Moving carefully so as not to wake them, he rolled to his feet and quietly removed the screen so he could add wood to the smoldering fire. For insurance, he tossed another handful of kindling into the mix and blew on it gently. Small flames danced and writhed as he took a medium-size log and positioned it across the coals.

The simple task rocked him in an indefinable way. How often did he pause in his daily schedule to enjoy something as elemental and magical as an honest-to-God wood fire? The elegant gas logs in his condo were nothing in comparison.

As he stared into the hearth, the temperature built. His skin burned, and yet he couldn't move away. Phoebe seemed to him more like this real fire than any woman he had been with in recent memory. Energetic…messy… mesmerizing. Producing a heat that warmed him down to his bones.

Most of his liaisons in Atlanta were brief. He spent an enormous amount of time, perhaps more than was warranted, growing and protecting the Cavallo bottom line. Sex was good and a necessary part of his life. But he had never been tempted to do what it took to keep a woman in his bed night after night.

Kneeling, he turned and looked at Phoebe. Should he wake her up? Did the baby need to be put to bed?

Uncharacteristically uncertain, he deferred a decision. Snagging a pillow from the sofa, he leaned back against the stone hearth, stretched out his legs and watched them sleep.

Phoebe awoke slowly, but in no way befuddled. Her situation was crystal clear. Like a coward, she kept her eyes closed, even though she knew Leo was watching her. Apparently, her possum act didn't fool him. He touched her foot with his. "Open your eyes, Phoebe."

She felt at a distinct disadvantage. There was no graceful way to get up with him so close. Sighing, she obeyed his command and stared at him with as much chutzpah as she could muster. Rolling onto her back, she tucked her hands behind her head. "Have I brought a voyeur into my home?" she asked with a tart bite in her voice. It would do no good to let him see how much he affected her.

Leo yawned and stretched, his eyes heavy-lidded. "It's not my fault you had too much wine at dinner."

"I did not," she said indignantly. "I'm just tired, because the baby—"

"Gotcha," he said smugly, his eyes gleaming with mischief.

She sat up and ran her hands through her hair, crossing her legs but being careful not to bump Teddy. "Very funny. How long was I out?"

He shrugged. "Not long." His hot stare told her more clearly than words what he was thinking. They had rocketed from acquaintances to sleeping partners at warp speed. It was going to be difficult to pretend otherwise.

Her breasts ached and her mouth was dry. Sexual tension

shimmered between them like unseen vines drawing them ever closer. The only thing keeping them apart was a baby.

A baby who was her responsibility. That reality drew her back from the edge, though the decision to be clear-headed was a painful one. "I think we'll say good-night," she muttered. "Feel free to stay up as long as you like. But please bank the fire before you go to bed."

His gaze never faltered as she scooped up Teddy and gathered his things. "We have to talk about this," he said, the blunt words a challenge.

It took a lot, but she managed to look him straight in the eyes with a calm smile. "I don't know what you mean. Good night, Leo."

At two o'clock, he gave up the fight to sleep. He was wired, and his body pulsed with arousal, his sex full and hard. Neither of which condition was conducive to slumber. The *New York Times* bestseller he had opened failed to hold his attention past the first chapter. Cursing as he climbed out of his warm bed to pace the floor, he stopped suddenly and listened.

Faintly, but distinctly, he heard a baby cry.

It was all the excuse he needed. Throwing a thin, gray wool robe over his navy silk sleep pants, he padded into the hall, glad of the thick socks that Hattie had packed for him. Undoubtedly she had imagined him needing them if it snowed and he wore his boots. But they happened to be perfect for a man who wanted to move stealthily about the house.

In the hallway, he paused, trying to locate his landlady. There was a faint light under her door, but not Teddy's. The kid cried again, a fretful, middle-of-the-night whimper. Without weighing the consequences, Leo knocked.

Seconds later, the door opened a crack. Phoebe peered

out at him, her expression indiscernible in the gloom. "What's wrong? What do you want?"

Her stage whisper was comical given the fact that Teddy was clearly awake.

"You need some backup?"

"I'm fine." She started to close the door, but he stuck his foot in the gap, remembering at the last instant that he wasn't wearing shoes.

She pushed harder than he anticipated, and his socks were less protection than he expected. Pain shot up his leg. He groaned, jerking backward and nearly falling on his ass. Hopping on one foot, he pounded his fist against the wall to keep from letting loose with a string of words definitely not rated for kid ears.

Now Phoebe flung the door open wide, her face etched in dismay. "Are you hurt? Oh, heavens, of course you are. Here," she said. "Hold him while I get ice."

Without warning, his arms were full of a squirmy little body that smelled of spit-up and Phoebe's light floral scent. "But I..." He followed her down the hall, wincing at every step, even as Teddy's grumbles grew louder.

By the time he made it to the living room, Phoebe had turned on a couple of lamps and filled a dish towel with ice cubes. Her fingers curled around his biceps. "Give me the baby and sit down," she said, sounding frazzled and irritated, and anything but amorous. She pushed him toward the sofa. "Put your leg on the couch and let me see if you broke anything."

Teddy objected to the jostling and cried in earnest. Leo lost his balance and flopped down onto the sofa so hard that the baby's head and Leo's chin made contact with jarring force.

"Damn it to hell." He lay back, half-dazed, as Phoebe plucked Teddy from his arms and sat at the opposite end of the sofa. Before he could object, she had his leg in her lap and was peeling off his sock.

When slim, cool fingers closed around the bare arch of his foot, Leo groaned again. This time for a far different reason. Having Phoebe stroke his skin was damned arousing, even if he was in pain. Her thumb pressed gently, moving from side to side to assess the damage.

Leo hissed, a sharp involuntary inhalation. Phoebe winced. "Sorry. Am I hurting you too badly?"

She glanced sideways and her eyes grew big. His robe had opened when he lost his balance. Most of his chest was bare, and it was impossible to miss the erection that tented his sleep pants. He actually saw the muscles in her throat ripple as she swallowed.

"It feels good," he muttered. "Don't stop."

But Teddy shrieked in earnest now, almost inconsolable.

Phoebe dropped Leo's foot like it was a live grenade, scooting out from under his leg and standing. "Put the ice on it," she said, sounding breathless and embarrassed. "I'll be back."

Phoebe sank into the rocker in Teddy's room, her whole body trembling with awareness. The baby curled into her shoulder as she rubbed his back and sang to him quietly. He wasn't hungry. She had given him a bottle barely an hour ago. His only problem now was that his mouth hurt. She'd felt the tiny sharp edge of a tooth on his bottom gum and knew it was giving him fits. "Poor darling," she murmured. Reaching for the numbing drops, she rubbed a small amount on his sore mouth.

Teddy sucked her fingertip, snuffled and squirmed, then gradually subsided into sleep. She rocked him an extra five minutes just to make sure. When he was finally out, she laid him in his crib and tiptoed out of the room.

Her bed called out to her. She was weaving on her feet,

wrapped in a thick blanket of exhaustion. But she had told Leo she would come back. And in truth, nothing but cowardice could keep her from fulfilling that promise.

When she returned to the living room, it was filled with shadows, only a single lamp burning, though Leo had started another fire in the grate that gave off some illumination. He was watching television, but he switched it off as soon as she appeared. She hovered in the doorway, abashed by the sexual currents drawing her to this enigma of a man. "How's the foot?"

"See for yourself."

It was a dare, and she recognized it as such. Her legs carried her forward, even as her brain shouted, *Stop. Stop.* She wasn't so foolish this time as to sit down on the sofa. Instead, she knelt and removed the makeshift ice pack, setting it aside on a glass dish. Leo's foot was bruising already. A thin red line marked where the sharp corner of the door had scraped him.

"How does it feel?" she asked quietly.

Leo sat up, wincing, as he pulled his thick wool sock into place over his foot and ankle. "I'll live."

When he leaned forward with his forearms resting on his knees, he was face-to-face with her. "Unless you have an objection," he said, "I'm going to kiss you now." A lock of hair fell over his forehead. His voice was husky and low, sending shivers down her spine. The hour was late, that crazy time when dawn was far away and the night spun on, seemingly forever.

She licked her lips, feeling her nipples furl tightly, even as everything else in her body loosened with the warm flow of honey. "No objections," she whispered, wondering if he had woven some kind of spell over her while she was sleeping.

Slowly, gently, perhaps giving her time to resist, he cupped her cheeks with his hands, sliding his fingers into her hair and massaging her scalp. His thumbs ran along her jawline, pausing when he reached the little indentation beneath her ear.

"God, you're beautiful," he groaned, resting his forehead against hers. She could feel the heat radiating from his bare chest. All on their own, her hands came up to touch him, to flatten over his rib cage, to explore miles of warm, smooth skin. Well-defined pectoral muscles gave way to a thin line of hair that led to a flat belly corded with more muscles.

She felt drunk with pleasure. So long…it had been so long. And though she had encountered opportunities to be intimate with men during the past three years, none of them had been as tempting as Leo Cavallo. "What are we doing?" she asked raggedly, almost beyond the point of reason.

He gathered handfuls of her hair and played with it, pulling her closer. "Getting to know each other," he whispered. His mouth settled over hers, lips firm and confident. She opened to him, greedy for more of the hot pleasure that built at the base of her abdomen and made her shift restlessly.

When his tongue moved lazily between her lips, she met it with hers, learning the taste of him as she had wanted to so badly, experimenting with the little motions that made him shudder and groan. He held her head tightly now, dragging her to him, forcing her neck to arch so he could deepen the kiss. He tasted of toothpaste and determination.

Her hands clung to his wrists. "You're good at this," she panted. "A little too good."

"It's you," he whispered. "It's you." He moved down beside her so that they were chest to chest. "Tell me to stop, Phoebe." Wildly he kissed her, his hands roving over her back and hips. They were so close, his erection pressed into her belly.

She was wearing her usual knit pajamas, nothing sexy about them. But when his big hands trespassed beneath the elastic waistband and cupped her butt, she felt like a desirable woman. It had been so long since a man had touched her. And this wasn't just any man.

It was Leo. Big, brawny Leo, who looked as if he could move mountains for a woman, and yet paradoxically touched her so gently she wanted to melt into him and never leave his embrace. "Make love to me, Leo. Please. I need you so much...."

He dragged her to her feet and drew her closer to the fireplace. Standing on the bearskin rug, he pulled her top over her head. As he stared at her breasts, he cradled one in each hand, squeezing them carefully, plumping them with an expression that made her feel wanton and hungry.

At last looking at her face, he rubbed her nipples lightly as he kissed her nose, her cheeks, her eyes. His expression was warmly sensual, wickedly hot. "You make a man weak," he said. "I want to do all sorts of things to you, but I don't know where to start."

She should have felt awkward or embarrassed. But instead, exhilaration fizzed in her veins, making her breathing choppy. His light touch was not enough. She twined her arms around his neck, rubbing her lower body against his. "Does this give you any ideas?"

Eight

Leo was torn on a rack of indecision. Phoebe was here… in his arms…willing. But some tiny shred of decency in his soul insisted on being heard. The timing wasn't right. *This* wasn't right.

Cursing himself inwardly with a groan of anguish for the effort it took to stop the train on the tracks, he removed her arms from around his neck and stepped back. "We can't," he said. "I won't take advantage of you."

Barely able to look at what he was saying no to, he grabbed her pajama top and thrust it toward her. "Put this on."

Phoebe obeyed instantly as mortification and anger colored her face. "I'm not a child, Leo. I make my own decisions."

He wanted to comfort her, but touching her again was out of the question. An explanation would have to suffice. He hoped she understood him. "A tree demolished one of your cabins. You're caring for a teething baby, who has kept you up big chunks of the past two nights. Stress and exhaustion are no basis for making decisions." He of all people should know. "I don't want to be that man you regret when the sun comes up."

She wrapped her arms around her waist, glaring at him with thinly veiled hurt. "I should toss you out on your ass," she said, the words holding a faint but audible tremor.

His heart contracted. "I hope you won't." There were things he needed to tell her before they became intimate, and if he wasn't ready to come clean, then he wasn't ready to have sex with Phoebe. He hurt just looking at her. With her hair mussed and her protective posture, she seemed far younger than he knew her to be. Achingly vulnerable.

She lifted her chin. "We won't do this again. You keep to yourself, and I'll keep my end of the bargain. Good night, Leo." Turning on her heel, she left him.

The room seemed cold and lonely in her absence. Had he made the most colossal mistake of his life? The fire between the two of them burned hot and bright. She was perfection in his arms, sensual, giving, as intuitive a lover as he had ever envisaged.

Despite his unfilled passion, he knew he had done the right thing. Phoebe wasn't the kind of woman who had sex without thinking it through. Despite her apparent willingness tonight to do just that, he knew she would have blamed both herself and him when it was all over.

What he wanted from her, if indeed he had a chance of ever getting close to her again, was trust. He had secrets to share. And he suspected she did, as well. So he could wait for the other, the carnal satisfaction. Maybe....

Phoebe climbed into her cold bed with tears of humiliation wetting her cheeks. No matter what Leo said, tonight had been a rejection. What kind of man could call a halt when he was completely aroused and almost at the point of penetration? Only one who wasn't fully involved or committed to the act of lovemaking.

Perhaps she had inadvertently stimulated him with her foot massage. And maybe the intimacy of their nap in front of the fire had given him a buzz. But in the end, Phoebe simply wasn't who or what he wanted.

The fact that she could be badly hurt by a man she had met only recently gave her pause. Was she so desperate? So lonely? Tonight's debacle had given her some painful truths to examine.

But self-reflection would have to wait, because despite her distress, she could barely keep her eyes open....

Leo slept late the next morning. Not intentionally, but because he had been up much of the night pacing the floor. Sometime before dawn he had taken a shower and pleasured himself, but it had been a hollow exercise whose only purpose was to allow him to find oblivion in much-needed sleep.

The clock read almost ten when he made his way to the front of the house. He liked the open floor plan of the living room and kitchen, because it gave fewer places for Phoebe to hide.

Today, however, he was dumbstruck to find that she was nowhere in the house. And Teddy's crib was empty.

A twinge of panic gripped him until he found both of them out on the front porch chatting with the man who had come to remove the enormous fallen oak tree. When he stepped outside, Phoebe's quick disapproving glance reminded him that he had neither shaved nor combed his hair.

The grizzled workman who could have been anywhere from fifty to seventy saluted them with tobacco-stained fingers and headed down the lane to where he had parked his truck.

"I'm sorry," Leo said stiffly. "I was supposed to be handling this."

Phoebe's lips smiled, but her gaze was wintry. "No problem. Teddy and I dealt with it. If you'll excuse me, I have to get him down for his morning nap."

"But I—"

She shut the door in his face, leaving him out in the cold…literally.

He paused on the porch to count to ten, or maybe a hundred. Then, when he thought he had a hold on his temper, he went back inside and scavenged the kitchen for a snack to hold him until lunch. A couple of pieces of cold toast he found on a plate by the stove would have to do. He slathered them with some of Phoebe's homemade strawberry jam and sat down at the table. When Phoebe returned, he had finished eating and had also realized that he needed a favor. Not a great time to ask, but what the heck.

She ignored him pointedly, but he wasn't going to let a little cold shoulder put him off. "May I use your phone?" he asked politely.

"Why?"

"I'm going to order a new phone from your carrier since mine is virtually useless, and I also want to get internet service going. I'll pay the contract fees for a year, but when I leave you can drop it if you want to."

"That's pretty expensive for a short-term solution. It must be nice to be loaded."

He ground his teeth together, reminding himself that she was still upset about last night. "I won't apologize for having money," he said quietly. "I work very hard."

"Is it really that important to stay plugged in? Can't you go cold turkey for two months?" Phoebe was pale. She looked at him as if she would put him on the first plane out if she could.

How had they become combatants? He stared at her until her cheeks flushed and she looked away. "Technology and business are not demons," he said. "We live in the information age."

"And what about your recovery?"

"What about it?"

"I got the impression that you were supposed to stay away from business in order to rest and recuperate."

"I can do that and still have access to the world."

She took a step in his direction. "Can you? Can you really? Because from where I'm standing, you look like a guy who is determined to get what he wants when he wants it. Your doctor may have given you orders. Your brother may have, as well. But I doubt you respect them enough to really do what they've asked."

Her harsh assessment hit a little too close to home. "I'm following doctor's orders, I swear. Though it's really none of your business." The defensive note in his voice made him cringe inwardly. Was he honestly the ass she described?

"Do what you have to do," she said, pulling her phone from her pocket and handing it to him. Her expression was a mix of disappointment and resignation. "But I would caution you to think long and hard about the people who love you. And why it is that you're here."

At that moment, Leo saw a large delivery truck pull up in front of the cabin. Good, his surprise had arrived. Maybe it would win him some brownie points with Phoebe. And deflect her from the uncomfortable subject of his recuperation.

She went to the door as the bell rang. "But I didn't order anything," she protested when the man in brown set a large box just inside the door.

"Please sign here, ma'am," he said patiently.

The door slammed and Phoebe stared down at the box as if it possibly contained dynamite.

"Open it," Leo said.

Phoebe couldn't help being a little anxious when she tore into the package. It didn't have foreign postage, so it was not from her sister. She pulled back the cardboard flaps and stared in amazement. The box was full of food—an expensive ham, casseroles preserved in freezer packs, desserts, fresh fruit, the list was endless.

She turned to look at Leo, who now lay sprawled on the sofa. "Did you do this?"

He shrugged, his arms outstretched along the back of the couch. "Before I lost my temper yesterday about my work email, I scrolled through my personal messages and decided to contact a good buddy of mine, a cordon bleu chef in Atlanta who owes me a favor. I felt bad about you agreeing to cook for me all the time, so I asked him to hook us up with some meals. He's going to send a box once a week."

Her mind reeled. Not only was this a beautifully thoughtful gesture, it was also incredibly expensive. She stared at the contents, feeling her dismal mood slip away. A man like Leo would be a lovely companion for the following two months, even if all he wanted from her was friendship.

Before she could lose her nerve, she crossed the room, leaned down and kissed him on the cheek. His look of shock made her face heat. "Don't worry," she said wryly. "That was completely platonic. I merely wanted to say thank-you for a lovely gift."

He grasped her wrist, his warm touch sending ripples of heat all the way up her arm. "You're welcome, Phoebe. But of course, it's partially a selfish thing. I get to enjoy the bounty, as well." His smile could charm the birds off the trees. In repose, Leo's rugged features seemed austere, even intimidating. But when he smiled, the force of his charisma increased exponentially.

Feeling something inside her soul ease at the cessation of hostilities, she returned the smile, though she pulled away and put a safe distance between them. It was no use being embarrassed or awkward around Leo. She wasn't so heartless as to throw him out, and truthfully, she didn't want to. Teddy was a sweetheart, but having another adult in the house was a different kind of stimulation.

Suddenly, she remembered what she had wanted to ask Leo before last night when everything ended so poorly. "Tell me," she said. "Would you object to having Christmas decorations in the house?"

"That's a strange segue, but why would I object?" he asked. "I'm not a Scrooge."

"I never thought you were, but you might have ethnic or religious reasons to abstain."

"No problems on either score," he chuckled. "Does this involve a shopping trip?"

"No. Actually, I have boxes and boxes of stuff in the attic. When I moved here, I wasn't in the mood to celebrate. Now, with Teddy in the house, it doesn't seem right to ignore the holiday. I wasn't able to take it all down on my own. Do you mind helping? I warn you…it's a lot of stuff."

"Including a tree?"

She smiled beseechingly. "My old one is artificial, and not all that pretty. I thought it might be fun to find one in the woods."

"Seriously?"

"Well, of course. I own thirty acres. Surely we can discover something appropriate."

He lifted a skeptical eyebrow. *"We?"*

"Yes, we. Don't be so suspicious. I'm not sending you out in the cold all on your own. I have one of those baby carrier things. Teddy and I will go with you. Besides, I don't think men are the best judge when it comes to locating the perfect tree."

"You wound me," he said, standing and clutching his chest. "I have excellent taste."

"This cabin has space limitations to consider. And admit it. Men always think bigger is better."

"So do women as a rule."

His naughty double entendre was delivered with a straight face, but his eyes danced with mischief. Phoebe knew her cheeks had turned bright red. She felt the heat. "Are we still talking about Christmas trees?" she asked, her throat dry as the Sahara.

"You tell me."

"I think you made yourself pretty clear last night," she snapped.

He looked abashed. "I never should have let things go that far. We need to take baby steps, Phoebe. Forced proximity makes for a certain intimacy, but I respect you too much to take advantage of that."

"And if *I* take advantage of you?"

She was appalled to hear the words leave her mouth. Apparently her libido trumped both her pride and her common sense.

Leo's brows drew together in a scowl. He folded his arms across his broad chest. With his legs braced in a fighting stance, he suddenly seemed far more dangerous. Today he had on old jeans and a cream wool fisherman's sweater.

Everything about him from his head to his toes screamed wealth and privilege. So why hadn't he chosen some exclusive resort for his sabbatical? A place with tennis courts and spas and golf courses?

He still hadn't answered her question. The arousal swirling in her belly congealed into a small knot of embarrassment. Did he get some kind of sadistic kick out of flirting with women and then shutting them down?

"Never mind," she said, the words tight. "I understand."

He strode toward her, his face a thundercloud. "You don't understand a single damn thing," he said roughly. Before she could protest or back up or initiate any other of a dozen protective moves, he dragged her to his chest, wrapped one arm around her back and used his free hand to anchor her chin and tip her face up to his.

His thick-lashed brown eyes, afire with emotion and seemingly able to peer into her soul, locked on hers and dared her to look away. "Make no mistake, Phoebe," he said. "I want you. And Lord willing, I'm going to have you. When we finally make it to a bed—or frankly any flat surface, 'cause I'm not picky—I'm going to make love to you until we're both too weak to stand. But in the meantime, *you're* going to behave. *I'm* going to behave. Got it?"

Time stood still. Just like in the movies. Every one of her senses went on high alert. He was breathing hard, his chest rising and falling rapidly. When he grabbed her, she had braced one hand reflexively on his shoulder, though the idea of holding him at bay was ludicrous. She couldn't manage that even if she wanted to. His strength and power were evident despite whatever illness had plagued him.

Dark stubble covered his chin. He could have been a pirate or a highwayman or any of the renegade heroes in the historical novels her sister read. Phoebe was so close she could inhale the warm scent of him. A great bear of a man not long from his bed.

She licked her lips, trembling enough that she was glad of his support. "Define *behave*." She kissed his chin, his wrist, the fingers caressing her skin.

Leo fought her. Not outwardly. But from within. His struggle was written on his face. But he didn't release her. Not this time.

The curse he uttered as he gave in to her provocation was heartfelt and earthy as he encircled her with both arms and half lifted her off her feet. His mouth crushed hers, taking…giving no quarter. His masculine force was exhilarating. She was glad she was tall and strong, because it gave her the ability to match him kiss for kiss.

Baby steps be damned. She and Leo had jumped over miles of social convention and landed in a time of desperation, of elemental reality. Like the prehistoric people who had lived in these hills and valleys centuries before, the base human instinct to mate clawed its way to the forefront, making a mockery of soft words and tender sentiments.

This was passion in its most raw form. She rubbed against him, desperate to get closer. "Leo," she groaned, unable to articulate what she wanted, what she needed. "Leo…"

Nine

He was lost. Months of celibacy combined with the uncertainty of whether his body would be the same after his attack walloped him like a sucker punch. In his brain he repeated a frenzied litany. *Just a kiss. Just a kiss, just a kiss…*

His erection was swollen painfully, the taut skin near bursting. His lungs had contracted to half capacity, and black dots danced in front of his eyes. Phoebe felt like heaven in his arms. She was feminine and sinfully curved in all the right places, but she wasn't fragile. He liked that. No. Correction. He loved that. She kissed him without apology, no half measures.

Her skin smelled like scented shower gel and baby powder. This morning her hair was again tamed in a fat braid. He wrapped it around his fist and tugged, drawing back her head so he could nip at her throat with sharp love bites.

The noise she made, part cry, part moan, hit him in the gut. He lifted her, grunting when her legs wrapped around his waist. They were fully clothed, but he thrust against her, tormenting them both with pressure that promised no relief.

Without warning, Phoebe struggled to get away from him. He held her more tightly, half crazed with the urge to take her hard and fast.

She pushed at his chest. "Leo. I hear the baby. He's awake."

Finally, her breathless words penetrated the fog of lust that chained him. He dropped her to her feet and staggered backward, his heart threatening to pound through the wall of his chest.

Afraid of his own emotions, he strode to the door where his boots sat, shoved his feet into them, flung open the door and left the cabin, never looking back.

Phoebe had never once seen Teddy's advent into her life as anything but a blessing. Until today. Collecting herself as best she could, she walked down the hall and scooped him out of his crib. "Well, that was a short nap," she said with a laugh that bordered on hysteria. Teddy, happy now that she had rescued him, chortled as he clutched her braid. His not-so-nice baby smell warned her that he had a messy diaper, probably the reason he had awakened so soon.

She changed him and then put him on a blanket on the floor while she tidied his room. Even as she automatically carried out the oft-repeated chores, her mind was attuned to Leo's absence. He had left without a coat. Fortunately, he was wearing a thick sweater, and thankfully, the temperature had moderated today, climbing already into the low fifties.

She was appalled and remorseful about what had happened, all of it her fault. Leo, ever the gentleman, had done his best to be levelheaded about confronting their attraction amidst the present situation. But Phoebe, like a lonely, deprived spinster, had practically attacked him. It was no wonder things had escalated.

Men, unless they were spoken for—and sometimes not even then—were not physically wired to refuse women who threw out such blatant invitations. And that's what

Phoebe had done. She had made it abysmally clear that she was his for the taking.

Leo had reacted. Of course. What red-blooded, straight, unattached male wouldn't? *Oh, God.* How was she going to face him? And how did they deal with this intense but ill-timed attraction?

A half hour later she held Teddy on her hip as she put away the abundance of food Leo's chef friend had sent. She decided to have the chimichangas for lunch. They were already prepared. All she had to do was thaw them according to the directions and then whip up some rice and salad to go alongside.

An hour passed, then two. She only looked out the window a hundred times or so. What if he was lost? Or hurt? Or sick? Her stomach cramped, thinking of the possibilities.

Leo strode through the forest until his legs ached and his lungs gasped for air. It felt good to stretch his physical limits, to push himself and know that he was okay. Nothing he did, however, erased his hunger for Phoebe. At first he had been suspicious of his immediate fascination. His life had recently weathered a rough patch, and feminine companionship hadn't even been on his radar. That was how he rationalized his response to Phoebe, even on the day they'd met.

But he knew it was more than that. She was a virus in his blood, an immediate, powerful affliction that was in its own way as dangerous as his heart attack. Phoebe had the power to make his stay here either heaven or hell. And if it were the latter, he might as well cut and run right now.

But even as he thought it, his ego *and* his libido shouted a vehement *hell, no.* Phoebe might be calling the shots as his landlady, but when it came to sex, the decision was already made. He and Phoebe were going to be lovers. The only question was when and where.

His head cleared as he walked, and the physical exertion gradually drained him to the point that he felt able to go back. He had followed the creek upstream for the most part, not wanting to get lost. In some places the rhododendron thickets were so dense he was forced to climb up and around. When he finally halted, he was partway up the mountainside. To his surprise, he could see a tiny section of Phoebe's chimney sticking up out of the woods.

Perhaps Luc had been right. Here, in an environment so antithetical to Leo's own, he saw himself in a new light. His world was neither bad nor good in comparison to Phoebe's. But it was different.

Was that why Phoebe had come here? To get perspective? And if so, had she succeeded? Would she ever go back to her earlier life?

He sat for a moment on a large granite boulder, feeling the steady pumping of his heart. Its quiet, regular beats filled him with gratitude for everything he had almost lost. Perhaps it was the nature of humans to take life for granted. But now, like the sole survivor of a plane crash, he felt obliged to take stock, to search for meaning, to tear apart the status quo and see if it was really worthy of his devotion.

Amidst those noble aspirations, he shamefully acknowledged if only to himself that he yearned to be back at his desk. He ran a billion-dollar company, and ran it well. He was Leo Cavallo, CFO of a textile conglomerate that spanned the globe. Like a recovering addict, his hands itched for a fix…for the pulse-pumping, mentally stimulating, nonstop schedule that he understood so intimately.

He knew people used *workaholic* as a pejorative term, often with a side order of pitying glances and shakes of the head. But, honest to God, he didn't see anything wrong with having passion for a job and doing it well. It irritated the hell out of him to imagine all the balls that were being dropped in his absence. Not that Luc and the rest of the team weren't as smart as he was…it wasn't that.

Leo, however, gave Cavallo his everything.

In December, the prep work began for year-end reports. Who was paying attention to those sorts of things while Leo was AWOL? It often became necessary to buy or sell some smaller arms of the business for the appropriate tax benefit. The longer he thought about it, the more agitated he became. He could feel his blood pressure escalating.

As every muscle in his body tensed, he had to force himself to take deep breaths, to back away from an invisible cliff. In the midst of his agitation, an inquisitive squirrel paused not six inches from Leo's boot to scrabble in the dirt for an acorn. Chattering his displeasure with the human who had invaded his territory, the small animal worked furiously, found the nut and scampered away.

Leo smiled. And in doing so, felt the burden he carried shift and ease. He inhaled sharply, filling his lungs with clean air. As a rule, he thrived on the sounds of traffic and the ceaseless hum of life in a big city. Yet even so, he found himself noticing the stillness of the woods. The almost imperceptible presence of creatures who went about their business doing whatever they were created to do.

They were lucky, Leo mused wryly. No great soul-searching for them. Merely point A to point B. And again. And again.

He envied them their singularity of purpose, though he had no desire to be a hamster on a wheel. As a boy, his teachers had identified him as gifted. His parents had enrolled him in special programs and sent him to summer camps in astrophysics and geology and other erudite endeavors.

All of it interested and engaged him, but he never quite fit in anywhere. His size and athletic prowess made him a target of suspicion in the realm of the nerds, and his academic successes and love for school excluded him from the jock circle.

His brother became, and still was, his best friend. They squabbled and competed as siblings did, but their bond ran deep. Which was why Leo was stuck here, like a storybook character, lost in the woods. Because Luc had insisted it was important. And Leo owed his brother. If Luc believed Leo needed this time to recover, then it was probably so.

Rising to his feet and stretching, he shivered hard. After his strenuous exercise, he had sat too long, and now he was chilled and stiff. Suddenly, he wanted nothing more than to see Phoebe. He couldn't share his soul-searching and his minor epiphanies with her, because he hadn't yet come clean about his health. But he wanted to be with her. In any way and for any amount of time fate granted him.

Though it was not his way, he made an inward vow to avoid the calendar and to concentrate on the moment. Perhaps there was more to Leo Cavallo than met the eye. If so, he had two months to figure it out.

Phoebe couldn't decide whether to cry or curse when Leo finally came through the door, his tall, broad silhouette filling the doorway. Her giddy relief that he was okay warred with irritation because he had disappeared for so long without an explanation. Of course, if he had been living in his own cabin, she would not have been privy to his comings and goings.

But this was different. He and Phoebe were cohabiting. Which surely gave her some minimal rights when it came to social conventions. Since she didn't have the guts to chastise him, her only choice was to swallow her pique and move forward.

As he entered and kicked off his muddy boots, he smiled sheepishly. "Have you already eaten?"

"Yours is warming in the oven." She returned the smile,

but stayed seated. It wasn't necessary to hover over him like a doting housewife. Leo was a big boy.

Teddy played with a plastic straw while Phoebe enjoyed a second cup of coffee. As Leo joined her at the table, she nodded at his plate. "Your friend is a genius. Please thank him for me. Though I'm sure I'll be ruing the additional calories."

Leo dug into his food with a gusto that suggested he had walked long and hard. "You're right. I've even had him cater dinner parties at my home. Makes me very popular, I can tell you."

As he finished his meal, Phoebe excused herself to put a drooping Teddy down for his nap. "I have a white noise machine I use sometimes in his room, so I think we'll be able to get the boxes down without disturbing him," she said. "And if he takes a long afternoon nap like he sometimes does, we can get a lot of the decorating done if you're still up for it."

Leo cocked his head, leaning his chair back on two legs. "I'm definitely *up* for it," he said, his lips twitching.

She couldn't believe he would tease about their recent insanity. "That's not funny."

"You don't have to tell me." He grinned wryly. "I realize in theory that couples with young children have sex. I just don't understand how they do it."

His hangdog expression made Phoebe burst into laughter, startling Teddy, who had almost fallen asleep on her shoulder. "Well, you don't have to worry about it," she said sharply, giving him a look designed to put him in his place. "All I have on the agenda this afternoon is decking the halls."

Leo had seldom spent as much time alone with a woman as he had with Phoebe. He was beginning to learn her expressions and to read them with a fair amount of accuracy.

When she reappeared after settling the baby, her excitement was palpable.

"The pull-down steps to the attic are in that far corner over there." She dragged a chair in that direction. "I'll draw the cord and you get ready to steady the steps as they come down."

He did as she asked, realizing ruefully that this position put him on eye level with her breasts. Stoically, he looked in the opposite direction. Phoebe dragged on the rope. The small framed-off section of the ceiling opened up to reveal a very sturdy set of telescoping stairs.

Leo grabbed the bottom section and pulled, easing it to the floor. He set his foot on the first rung. "What do you want me to get first?"

"The order doesn't really matter. I want it all. Except for the tree. That can stay. Here," she said, handing him a flashlight from her pocket. "I almost forgot."

Leo climbed, using the heavy flashlight to illuminate cobwebs so he could swat them away. Perhaps because the cabin was fairly new, or maybe because Phoebe was an organized sort, her attic was not a hodgepodge of unidentified mess. Neatly labeled cardboard cartons and large plastic tubs had been stacked in a tight perimeter around the top of the stairs within easy reach.

Some of the containers were fairly heavy. He wondered how she had managed to get them up here. He heard a screech and bent to stick his head out the hole. "What's wrong?"

Phoebe shuddered. "A spider. I didn't think all this stuff would have gotten so icky in just three years."

"Shall I stop?"

She grimaced. "No. We might as well finish. I'll just take two or three showers when we're done."

He tossed her a small box that was light as a feather. In neat black marker, Phoebe had labeled *Treetop Angel*.

When she caught it, he grinned at her. "I'd be glad to help with that body check. I'll search the back of your hair for creepy-crawlies."

"I can't decide if that's revolting or exciting. Seems like you made a similar offer when you were convincing me to let you stay. Only then, you promised to kill *hypothetical* bugs."

"Turns out I was right, doesn't it?" He returned to his task, his body humming with arousal. He'd never paid much attention to the holidays. But with Phoebe, suddenly all the chores surrounding Christmas took on a whole new dimension.

By the time he had brought down the last box and stored away the stairs, Phoebe was elbows-deep into a carton of ornaments.

She held up a tiny glass snowman. "My grandmother gave me this when I was eight."

He crouched beside her. "Is she still alive?"

"No. Sadly."

"And your parents?" He was close enough to brush his lips across the nape of her neck, but he refrained.

Phoebe sank back on her bottom and crossed her legs, working to separate a tangle of glittery silver beads. "My parents were hit by a drunk driver when my sister and I were in high school. A very kind foster family took us in and looked after us until we were able to graduate and get established in college."

"And since then?"

"Dana and I are very close."

"No significant others in your past?"

She frowned at the knot that wouldn't give way. "What about your family, Leo?"

He heard the unspoken request for privacy, so he backed off. "Oddly enough, you and I have that in common. Luc and I were seventeen and eighteen when we lost our parents. Only it was a boating accident. My father loved his nautical toys, and he was addicted to the adrenaline rush of speed. We were in Italy visiting my grandfather one spring break. Dad took a friend's boat out, just he and my mom. On the way back, he hit a concrete piling at high speed as they were approaching the dock."

"Oh, my God." Her hands stilled. "How dreadful."

He nodded, the memory bleak even after all this time. "Grandfather insisted on having autopsies done. My mother wasn't wearing a life jacket. She drowned when she was flung into the water. I took comfort in the fact that she was probably unconscious when she died, because she had a severe head wound."

"And your father?"

Leo swallowed. "He had a heart attack. That's what caused him to lose control of the boat." Repeating the words stirred something dark and ugly in his gut. To know that he was his father's son had never pained him more than in the past few months.

Phoebe put a hand on his arm. "But wasn't he awfully young?"

"Forty-one."

"Oh, Leo. I'm so very sorry."

He shrugged. "It was a long time ago. After the funerals, Grandfather took Luc and I back to Italy to live with him. He insisted we attend college in Rome. Some would say we were lucky to have had such an education, but we were miserable for a long time. Our grief was twofold, of course. On top of that, Grandfather is not an easy man to love." He hesitated for a moment. "I don't tell many people that story, but you understand what it feels like to have the rug ripped out from under your feet."

"I do indeed. My parents were wonderful people. They always encouraged Dana and me to go for any goal we wanted. Never any question of it being *too hard* or *not a girl thing*. Losing them changed our lives."

Silence fell like a pall. Leo tugged at her braid. "Sorry. I didn't mean to take us down such a dismal path."

She rested her head against his hand. "It's hard not to think of family at this time of year, especially the ones we've lost. I'm glad you're here, Leo."

Ten

She wasn't sure who initiated the intimate contact. Their lips met briefly, sweetly. The taste of him was as warm and comfortable as a summer rain. She felt the erotic river of molten lava hidden just beneath the surface, but as if by unspoken consent, the kiss remained soft and easy.

Leaning into him, she let herself be bolstered by his strength. One big arm supported her back. He was virile and sexy. She couldn't be blamed for wanting more. "Leo," she muttered.

All she said was his name, but she felt the shudder that ran through him. "What?" he asked hoarsely. "What, Phoebe?"

A million different answers hovered at the tip of her tongue. *Undress me. Touch my bare skin. Make love to me.* Instead, she managed to be sensible. "Let me put some music on to get us in the mood for decorating."

"I *am* in the mood," he grumbled. But he smiled when he said it and kissed the tip of her nose. Then he sobered. "To be absolutely clear, I want you in my bed, tonight, Phoebe. When the little man is sound asleep and not likely to interrupt us."

His eyes were dark chocolate, sinful and rich and designed to make a woman melt into their depths. She stared at him, weighing the risks. As a financial speculator, she played hunches and often came out on top. But taking Leo as a lover was infinitely more dangerous.

He was here only for a short while. And though Phoebe had made peace with her demons and embraced her new lifestyle, she was under no illusions that Leo had done the same. He was anxious to return home. Coming to the mountains had been some sort of penance for him, a healing ritual that he accepted under protest.

Leo would never be content to stagnate. He had too much energy, too much life.

She touched his cheek, knowing that her acquiescence was a forgone conclusion. "Yes. I'd like that, too. And I'm sorry that we can't be more spontaneous. A new relationship should be hot and crazy and passionate." *Like this morning when you nearly took me standing up.* Her pulse tripped and stumbled as her thighs tightened in remembrance.

Leo cupped her hand to his face with one big palm. "It will be, Phoebe, darlin'. Don't you worry about that."

To Phoebe's surprise and delight, the afternoon became one long, drawn-out session of foreplay. Leo built a fire so high and hot they both had to change into T-shirts to keep cool. Phoebe found a radio station that played classic Christmas songs. She teased Leo unmercifully when she realized he never remembered any of the second verses, and instead made up his own words.

Together, they dug out a collection of balsam-scented candles, lit them and set them on the coffee table. During the summer, the trapped heat in the attic had melted the wax a bit, so the ones that were supposed to be Christmas trees looked more like drunken bushes.

Phoebe laughed. "Perhaps I should just throw them away."

Leo shook his head. "Don't do that. They have *character*."

"If you say so." She leaned down and squinted at them. "They look damaged to me. Beyond repair."

"Looks can be deceiving."

Something in his voice—an odd note—caught her attention. He was staring at the poor trees as if all the answers to life's great questions lay trapped in green wax.

What did Leo Cavallo know about being damaged? As far as Phoebe could see, he was at the peak of his physical strength and mental acuity. Sleek muscles whispered of his ability to hold a woman…to protect her. And in a contest of wits, she would need to stay on her toes to best him. Intelligence crackled in his eyes and in his repartee.

Leo was the whole package, and Phoebe wanted it all.

Gradually, the room was transformed. With Leo's assistance, Phoebe hung garland from the mantel and around the doorways, intertwining it with tiny white lights that sparkled and danced even in the daytime. She would have preferred fresh greenery. But with a baby to care for and a cabin to repair, she had to accept her limits.

Leo spent over an hour tacking silver, green and gold snowflakes to the ceiling. Far more meticulous than she would have been, he measured and arranged them until every glittering scrap of foil was perfectly placed. The masculine satisfaction on his face as he stood, neck craned, and surveyed his handiwork amused her, but she was quick to offer the appropriate accolades.

In addition to the misshapen candles, the coffee table now sported a red wool runner appliquéd in reindeer. The *Merry Christmas* rug she remembered from her home in Charlotte now lay in front of a new door. The kitchen table boasted dark green place mats and settings of Christmas china.

At long last, Leo flopped down on the sofa with a groan. "You *really* like Christmas, don't you?"

She joined him, curling into his embrace as naturally as if they were old friends. "I lost the spirit for a few years, but with Teddy here, this time I think it will be pretty magical." Weighing her words, she finally asked the question she had been dying to have him answer. "What about you, Leo? Your sister-in-law made your reservation for two months. But you'll go home for the holidays, won't you?"

Playing lazily with the ends of her braid, he sighed. "I hadn't really thought about it. Many times in the past six or eight years, Luc and I flew to Italy to be with Grandfather for Christmas. But when Luc and Hattie married the year before last, Grandfather actually came over here, though he swore it wouldn't be an annual thing, because the trip wore him out. Now, with two little ones, I think Luc and Hattie deserve their own family Christmas."

"And what about you?"

Leo shrugged. "I'll have an invitation or two, I'm sure."

"You could stay here with Teddy and me." Only when she said the words aloud did she realize how desperately she wanted him to say yes.

He half turned to face her. "Are you sure? I wouldn't want to intrude."

Was he serious? She was a single woman caring for a baby that wasn't hers in a lonely cabin in the woods. "I think we can make room," she said drily. Without pausing to think of the ramifications, she ran a hand through his thick hair. The color, rich chestnut shot through with dark gold, was far too gorgeous for a man, not really fair at all.

Leo closed his eyes and leaned back, a smile on his face, but fine tension in his body. "That would be nice...." he said, trailing off as though her gentle scalp massage was making it hard to speak.

She put her head on his chest. With only a thin navy

T-shirt covering his impressive upper physique, she could hear the steady *ka-thud, ka-thud, ka-thud* of his heart. "Perhaps we should wait and see how tonight goes," she muttered. "I'm out of practice, to be honest." Better he know now than later.

Moving so quickly that she never saw it coming, he took hold of her and placed her beneath him on the sofa, his long, solid frame covering hers as he kissed his way down her throat. One of his legs lodged between her thighs, opening her to the possibility of something reckless. She lifted her hips instinctively. "Don't stop," she pleaded.

He found her breasts and took one nipple between his teeth, wetting the fabric of her shirt and bra as he tormented her with a bite that was just short of pain. Fire shot from the place where his mouth touched her all the way to her core. Shivers of pleasure racked her.

Suddenly, Leo reared back, laughing and cursing.

Blankly, she stared up at him, her body at a fever pitch of longing. "What? Tell me, Leo."

"Listen. The baby's awake."

When a knock sounded at the door minutes later, Leo knew he and Phoebe had narrowly escaped embarrassment on top of sexual frustration. She was out of sight tending to Teddy, so Leo greeted the man at the door with a smile. "Can I help you?"

The old codger in overalls looked him up and down. "Name's Buford. These sugared pecans is from my wife. She knowed they were Miss Phoebe's favorite, so she made up an extra batch after she finished the ones for the church bazaar. Will you give 'em to her?"

Leo took the paper sack. "I'd be happy to. She's feeding the baby a bottle, I think, but she should be finished in a moment. Would you like to come in?"

"Naw. Thanks. Are you the fella that was going to rent the other cabin?"

"Yes, sir, I am."

"Don't be gettin' any ideas. Miss Phoebe's pretty popular with the neighbors. We look out fer her."

"I understand."

"You best get some extra firewood inside. Gonna snow tonight."

"Really?" The afternoon sunshine felt more like spring than Christmas.

"Weather changes quicklike around here."

"Thanks for the warning, Buford."

With a tip of his cap, the guy ambled away, slid into a rust-covered pickup truck and backed up to turn and return the way he had come.

Leo closed the door. Despite feeling like a sneaky child, he unfolded the top of the sack and stole three sugary pecans.

Phoebe caught him with his hand in the bag…literally. "What's that?" she asked, patting Teddy on the back to burp him.

Leo chewed and swallowed, barely resisting the urge to grab another handful of nuts. "Your farmer friend, Buford, came by. How old is he anyway?"

"Buford is ninety-eight and his wife is ninety-seven. They were both born in the Great Smoky Mountains before the land became a national park. The house Buford and Octavia now live in is the one he built for her when they married in the early 1930s, just as the Depression was gearing up."

"A log cabin?"

"Yes. With a couple of rambling additions. They still used an actual outhouse up until the mid-eighties when their kids and grandkids insisted that Buford and Octavia were getting too old to go outside in the dead of winter to do their business."

"What happened then?"

"The relatives chipped in and installed indoor plumbing."

"Good Lord." Leo did some rapid math. "If they married in the early thirties, then—"

"They'll be celebrating their eightieth anniversary in March."

"That seems impossible."

"She was seventeen. Buford one year older. It happened all the time."

"Not their ages. I mean the part about eighty years together. How can anything last that long?"

"I've wondered that myself. After all, even a thirty-five-year marriage is becoming harder to find among my peers' parents."

Leo studied Phoebe, trying to imagine her shoulders stooped with age and her beautiful skin lined with wrinkles. She would be lovely still at sixty, and even seventy. But closing in on a hundredth birthday? Could any couple plan on spending 85 percent of an entire life looking at the same face across the breakfast table every morning? It boggled the mind.

Somehow, though, when he really thought about it, he *was* able see Phoebe in that scenario. She was strong and adaptable and willing to step outside her comfort zone. He couldn't imagine ever being bored by her. She had a sharp mind and an entertaining sense of humor. Not to mention a body that wouldn't quit.

Leo, himself, had never fallen in love even once. Relationships, good ones, took time and effort. Until now, he'd never met a woman capable of making him think long term.

Phoebe was another story altogether. He still didn't fully understand the decision that had brought her to the mountains, but he planned on sticking around at least long enough to find out. She intrigued him, entertained him and aroused him. Perhaps it was their isolation, but he felt a connection that transcended common sense and entered the realm of the heart. He was hazy about what he wanted from her in the long run. But tonight's agenda was crystal clear.

He desired Phoebe. Deeply. As much and as painfully as a man could hunger for a woman. Barring any unforeseen circumstances, she was going to be his.

To Phoebe's eyes, Leo seemed to zone out for a moment. She didn't feel comfortable demanding an explanation, not even a joking "Penny for your thoughts." Instead, she tried a distraction. "Teddy is fed and dry and rested at the moment. If we're going to get a tree, the time is right."

Leo snapped out of his fog and nodded, staring at the baby. "You don't think it will be too cold?"

"I have a snowsuit to put on him. That should be plenty of insulation for today. I'll get the two of us ready. If you don't mind going out to the shed, you can get the ax. It's just inside the door."

"You have an ax?" He was clearly taken aback.

"Well, yes. How else would we cut down a tree?"

"But you told me you haven't had a Christmas tree since you've been here. Why do you need an ax?"

She shrugged. "I split my own wood. Or at least I did in the pre-Teddy days. Now I can't take the chance that something might happen to me and he'd be in the house helpless. So I pay a high school boy to do it."

"I'm not sure how wise it is for you to be so isolated and alone. What if you needed help in an emergency?"

"We have 911 access. And I have the landline phone in addition to my cell. Besides, the neighbors aren't all that far away."

"But a woman on her own is vulnerable in ways a man isn't."

She understood what he wasn't saying. And she'd had those same conversations with herself in the beginning. Sleeping had been difficult for a few months. Her imagination had run wild, conjuring up rapists and murderers and deviants like the Unabomber looking for places to hide out in her neck of the woods.

Eventually, she had begun to accept that living in the city carried the same risks. The only difference being that they were packaged differently.

"I understand what you're saying," Phoebe said. "And yes, there have been nights, like the recent storm for instance, when I've questioned my decision to live here. But I decided over time that the benefits outweigh the negatives, so I've stayed."

Leo looked as if he wanted to argue the point, but in the end, he shook his head, donned his gear and left.

It took longer than she expected to get the baby and herself ready to brave the outdoors. That had been the biggest surprise about keeping Teddy. Everything about caring for him was twice as complicated and time-consuming as she had imagined. Finally, though, she was getting the hang of things, and already, she could barely remember her life without the little boy.

Eleven

It was the perfect day for an excursion. Since men were still working at the cabin removing the last of the tree debris and getting ready to cover the whole structure with a heavy tarp, Phoebe turned in the opposite direction, walking side by side with Leo back down the road to a small lane which turned off to the left and meandered into the forest.

She had fastened Teddy into a sturdy canvas carrier with straps that crisscrossed at her back. Walking was her favorite form of exercise, but it took a quarter mile to get used to the extra weight on her chest. She kept her hand under Teddy's bottom. His body was comfortable and warm nestled against her.

Leo carried the large ax like it weighed nothing at all, when Phoebe knew for a fact that the wooden-handled implement was plenty heavy. He seemed pleased to be out of the house, whistling an off-key tune as they strode in amicable silence.

The spot where she hoped to find the perfect Christmas tree was actually an old home site, though only remnants of the foundation and the chimney remained. Small weather-roughened headstones nearby marked a modest family cemetery. Some of the writing on the stones was still legible, including several that read simply, Beloved Baby. It pained her to think of the tragic deaths from disease in those days.

But she had suffered more than her share of hurt. She liked to think she understood a bit of what those families had faced.

Leo frowned, seeing the poignant evidence of human lives loved and lost. "Does this belong to you?" The wind soughed in the trees, seeming to echo chattering voices and happy laughter of an earlier day.

"As much as you can own a graveyard, I guess. It's on my property. But if anyone ever showed up to claim this place, I would give them access, of course. If descendants exist, they probably don't even know this is here."

One of the infant markers caught his attention. "I can't imagine losing a child," he said, his expression grim. "I see how much Luc and Hattie love their two, and even though I'm not a parent, sometimes it terrifies me to think of all the things that happen in the world today."

"Will you ever want children of your own?" Her breath caught in her throat as she realized that his answer was very important to her.

He squatted and brushed leaves away from the base of the small lichen-covered stone. "I doubt it. I don't have the time, and frankly, it scares the hell out of me." Looking up at her, his smile was wry. But despite the humor, she realized he was telling the absolute truth.

Her stomach tightened in disappointment. "You're still young."

"The business is my baby. I'm content to let Luc carry on the family lineage."

Since she had no answer to that, the subject lapsed, but she knew she had been given fair warning. Not from any intentional ultimatum on Leo's part. The problem was, Phoebe had allowed her imagination to begin weaving fantasies. Along the way, her heart, once broken but well on the way to recovery, had decided to participate.

The result was an intense and sadly dead-end infatuation with Leo Cavallo.

She stroked Teddy's hair, smiling to see the interest he demonstrated in his surroundings. He was a happy, inquisitive baby. Since the day he was born, she had loved him terribly. But this time alone, just the two of them, and now with Leo, had cemented his place in her heart. Having to return him to his parents was going to be a dreadful wrench. The prospect was so dismal, she forced the thought away. Much more of this, and she was going to start quoting an infamous Southern belle. *I'll think about that tomorrow.*

Leo stood and stretched, rolling his shoulders, the ax on the ground propped against his hip. "I'm ready. Show me which one."

"Don't be silly. We have to make a careful decision."

"This is the world's biggest Christmas tree farm. I'd say you won't have too much trouble. How about that one right there?" He pointed at a fluffy cedar about five feet tall.

"Too small and the wrong variety. I'll know when I see it."

Leo took her arm and steered her toward a grouping of evergreens. "Anything here grab your fancy?"

She and Leo were both encased in layers of winter clothes. But she fancied she could feel the warmth of his fingers on her skin. A hundred years ago, Leo would have worked from dawn to dusk, providing for his family. At night, when the children were asleep in the loft, she could see him making love to his wife on a feather tick mattress in front of the fire. Entering *her,* Phoebe, with a fire, a passion he had kept banked during the daylight hours. Saving those special moments of intimacy for the dark of night.

Wishing she could peel out of her coat, she stripped off her gloves and removed her scarf. The image of a more primitive Leo was so real, her breasts ached for his touch. She realized she had worn too many clothes. The day was warm for a winter afternoon. And thoughts of Leo's expertise in bed made her feel as if she had a fever.

She cleared her throat, hoping he wouldn't notice the hot color that heated her neck and cheeks. "Give me a second." Pretending an intense interest in the grouping of trees, she breathed deeply, inhaling the scent of the fresh foliage. "This one," she said hoarsely, grabbing blindly at the branches of a large Fraser fir.

At her back, Leo stood warm and tall. "I want you to have your perfect Christmas, Phoebe. But as the voice of reason I have to point out that your choice is a little on the big side." He put his hands on her shoulders, kissing her just below the ear. "If it's what you want, though, I'll trim it or something."

She nodded, her legs shaky. "Thank you."

He set her aside gently, and picked up the ax. "Move farther back. I don't know how far the wood chips will fly."

Teddy had dozed off, his chubby cheeks a healthy pink. She kept her arms around him as Leo notched the bottom of the tree trunk and took a few practice chops. At the last minute, he shed his heavy parka, now clad above the waist in only a thermal weave shirt, green to match his surroundings.

It was ridiculous to get so turned on by a Neanderthal exhibition of strength. But when Leo took his first powerful swing and the ax cut deeply into the tree, Phoebe felt a little faint.

Leo was determined to make Phoebe happy. The trunk of this particular fir was never going to fit into a normal-size tree stand. He'd have to cobble something together with a large bucket and some gravel. Who knew? At the moment, his first task was to fell the sucker and drag it home.

At his fifth swing, he felt a twinge in his chest. The feeling was so unexpected and so sharp, he hesitated half a second, long enough for the ax to lose its trajectory and land out of target range. Now, one of the lower branches was about two feet shorter than it had been.

Phoebe, standing a good ten feet away, called out to him. "What's wrong?"

"Nothing," he said, wiping his brow with the back of his hand. Tree chopping was damned hard work. Knowing that her eyes were on him, he found his stride again, landing four perfect strikes at exactly the same spot. The pain in his chest had already disappeared. Probably just a muscle. His doctor had reassured him more than once that Leo's health was perfect. Trouble was, when a man had been felled by something he couldn't see, it made him jumpy.

Before severing the trunk completely, he paused before the last swing and tugged the tree to one side. The fragrance of the branches was alluring. Crisp. Piquant. Containing memories of childhood days long forgotten. Something about scent leaped barriers of time and place.

Standing here in the forest with sap on his hands and his muscles straining from exertion, he felt a wave of nostalgia. He turned to Phoebe. "I'm glad you wanted to do this. I remember Christmases when I begged for a real tree. But my dad was allergic. Our artificial trees were always beautiful—Mom had a knack for that—but just now, a whiff of the air brought it all back. It's the smell of the holidays."

"I'm glad you approve," she said with a charming grin. Standing as she was in a splash of sunlight, her hair glistened with the sheen of a raven's wing. The baby slept against her breast. Leo wondered what it said about his own life that he envied a little kid. Phoebe's hand cradled Teddy's head almost unconsciously. Every move she made to care for her sister's child spoke eloquently of the love she had for her nephew.

Phoebe should have kids of her own. And a husband. The thought hit him like a revelation, and he didn't know why it was startling. Most women Phoebe's age were looking to settle down and start families. But maybe she wasn't. Because, clearly, she had hidden herself away like the unfortunate heroine in Rapunzel's castle. Only in Phoebe's case, the incarceration was voluntary.

Why would a smart, attractive woman isolate herself in an out-of-the-way cabin where her nearest neighbors were knocking on heaven's door? When was the last time she'd had a date? Nothing about Phoebe's life made sense, especially since she had admitted to working once upon a time in a highly competitive career.

A few thin clouds had begun to roll in, dropping the temperature, so he chopped one last time and had the satisfaction of hearing the snap that freed their prize. Phoebe clapped softly. "Bravo, Paul Bunyan."

He donned his coat and lifted an eyebrow. "Are you making fun of me?"

She joined him beside the tree and reached up awkwardly to kiss his cheek, the baby tucked between them. "Not even a little. You're my hero. I couldn't have done this on my own."

"Happy to oblige." Her gratitude warmed him. But her next words gave him pause.

"If we eat dinner early, we can probably get the whole thing decorated before bedtime."

"Whoa. Back up the truck. I thought we had *plans* for bedtime." He curled a hand behind her neck and stopped her in her tracks by the simple expedient of kissing her long and slow. Working around the kid was a challenge, but he was motivated.

Phoebe's lashes fluttered downward as she leaned into him. "We do," she whispered. The fact that she returned his kiss was noteworthy, but even more gratifying was her enthusiasm. She went up on tiptoes, aligned their lips perfectly and kissed him until he shuddered and groaned. "Good Lord, Phoebe."

She smoothed a strand of hair behind his ear, her fingers warm against his chilled skin. "Are you complaining, Mr. Cavallo?"

"No," he croaked.

"Then let's get crackin'."

Even though Phoebe carried a baby, and had been for some time, Leo was equally challenged by the difficulty of dragging the enormous tree, trunk first, back to the house. He walked at the edge of the road in the tall, dead grass, not wanting to shred the branches on gravel. By the time they reached their destination, he was breathing hard. "I think this thing weighs a hundred pounds."

Phoebe looked over her shoulder, her smile wickedly teasing. "I've seen your biceps, Leo. I'm sure you can bench-press a single measly tree." She unlocked the front door and propped it open. "I've already cleared a spot by the fireplace. Let me know if you need a hand."

Phoebe couldn't remember the last time she'd had so much fun. Leo was a good sport. Chopping down the large tree she had selected was not an easy task, but he hadn't complained. If anything, he seemed to get a measure of satisfaction from conquering *O Tannenbaum*.

Phoebe unashamedly used Teddy as a shield for the rest of the day. It wasn't that she didn't want to be alone with Leo. But there was something jarring about feeling such wanton, breathless excitement for a man when she was, at the same time, cuddling a little baby.

It would probably be different if the child were one they shared. Then, over Teddy's small, adorable head, she and Leo could exchanges smiles and loving glances as they remembered the night they created this precious bundle of joy. With no such scenario in existence, Phoebe decided her feelings were fractured…much like the time she'd had a high school babysitting job interrupted by the arrival of her boyfriend. That long-ago night as a sixteen-year-old, it had been all she could do to concentrate on her charges.

Almost a decade and a half later, with Leo prowling the interior of the cabin, all grumpy and masculine and gorgeous, she felt much the same way. Nevertheless, she focused on entertaining her nephew.

Fortunately, the baby was in an extremely good mood. He played in his high chair while Phoebe threw dinner together. Thanks to the largesse of Leo's buddy—which Leo no doubt cofunded—it was no trouble to pick and choose. Chicken Alfredo. Spinach salad. Fruit crepes for dessert. It would be easy to get spoiled by having haute cuisine at her fingertips with minimal effort. She would have to resist, though. Because, like Leo's presence in her life, the four-star meals were temporary.

Leo, after much cursing and struggling, and with a dollop of luck, finally pronounced himself satisfied with the security of their Christmas pièce de résistance. After changing the baby's diaper, Phoebe served up two plates and set them on the table. "Hurry, then. Before it gets cold."

Leo sat down with a groan. "Wouldn't matter to me. I'm starving."

She ended up sitting Teddy in his high chair and feeding him his bottle with one hand while she ate with the other. At the end of the meal, she scooped Teddy up and held him out to Leo. "If you wouldn't mind playing with him on the sofa for a little while, I'll clean up the kitchen, and we can start on the tree."

A look of discomfort crossed Leo's face. "I'm more of an observer when it comes to babies. I don't think they like me."

"Don't be silly, Leo. And besides, you did offer to help with Teddy when I let you stay. Remember?"

He picked up his coat. "Buford says it's going to snow tonight. I need to move half of that pile of wood you have out by the shed and stack it on the front porch. If it's a heavy snow, we might lose power." Before Phoebe could protest, he bundled up in his winter gear and was gone.

Phoebe felt the joy leach out of the room. She wanted Leo to love Teddy like she did, but that was silly. Leo had his own family, a brother, a sister-in-law, a niece, a nephew and a grandfather. Besides, he'd been pretty clear about not wanting kids. Some people didn't get all warm and fuzzy when it came to infants.

Still, she felt a leaden sense of disappointment. Leo was a wonderful man. Being squeamish about babies was hardly a character flaw.

She put Teddy back in the high chair. "Sorry, kiddo. Looks like it's you and me on KP duty tonight. I'll be as quick as I can, and then I'll read you a book. How about that?"

Teddy found the loose end of the safety strap and chewed it. His little chortling sounds and syllables were cute, but hardly helpful when it came to the question of Leo.

Tonight was a big bridge for Phoebe to cross. She was ready. She wanted Leo, no question. But she couldn't help feeling anxiety about the future. In coming to the mountains, she had learned to be alone. Would agreeing to be Leo's lover negate all the progress she had made? And would ultimately losing him—as she surely would—put her back in that dark place again?

Even with all her questions, tonight's outcome was a forgone conclusion. Leo was her Christmas present to herself.

Twelve

Leo pushed himself hard, carrying five or six heavy logs at a time. He took Buford's warning seriously, but the real reason he was out here was because staying in the cabin with Phoebe was torture. It was one thing to casually say, "We'll wait until bedtime." It was another entirely to keep himself reined in.

Every time she bent over to do something with the baby or to put something in the oven, her jeans cupped a butt that was the perfect size for a man's hands to grab hold of. The memory of her naked breasts lodged in his brain like a continuous, R-rated movie reel.

Earlier, he had called Luc, explaining the isolation of Phoebe's cabin and promising to stay in touch. His new phone should arrive in the morning, and the satellite internet would be set up, as well. By bedtime *tomorrow* night, Leo would be plugged in, all of his electronic devices at his fingertips. A very short time ago, that notion would have filled him with satisfaction and a sense of being on track. Not today. Now he could think of nothing but taking Phoebe to bed.

When he had a healthy stack of logs tucked just outside the front door in easy reach, he knew it was time to go in and face the music. His throat was dry. His heart pounded far harder than warranted by his current task. But the worst part was his semipermanent erection. He literally ached all over…wanting Phoebe. *Needing* her with a ferocious appetite that made him grateful to be a man with a beating heart.

He told himself he was close to having everything he craved. All he had to do was make it through the evening. But he was jittery with arousal. Testosterone charged through his bloodstream like a devil on his shoulder. Urging him on to stake a claim. Dismissing the need for gentleness.

Phoebe was his for the taking. She'd told him as much. A few more hours, and everything he wanted would be his.

Phoebe moved the portable crib into the living room near the fireplace, on the opposite side from the tree. Her hope was that Teddy would amuse himself for a while. He'd been fed, changed, and was now playing happily with several of his favorite teething toys.

When Leo came through the door on a blast of cold air, her stomach flipped. She'd given herself multiple lectures on remaining calm and cool. No need for him to know how agitated she was about the evening to come. Her giddiness was an odd mixture of anticipation and reservation.

Never in her life had she been intimate with a man of whom she knew so little. And likewise, never had she contemplated sex with someone for recreational purposes. She and Leo were taking advantage of a serendipitous place and time. Neither of them made any pretense that this was more. No passionate declarations of love. No tentative plans for the future.

Just sex.

Did that cheapen what she felt for him?

As he removed his coat and boots, she stared. The look in his eyes was hot and predatory. A shiver snaked down her spine. Leo was a big man, both in body and in per-

sonality. His charisma seduced her equally as much as his
honed, masculine body.

She licked her lips, biting the lower one. "Um…there's
hot chocolate on the stove. I made the real stuff. Seemed
appropriate."

He rubbed his hands together, his cheeks ruddy from
the cold. "Thanks."

The single syllable was gruff. Phoebe knew then, beyond the shadow of a doubt, that Leo was as enmeshed in
whatever was happening between them as she was. The
knowledge settled her nerves. She had been afraid of seeming gauche or awkward. Leo's intensity indicated that he
was perhaps as off balance as she felt.

As he poured his drink, she expected him to come sit on
the sofa. Instead, he lingered in the kitchen. She dragged a
large red plastic tub nearer the tree. "If you'll do the lights,
I'll sort through the ornaments and put hangers on them so
that part will go quickly."

He set his mug in the sink. "Lights?"

She shot him an innocent look. "It's the man's job. Always."

"And if there were no man around?"

"I'd have to handle it. But I'm sure the tree would not
look nearly as pretty."

Finally, he joined her, his body language somewhat more
relaxed. "You are so full of it," he said with a fake glower
as he bent and picked up the first strand. "You realize,
don't you, that many people buy pre-lit trees these days."

"True." She plugged in the extension cord and handed
him the end. "But not live ones. Think how proud you're
going to be when we're finished, how satisfied with a job
well done."

Tugging her braid, he deliberately brushed the backs of
his fingers down her neck. "I'm a long way from satisfied."

His chocolate-scented breath was warm on her cheek. If she turned her head an inch or two, their lips would meet.

She closed her eyes involuntarily, her body weak with longing. Leo had to know what he was doing to her. And judging by the smirk on his face when she finally managed to look at him, he was enjoying her discomfiture.

Turnabout was fair play. "Good things come to those who wait," she whispered. She stroked a hand down the middle of his rib cage, stopping just above his belt buckle.

Leo sucked in a sharp breath as his hands clenched on her shoulders. "Phoebe..."

"Phoebe, what?" Toying with the hem of his shirt, she lifted it and touched his bare skin with two fingertips. Teasing him like this was more fun than she could have imagined. Her long-buried sensual side came out to play. Taking one step closer so that their bodies touched chest to knee, she laid her cheek against him, hearing the steady, though rapid, beat of his heart.

Between them, she felt the press of his erection, full and hard, at her stomach. For so long she had hidden from the richness of life, afraid of making another tragic misstep. But one lesson she had learned well. No matter how terrible the mistake and how long the resultant fall, the world kept on turning.

Leo might well be her next blunder. But at least she was living. Feeling. Wanting. Her emotions had begun to thaw with the advent of Teddy. Leo's arrival in the midst of her reawakening had been fortuitous. Six months ago, she would not have had the courage to act on her attraction.

Now, feeling the vestiges of her grief slide into the realm of the past, her heart swelled with joy in the realization that the Phoebe Kemper she had once known was still alive. It had been a long road. And she didn't think she would ever want to go back and reclaim certain remnants of that woman's life.

But she was ready to move forward. With Leo.

He set her away from him, his expression strained. "Give me the damn lights."

Leo was at sixes and sevens, his head muddled with a million thoughts, his body near crippled with desire. Fortunately for him, Phoebe was the meticulous sort. There were no knots of wire to untangle. Every strand of lights had been neatly wrapped around pieces of plywood before being stored away. He sensed that this Christmas decorating ritual was far more important to Phoebe than perhaps he realized. So despite his mental and physical discomfort, he set his mind to weaving lights in amongst the branches.

Phoebe worked nearby, unwrapping tissue-wrapped ornaments, discarding broken ones, tending to Teddy now and again. Music played softly in the background. One tune in particular he recognized. He had always enjoyed the verve and tempo of the popular modern classic by Mariah Carey. But not until this exact minute had he understood the songwriter's simple message.

Some things were visceral. It was true. He needed no other gift but Phoebe. When a man was rich enough to buy anything he wanted, the act of exchanging presents took on new meaning. He had always given generously to his employees. And he and Luc knew each other well enough to come up with the occasional surprise gift that demonstrated thought and care.

But he couldn't remember a Christmas when he'd been willing to strip the holiday down to its basic component. Love.

His mind shied away from that thought. Surely a man of his age and experience and sophistication didn't believe in love at first sight. The heart attack had left him floundering, grasping at things to stay afloat in a suddenly changing world. Phoebe was here. And it was almost Christmas.

He wanted her badly. No need to tear the situation apart with questions.

He finished the last of the lights and dragged one final tub over to the edge of the coffee table so he could sit and sift through the contents. Though the tree was large, he wasn't sure they were going to be able to fit everything on the limbs.

Spying a small, unopened green box, he picked it up and turned it over. Visible through the clear plastic covering was a sterling sliver rocking horse with the words *Baby's First Christmas* engraved on the base. And a date. An old date. His stomach clenched.

When he looked up, Phoebe was staring at the item in his hands, her face ashen. Cursing himself for not moving more quickly to tuck it out of sight, he stood, not knowing what to say. A dozen theories rushed through his mind. But only one made sense.

Tears rolled from Phoebe's huge pain-darkened eyes, though he was fairly certain she didn't know she was crying. It was as if she had frozen, sensing danger, not sure where to run.

He approached her slowly, his hands outstretched. "Phoebe, sweetheart. Talk to me."

Her eyes were uncomprehending…even when she wiped one wet cheek with the back of her hand.

"Let me see it," she whispered, walking toward the tub of ornaments.

He put his body in front of hers, cupping her face in his hands. "No. It doesn't matter. You're shaking." Wrapping his arms around her and holding her as tightly as he could, he tried to still the tremors that tore through her body cruelly.

Phoebe never weakened. She stood erect, not leaning into him, not accepting his comfort. He might as well have been holding a statue. At last, he stepped back, staring into her eyes. "Let me get you a drink."

"No." She wiped her nose.

Leo reached into his pocket for a handkerchief and handed it to her. He was torn, unsure if talking about it would make things better or worse. As he stood there, trying to decide how to navigate the chasm that had opened at his feet, the fraught moment was broken by a baby's cry.

Phoebe whirled around. "Oh, Teddy. We were ignoring you." She rushed to pick him up, holding him close as new tears wet her lashes. "It's your bedtime, isn't it, my sweet? Don't worry. Aunt Phoebe is here."

Leo tried to take the boy. "You need to sit down, Phoebe." He was fairly certain she was in shock. Her hands were icy cold and her lips had a blue tinge.

Phoebe fought him. "No. You don't like babies. I can do it."

The belligerence in her wild gaze shocked him, coming as it did out of nowhere. "I never said that." He spoke softly, as though gentling a spooked animal "Let me help you."

Ignoring his plea, she exited the room, Teddy clutched to her chest. He followed the pair of them down the hall and into the baby's nursery cum storage room. He had never seen this door open. Phoebe always used her own bedroom to access Teddy's.

She put the child on the changing table and stood there. Leo realized she didn't know what to do next.

Quietly, not making a fuss, he reached for the little pair of pajamas hanging from a hook on the wall nearby. The diapers were tucked into a cheerful yellow plastic basket at the boy's feet. Easing Phoebe aside with nothing more than a nudge of his hip, he unfastened what seemed like a hundred snaps, top and bottom, and drew the cloth up over Teddy's head. Teddy cooed, smiling trustingly as Leo stripped him naked. The baby's skin was soft, his flailing arms and legs pudgy and strong.

The diaper posed a momentary problem, but only until Leo's brain clicked into gear and he saw how the assembly worked. Cleaning the little bottom with a baby wipe, he gave thanks that he was only dealing with a wet diaper, not a messy one.

Phoebe hadn't moved. Her hands were clenched on the decorative edge of the wooden table so hard that her knuckles were white.

Leo closed up the diaper, checked it for structural integrity, and then held up the pajamas. He couldn't really see much difference between these pj's and the daytime outfits the kid wore, but apparently there was one. This piece of clothing was even more of a challenge, because the snaps ran from the throat all the way down one leg. It took him three tries to get it right.

Through it all, Phoebe stood unaware. Or at least it seemed that way.

Cradling the child in one arm, Leo used his free hand to steer Phoebe out of the room. "You'll have to help me with the bottle," he said softly, hoping she was hearing him.

Her brief nod was a relief.

Leo installed Phoebe in a kitchen chair. Squatting in front of her, he waited until her eyes met his. "Can you hold him?"

She took the small, squirmy bundle and bowed her head, teardrops wetting the front of the sleeper. "I have a bottle ready," she said, the words almost inaudible. "Put it in a bowl of hot water two or three times until the formula feels warm when you sprinkle it on your wrist."

He had seen her perform that task several times, so it was easy to follow the instructions. When the bottle was ready, he turned back to Phoebe. Her grip on Teddy was

122 A BILLIONAIRE FOR CHRISTMAS

firm. The child was in no danger of being dropped. But Phoebe had ceased interacting with her nephew.

Leo put a hand on her shoulder. "Would you like to feed him, or do you want me to do it? I'm happy to."

Long seconds ticked by. Phoebe stood abruptly, handing him the baby. "You can. I'm going to my room."

He grabbed her wrist. "No. You're not. Come sit with us on the sofa."

Thirteen

Phoebe didn't have the emotional energy to fight him. Leo's gaze was kind but firm. She followed him to the living room and sat down with her legs curled beneath her. Leo sat beside her with Teddy in his arms. Fortunately, Teddy didn't protest the change in leadership. He took his bottle from Leo as if it were an everyday occurrence.

Despite the roaring fire that Leo had built, which still leaped and danced vigorously, she felt cold all over. Clenching her jaw to keep her teeth from chattering, she wished she had thought to pick up an afghan. But the pile neatly folded on the hearth was too far away. She couldn't seem to make her legs move.

Trying to distract her thoughts, she studied Leo out of the corner of her eye. The powerful picture of the big man and the small baby affected her at a gut-deep level. Despite Leo's professed lack of experience, he was doing well. His large hands were careful as he adjusted Teddy's position now and again or moved the bottle to a better angle.

Beyond Leo's knee she could see the abandoned ornaments. But not the little green box. He must have shoved it out of sight beneath the table. She remembered vividly the day she'd purchased it. After leaving her doctor's office, she was on her way back to work. On a whim, she stopped by the mall to grab a bite of lunch and to walk off some of her giddy euphoria.

It was September, but a Christmas shop had already opened its doors in preparation for the holidays. On a table near the front, a display of ornaments caught her eyes. Feeling crazily joyful and foolishly furtive, she picked one out and paid for it.

Until this evening she had suppressed that memory. In fact, she didn't even realize she had kept the ornament and moved it three years ago.

Leo wrapped an arm around her shoulders, pulling her closer to his side. "Lean on me," he said.

She obeyed gladly, inhaling the scent of his aftershave and the warm "man" smell of him. Gradually, lulled by the fire and the utter security of Leo's embrace, she closed her eyes. Pain hovered just offstage, but she chose not to confront it at the moment. She had believed herself to be virtually healed. As though all the dark edges of her life had been sanded away by her sojourn in the woods.

How terribly unfair to find out it wasn't true. How devastating to know that something so simple could trip her up.

Perhaps because the afternoon and evening had been so enjoyable, so delightfully *homey,* the harshness of being thrust into a past she didn't want to remember was all the more devastating.

Teddy drained the last of the bottle, his little eyelashes drooping. Leo coaxed a muffled burp from him and then put a hand on Phoebe's knee. "Is it okay for me to lay him down? Anything I need to know?"

"I'll take him," she said halfheartedly, not sure if she could make the effort to stand up.

He squeezed her hand. "Don't move. I'll be right back."

She stared into space, barely even noticing when he returned and began moving about the kitchen with muffled sounds. A few minutes later he handed her a mug of cocoa. She wrapped her fingers around the warm stoneware, welcoming the heat against her frozen skin.

Leo had topped her serving with whipped cream. She sipped delicately, wary of burning her tongue.

He sat down beside her and smiled. "You have a mustache," he teased. Using his thumb, he rubbed her upper lip. Somewhere deep inside her, regret surfaced. She had ruined their sexy, fun-filled evening.

Leo appeared unperturbed. He leaned back, his legs outstretched, and propped his feet on the coffee table. With his mug resting against his chest, he shot her a sideways glance. "When you're ready, Phoebe, I want you to tell me the story."

She nodded, her eyes downcast as she studied the pale swirls of melted topping in the hot brown liquid. It was time. It was beyond time. Even her sister didn't know all the details. When the unthinkable had happened, the pain was too fresh. Phoebe had floundered in a sea of confused grief, not knowing how to claw her way out.

In the end, her only choice had been to wait until the waves abated and finally receded. Peace had eventually replaced the hurt. But her hard-won composure had been fragile at best. Judging by today, she had a long way to go.

Leo got up to stoke the fire and to add more music to the stereo. She was struck by how comfortable it felt to have him in her cabin, in her life. He was an easy man to be with. Quiet when the occasion demanded it, and drolly amusing when he wanted to be.

He settled back onto the couch and covered both of them with a wool throw. Fingering the cloth, he wrinkled his nose. "We should burn this," he said with a grin. "Imported fabric, cheap construction. I could hook you up with something far nicer."

"I'll put it on my Christmas list." She managed a smile,

not wanting him to think she was a total mental case. "I'm sorry I checked out on you," she muttered.

"We're all entitled now and then."

The quiet response took some of the sting out of her embarrassment. He was being remarkably patient. "I owe you an explanation."

"You don't *owe* me anything, sweet Phoebe. But it helps to talk about it. I know that from experience. When our parents were killed, Grandfather was wise enough to get us counseling almost immediately. We would never have shown weakness to him. He was and still is a sharp-browed, blustering tyrant, though we love him, of course. But he knew we would need an outlet for what we were feeling."

"Did it work?"

"In time. We were at a vulnerable age. Not quite men, but more than boys. It was hard to admit that our world had come crashing down around us." He took her hand. She had twisted one piece of blanket fringe so tightly it was almost severed. Linking their fingers, he raised her hand to his lips and kissed it. "Is that what happened to you?"

Despite her emotional state, she was not above being moved by the feel of his lips against her skin. Hot tears stung her eyes, not because she was so sad, but in simple recognition of his genuine empathy. "You could say that."

"Tell me about your baby."

There was nothing to be gained from denial. But he would understand more if she began elsewhere. "I'll go back to the beginning if you don't mind."

"A good place to start." He kissed her fingers again before tucking her hand against his chest. The warmth of him, even through his clothing, calmed and comforted her.

"I told you that I was a stockbroker in Charlotte."

"Yes."

"Well, I was good, really good at my job. There were a half dozen of us, and competition was fierce. Gracious for the most part, but inescapable. I had a knack for putting together portfolios, and people liked working with me, because I didn't make them feel stupid or uninformed about their money. We had a number of very wealthy clients with neither the time nor the inclination to grow their fortunes, so we did it for them."

"I'm having a hard time reconciling *killer* Phoebe with the woman who bakes her own bread."

His wry observation actually made her laugh. "I can understand your confusion. Back then I focused on getting ahead in my profession. I was determined to be successful and financially comfortable."

"Perhaps because losing your parents left you feeling insecure in so many other ways."

His intuitive comment was impressive. "You should hang out a shingle," she said. "I'm sure people would pay for such on-the-mark analysis."

"Is that sarcasm I hear?"

"Not at all."

"I can't take too much credit. You and I have more in common than I realized. Getting the foundations knocked out from under you at a time when most young people are getting ready to step out into the big wide world breeds a certain distrust in the system. Parents are supposed to help their children with the shift into adulthood."

"And without them, everything seems like a scary gamble at best."

"Exactly. But there's more, isn't there?"

She nodded, fighting the lump in her throat. "I was engaged," she croaked. "To another broker. We had an ongoing battle to see who could bring in the most business. I thought we were a team, both professionally *and* personally, but it turns out I was naive."

"What happened?"

Taking a deep breath, she ripped off the Band-Aid of her

old wound and brought it all back to life…to ugly life. "We had plans to get married the following year, but no specific date. Then—in the early fall—I found out I was pregnant."

"Not planned, I assume?"

"Oh, gosh, no. I assumed that motherhood, if it ever rolled around, was sometime *way* in the future. But Rick and I—that was his name—well…once we got over the shock, we started to be happy about it. Freaked-out, for sure. But happy nevertheless."

"Did you set a date then for a wedding?"

"Not at first. We decided to wait a bit, maybe until we knew the sex of the baby, to tell our coworkers. I thought everything was rocking along just fine, and then Rick began dropping subtle and not-so-subtle hints that I should think about taking a leave for a while."

"Why? It wasn't a physically demanding job, was it?"

"No. But he kept bringing up the stress factor. How my intensity and my long hours could be harmful to the baby. At first, I was confused. I honestly didn't see any problem."

"And was there?"

"Not the one he was trying to sell to me. But the truth was, Rick knew he could be top dog at the company if I were gone. And even when I came back after maternity leave, he would have made so much progress that I would never catch up."

"Ouch."

She grimaced. "It was a nasty smack in the face. We had a huge fight, and he accused me of being too ambitious for my own good. I called him a sexist pig. Things degenerated from there."

"Did you give the ring back?"

"How could I? Even if I now knew that my fiancé was a jerk, he was the father of my baby. I decided I had no choice but to make it work. But no matter how hard I tried, things only got worse."

"Did you have an abortion?"

Leo's quiet query held no hint of judgment, only a deep compassion. From where he was standing, that assumption made perfect sense.

She swallowed. The trembling she had managed to squelch started up again. "No. I wanted the baby by then. Against all odds. I was three and a half months along, and then…" Her throat tightened. Leo rubbed her shoulder, the caress comforting rather than sexual.

"What happened, Phoebe?"

Closing her eyes, she saw the moment as if it had been yesterday. "I started bleeding at work one day. Terribly. They rushed me to the hospital, but I lost the baby. All I could think about when I was lying in that bed, touching my empty belly, was that Rick had been right."

"You were young and healthy. I can't imagine there was a reason you shouldn't have been working."

"That's what my doctor said. She tried to reassure me, but I wasn't hysterical. Just cold. So cold. They told me the baby had developed with an abnormality. I would never have carried it to term. One of those random, awful things."

She didn't cry again. The emptiness was too dry and deep for that…a dull, vague feeling of loss.

Leo lifted her onto his lap, turning her sideways so her cheek rested on his chest. His arms held her tightly, communicating without words his sympathy and his desire to comfort her. He brushed a stray hair from her forehead. "I'm so sorry, Phoebe."

She shrugged. "Lots of people lose babies."

"But usually not a fiancé at the same time. You lost everything. And that's why you came here."

"Yes. I was a coward. I couldn't bear people staring at me with pity. And with Rick still working at the company, I knew I was done. My boss wasn't happy about it. I think he would have liked to fire Rick and keep me, but you can't terminate a guy for being a selfish, self-absorbed bastard."

"I would have." The three words encompassed an icy intensity that communicated his anger toward a man he had never met. "Your boss shouldn't have been so spineless. You were good at your job, Phoebe. If you had stayed, you might have recovered from your loss much sooner. The work would have been a healthy distraction. Perhaps even fulfilling in a new way."

Here was the crux of the matter. "The thing is," she said slowly. "I have my doubts. Looking back, I can see that I had all the makings of a workaholic. It's bad enough when a man falls into that trap. But women are traditionally the caregivers, the support system for a spouse or a family. So even though the doctor told me I had done nothing wrong, I felt as if I had betrayed my child by working nonstop."

Leo's arms tightened around her, his chest heaving in a startled inhalation. "Good Lord, Phoebe. That's totally irrational. You were an unencumbered woman on the upswing of your career. Female pioneers have fought for decades so you could be exactly where you were."

"And yet we still have battles within the sisterhood between stay-at-home moms and those who work outside the home. I've seen both groups sneer at each other as though one choice is more admirable than the other."

"I'll give you that one. In reality, though, I assume women work for many reasons. Fulfillment. Excitement. Or in some cases, simply to put food on the table."

"But it's about balance, Leo. And I had none. It's not true that women can have it all. Life is about choices. We only have twenty-four hours in a day. That never changes. So if I don't learn how to fit *work* into a box of the appropriate size, I don't know that I'll ever be able to go back."

"That's it, then? You're never going to be employed

again? Despite the fact that you've been gifted with financial talents and people skills?"

"I'd like to have a family someday. And even more importantly, find peace and contentment in the way I live my life. Is that so wrong?"

"How are you supposed to accomplish that by hiding out? Phoebe, you're not doing what you're good at…and borrowing a baby from your sister isn't exactly going after what you want."

"I don't know if I'm ready yet. It sounds like a cliché, but I've been trying to find myself. And hopefully in the process learning something about balance."

"We all have to live in the real world. Most of the life lessons I've learned have come via failure."

"Well, that's depressing."

"Not at all. You have to trust yourself again."

"And if I crash and burn?"

"Then you'll pick yourself up and start over one more time. You're more resilient than you think."

Fourteen

Leo was more bothered by Phoebe's soul-searching than he should have been. Her self-evaluation proved her to be far more courageous than he was in facing up to painful truths. But in his gut, he believed she was missing the bigger picture. Phoebe had clearly excelled in her previous career. And had loved the work, even with overt competition…perhaps *because* of it.

She was lucky to have had the financial resources to fund her long sabbatical. In the end, though, how would she ever know if it was time to leave the mountains? And what if she decided to stay? She had proved her independence. And in her eyes and in her home he saw peace. Did that mean she couldn't see herself finding happiness—and perhaps a family—anywhere but here?

He played with her hair, removing the elastic band that secured her braid. Gently, he loosened the thick ropes, fanning out the dark, shiny tresses until they hung down her back, covering his hand in black silk. Holding her in his arms as a friend and not a lover was difficult, but he couldn't push her away.

Phoebe saw herself as a coward, but that was far from the truth. Though she had been at the top of her game, she had wanted the baby that threatened to disrupt her life. Even in the face of disappointment, knowing that her fiancé was not the man she thought he was, she had been prepared to work at the relationship so they could be a family.

Leo admired her deeply.

Her eyes were closed, her breathing steady. It had been a long, busy day, and an emotional one for her. Leo knew their timing was off. Again. Even with Teddy sleeping soundly, Phoebe was in no shape to initiate a sexual relationship with a new partner. Perhaps if they had been a couple for a long time, Leo could have used the intimacy of sex to comfort and reassure her. As it was, his role would have to be that of protector.

A man could do worse when it came to Phoebe Kemper.

He stood, prepared to carry her to her room. Phoebe stirred, her long lashes lifting to reveal eyes that were still beautiful, though rimmed in red. "What are you doing?"

"You need to be in bed. Alone," he clarified, in case there was any doubt about his intentions.

She shook her head, a stubborn expression he had come to know all too well painting her face with insistence. "I want to sleep in here so I can see the tree. I'll keep the monitor with me. You go on to bed. I'm fine."

He nuzzled her nose with his, resisting the urge to kiss her. Her aching vulnerability held him back. "No," he said huskily. "I'll stay with you." He set her on her feet and went to his room to get extra blankets and a pillow. The bearskin rug in front of the fire would be a decent enough bed, and from there, he'd be able to keep the fire going. He brushed his teeth and changed into his pajama pants and robe.

By the time he returned, Phoebe had made the same preparations. It was colder tonight. Instead of her knit pj's, she had donned a high-necked flannel nightgown that made her look as if she had stepped right out of the pages of *Little*

House on the Prairie. The fabric was pale ivory with little red reindeer cavorting from neck to hemline.

The old-fashioned design should have made her look as asexual as a nun. But with her hair spilling around her shoulders and her dark eyes heavy-lidded, all Leo could think about was whether or not she had on panties beneath that fortress of a garment.

If the utilitarian cloth and enveloping design was meant to discourage him, Phoebe didn't know much about men. When the castle was barricaded, the knights had to fight all the harder to claim their prize.

She clutched a pillow to her chest, her cheeks turning pink. "You don't have to stay with me. I'm okay…really."

"What if I want to?" The words came out gruffer than he intended.

Her eyes widened. He could swear he saw the faint outline of pert nipples beneath the bodice of her nightwear. She licked her lips. "You've been very sweet to me, Leo. I'm sorry the night didn't go the way we planned. But maybe it's for the best. Perhaps we were rushing into this."

"You don't want me?" He hadn't meant to ask it. Hated the way the question revealed his need.

Phoebe's chin wobbled. "I don't know. I mean, yes. Of course I want you. I think that's painfully obvious. But we're not…"

"Not what?" He took the pillow from her and tossed it on the couch. Gathering her into his arms, he fought a battle of painful scale. It seemed as if he had wanted her for a lifetime. "Only a fool would press you now…when you've dealt with so much tonight. But make no mistake, Phoebe. I'm going to have you. No matter how long the wait." He stroked his hands down her back, pulling her hips to his, establishing once and for all that she was *not* wearing underwear.

Had he detected any resistance at all on her part, he

would have been forced to release her. But she melted into him, her body warm and soft and unmistakably feminine through the negligible barrier of her gown. He had belted his robe tightly before leaving his bedroom, not wanting to give any appearance of carnal intent.

To his intense shock and surprise, a small hand made its way between the thin layers of cashmere and found his bare chest. Within seconds his erection lifted and thickened. His voice locked in his throat. He was positive that if he spoke, the words would come out wrong.

Phoebe's hand landed over his heart and lingered as if counting the beats. Could she hear the acceleration? Did she feel the rigidity of his posture? He gulped, his breathing shallow and ragged. There was no way she could miss his thrusting sex, even through her pseudo armor.

The woman in his arms sighed deeply. "You should go to your room," she whispered. "The floor will be too hard."

"I'll manage." He thrust her away, hoping the maneuver wasn't as awkward as it felt. Turning his back, he added logs to the fire and then prepared his makeshift bed.

In his peripheral vision he saw Phoebe ready the sofa with a pile of blankets and her own pillow. When she sat down, removed her slippers and swung her legs up onto the couch, he caught one quick glimpse of bare, slender thighs. *Holy hell.*

A shot of whiskey wouldn't come amiss, but Phoebe's fridge held nothing stronger than beer. Quietly, keeping a wide perimeter between himself and temptation, he went about the cabin turning off lights. Soon, only the glow of the fire and the muted rainbow colors of the tree illuminated the room.

He checked the lock on the front door and closed a gap in the drapes. When he could think of nothing else as a distraction, he turned reluctantly and surveyed the evocative scene Phoebe's love of Christmas had created. Even the most hardened of "Scrooge-ish" hearts surely couldn't resist the inherent emotion.

Peace. Comfort. Home. All of it was there for anyone with eyes to see. Had his luxurious condo in Atlanta ever been as appealing?

Phoebe's eyes were closed, a half smile on her lips. She lay like a child with one hand tucked beneath her cheek. He didn't know if she was already asleep or simply enjoying the smell of the outdoors they had managed to capture in a tree. Perhaps it was the sound of the fire she savored, the same life-affirming heat that popped and hissed as it had for generations before.

Exhaustion finally overrode his lust-addled brain and coaxed him toward sleep. He fashioned his bed in front of the hearth and climbed in. It wasn't the Ritz-Carlton, but for tonight, there was nowhere he would rather be. After no more than five minutes, he realized that his robe was going to be far too warm so close to the fire.

Shrugging out of it, he tossed it aside and lay back in the covers with a yawn. A month ago if anyone had told him he'd be camping out on a hard floor in dangerous proximity to a fascinating woman he wanted desperately, he'd have laughed. Of course, he would have had a similar reaction if that same someone had told him he'd have a heart attack at thirty-six.

He had to tell Phoebe the truth about why he had come to the Smoky Mountains…to her cabin in the woods. She had bared her soul to him. Perhaps tomorrow he would find the opportunity and the words to reveal the truth. The prospect made him uneasy. He hated admitting weakness. Always had. But his pride should not stand in the way of his relationship to a woman he had come to respect as much or more than he desired her.

He shifted on the furry pallet, searching for a position that was comfortable. With Phoebe in the same room, he didn't even have the option of taking his sex in hand and finding relief. Hours passed, or so it seemed, before he slept....

Phoebe jerked awake, her heart pounding in response to some unremembered dream. It took her several seconds to recognize her surroundings. In the next instant, she glanced at the baby monitor. Reassurance came in the form of a grainy picture. Teddy slept in his usual position.

Sighing shakily as adrenaline winnowed away, she glanced at the clock on the far wall. Two in the morning. The fire burned brightly, so Leo must have been up tending to it recently. The room was warm and cozy. Despite her unaccustomed bed and the late hour, she felt momentarily rested and not at all sleepy.

Warily, she lifted her head a couple of inches, only enough to get a clear view of Leo over the top of the coffee table. Her breath caught at the picture he made. Sprawled on his back on the bearskin rug, he lay with one arm flung outward, the other bent and covering his eyes.

He was bare-chested. Firelight warmed skin that was deep gold dusted with a hint of dark hair that ran down the midline of his rib cage. Smooth muscles gave definition to a torso that was a sculptor's dream.

Arousal swam in her veins, sluggish and sweet, washing away any vestige of sadness from earlier in the evening. A wave of yearning tightened her thighs. Moisture gathered in her sex, readying her for his possession. Leo would never have made a move on her this evening in light of what she had shared with him.

Which meant that Phoebe had to take the initiative.

Telling herself and her houseguest that intimacy between them wasn't a good idea was as realistic as commanding the moon not to rise over the mountain. She *wanted* Leo. She trembled with the force of that wanting. It had been aeons since she had felt even the slightest interest in a man, longer still since she had paid any attention to the sexual needs of her body.

It was foolish to miss this chance that might never come her way again. Leo was not only physically appealing, he was also a fascinating and complex man. She was drawn to him with a force that was as strong as it was unexpected. Some things in life couldn't be explained. Often in her old life, she had picked stocks based on hunches. Nine times out of ten she was right.

With Leo, the odds might not be as good. Heartbreak and loss were potential outcomes. But at this barren time in her life, she was willing to take that chance.

Before she could change her mind, she drew her gown up and over her head. Being naked felt wanton and wicked, particularly in the midst of winter. Too long now she had bundled herself up in every way…mentally…emotionally. It was time to face life and be brave again.

She knelt beside him and sat back on her haunches, marveling at the beauty of his big, elegant body. His navy sleep pants hung low on his hips, exposing his navel. The tangle of bedding, blankets and all, reached just high enough to conceal his sex. Though she was pushing her limits, she didn't quite have the courage to take a corner of the sheet and pull.

Would he reject her, citing her emotional distress and bad timing? Or was Leo's need as great as hers? Did he want her enough to ignore all the warning signs and go for it regardless of possible catastrophe?

There was only one way to find out. Slipping her hand beneath the blanket, she encountered silk warmed by his skin. Carefully, she stroked over the interesting mound that was his sex. She had no more than touched him when he began to swell and harden.

Fifteen

Leo was having the most amazing dream. One of Phoebe's hands touched him intimately, while the other moved lightly over his chest, toying with his navel, teasing his nipples with her thumb. He groaned in his sleep, trying not to move so the illusion wouldn't shatter.

He sensed her leaning over him, her hair brushing his chest, his shoulders, his face, as she found his mouth. The kiss tasted sweet and hot. Small, sharp teeth nipped his bottom lip. He shuddered, bound in thrall to a surge of arousal that left him weak and gasping for breath. His chest heaved as he tried to pull air into his lungs.

His heart pounded like the hooves of a racehorse in the last turn. For a split second, a dash of cold fear dampened his enthusiasm. He hadn't had sex since his heart attack. All medical reassurances to the contrary, he wasn't sure what would happen when he was intimate with a woman. His hand—and the process of self-gratification—he trusted. Would the real deal finish him off?

But this was a dream. No need for heartburn. He laughed inwardly at his own pun. Nothing mattered but hanging onto the erotic fantasy and enjoying it until the end.

He felt Phoebe slide his loose pants down his legs and

over his feet. In the next second she was up on her knees straddling him. Grabbing one smooth, firm thigh, he tugged, angling her leg over his shoulder so he could pleasure her with his mouth. When he put his tongue at her center and probed, he shot from the realm of slumber to delicious reality in a nanosecond. The taste of Phoebe's sweet, hot sex was all too authentic.

His hands cupped her ass to hold her steady, even as his brain struggled to catch up. "Phoebe?" The hoarse word was all he could manage. Blinking to clear his sleep-fogged eyes, he looked up and found himself treated to the vision of soft, full breasts half hidden in a fall of silky black hair. Curvy hips nipped into a narrow waist.

Phoebe's wary-eyed gaze met his. She licked her lips, uncertainty in every angle of her body. "I didn't ask," she said, looking delightfully guilty.

"Trust me, honey. There's not a man living who would object. But you should have woken me up sooner. I don't want to miss anything." He loved the fact that she had taken the initiative in their coming together, because it told him she was as invested in this madness as he was. He scooted his thumb along the damp crevice where her body was pink and perfect. When he concentrated on a certain spot, Phoebe moaned.

Inserting two fingers, he found her swollen and wet. *Sweet Lord.* The driving urge he had to take her wildly and immediately had to be subdued in favor of pleasuring such an exquisite creature slowly. Making her yearn and burn and ultimately reach the same razor-sharp edge of arousal on which he balanced so precariously.

"Put your hair behind your shoulders," he commanded.

Phoebe lifted her arms and obeyed.

"Link your hands behind your back."

A split second of hesitation and then compliance. The

docile acquiescence gave him a politically incorrect rush of elation. She was his. She was his.

Watching her face for every nuance of reaction, he played with her sex…light, teasing strokes interspersed with firmer pressure. Her body bloomed for him, the spicy sent of her making him drunk with hunger. Keeping his thumb on the little bud that encompassed her pleasure center, he entered her with three fingers this time, stretching her sheath.

Phoebe came instantly, with a keening cry. He actually felt the little flutters inside her as she squeezed. Imagining what that would feel like on his shaft made him dizzy.

When the last ripple of orgasm released her, he sat up, settling Phoebe in his lap and holding her tightly. His eager erection bumped up against her bottom. Her thighs were draped over his, her ankles linked at his back.

Emotions hit him hard and fast. The one he hadn't anticipated was regret. Not for touching her, never that. But sorrow that they hadn't met sooner. And fear that she would be dismissive of their intimacy because their time together had been so brief.

He waited as long as he could. At least until her breathing returned to normal. Then he pulled back and searched her face. "Don't think for a minute that we're almost done. That was only a tiny prelude. I'm going to devote myself to making you delirious with pleasure."

Her smile was smug. "Been there, done that, bought the T-shirt."

Leo knew that if things were to progress he had to get up. But knowing and doing were two different matters. "Can I ask you a very important question, my Phoebe?"

She rested her forehead on his shoulder. "Ask away."

"If I go fetch a bushel of condoms, will you change your mind about this while I'm gone?"

He felt her go still. "No." The voice was small, but the sentiment seemed genuine.

"And if Teddy wakes at an inopportune moment, will that be an excuse? Or even a sign from the universe that we should stop?"

She lifted her head, her eyes searching his. For what? Encouragement? Sincerity? "If that happens," she said slowly, "we'll settle him back to sleep and pick up where we left off."

"Good." He told himself to release her. Until he rustled up some protection, he couldn't take her the way he wanted to. But holding her like this was unutterably sweet. A real conundrum, because he couldn't ever remember feeling such a thing with another lover. This mix of shivering need and overwhelming tenderness.

Phoebe smiled. "Shall I go get them?"

He shook his head. "No. Just give me a minute." The actual fire had died down, and he needed to take care of that, as well.

While he sat there, desperately trying to find the will to stand up, Phoebe reached behind her bottom and found his shaft, giving it a little tug. The teasing touch was almost more than he could stand. The skin at the head was tight and wet with fluid that had leaked in his excitement.

Her fingers found the less rigid part of his sex and massaged him gently. "Don't. Ah, God, don't," he cried. But it was too late. He came in a violent climax that racked him with painful, fiery release. Gripping Phoebe hard enough to endanger her ribs, he groaned and shuddered, feeling the press of her breasts against his chest.

In the pregnant silence that followed, the witch had the temerity to laugh. "Perhaps we should quit while we're ahead. I don't think you're going to make it down the hall anytime soon."

He pinched her ass, gasping for breath. "Impertinent hussy."

"Well, it's true. I suppose I should have thought through all the ramifications before I jumped your bones."

"You *were* a tad eager," he pointed out, squeezing her perfectly plump butt cheeks.

Phoebe wriggled free and wrapped a blanket around her shoulders. "Go, Leo. Hurry. I'm getting cold."

Dragging himself to his feet, he yawned and stretched. Just looking at her had his erection bobbing hopefully again. *Down, boy.* He removed the fire screen, threw on a couple of good-size logs and poked the embers until they blazed up again. "Don't go anywhere," he ordered. "I'll be right back."

Phoebe watched him walk away with stars in her eyes. This was bad. This was very bad. Leo in the buff was one spectacular sight. Aside from his considerable *assets,* the view from the rear was impressive, as well. Broad shoulders, trim waist, taut buttocks, nicely muscled thighs. Even his big feet were sexy.

Despite everything they had done in the last forty-five minutes, her body continued to hum with arousal. She still couldn't believe she had stripped naked and attacked him in his sleep. That was something the old Phoebe might have done. But only if the man in question were Leo. He had the ability to make a woman throw caution to the wind.

She tidied the pile of bedding and smoothed out the wrinkles. Just like a cavewoman preparing for the return of her marauding spouse. It struck her as funny that Leo really had provided food for her. Not by clubbing anything over the head, but still…

Now that he was gone, she felt a bit bashful. She had seen the size of his sex. Wondering how things would fit together made her nipples furl in anticipation.

His return was rapid and startling. From his hand dangled a long strip of connected condom packages. She licked her lips. "I don't think the night is that long."

Dropping down beside her, he bit her shoulder. "Trust me, sweetheart."

He took her chin in his hand, the lock of hair falling across his forehead making him look younger and more carefree. "I'm thinking we'll go hard and fast the first time and then branch out into variations."

As he cupped her breast, her eyelids fluttered shut all of their own accord. Despite the fact that he had paraded nude through the house, his skin was as warm as ever. She burrowed closer. "Merry Christmas to me," she muttered.

"Look at me, Phoebe."

When she obeyed, she saw that every trace of his good humor had fled. His face was no more than planes and angles, painted by firelight to resemble an ancient king. Eyes so dark they appeared black. Still he held her chin. "I'm looking," she quipped with deliberate sass. "What am I supposed to see?" His intensity aroused and agitated her, but she wouldn't let him know how his caveman antics affected her. Not yet.

He flipped her onto her back without warning, her brief fall cushioned by the many-layered pallet. Instead of answering her provocative question, he *showed* her. Kneeling between her thighs, he yanked a single packet free, ripped it open with his teeth and extracted the contents. Making sure she watched him—by the simple expedient of locking her gaze to his—he rolled the condom over his straining erection.

She doubted he meant for her to see him wince. But the evidence of his arousal lit a fire low in her belly. Leo was in pain. Because of her. He wanted her so badly his hands were shaking. That meant he was more vulnerable than she had imagined. And knowing she was not the only one falling apart calmed her nerves.

Clearly, Leo did not see her as one in a line of faceless women. Whatever their differences in lifestyle, or world view, or even sexual experience, tonight was special.

She grabbed his wrist. "Tell me what you're going to do to me." She breathed the words on a moan as his legs tangled with hers and he positioned the head of his sex at her opening.

Still he didn't smile. His expression was a mask of frayed control…jaw clenched, teeth ground together. "I'm going to take you, my sweet. To heaven and back."

At the first push of his rigid length, she lost her breath. Everything in the room stood still. Her body strained to accommodate him. Though she was more than ready, she had been celibate a long time, and Leo was a big man.

He paused, though the effort brought beads of perspiration to his forehead. "Too much?" he asked, his voice raw.

"No." She concentrated on relaxing, though everything inside her seemed wound tight. "I want all of you."

Her declaration made him shudder as though the mental picture was more stimulating than the actual joining of their flesh. Steadily, he forced his way in. Phoebe felt his penetration in every inch of her soul. She knew in that instant that she had been deceiving herself. Leo was more than a mere fling. He was the man who could make her live again.

When he was fully seated, he withdrew with a hoarse shout and slammed into her, making her grab the leg of the coffee table as a brace. "I don't want to hurt you," he rasped.

"Then don't stop, Leo. I can handle whatever you have to give."

Sixteen

Leo was out of control. In some sane corner of his mind, he knew it. But Phoebe…God, Phoebe…she milked the length of him every time he withdrew, and on the downstroke arched her back, taking him a centimeter deeper with each successive thrust.

Her legs had his waist in a vise. Her cloud of night-dark hair fanned out around them. He buried his face in it at one point, stilling his frantic motions, desperately trying to stave off his release. She smelled amazing. Though he couldn't pinpoint the fragrance, he would have recognized her scent in a pitch-black room.

Her fingernails dug into his back. He relished the stinging discomfort…found his arousal ratcheting up by a degree each time she cried out his name and marked his flesh.

But nothing prepared him for the feel of her climax as she tightened on his shaft and came apart in release. He held her close, feeling the aftershocks that quivered in her sex like endless ripples of sensation.

When he knew she was at peace, he lost it. Slamming into her without finesse or reason, he exploded in a white-hot flash of lust. He lost a few seconds in the aftermath, his mouth dry and his head pounding.

Barely conscious, he tried to spare her most of his weight. He had come twice in quick succession, and his brain was muddled, incredulous that he wanted her still.

Phoebe stirred restlessly. "We should get some sleep." Her words were barely audible, but he caught the inference.

No way. She wasn't leaving him. No way in hell. Rolling onto his side, he scooped her close, spooning her with a murmur of satisfaction. Though her soft bottom pressed into the cradle of his thighs, his arousal was a faint whisper after two incredible climaxes. The need he felt was more than physical.

Her head pillowed on his arm, he slept.

He couldn't mark the moment consciousness returned, but he knew at once that he was alone. Sunlight peeked in around the edges of the drapes, the reflection strangely bright. He could hear the furnace running, and although the fire had long since burned out, he was plenty warm.

Sitting up with a groan, he felt muscle twinges that came from a night of carnal excess. Thinking about it made him hard. He cursed, well aware that any repeat of last night's sexual calisthenics was hours in the future.

Phoebe had put away all the bedding she had used on the sofa. But on the kitchen counter he saw a pot of coffee steaming. He stood up, feeling as if he'd been on a weekend bender. Grabbing his robe that had gotten wedged beneath the edge of the sofa, he slid his arms into the sleeves and zeroed in on the life-saving caffeine.

After two cups he was ready to go in search of his landlady. He found her and Teddy curled up on Phoebe's bed reading books. She sat up when she saw him, her smile warm but perhaps tinged with reserve. "I hope we didn't wake you."

He put his hands on top of the door frame and stretched

hard, feeling the muscles loosen bit by bit. "I didn't hear a thing. Has he been up long?"

"An hour maybe. I gave him his bottle in here."

They were conversing like strangers. Or perhaps a married couple with nothing much to say.

He sat down on the edge of the bed and took her hand. "Good morning, Phoebe."

Hot color flushed her cheeks and reddened her throat. "Good morning."

He dragged her closer for a scorching kiss. "It sure as hell is."

That surprised a laugh from her, and immediately he felt her relax. "Have you looked outside?" she asked.

He shook his head. "No. Why? Did it snow?"

She nodded. "We got three or four inches. Buford's grandson will plow the driveway by midmorning. I know you were expecting some deliveries."

Shock immobilized him. It had been hours since he had checked his email on Phoebe's phone or even sent his brother a text. Never in his adult life could he remember going so long without his electronic lifelines. Yet with Phoebe, tucked away from the world, he had gradually begun to accept the absence of technology as commonplace.

Not that she was really rustic in her situation. She had phones and television. But beyond that, life was tech-free. He frowned, not sure he was comfortable with the knowledge that she had converted him in a matter of days. It was the sex. That's all. He'd been pleasantly diverted. Didn't mean he wanted to give up his usual M.O. on a permanent basis.

Smiling to cover his unease, he released her. "I'm going to take a shower. I can play with the kid after that if you want to clean up."

* * *

Phoebe watched him go, her heart troubled. Something was off, but she couldn't pinpoint it. Maybe nothing more than a bad case of *morning after*.

By the time both adults were clean and dressed, the sound of a tractor echoed in the distance. Soon the driveway was passable, and in no time at all, vehicles began arriving. A truck dealing with Leo's satellite internet. The express delivery service with his new phone. A large moving van that somehow managed to turn and back up to the damaged cabin.

With the felled tree completely gone now, a small army of men began carrying out everything salvageable to place into storage until the repairs were complete. Leo didn't even linger for breakfast. He was out the door in minutes, wading into the midst of chaos…coordinating, instructing, and generally making himself indispensable. Phoebe wasn't sure what she would have done without his help. If she had not been laden with the responsibility of Teddy, she would have managed just fine. But caring for a baby and trying to deal with the storm damage at the same time would have made things extremely difficult.

She was amazed that she could see a difference in the baby in two weeks. He was growing so quickly and his personality seemed more evident every day. This morning he was delighting himself by blowing bubbles and babbling nonsense sounds.

After tidying the kitchen, Phoebe picked him up out of his high chair and carried him over to the tree. "See what Leo and I did, Teddy? Isn't it pretty?" The baby reached for an ornament, and she tucked his hand to her cheek. "I know. It isn't fair to have so many pretty baubles and none of them for you to play with."

Teddy grabbed a strand of her hair that had escaped her braid and yanked. She'd been in a hurry that morning after her shower and had woven her hair in its usual style with less than her usual precision. It was beginning to be clear to her why so many young mothers had simple hairstyles. Caring for an infant didn't leave much time for primping.

In another half hour Teddy would be ready for a nap. Already his eyes were drooping. After last night's excess, Phoebe might try to sneak in a few minutes of shut-eye herself. Thinking about Leo made her feel all bubbly inside. Like a sixteen-year-old about to go to prom with her latest crush.

Even in the good days with her fiancé, sex had never been like that. Leo had devoted himself to her pleasure, proving to her again and again that she had more to give and receive. Her body felt sensitized…energized…eager to try it all over again.

She walked the baby around the living room, humming Christmas carols, feeling happier than she had felt in a long time.

When the knock sounded at the front door, she looked up in puzzlement. Surely Leo hadn't locked himself out. She had made sure to leave the catch undone when he left. Before she could react, the door opened and a familiar head appeared.

"Dana!" Phoebe eyed her sister with shock and dismay. "What's wrong? Why are you here?"

Leo jogged back to the cabin. He was starving, but more than that, he wanted to see Phoebe. He didn't want to give her time to think of a million reasons why they shouldn't be together. When he burst through the front door, he ground to a halt, immediately aware that he had walked into a tense situation. He'd seen an unfamiliar car outside, but hadn't paid much attention, assuming it belonged to one of the workmen.

Phoebe's eyes met his across the room. For a split second, he saw into her very soul. Her anguish seared him, but the moment passed, and now her expression seemed normal. She smiled at him. "You're just in time. My sister, Dana, arrived unexpectedly. Dana, this is Leo."

He shook hands with the other woman and tried to analyze the dynamic that sizzled in the room. Dana was a shorter, rounder version of her sister. At the moment, she seemed exhausted and at the point of tears.

Phoebe held Teddy on her hip. "What are you doing here, Dana? Why didn't you let me know you were coming? I would have picked you up at the airport. You look like you haven't slept in hours."

Dana plopped onto the sofa and burst into tears, her hands over her face. "I knew you would try to talk me out of it," she sobbed. "I know it's stupid. I've been on a plane for hours, and I have to be back on a flight at two. But I couldn't spend Christmas without my baby. I thought I could, but I can't."

Leo froze, realizing at once what was happening. Phoebe…dear, beautiful, strong Phoebe put whatever feelings she had aside and went to sit beside her sister. "Of course you can't. I understand. Dry your eyes and take your son." She handed Teddy over to his mother as though it were the most natural thing in the world.

Leo knew it was breaking her heart.

Dana's face when she hugged her baby to her chest would have touched even the most hardened cynic. She kissed the top of his head, nuzzling the soft, fuzzy hair. "We found a lady in the village who speaks a little English. She's agreed to look after him while we work."

Phoebe clasped her hands in her lap as if she didn't know what to do with them. "How are things going with your father-in-law's estate?"

Dana made a face. "It's a mess. Worse than we thought. So stressful. The house is chock-full of junk. We have to go through it all so we don't miss anything valuable. I know it doesn't make sense to take Teddy over there, but if I can just have him in the evenings and be able to see him during the day when we take breaks, I know I'll feel so much better."

Phoebe nodded. "Of course you will."

Dana grabbed her sister's wrist. "You don't know how much we love you and appreciate all you've done for Teddy. I have an extra ticket on standby if you want to come back with me…or even in a day or two. I don't want you to be alone at Christmas, especially because it was that time of year when you lost—" She clapped her hand over her mouth, her expression horrified. "Oh, God, honey. I'm sorry. I'm exhausted and I don't know what I'm saying. I didn't mean to mention it."

Phoebe put an arm around the frazzled woman and kissed her cheek. "Take a deep breath, Dana. Everything's fine. I'm fine. If you're really on such a time crunch, let's start packing up Teddy's things. He'll nap in the car while you drive."

Phoebe paused in the back hallway, leaning against the wall and closing her eyes. Her smile felt frozen in place. Leo wasn't fooled. She could see his concern. But the important thing was for Dana not to realize what her unexpected arrival had done to Phoebe's plans for a cozy Christmas.

In less than an hour from start to finish, Dana came and went, taking Teddy with her. The resultant silence was painful. The only baby items left behind were the high chair in the kitchen and the large pieces of furniture in Teddy's room. Without asking, Leo took the high chair, put it in with the other stuff and shut the door. Phoebe watched him, her heart in pieces at her feet.

When he returned, she wrapped her arms around her

waist, her mood as flat as a three-day-old helium balloon. "I knew he wasn't my baby."

"Of course you did."

Leo's unspoken compassion took her close to an edge she didn't want to face. "Don't be nice to me or I may fall apart."

He grinned, taking her in his arms and resting his cheek on her head. "I'm very proud of you, Phoebe."

"For what?"

"For being such a good sister and aunt. For not making Dana feel guilty. For doing what had to be done."

"I was looking forward to Christmas morning," she whispered, her throat tight with unshed tears. "His presents are all wrapped." She clung to Leo, feeling his warm presence like a balm to her hurting spirit.

He squeezed her shoulders. "I have an idea to cheer you up."

She pulled back to look at him, only slightly embarrassed that her eyes were wet. "Having recently participated in some of your ideas, I'm listening," she said.

He wiped the edge of her eye with his thumb. "Get your mind out of the gutter, Ms. Kemper. I wanted to propose a trip."

"But you just arrived."

Putting a finger over her lips, he drew her to the sofa and sat down with her, tucking her close to his side. "Let me get it all out before you interrupt."

Phoebe nodded. "Okay."

"You asked me earlier about my plans for Christmas, and I had pretty much decided to stay here with you and Teddy. But I did feel a twinge of sadness and guilt to be missing some things back home. This weekend is the big Cavallo Christmas party for all our employees and their families. We have it at Luc's house. I'd like you to go with me."

She opened her mouth to speak, but he shushed her.

"Hear me out," he said. "I have an older friend who retired from Cavallo ten years ago, but he likes to keep busy. So now and again when the need arises, he does jobs for me. I know he would jump at the chance to come up here and oversee your cabin renovation. I trust him implicitly. He could stay in my room if it's okay with you. What do you think?"

"So I'm allowed to speak now?" She punched his ribs.

He inclined his head. "You have my permission."

"Where would *I* stay?"

"You mean in Atlanta?"

She nodded. "Yes."

"I was hoping you'd be at my place. But I can put you up at a nice hotel if you'd rather do that."

She scooted onto his lap, facing him, her hands on his shoulders. "But what about all my decorations and the tree?"

He pursed his lips. "Well, we could replicate the ambience at my place. You *do* like decorating. But I was also thinking that maybe you and I could come back here in time for Christmas Eve. Just the two of us. I know it won't be the same without Teddy, so if that's a bad idea, you can say so."

Seventeen

Leo held his breath, awaiting her answer. The fact that she felt comfortable enough with him to be sitting as she was reassured him. Last night a noticeable dynamic between them had shifted. She felt a part of him now. In ways he couldn't quite explain.

It had killed him to know she was so hurt this morning. Yet in the midst of her pain, she had handled herself beautifully, never once letting her sister realize how much Phoebe had been counting on Christmas with her nephew. By Phoebe's own admission, this was the first time in three years she had felt like celebrating. Yet when everything seemed to be going her way, she was blindsided by disappointment and loss.

Not a tragedy or a permanent loss, but deeply hurtful nevertheless.

Phoebe ran her fingers across his scalp, both hands… messing up his hair deliberately. "Do I have to decide now?"

"You mean about Christmas Eve?"

"Yes."

"I think that can wait. But does that mean you'll go with me?"

"I suppose I'll need a fancy dress." She traced the outer edges of his ears, making him squirm restlessly.

"Definitely. Is that a problem?" Holding her like this was a torment he could do without at the moment. He heard too much activity going on outside to be confident of no interruptions. When she slid a hand inside his shirt collar, he shivered. His erection was trapped uncomfortably beneath her denim-clad butt.

"No problem at all," she said breezily, unfastening the top two buttons of his shirt. "I have a whole closet full of nice things from my gainfully employed days."

"Define nice…."

She kissed him softly, sliding her tongue into his mouth and making him crazy. "Backless," she whispered. "Not much of a front. Slit up the leg. How does that sound?"

He groaned. "Lord, have mercy." He wasn't sure if he was talking about the dress or about the way her nimble fingers were moving down his chest. "Phoebe," he said, trying to sound more reasonable and less desperate. "Was that a *yes?*"

She cupped his face in her hands, her expression suddenly sweet and intense. "Thank you, Leo. You've saved Christmas for me. As hard as it was to say goodbye to little Teddy, you're the only other male of my acquaintance who could make me want to enjoy the season. So yes. I'd love to go with you to Atlanta."

He had to talk fast, but he managed to convince her they should leave that afternoon. Already he was fantasizing about making love to her in his comfy king-size bed. Last night's spontaneous lunacy had been mind-blowing, but there was something to be said for soft sheets and a firm mattress. Not to mention the fact that he wanted to wine and dine her and show her that the big city had its own appeal.

When she finally emerged from her bedroom, he stared.

Phoebe had one large suitcase, two smaller ones and a garment bag.

He put his hands on his hips, cocking his head. "You did understand that this was a *brief* visit...right?"

She was hot and flushed and wisps of hair stood out from her head like tiny signals saying, *Don't mess with me!* Dumping the bags at his feet, she wiped her forehead with the back of her hand. "I want to be prepared for any eventuality."

He nudged the enormous bag with his toe. "The NASA astronauts weren't *this* prepared," he joked. But inside he was pleased that the sparkle was back in her eyes. "Anything else I should know about? You do know I drive a Jag."

Phoebe smiled sweetly. "We could take my van."

He shuddered theatrically. "Leo Cavallo has a reputation to uphold. No, thank you."

While Phoebe went through the cabin turning off lights and putting out fresh sheets and towels, Leo studied the phone he had ordered. No point in taking it with him. He would only need it if he came back. If. Where had that thought come from? His reservation was fixed until the middle of January with a possible two-week extension.

Simply because he and Phoebe were going to make an appearance at the Christmas party didn't mean that his doctor and Luc were going to let him off the hook. He was painfully aware that he still hadn't told Phoebe the truth. And the reasons were murky.

But one thing stood out. Vanity. He didn't want her to see him as weak or broken. It was a hell of a thing to admit. But would she think of him differently once she knew?

By the time the car was loaded and they had dropped off the keys at Buford's house, Leo was starving. In blissful disregard of the calendar date, Phoebe had packed a picnic. To eat in the car, she insisted.

Instead of the way he had come in before, Phoebe suggested another route. "If you want to, we can take the scenic route, up over the mountains to Cherokee, North Carolina, and then we'll drop south to Atlanta from there. The road was closed by a landslide for a long time, but they've reopened it."

"I'm game," he said. "At least this time it will be daylight."

Phoebe giggled, tucking her legs into the car and waiting for him to shut the door. "You were so grumpy that night."

"I thought I was never going to get here. The rain and the fog and the dark. I was lucky I didn't end up nose deep in the creek."

"It wasn't that bad."

He shook his head, refusing to argue the point. Today's drive, though, was the complete opposite of his introduction to Phoebe's home turf. Sun shone down on them, warming the temperatures nicely. The winding two-lane highway cut through the quaint town of Gatlinburg and then climbed the mountain at a gentle grade. The vistas were incredible. He'd visited here once as a child, but it had been so long ago he had forgotten how peaceful the Smokies were… and how beautiful.

The trip flew by. Part of the time they talked. At other moments, they listened to music, comparing favorite artists and arguing over the merits of country versus pop. If driving to Tennessee had initially seemed like a punishment, today was entirely the opposite. He felt unreasonably lucky and blessed to be alive.

As they neared the city, he felt his pulse pick up. This was where he belonged. He and Luc had built something here, something good. But what if the life he knew and loved wasn't right for Phoebe?

Was it too soon to wonder such a thing?

All day he had been hyperaware of her…the quick flash of her smile, her light flowery scent, the way she moved her hands when she wanted to make a point. He remained in a state of constant semi-arousal. Now that they were almost at their destination, he found himself subject to a surprising agitation.

What if Phoebe didn't like his home?

She was silent as they pulled into the parking garage beneath his downtown high-rise building and slowed to a halt beside the kiosk. "Hey, Jerome," he said, greeting the stoop-shouldered, balding man inside the booth with a smile. "This is where we get out, Phoebe." He turned back to Jerome. "Do you mind asking one of the boys to unload the car and bring up our bags?"

"Not at all, Mr. Cavallo. We'll get them right up."

Leo took Phoebe's elbow and steered her toward the elevator, where he used his special key to access and press the penthouse button. "Jerome's a retired army sergeant. He runs this place with an iron fist."

Phoebe clutched her purse, her expression inscrutable. Because the video camera in this tiny space was recording everything they said, Leo refrained from personal chitchat. He preferred to keep his private life private.

Upstairs, they stepped out into his private hallway. He generally took the recessed lighting and sophisticated decor for granted, but Phoebe looked around with interest. Once inside, he tossed his keys on a console table and held out a hand. "Would you like the tour?"

Phoebe felt like Alice in Wonderland. To go from her comfortable though modest cabin to this level of luxury was the equivalent of situational whiplash. She had realized on an intellectual level that Leo must be wealthy. Though she hadn't known him personally before he arrived on her doorstep, she was well aware of the Cavallo empire and the pricey goods it offered to high-end consumers. But somehow, she hadn't fully understood *how* rich Leo really was.

The floors of his penthouse condo, acres of them it seemed, were laid in cream-colored marble veined with gold. Expensive Oriental rugs in hues of cinnamon and deep azure bought warmth and color to what might otherwise have been too sterile a decorating scheme.

Incredible artwork graced the walls. Some of the paintings, to Phoebe's inexperience gaze, appeared to be priceless originals. Two walls of the main living area were made entirely of glass, affording an unparalleled view of Atlanta as far as the eye could see. Everything from the gold leaf–covered dome of the Capitol building to the unmistakable outline of Stone Mountain in the far distance.

A variety of formal armchairs and sofas were upholstered in either pale gold velvet or ecru leather. Crimson and navy pillows beckoned visitors to sit and relax. Overhead, a massive modern chandelier splayed light to all corners of the room.

Undoubtedly, all of the fabrics were of Italian Cavallo design. Phoebe, who had always adored vivid color and strong statements in decor, fell in love with Leo's home immediately. She turned in a circle. "I'm speechless. Should I take off my shoes?"

He stepped behind her, his hands on her shoulders. Pushing aside her hair, left loose for a change, he kissed her neck just below her ear. "It's meant to be lived in. May I say how glad I am that you're here?"

She turned to face him, wondering if she really knew him at all. At her old job, she had earned a comfortable living. But in comparison to all this, she was a pauper. How did Leo know she was not interested in him for his money? Unwilling to disclose her unsettling thoughts, she linked her arms around his neck. "Thank you for inviting me."

She tugged at his bottom lip with the pad of her thumb. "Surely there are bedrooms I should see."

His eyes darkened. "I didn't want to rush you."

Her hand brushed the front of his trousers. "I've noticed this fellow hanging around all day."

The feel of her slim fingers, even through the fabric of his pants, affected him like an electric shock. "Seems to be a permanent condition around you."

"Then I suppose it's only fair if I offer some…um…"

His grin was a wicked flash of white teeth. "While you're thinking of the appropriate word, my sweet," Leo said, scooping her into his arms, "I could show you my etchings."

She tweaked his chin. "Not in here, I presume?"

"Down the hall." He held her close to his chest, his muscular arms bearing her weight as if she were no more than a child.

Being treated like Scarlett O'Hara seemed entirely appropriate here in the Peach State. Leo's power and strength seduced her almost as much as the memory of last night's erotic play. "The sofa is closer," she whispered, noting the shadow of his stubble and the way his golden-skinned throat moved when he spoke huskily.

He nodded his head, hunger darkening his eyes. "I like the way you think." He kissed her cheek as he strode across the room.

"No one knows you're home, right?"

"Correct."

"And there's no one else on this floor?"

He shook his head, lowering her onto the soft cushions. "No."

"So I can be as loud as I like?"

He stared at her in shock as her outrageous taunt sank in. "Good God Almighty." Color crept from his throat to his hairline. "I thought you were a sweet young thing when I first met you. But apparently I was wrong."

"Never judge a book by its cover, Mr. Cavallo." She ripped her sweater off over her head. "Please tell me you have some more of those packets."

Leo seemed fixated on the sight of her lace-covered breasts, but he recovered. "Damn it." His expression leaned toward desperation.

"What's wrong?"

"All of our luggage is downstairs."

"Your bathroom. Here?"

"Well, yes, but somebody will be coming up that elevator any moment now."

"Leo…" she wailed, not willing to wait another second. "Call them back. Tell them we're in the shower."

"Both of us?" He glanced at the door and back at her, frustration a living, breathing presence between them. An impressive erection tented his slacks. "It won't be long. Fifteen minutes tops."

The way she felt at the moment, five minutes was too long. She wanted Leo. Now.

Fortunately for both of them, a quiet chime sounded, presumably a doorbell, though it sounded more like a heavenly harp. Leo headed for the entrance and stared back at her. "You planning on staying like that?"

Her jaw dropped. She was half naked and the doorknob was turning in Leo's hand. With a squeak, she clutched her sweater to her breasts and ran around the nearest wall, which happened to conceal the kitchen. Not even bothering to envy the fabulous marble countertops and fancy appliances, she listened with bated breath as Leo conversed with the bellman. At long last, she heard the door close, and the sound of footsteps.

As she hovered amidst gourmet cookware and the scent of unseen spices, Leo appeared. "He's gone." In his hand he held a stack of condoms. "Is this what you wanted?"

Eighteen

Leo had never particularly considered his kitchen to be a sexy place. In truth, he spent little time here. But with Phoebe loitering half naked, like a nymph who had lost her way, he suddenly began to see about a zillion possibilities.

He leaned a hip against the counter. "Take off the rest of your clothes." Would she follow his lead, or had he come on too strong?

When perfect white teeth mutilated her bottom lip, he couldn't decide if she was intending to drive him crazy by delaying or if she was perhaps now a bit shy. Without responding verbally, she tugged off her knee-length boots and removed her trim black slacks. The only article of clothing that remained, her tiny panties, was a perfect match to her blush-pink bra.

"The floor is cold," she complained as she kicked aside the better part of her wardrobe.

His hands clenched the edge of the counter behind him. Lord, she was a handful. And gorgeous to boot. "You're not done," he said with far more dispassion than he felt.

Phoebe thrust out her bottom lip and straightened her shoulders. "I don't know why you have to be so bossy."

"Because you like it." He could see the excitement building in her wide-eyed stare as she reached behind her back and unfastened her bra. It fell to the floor like a wispy pink cloud. Though she hesitated for a brief moment, she continued disrobing, stepping out of her small undies with all the grace of a seasoned stripper.

She twirled the panties on the end of her finger. "Come and get me."

He literally saw red. His vision hazed and he felt every molecule of moisture leach from his mouth. Quickly, with razor-sharp concentration that belied the painful ache in his groin, he assessed the possibilities. Beside the refrigerator, some genius architect had thought to install a desk that matched the rest of the kitchen. The marble top was the perfect height for what Leo had in mind.

Forget the sofa or the bedroom or any other damned part of his house. He was going to take her here.

He could barely look at Phoebe without coming apart at the seams. Young and strong and healthy, she was the epitome of womanhood. Her dark hair fell over one shoulder, partially veiling one raspberry nipple. "You're beautiful, Phoebe."

The raw sincerity in his strained voice must have told her that the time for games was over. Surprised pleasure warmed her eyes. "I'm glad you think so." She licked her lips. "Do you plan on staying over there forever?"

"I don't know," he said in all seriousness. "The way I feel at the moment, I'm afraid I'll take you like a madman."

Her lips curved. "Is that a bad thing?"

"You tell me." Galvanized at last into action by a yearning that could no longer be denied, he picked her up by the waist and sat her on the desk. Phoebe yelped when the cold surface made contact with her bottom, but she exhaled on a long, deep sigh as the sensation subsided.

He ripped at his zipper and freed his sex. He was as hard as the marble that surrounded them, but far hotter. Sheathing himself with fumbling hands, he stepped between her legs. "Prop your feet on the desk, honey."

Phoebe's cooperation was instant, though her eyes rounded when she realized what he was about to do.

He positioned himself at the opening of her moist pink sex and shoved, one strong thrust that took him all the way. He held her bottom for leverage and moved slowly in and out. Phoebe's arms linked around his neck in a stranglehold. Her feet lost their purchase and instead, she linked her ankles behind his waist.

It would be embarrassing if she realized that his legs were trembling and his heart was doing weird flips and flops that had nothing to do with his recent health event. Phoebe made him forget everything he thought was important and forced him to concentrate on the two of them. Not from any devious machinations on her part, but because she was so damned cute and fun.

Even as he moved inside her, he was already wondering where they could make love next. Heat built in his groin, a monstrous, unstoppable force. "I'm gonna come," he groaned.

She had barely made a sound. In sudden dismay, he leaned back so he could see her face. "Talk to me, Phoebe." Reaching down, he rubbed gently at the swollen nub he'd been grazing again and again with the base of his sex. When his fingers made one last pass, Phoebe arched her back and cried out as she climaxed. Inside, her body squeezed him with flutters that threatened to take off the top of his head because the feeling was so intense.

With his muscles clenched from head to toe, he held back his own release so he could relish every moment of her shuddering finale. As she slumped limp in his embrace, he cursed and thrust wildly, emptying himself until he was wrung dry. With one last forceful thrust, he finished, but as he did, his forehead met the edge of the cabinet over Phoebe's head with enough force to make him stagger backward.

"Hell..." His reverse momentum was halted by the large island in the center of the kitchen. He leaned there, dazed.

Phoebe slid to her feet. "Oh, Leo. You're bleeding." Her face turned red, and she burst out laughing. Mortification and remorse filled her eyes in addition to concern, but she apparently couldn't control her mirth, despite the fact that he had been injured in battle.

Okay. So it *was* a little funny. His lips quirking, he put a hand to his forehead and winced when it came away streaked in red. "Would you please put some clothes on?" he said, trying not to notice the way her breasts bounced nicely when she laughed.

Phoebe rolled her eyes. "Take them off. Put them on. You're never satisfied."

He looked down at his erection that was already preparing for duty. "Apparently not." When she bent over to step into her underwear and pants, it was all he could do not to take her again.

Only the throbbing in his head held him back. When she was decent, he grimaced. "We're going to a party tomorrow night. How am I going to explain this?"

Phoebe took his hand and led him toward the bedrooms. "Which one is yours?" she asked. When he pointed, she kept walking, all the way to his hedonistic bathroom. "We'll put some antibiotic ointment on it between now and then. Plus, there's always makeup."

"Great. Just great."

She opened the drawer he indicated and gathered the needed supplies. "Sit on the stool."

He zipped himself back into his trousers, more to avoid temptation than from any real desire to be dressed. "Is this going to hurt?"

"Probably."

The truth was the truth. When she moistened a cotton ball with antiseptic and dabbed at the cut, it stung like fire. He glanced in the mirror. The gash, more of a deep scrape really, was about two inches long. And dead in the center of his forehead. Now, every time he saw his reflection for the next week or so, all he would remember was debauching Phoebe in his kitchen.

She smeared a line of medicated cream along the wound and tried covering it with two vertical Band-Aids. Now he looked like Frankenstein.

Their eyes met in the large mahogany-framed mirror. Phoebe put a hand over her mouth. "Sorry," she mumbled. But she was shaking all over, and he wasn't fooled. Her mirth spilled out in wet eyes and muffled giggles.

"Thank God you didn't go into nursing," he groused. He stood up and reached for a glass of water to down some ibuprofen. "Are you hungry, by any chance?" The kitchen episode had left him famished. Maybe it was the subliminal message in his surroundings.

Phoebe wiped her eyes and nodded. "That picnic food was a long time ago."

"In that case, let me show you to your room and you can do whatever you need to do to get ready. The place I want to take you is intimate, but fairly casual. You don't really have to change if you don't want to. But I'll drag your three dozen suitcases in there to be on the safe side."

Phoebe wasn't sure what to think about the opulent suite that was apparently hers for the duration of her visit. It was amazing, of course. Yards of white carpet. French country furniture in distressed white wood. A heavy cotton bedspread that had been hand embroidered with every wildflower in the world. And a bathroom that rivaled Leo's. But in truth, she had thought she would be sleeping with him.

Nevertheless, when Leo disappeared, she wasted no time

in getting ready. She took a quick shower, though she made sure to keep her hair dry. It had grown dramatically in three years, far longer than she had ever worn it. Once wet, it was a pain to dry. She brushed it quickly and bound it loosely at the back of her neck with a silver clasp.

Given Leo's description of their destination, she chose black tights and black flats topped with a flirty black skirt trimmed at the hem in three narrow layers of multicolored chiffon. With a hot-pink silk chemise and a waist-length black sweater, she looked nice, but not too over-the-top.

She had forgotten how much fun it was to dress up for a date. Fastening a silver chain around her neck, she fingered the charm that dangled from it. The letter *P* was engraved on the silver disc in fancy cursive script. Her mother's name had started with the same letter as Phoebe's. And Phoebe had decided that if her baby was a girl, she wanted to name her Polly. An old-fashioned name maybe, but one she loved.

It was hard to imagine ever being pregnant again. Would she be terrified the entire nine months? The doctor had insisted there was no reason her next pregnancy shouldn't be perfectly normal. But it would be hard, so hard, not to worry.

Pregnancy was a moot point now. There was no man in her life other than Leo. And the two of them had known each other for no time at all. Even if the relationship were serious—which it definitely was not—Leo wasn't interested in having kids. It hadn't been difficult to pick up on that.

He clearly loved his niece and nephew, and he had been great with Teddy. But he was not the kind of guy to settle for home and hearth. Running the Cavallo conglomerate required most of his devotion. He loved it. Was proud of it. And at the level of responsibility he carried, having any substantive personal life would be tricky.

His brother, Luc, seemed to have mastered the art of balance, from what Leo had said. But maybe Luc wasn't quite as single-mindedly driven as his intense brother.

When she was content with her appearance, she returned to the living room. Leo was standing in front of the expanse of glass, his hands clasped behind his back. He turned when he heard her footsteps. "That was quick."

He looked her over from head to toe. "I'll be the envy of every guy in the restaurant."

She smiled, crossing the room to him and lightly touching his forehead. "You okay?"

"A little headache, but I'll live. Are you ready?"

She nodded. "Perhaps we should stop by a pharmacy and grab some tiny Band-Aids so you don't scare children."

"Smart-ass." He put an arm around her waist and steered her toward the door.

"I'm serious."

"So am I...."

Nineteen

After a quick stop for medical supplies, they arrived at a small bistro tucked away in the heart of downtown Atlanta. The maître d' recognized Leo and escorted them to a quiet table in the corner. "Mr. Cavallo," he said. "So glad to see you are well."

An odd look flashed across Leo's face. "Thank you. Please keep our visit quiet. I hope to surprise my brother tomorrow."

"At the Christmas party, yes?" The dumpy man with the Italian accent nodded with a smile. "My nephew works in your mail room. He is looking forward to it."

"Tell him to introduce himself if he gets a chance."

Leo held Phoebe's chair as she was seated and then joined her on the opposite side of the table. He handed her a menu. "I have my favorites, but you should take a look. They make everything from scratch, and it's all pretty amazing."

After they ordered, Phoebe cocked her head and stared at him with a smile. "Does everyone in Atlanta know who you are?"

"Hardly. I'm just the guy who writes the checks."

"Modest, but suspect."

"It's true," he insisted. "I'm not a player, if that's what you're thinking."

"You don't have the traditional little black book full of names?"

"My phone is black. And a few of the contacts are women."

"That's not an answer."

"I'll plead the Fifth Amendment."

Phoebe enjoyed the dinner immensely. Leo was wearing a beautiful navy-and-gray tweed blazer with dark slacks. Even battle-scarred, he was the most impressive man in the room. Despite his size, he handled his fragile wineglass delicately, his fingers curled around the stem with care.

Thinking about Leo's light touch made Phoebe almost choke on a bite of veal. When she had drained her water glass and regained her composure, Leo grinned. "I don't know what you were thinking about, but your face is bright red."

"You're the one with the sex injury," she pointed out.

"Fair enough." His lips twitched, and his gaze promised retribution later for her refusal to explain.

On the way home, it started to rain. Phoebe loved the quiet swish of the wipers and the fuzzy glow of Christmas decorations in every window. Leo turned down a side street and parked at the curb. He stared through the windshield, his expression oddly intent, his hands clenched on the steering wheel.

"What is it?" she asked. "What's wrong?"

He glanced at her, eyes hooded. "Nothing's *wrong*. Would you mind if we go up to my office?"

She craned her neck, for the first time seeing the Cavallo name on the building directory. "Of course not." He was acting very strangely.

Leo exited the car, opened an umbrella and came around the car to help her out. Fortunately her shoes were not expensive, because her feet tripped through the edge of a puddle as they accessed the sidewalk.

She shivered while he took a set of keys from his pocket and opened the main door. The plate glass clunked shut behind them. "Over there," Leo said. Again, using his private keys, they entered a glossy-walled elevator.

Phoebe had seen dozens of movies where lovers used a quick ride to sneak a passionate kiss. Leo clearly didn't know the plot, because he leaned against the wall and studied the illuminated numbers as they went higher and higher. Cavallo occupied the top twelve floors.

When they arrived at their destination, Phoebe was not surprised to see all the trappings of an elite twenty-first-century business. A sleek reception area decorated for the season, secretarial cubicles, multiple managerial offices and, at the far end of the floor on which they entered, an imposing door with Leo's name inscribed on a brass panel.

Another key, another entry. They skirted what was obviously the domain of an executive assistant and walked through one last door.

Leo stopped so suddenly, she almost ran into his back. She had a feeling he had forgotten her presence. He moved forward slowly, stopping to run a hand along the edge of what was clearly *his* desk. The top was completely bare, the surface polished to a high sheen.

Leo turned to her suddenly, consternation on his face. "Make yourself comfortable," he said, pointing to a leather chair and ottoman near the window. "That's where I like to sit when I have paperwork to read through. I won't be long."

She did as he suggested, noting that much like his sophisticated home, his place of business, arguably the epicenter of his life, had two transparent walls. The dark, rainy night beyond the thick glass was broken up by a million pinpoints of light, markers of a city that scurried to and fro.

As she sat down and propped her feet on the ottoman,

she relaxed into the soft, expensive seat that smelled of
leather and Leo's distinctive aftershave. The faint aroma
made her nostalgic suddenly for the memory of curling
up with him on her sofa, enjoying the Christmas tree and
watching the fire.

Leo prowled, tension in the set of his shoulders. He
opened drawers, shuffled papers, flicked the leaves of
plants on the credenza. He seemed lost. Or at the very
least confused.

Hoping to give him the semblance of privacy, she picked
up a book from the small table at her elbow. It was a techni-
cal and mostly inaccessible tome about third-world econo-
mies. She read the first two paragraphs and turned up her
nose. Not exactly escape reading.

Next down the pile was a news magazine. But the date
was last month's, and she was familiar with most of the
stories. Finally, at the bottom, was a collection of Sunday
newspapers. Someone had taken great care to stack them
in reverse order. Again, they were out of date, but that same
someone had extracted the "Around Town" section of the
most recent one and folded it to a story whose accompanying photograph she recognized instantly. It was Leo.

Reading automatically, her stomach clenched and her
breathing grew choppy. No. This had to be a mistake.

She stood up, paper in her hand, and stared at him. Disbelief, distress and anger coursed through her veins in a
nauseating cocktail. "You had a heart attack?"

Leo froze but turned around to face her, his shoulders
stiff and his whole body tensed as if facing an enemy. "Who
told you that?"

She threw the paper at him, watching it separate and
rain down on the thick pile carpet with barely a sound. "It's
right there," she cried, clutching her arms around her waist.
Prominent Atlanta Businessman Leo Cavallo, Age 36, Suf-
fers Heart Attack. "My God, Leo. Why didn't you tell me?"

He opened his mouth to speak, but she interrupted him with an appalled groan. "You carried wood for me. And chopped down a tree. I made you drag heavy boxes from the attic. Damn it, Leo, how could you not tell me?"

"It wasn't that big a deal." His expression was blank, but his eyes burned with an emotion she couldn't fathom.

She shivered, her mind a whirl of painful thoughts. He could have died. He could have died. He could have died. And she would never have known him. His humor. His kindness. His incredibly sexy and appealing personality. His big, perfect body.

"Trust me," she said slowly. "When a man in his thirties has a heart attack, it's a big freaking deal."

He shoved his hands into his pockets, the line of his mouth grim. "I had a very mild heart attack. A minor blockage. It's a hereditary thing. I'm extraordinarily healthy. All I have to do now is keep an eye on certain markers."

As she examined the days in the past week, things kept popping up, memories that made her feel even worse. "Your father," she whispered. "You said he had a heart attack. And that's why the boat crashed."

"Yes."

"That's it. Just *yes?* Did it ever occur to you when you were screwing me that your medical history was information I might have wanted to know? Hell, Leo, I gave you every intimate detail of my past and you couldn't be bothered to mention something as major as a heart attack?" She knew she was shouting and couldn't seem to stop. Her heart slammed in her chest.

"I've never heard you curse. I don't like it."

"Well, that's just too damn bad." She stopped short, appalled that she was yelling like a shrew. Hyperventilation threatened. "That's why you came to my cabin, isn't it? I thought maybe you'd had a bad case of the flu. Or complications from pneumonia. Or even, God forbid, a mental breakdown of some sort. But a heart attack..." Her legs gave out, and she sank back into the chair, feeling disappointed and angry and, beneath it all, so scared for him. "Why didn't you tell me, Leo? Why couldn't you trust me with the truth? Surely I deserved that much consideration."

But then it struck her. He hadn't shared the intimate details of his illness with her because she didn't matter. The bitter realization sat like a stone in her stomach. Leo had kept his secrets, because when all was said and done, Phoebe was nothing more than a vacation romance of sorts. Leo wasn't serious about any kind of a future with her. He fully planned to return to his old life and take up where he left off. As soon as his doctor gave permission.

He came to her then, sat on the ottoman and put a hand on her leg. "It wasn't something I could easily talk about, Phoebe. Try to understand that. I was a young man. One minute I was standing in a room, doing my job, and the next I couldn't breathe. Strangers were rushing me out to an ambulance. It was a hellish experience. All I wanted to do was forget."

"But you didn't want to come to the mountains."

"No. I didn't. My doctor, who happens to be a good friend, and my brother, who I consider my *best* friend, gave me no choice. I was supposed to learn how to control my stress levels."

She swallowed, wishing he wasn't touching her. The warmth of his hand threatened to dissolve the fragile hold she had on her emotions. "We had *sex,* Leo. To me, that's pretty intimate. But I can see in retrospect that I was just a piece of your convalescent plan, not dictated by your doctor friend, I'm sure. Did it even cross your mind to worry about *that?*"

He hesitated, and she knew she had hit a nerve.

She saw him swallow. He ran a hand through his hair, unintentionally betraying his agitation. "The first time I was with you…in that way, I hadn't had sex since my heart attack. And to be honest, not for several months before that. Do you want me to tell you I was scared shitless? Is that going to make you feel better?"

She knew it was the nature of men to fear weakness. And far worse was having someone witness that vulnerability. So she even understood his angry retort to some extent. But that didn't make her any less despairing. "You haven't taken any of this seriously, have you, Leo? You think you're invincible and that your exile to Tennessee was just a momentary inconvenience. Do you even want to change your ways?" Coming to the office tonight said louder than words what he was thinking.

"It's not that easy."

"Nothing important ever is," she whispered, her throat almost too tight for speech. She stood up and went to the window, blinking back tears. If he couldn't admit that he needed a life outside of work, and if he couldn't be honest with himself *or* with her, then he wasn't ready for the kind of relationship she wanted.

In that moment, she knew that any feeble hope she had nurtured for intimacy with Leo, even in the short term, was futile. "May we leave now?" she asked, her emotions at the breaking point. "I'm tired. It's been a long day."

Twenty

Leo knew he had hurt Phoebe. Badly. But for the life of him, he couldn't see a way to fix things. She disappeared into her room as soon as they got home from his office. The next day, they barely spoke. He fooled around on the internet and watched MSNBC and CNN, particularly the financial pundits.

Being in his office last night had unsettled him. The room had been cold and clinically clean, as if the last occupant had died and the desk was awaiting a new owner.

Somehow he'd thought he might get some kind of revelation about his life if he could stand where he'd once stood. As though in the very air itself he would be able to make sense of it all.

If he had gone straight home from the restaurant, he and Phoebe would no doubt have spent the night in bed dreaming up one way after another to lose themselves in pleasure.

Instead, his impulsive action had ruined everything.

He didn't blame her for being upset. But if he had it to do over again, he still wouldn't have told her about his heart attack. It wasn't the kind of news a man shared with the woman he wanted to impress.

And there it was. He wanted to impress Phoebe. With

his intellect, his entrepreneurial success, his life in general. As if by comparison she could and would see that her hermitlike retreat was not valid. That she was the one with lessons to learn.

As he remembered his brief time in Phoebe's magical mountain home, suddenly, everything clicked into focus. The reason his office had seemed sterile and empty last night was not because Leo had been gone for several weeks. The odd feelings he had experienced were a reluctant recognition of the difference between his work domain and the warm, cheerful home Phoebe had created.

In the midst of her pain and heartbreak, she hadn't become a bitter, angry woman. Instead, she had stretched her wings. She'd had the courage to step out in faith, trusting that she would find the answers she needed. Her solitude and new way of life had taught her valuable lessons about what was important. And she'd been willing to share her wisdom with Leo. But he had been too arrogant to accept that her experience could in any way shed light on his own life.

What a jackass he had been. He had lied to her by omission and all along had been patronizing about her simple existence. Instead of protecting his macho pride, he should have been begging her to help him make a new start.

He *needed* to find balance in his life. His brother, Luc, had managed that feat. Surely Leo could follow his example. And even beyond that, Leo needed Phoebe. More than he could ever have thought possible. But by his selfish actions, he had lost her. Perhaps forever. It would take every ounce of genius he possessed to win back her trust.

The magnitude of his failure was humbling. But as long as there was life, there was hope.

At his request, she consented to stay for the party. He knew she had booked a flight home for the following morning, because he had eavesdropped unashamedly at her door while she made the reservation.

When she appeared in the foyer at a quarter 'til seven that evening, his heart stopped. But this time he recognized the interruption. A lightning bolt of passion or lust or maybe nothing more complicated than need shattered his composure.

She wore a dress that many women would avoid for fear they couldn't carry it off. The fabric was red. An intense crimson that spoke for itself. And Phoebe hadn't been teasing when she described it. Cut low in the back and the front and high on the leg, it fit her as if it had been created with exactly her body in mind.

Stiletto heels in matte black leather put her almost on eye level with him. As equals.

Her hair was stunning. She had braided two tiny sections from the front and wound them at her crown. The rest cascaded in a sleek fall halfway down her back. On her right upper arm she wore a three-inch wide hammered silver band. Matching earrings dangled and caught the light.

He cleared his throat. "You look sensational."

"Thank you." Her expression was as remote as the Egyptian queen she resembled.

He had hoped tonight to strengthen the connection between them by showing her a slice of his life. His family. His employees. The way the company was built on trust and integrity. But now there was this chasm between Phoebe and him.

He hated the emotional distance, but he would use their physical attraction to fight back, to get through to her, if he had to. She had accused him of not taking his recovery seriously, but by God, he was serious now. His future hung in the balance. Everything he had worked for up until this point was rendered valueless. Without Phoebe's love and trust, he had nothing.

* * *

Fortunately his brother's home was close…on West Paces Ferry Road, an old and elegant established neighborhood for Atlanta's wealthy and powerful. But Luc and Hattie had made their home warm and welcoming amidst its elegant personality, a place where children could run and play, though little Luc Jr. was still too small for that.

Leo handed the keys of his Jag to the attendant and helped Phoebe out of the car. The college kid's eyes glazed over as he caught a glimpse of Phoebe's long, toned legs. Glaring at the boy, Leo wrapped her faux fur stole around her shoulders and ushered her toward the house.

Every tree and bush on the property had been trimmed in tiny white lights. Fragrant greenery festooned with gold bows wrapped lampposts and wrought-iron porch rails.

Phoebe paused on the steps, taking it all in. "I love this place," she said simply. "It feels like a classy Southern lady."

"Luc and Hattie will probably be at the door greeting their guests, but perhaps we can sit down with them later and catch up." The timing was off. Phoebe was leaving in the morning, and their relationship was dead in the water, but he still wanted her to meet his brother.

As it turned out, Leo was correct. His dashing brother took one look at Leo and wrestled him into a long bear hug that brought tears to Phoebe's eyes. Leo's sister-in-law wore the very same expression as she watched the two men embrace. Both brothers wore classic formal attire, and in their tuxes, they were incredibly dashing, almost like old film stars with their chiseled features.

Luc shook Phoebe's hand as they were introduced. "I wasn't sure Leo was going to come back for the holidays, or even if he should. I'm happy to see he has such a lovely woman looking after him."

Leo's jaw tightened, though his smile remained. "Phoebe's my date, not my nurse."

Phoebe saw from Luc's abashed expression that he knew he had stepped in it. Hattie whispered something in his ear, and he nodded.

Other people crowded in behind them, but Leo lingered for a moment longer. "Can we see the kids?"

Hattie touched his cheek, her smile warm and affectionate. "We have them asleep upstairs with a sitter, but you're welcome to take a peek." She smiled at Phoebe. "Leo dotes on our babies. Lord help us when he has some of his own. I've never known a man with a softer heart."

"Hey," Luc said, looking indignant. "I'm standing right here."

Hattie kissed his cheek. "Don't worry, sweetheart. I'll always love you best."

On the cloud of laughter that followed, Leo and Phoebe moved into the thick of the party. It was soon clear to her that Leo Cavallo was popular and beloved. Despite his reputation as a hard-hitting negotiator in the boardroom, everyone under Luc's roof treated Leo not only with respect, but with genuine caring and concern.

After an hour, though, she sensed that his patience was wearing thin. Perhaps he hadn't anticipated the many questions about his recovery. At any rate, she recognized his growing tension. She hated the unmistakable awkwardness between them as the evening progressed, but despite her hurt, she couldn't stop wanting to help him. Even if he couldn't be hers, she wanted him to be happy.

In a lull between conversations, she touched his arm. "Do you want to go upstairs and see your niece and nephew?"

He nodded, relief in his harried gaze.

Luc and Hattie's home was far different than Leo's, but spectacular in its own right. Phoebe experienced a frisson of envy for the couple who had created such a warm and nurturing family environment. The little girl's room was done in peach and cream with Disney fairies. The baby boy's nursery sported a delightful zoo animal theme.

Leo stroked his nephew's back and spoke to him softly, but he stayed the longest in Deedee's room. His eyes were somber as he watched the toddler sleep. "She's not their biological child, you know. When Hattie's sister died, Hattie took her baby to raise, and then after the wedding, Luc and Hattie adopted her."

"Has your brother been married long?"

"Less than two years. He and Hattie were pretty serious back in college. The relationship didn't work out, but they were lucky enough to find their way back to each other."

Phoebe stared at Leo's bent head as he sat carefully on the corner of the bed and touched his niece's hand. He took her tiny fingers in his and brought them to his lips. It would have been clear to a blind man that Leo was capable of great love and caring. He felt about these two little ones the way Phoebe did about Teddy.

He turned his head suddenly and caught her watching him, probably with her heart in her eyes. "Will you take a walk with me?" he asked gravely.

"Of course."

Tiny flurries of snow danced around them when they exited the back of the house. Leo had retrieved her wrap, but even so, the night was brisk. In the center of the upper terrace a large, tiled fire pit blazed with vigor, casting a small circle of warmth. Other than the old man adding logs now and again, Leo and Phoebe were alone. Apparently no one else was eager to brave the cold.

A wave of sadness, deep and poignant, washed over Phoebe. If only she and Leo had met under other circumstances. No pain and heartache in her past. No devastating illness in his. Just two people sharing a riveting attraction.

They could have enjoyed a sexual relationship that might have grown into something more.

Now, they stood apart, when only twenty-four hours ago, give or take, Leo had been turning her world upside down with his lovemaking. Their recent fight echoed in her mind. She had accused Leo of not wanting to change, but wasn't she just as cowardly? She had gone from one extreme to the other. Workaholic to hermit. Such a radical swing couldn't be considered balance at all.

In the faces of the crowd tonight, she saw more than the bonhomie of the season. She saw a kinship, a trust that came from working side by side. That was what she had given up, and she realized that she missed it. She missed all of it. The hard challenges, the silly celebrations, the satisfaction of a job well done.

So lost in her thoughts was she, that she jumped when Leo took her by the shoulders and turned her to face him. Again, as at her cabin, firelight painted his features. His eyes were dark, unfathomable. "I have a proposition for you, Phoebe, so hear me out before you say anything."

Her hands tightened on her wrap. "Very well." A tiny piece of gravel had found its way into her shoe. And she couldn't feel her toes. But not even a blizzard could have made her walk away.

He released her as though he couldn't speak freely when they were touching. She thought she understood. Passion had flared so hot and so quickly between them when they first met, its veracity was suspect given the length of their acquaintance.

"First of all," he said quietly, "I'm sorry I didn't tell you about the heart attack. It was an ego thing. I didn't want you to think less of me."

"But I…" She bit her lip and stopped, determined to listen as he had requested.

He ran a hand across the back of his neck. "I was angry

and bitter and confused when I met you. I'd spent a week at the hospital, a week here at Luc's, and then to top it all, they exiled me to Tennessee."

"Tennessee is a very nice state," she felt bound to point out.

A tiny smile flickered across his lips. "It's a lovely state, but that's not the point. I looked at you and saw a desirable woman. You had your hang-ups. We all do. But I didn't want you to look too closely at mine. I wanted you to see me as a strong, capable man."

"And I did."

"But you have to admit the truth, Phoebe. Last night in my office. You stared at me and saw something else." The defeat in his voice made her ill with regret.

"You don't understand," she said, willing him to hear her with an open mind. "I was upset, yes. It terrified me that you had been in such a dangerous situation. And I was angry that you didn't trust me enough to share that with me. But it never changed the way I saw you. If you felt that, then you were wrong."

He paced in silence for several long minutes. She wondered if he believed her. Finally, he stopped and lifted a hand to bat away the snowflakes that were increasing in size and frequency. "We jumped too far ahead," he said. "I want to say things to you that are too soon, too serious."

Her heart sank, because she knew he was right. "So that's it?" she asked bleakly. "We just chalk this up to bad timing and walk away?"

"Is that what you want?" He stood there…proud, tall and so alone her heart broke for him.

"No. That's not what I want at all," she said, daring to be honest with so much at stake. "So if you have a plan, I'm listening."

He exhaled noisily as if he'd been holding his breath. "Well, okay, then. Here it is. I propose that we go back to your place and spend Christmas Eve together when it rolls around. I'll stay with you for the remainder of the time I have reserved and work on learning how not to obsess about business."

"Is that even possible?" She said it with a grin so he would know she was teasing. Mostly.

"God, I hope so. Because I want you in my life, Phoebe. And you deserve a man who will not only make a place for you, but will put you front and center."

One hot tear rolled down her cheek. "Is there more?"

"Yes. And this is the scary part. At the end of January, assuming we haven't killed each other or bored each other to death, I want you to come back to Atlanta and move in with me…as my fiancée. Not now," he said quickly. "As of this moment, we are simply a man and a woman who are attracted to each other."

"Very attracted," Phoebe agreed, her heart lifting to float with the snowflakes.

She took a step in his direction, but he held up a hand. "Not yet. Let me finish."

His utter seriousness and heartfelt sincerity gave her hope that what had begun as a serendipitous fling might actually have substance and a solid foundation. Cautious elation fluttered inside her chest. But she kept her cool… barely. "Go on."

"I'm not criticizing you, Phoebe, but you have to admit— you have issues with balance, too. Work is valid and important. But when you left Charlotte, you cut off that part of yourself."

She grimaced, feeling shame for the holier-than-thou way she had judged his life. "You're right. I did. But I'm not sure how to step back in the opposite direction."

A tiny smile lifted the corners of his mouth. "When we get back to Atlanta, I want you to work for Cavallo. I could use someone with your experience and financial instincts.

Not only that, but it would make me very happy for us to share that aspect of who we are. I understand why you ran away to the mountains. I do. And I strongly suspect that knowing each of us, we'll need your cabin as an escape when work threatens to become all-encompassing."

Anxiety dampened her burgeoning joy. "I'm afraid, Leo. I messed things up so badly before."

He shook his head. "You had a man who didn't deserve you and you lost your baby, a miscarriage that was one of those inexplicable tragedies of life. But it's time to live again, Phoebe. I want that for both of us. It's not wrong to have a passion for work. But we can keep each other grounded. And I think together we can find that balance and peace that are so important." He paused. "There's one more thing."

She was shaking more on the inside than she was on the outside. Leo was so confident, so sure. Could she take another chance at happiness? "What is it?" she asked.

At last, he took her in his arms, warming her with his big, solid frame. He cupped her cheeks in his hands, his gaze hot and sweet. "I want to make babies with you, Phoebe. I thought my life was great the way it was. But then I had the heart attack, and I met you, and suddenly I was questioning everything I had ever known about myself. Watching you with Teddy did something to me. And now tonight, with Luc and Hattie's babies upstairs asleep, I see it all clearly. You and I, Phoebe, against all odds…we have a shot at the brass ring. Having the whole enchilada. I think you were wrong about that, my love. I think with the right person, life can be just about perfect."

He bent his head and took her mouth in a soft, firm kiss that was equal parts romance and knee-weakening passion. "Will you be my almost-fiancée?" he whispered, his voice hoarse and ragged. His hands slid down the silky fabric of her dress all the way to her hips. Dragging her closer still, he buried his face in her neck. She could feel him trembling.

Emotions tumbled in her heart with all the random patterns of the snowflakes. She had grieved for so long, too long in fact. Cowardice and the fear of being hurt again had constrained her equally as much as Leo's workaholic ways had hemmed him in.

The old man tending the fire had gone inside, probably to get warm. Phoebe gasped when Leo used the slit in her skirt to his advantage, placing a warm palm on her upper thigh. His fingers skated perilously close to the place where her body ached for him.

Teasing her with outrageous caresses, he nibbled her ear, her neck, the partially exposed line of her collarbone. "I need an answer, my love. Please."

Heat flooded her veins, negating the winter chill. Her body felt alive, spectacularly alive. Leo held her tightly, as if he were afraid she might run. But that was ludicrous, because there was no place she would rather be.

She gave herself a moment to say goodbye to the little child she would never know. So many hopes and dreams she had cherished had been ripped away. But the mountains had taught her much about peace, and in surviving, she had been given another chance. A wonderful, exciting, heart-pounding second chance.

Laying her cheek against Leo's crisp white shirt, feeling the steady beat of his wonderfully big heart, she nodded. "Yes, Leo Cavallo. I believe I will."

Epilogue

Leo paced the marble floor, his palms damp. "Hurry, Phoebe. They'll be here in a minute." He was nervous about his surprise, and if Phoebe lollygagged too much longer, it would be ruined. He gazed around his familiar home, noting the addition this year of a gigantic Christmas tree, its branches heavy with ornaments. In the chandelier overhead, tiny clumps of mistletoe dangled, tied with narrow red velvet ribbons.

His body tightened and his breath quickened as he recalled the manner in which he and Phoebe had christened that mistletoe, making love on the rug beneath. In truth, they had christened most of his condo in such a way. Including a repeat of what he liked to call "the kitchen episode."

He tugged at his bow tie, feeling much too hot all of a sudden.

At long last, his beloved wife appeared, her usual feminine stride hampered by a certain waddling movement. She grimaced. "This red dress makes me look like a giant tomato."

He pulled her in close for a kiss, running his hand over the fascinating swell of her large abdomen. "Red is my new favorite color. And besides, it's Christmas." Feeling the life growing inside his precious Phoebe tightened his throat and wet his eyes. So many miracles in his life. So much love.

She returned the kiss with passion. The force that drew them together in the beginning had never faded. In fact, it grew deeper and more fiery with each passing month.

This evening, though, they were headed for a night out on the town with Luc and Hattie. Dinner, followed by a performance of *The Nutcracker*.

Phoebe rubbed her back. "I hope I'm going to fit into a seat at the theater."

He grinned broadly. "Quit fishing for compliments. You know you're the sexiest pregnant woman in the entire state. But sit down, my love. I have something I want to give you before they get here."

Phoebe eased into a comfy armchair with a grimace. "It's five days 'til Christmas."

"This is an *early* present."

From his jacket pocket he extracted a ruby velvet rectangle. Flipping it open, he handed it to her. "I had it made especially for you."

Phoebe took the box from him and stared. Inside, nestled on a bed of black satin, was an exquisite necklace. Two dozen or more tiny diamond snowflakes glittered with fire on a delicate platinum chain. She couldn't speak for the emotion that threatened to swamp her with hormonal tears.

Leo went down on one knee beside her, removed the jewelry from the box and gently fastened it around her neck.

She put a hand to her throat, staring at his masculine beauty, feeling the tangible evidence of his boundless, generous love. "Thank you, Leo. It's perfect."

He wrapped a hand in her hair and fingered it. "I could have waited until our anniversary. But tonight is special to me. It was exactly a year ago that you stood in the snow and gave me a new life. A wonderful life."

Running one hand through his hair, she cupped his neck with the other and pulled him back for another kiss. "Are you channeling Jimmy Stewart now?" she teased, her heart full to bursting.

He laid a hand on her round belly, laughing softly when their son made an all too visible kick. "Not at all, my dear Phoebe. I'm merely counting my blessings. And I always count you twice."

* * * * *

Merry Christmas
& A Happy New Year!

Thank you for a wonderful
2013...

A sneaky peek at next month...

Desire™

PASSIONATE AND DRAMATIC LOVE STORIES

My wish list for next month's titles...

In stores from 20th December 2013:

☐ Beneath the Stetson – Janice Maynard

❧ For the Sake of Their Son – Catherine Mann

☐ Pregnant by Morning – Kat Cantrell

❧ The Nanny's Secret – Elizabeth Lane

☐ At Odds with the Heiress – Cat Schield

❧ Project: Runaway Bride – Heidi Betts

2 stories in each book - only **£5.49!**

Available at WHSmith, Tesco, Asda, Eason, Amazon and Apple

Just can't wait?

Visit us Online

You can buy our books online a month before they hit the shops!

Come in from the cold this Christmas with two of
our favourite authors. Whether you're jetting off to
Vermont with Sarah Morgan or settling down for
Christmas dinner with Fiona Harper, the smiles
won't stop this festive season.

Visit:
www.millsandboon.co.uk

MILLS & BOON® Book Club

Join the Mills & Boon Book Club

Want to read more **Desire**™ books?
We're offering you **2 more** absolutely **FREE!**

We'll also treat you to these fabulous extras:

- 🌹 **Exclusive offers and much more!**

- 🌹 **FREE home delivery**

- 🌹 **FREE books and gifts with our special rewards scheme**

Get your free books now!

visit www.millsandboon.co.uk/bookclub
or call Customer Relations on 020 8288 2888